Tantalizing Treats

Cris Anson
Amy Ruttan
Lolita Lopez
Lacey Savage
Brigit Zahara
Jenna Castille
Cindy Spencer Pape

Enjoy!
Cindy Spencer Pape

ELLORA'S CAVE
ROMANTICA PUBLISHING

What the critics are saying...

MASQUE OF DESIRE
Amy Ruttan

4 Hearts "This reviewer really enjoyed reading MASQUE OF DESIRE and it's a quickie so it can be read in one sitting. Overall this reviewer would recommend this book to any lover of the paranormal." ~ *Love Romances and More*

BETWEEN A ROCK AND A HARD-ON
Cindy Spencer Pape

4 Enchantments "This short novella will meet your expectations for a passionate, sizzling quickie. The heat between Bram and Twyla would scorch mere mortals (good thing one of them is a dragon and used to producing fire—I wasn't too worried when my computer started smoking). If this is a sip of Ms. Spencer Pape's writing, I can't wait to consume more. Next time, though, I will keep the fire extinguisher close by (computers are expensive, you know) and the fire department on speed dial." ~ *Enchanting Reviews*

MISCHIEF NIGHT
Cris Anson

4.5 Blue Ribbons "Cris Anson has me hooked yet again on another extremely sexy read! MISCHIEF NIGHT is Halloween at its most alluring!" ~ *Romance Junkies Reviews*

SPELLS AT MIDNIGHT
Jenna Castille

"*Spells at Midnight* is an intriguing and heart-felt read that brings you along a smooth and satisfying path where you can cheer our lovers on. Jenna Castille has given us two romantic souls who are destined to be together. Forever." ~ *ParaNormal Romance Reviews*

GHOSTLY AWAKENING
Lacey Savage

5 Hearts "This reviewer's favorite author, Lacey Savage never disappoints and always gives her readers a hot, sensuous story, alive and vibrant characters and sex to make your socks sizzle off. She infuses her stories with lots of emotions that carry the reader away on a wonderful journey. Ms. Savage's stories will always thrill, chill and get the readers toes curling. [...] Readers cannot go wrong with a story from Lacey Savage, if you like a lot of hot sex, characters to fall in love with and a good plot, then this author can fulfill all your reading dreams. This reviewer can always highly recommend any story that Ms. Savage has written." ~ *Love Romances and More*

CONJURED BLISS
Brigit Zahara

4.5 Lips "This short story was so heated it steamed up my glasses. Callie's stamina, in keeping up with her undead employers, was truly amazing. This woman, who was so cautious since her husband's departure—and so starved for sex—melts the pages. Brigit Zahara's *Conjured Bliss* is a great read for those who love hot vampires, and have only a little time to spare!" ~ *Two Lips Reviews*

NOCTURNAL OBSESSION
Lolita Lopez

4 Enchantments "What a delightful holiday quickie! Full of gratifying, erotic encounters and gentle, wistful moments. [...] Read *Nocturnal Obsession* for a story with interesting characters, inventive sex and an unusual resolution." ~ *Enchanting Reviews*

An Ellora's Cave Romantica Publication

www.ellorascave.com

Tantalizing Treats

ISBN 9781419958328

This book printed in the U.S.A. by Jasmine–Jade Enterprises, LLC.

Trade paperback Publication October 2008

TANTALIZING TREATS

ဢ

MASQUE OF DESIRE

Amy Ruttan

ဢ

Trademarks Acknowledgement

Chapter One

෨

"I don't really want to go, Deanna," Miranda Carter protested as her best friend tightened her corset. "Christ, don't pull the damn thing so tight."

"Miranda, you want your costume to be authentic, don't you? You want to win best costume, don't you?"

"No, you want me to win best costume. I couldn't care less," Miranda said as she ran her hands down her even thinner waist. "How did these women breathe?"

"Who needed to breathe when you had sexy cavaliers at your disposal?" Deanna sighed, sitting down on Miranda's bed to survey her handiwork. "I wish I were going to the masquerade. I would love to wear a costume like that."

"Do you want to go in my place?" Miranda asked, spinning around. "I mean, if you want to go instead of me, feel free. I would be more than happy to oblige you."

"No thanks, Miranda. Besides, you're the attorney who helped that zillionaire client of yours from Europe buy and fix up the place. You have to represent your firm."

Miranda snorted. *Sure, there was representing your firm and then there was acting like a fool on Halloween.* When was the last time she dressed up like this and trick-or-treated? Not in a long time, not since her parents split up when she was eight, then there was no time to trick or treat with two younger siblings to take care of.

All her life she had strived to survive and take care of her family since her father had left them. She took on the role of father figure. Miranda wanted to succeed where her father had failed.

She worked her way through Harvard Law and worked her way to youngest partner in her firm. At the age of thirty-three she had it all. Except a man.

Miranda had no time for relationships and any brief liaisons she did have had been short and unfulfilling. Then again, who needed a man when she had a perfectly good vibrator in her nightstand drawer?

"Besides, I have a hot date with Nick tonight," Deanna said, happily interrupting her thoughts.

"So tonight's the night?"

"Yes, tonight it is. I've rented all the old horror classics to snuggle up and, well, you know." Deanna waggled her eyebrows suggestively.

"Yeah, I remember," Miranda said offhandedly. She smoothed down the skirt of her eighteenth-century French costume. It was very beautiful but too constricting. *How the heck did women live in these things?* Miranda wondered bitterly again. "I really wish it wasn't themed. If I had my choice to dress up I would have gone as—"

"Either an attorney or something equally boring!" Deanna said, throwing her hands up in the air. "Have fun tonight, Miranda. For once let your hair down, it's a masquerade, for crying out loud. You'll be masked the whole night. No one will know who you were if you want to have some fun."

"Come on, Dee. Don't be silly."

"I'm not and you should be for once," Deanna said seriously, handing her the black sequined velveteen mask. Miranda put the mask up to her face. "Let loose, you're uptight. It's one night. Have some fun."

Miranda stared at herself in the mirror. The mask certainly covered most of her face, except for her brilliant blue eyes and red lips. *Maybe tonight would be a good opportunity for a one-night stand.*

* * * * *

As the limo pulled up the long gravel drive of the restored Georgian plantation on the outskirts of New Orleans, Miranda felt the butterflies in her stomach go ballistic.

Just tell the driver to turn around, you don't have to do this. She still couldn't figure out why she had finally agreed and actually came to this foolhardy masquerade. She had finally convinced herself that it was for a client, a very important client. Now under the light of a full harvest moon, the realization of the foolishness of a bunch of business-men and - women dressing in eighteenth-century French costumes was ridiculous. And attending a mock masquerade of the time of the great plantation owners in New Orleans seemed utterly unrealistic.

"We're here, Ms. Carter," the driver said as he opened the door. He held out his hand and she, for once, took it, as the crazy getup she was wearing prevented her from exiting gracefully.

"Bloody hoops," she cursed under her breath.

She climbed from the limo with as much dignity as she could muster. She could barely see a thing with the damn mask on.

The house, which had once been rotting to nothing, had been easily purchased for her client, Aleksandr Valquet, for a nominal fee. Through his aides and his assistants Miranda had helped the French billionaire get building permits, contractors and materials to restore the plantation to its former glory.

And she must admit that it was beautiful. She stared up at the white stucco masterpiece, lit up against the verdant moss-covered willows under the bright harvest moon. It was like something from *Interview with the Vampire*. A shiver raced down her spine as she looked up at the spectacular Georgian home. Torches lit the path all the way up to the mahogany double doors.

As the limo pulled away Miranda had the strangest feeling she was being watched. She looked over her shoulder and a small old woman dressed in black stood in the shadows by the trees. The woman's eyes were fixed intently on her.

The woman was cloaked in black, her long gray hair blowing around her face in the gentle breeze. Miranda couldn't help but stare at her. The little old woman seemed familiar to her. Then suddenly Miranda had a vision that washed over her like a wave. She saw a roaring bonfire and the old woman clapping her hands in time with the sensuous sound of the violin.

Gypsies was Miranda's first thought. She knew over a century ago this land was covered in caravans. Heck, even now New Orleans peddled voodoo priests and other forms of magic to tourists.

"*Mira*," came a whispered voice on the wind. Miranda quickly looked toward the house, when she saw no one there she turned back to the trees but the old woman was gone. "*Mira, welcome home*," the voice said faintly in the breeze that rustled the leaves in the trees. The hair on the back of her neck stood on end as she listened to the voice calling her name — a rich, deep, male voice. "*Mira*."

"Welcome to Violet Hall. May I see your invitation please?"

Miranda startled at the sound of the doorman's Cajun accent, before handing the liveried and powdered-wigged man her gilded invitation. He scanned it quickly in the torchlight. He smiled and bowed, adding to the old-world charm.

"Very good, Ms. Carter. Again, welcome to Violet Hall. Monsieur Valquet asks that all guests remain masked until midnight, when all will be revealed. If you will follow me up to the house."

A shiver passed down Miranda's spine. All will be revealed, what did that mean? She brushed it off as she followed the doorman up the gravel path toward Violet Hall.

As they neared the house, she paused briefly, feeling that someone was still watching her. She stared back and saw a marble statue of a man. A mausoleum, unmarked and lit up by floodlights. The bust of the occupant of the tomb was what intrigued her. Without a doubt, the occupant had been a handsome man. She could not tell the color of his hair, or his eyes, because he had been carved in white marble. He had a strong face, with a delectable cleft in his chin.

She just stared up at the man's face, mesmerized by the poignant expression set deep within the stone. She felt a rush of heat flood her veins as she stared up at the cold, marble face. It seemed familiar to her, as if she had seen that stone face before.

"Ms. Carter?" the doorman asked from a few feet away.

"Do you know who this is?" she asked.

"Ah, no one knows his name but he was the original owner of Violet Hall over two hundred and fifty years ago. Have you never heard of the curse of Violet Hall before?"

"No, I haven't," Miranda said quickly.

"Apparently, the previous owner crossed the paths of a mad voodoo priestess. She condemned him to sleep forever until his one true love wakens him."

Miranda snorted. "A reverse sleeping beauty, huh?"

"Sort of. The man disappeared two hundred and fifty years ago today. Myths are that the original owner appears every Halloween looking for his one true love to break the curse." The doorman chuckled. "Of course, it's all a romantic myth. The mausoleum was opened, there was a body that had obviously been in there for over two hundred years."

"Hmmm," Miranda said seductively, returning her attention to the marble bust. "Too bad it was only a myth." As she spoke those words, the wind whipped through the trees, the flame in the torches around her snapped and sparked. She felt a chill run down her spine.

"Come, Ms. Carter, it's much more hospitable inside."

Miranda nodded and followed the doorman back down the path. The night was suddenly silent and all she heard was the crunching of gravel beneath her feet. She looked back at the mausoleum and thought she saw the fleeting glimpse of a figure in the shadow of the crypt.

Chapter Two

Miranda walked around the room. She was dying of heat. The crush of bodies, the heat from the electric and the authentic oil lamps made the ballroom absolutely sweltering. *This must be how our forefathers felt, poor bastards.* She felt the sweat trickle down from the nape of her neck and pool between her breasts, which had been smashed and pushed out by the strict confines of the corset beneath her mantua, height of fashion in the mid-eighteenth century, or at least that's what Dee had told her when she complained about the complex costume.

She waved her fan, the one that Deanna had included with her costume when Dee made it. *Note to self, kiss Dee when this is all over.*

She stood by the open double patio doors, leaning against the doorjamb, letting the tepid autumn breeze lick at her skin. She could see the other homes surrounding the grounds by the glow of jack-o'-lanterns. *Why am I here?* she thought.

She didn't recognize anyone because of the masks. Apparently, Monsieur Valquet felt that it added to the mystery.

Everything about this masquerade was historically accurate, the music, the trained dancers performing minuets and quadrilles for the guests' entertainment. The food was accurate to eighteenth-century Louisiana. That's what the invitation had boasted about this shindig. *An eighteenth-century masquerade on All Hallow's Eve, a Masque of Desire.* Totally cheesy but Monsieur Valquet had done a good job pulling it off.

As Miranda looked over the estate she almost expected to see one of Anne Rice's vampires strolling up the path.

"May I ask what you are thinking about, mademoiselle?"

Miranda startled at the heavy French accent that purred in her ear. She turned her head to see a tall, broad-chested masked man leaning over her, smiling. He had a cleft in his chin and sparkling green eyes. That was all Miranda could see from behind the black scarf mask tied around his face. She leisurely perused the rest of his body. He was decked out all in black—his waistcoat, vest and shirt. What intrigued her most were the very tight breeches he wore that showed off very muscular thighs. Miranda had to admit that men's clothing of the eighteenth century left nothing to the imagination.

She could feel the heat emanating from his body, due to the closeness. His breath was cool on her hot skin, causing goose bumps to rise down her neck. She felt her heart beat faster. He was so close she could smell the spiciness of his warm body.

"I don't share my thoughts with strange men."

He looked surprised. "Well, how about just for tonight. I cannot tell you my name, yet."

"Look." Miranda was about to tell this man where to stick it and she wasn't in the mood to play these silly games. *Play along, have some fun, it's been so long since a man paid attention to you.* "All right, I was thinking about vampires," she said coyly, waiting for his response.

He chuckled. His voice, rich and deep. "Vampires, now that is something I have not heard of before. Could it be the date that reminds you of vampires so?" he asked, his voice heavily accented.

She laughed. She liked the sound of his voice—it had an old-world quality to it. "Well…no, not really. It has nothing to do with Halloween."

"Ah, Halloween. Yes, that is what you call it. Halloween."

"What do you call it then?"

"All Hallow's Eve."

Miranda laughed. "Maybe, you're certainly taking on this role seriously."

"Role?" he asked frowning. "What do you mean by role?"

Damn, Miranda, stick with the act. Don't blow it. "Sorry, monsieur. You can forget my last remark."

He seemed happy then he nodded his head. "*Bonne*." He held out his arm. "Dare you take a walk with a complete stranger?"

Warning bells immediately went off in her head. She would never, under any circumstances, walk into unfamiliar territory with a stranger but Monsieur Valquet would hardly invite any dangerous criminals to his party. *Do it*, a little voice inside her head said. *Do whatever he wants, you'll never have another chance. Live a little.*

"All right, I shall." She took his arm and she could feel his muscles under the sleeve of his tight black waistcoat.

"Would you like a tour of the house, or perhaps the garden?"

"House, I think," she replied. He smiled and led her across the ballroom to the double doors that led out into a dark hallway.

She'd rather walk with a stranger in a house occupied by fifty or so partygoers, than wander unlit grounds with a stranger. Although, she wasn't thinking he was a stranger anymore. Only the owner would offer her a tour, which meant her handsome stranger was probably Monsieur Valquet, whom she had yet to meet.

This was the man her firm wanted to impress and she would impress him and play along with his games. *It might be fun*, Miranda thought to herself. It also didn't hurt that Monsieur Valquet seemed a prime specimen. She couldn't remember the last time she had seen such a hot man before. *You can have your cake and eat it too.*

Miranda could feel his rippled muscles under the taut fabric of his waistcoat. She could feel the heat of his body and the feel of his breath against her neck, which caused her heart to beat faster, her pulse quicken. She thought about what it would be like to be wrapped up in his warmth.

"Follow me then, *ma chere*," he whispered in her ear.

He was so close to her, her lips went dry as she thought of him pressed against her. A mental image flashed through her mind. She saw herself against the wall, her bare legs wrapped around him, her skirt hiked to her waist as he pounded into her.

Miranda fanned herself as she walked into the entranceway. She realized the image of them together was from this hallway. She had a sudden, intense feeling of déjà vu.

As they walked out into the hallway, he immediately led her to the stairs.

"Shall we start with the upstairs first?" he asked.

"I don't see why not," she replied. She had been longing to see what kind of restoration had been made to the house.

He led her up the stairs and she saw that apparently they were not the only ones who had that idea. She heard the steady creak of a bed from one of the chambers at the top of the stairs. The closer they got to the upper floor, the louder the moaning became.

The nerve of some people! was her first thought, then, she envied them. Envied their unbridled want to be able to fuck in someone else's house.

She felt her blood heat and her pulse race at the thought. She wished it was her.

"Are you jealous of them?" her companion asked, shattering her reverie.

"What?" she asked hoarsely.

"I asked you, *ma chere*, if you were jealous."

"No—I," she faltered. She couldn't think of a plausible excuse. He pushed her up against a paneled wall with his arms on either side of her face.

"I could accommodate you," he whispered huskily into her ear. "That's what we're all here for, is it not?"

She felt him press his hard body into hers. Even through the folds of fabric she could feel his hard cock against her thigh. His lips mere inches from hers. His spicy scent wrapped her up, enveloping her body, enflaming her senses.

Her initial reaction was to knee him in the groin and tell him to fuck off before she called the cops but she didn't do that. Instead, she pictured herself impaled on his cock, riding him up and down. She pictured him going down on her, his tongue tracing the lips of her pussy. It had been too long since she had a good, hard fuck.

"*Ma chere*, that is the purpose of these masquerades. To let the inhibitions flow free, you will remain masked, as will I. We can enjoy each other, as strangers. Neither one of us would know."

He bent down and captured her lips, sucking on them, and she felt the heat in her loins, the undeniable ache and longing for male attention that had been denied her for far too long. As he tongue delved deeper for a taste, she ground her hips up against his cock in a total reflex action.

He broke off the kiss and rubbed his thumb against her swollen red lips. "Don't deny me."

Miranda shook her head. "I'll do whatever you want."

He smiled down at her, a pleased expression on his face. "Anything I want? Are you certain?"

"Yes," Miranda heard herself reply.

"Good." He leaned in and placed a feathery-soft kiss against her lips. That alone was enough to cause her knees to buckle and her heart to race. He backed away from her then and she hated the feeling of emptiness he left behind. Even though he was only an arm's length away, she could feel the loss of not having him close.

He held out his arm, in the old-world tradition, like something from *Pride and Prejudice*. Miranda placed her hand on top of his arm.

"Ah, *chere*, you do this, how you say, like a pro."

She giggled. "Like a pro?"

"The masquerade, you play your role in this masque so well."

"And what role is that, monsieur?"

He leaned in and whispered, "Lover," so softly it caused her skin to break out in gooseflesh.

"And what is your role?" she asked, hoping to trick him into divulging his secret identity as Monsieur Valquet.

He laughed a deep sultry laugh. "Seducer. That is what this night is for."

They walked down the hall. Through the partially open doors she could see couples playing their parts in the masquerade all too well. He stopped in front of a door where a man and a woman were making love.

Unabashedly he pushed open the door and Miranda squeaked and ducked out of the way of the open door.

Her companion stood in the doorway and seemed alarmed by her behavior. "What is wrong, *cherie*?"

"They'll see us," she hissed from the shadows.

"*Non*, they will not. They only see each other. Nothing else matters to them." He held out his hand. "Come, I want you to see."

She shook her head. *You want to look, you know you do*, her inner devil said. *No, don't, you can't*, her inner conscience said.

"*Ma chere*, you promised me you would do anything I asked." He gazed into her eyes intently, she felt drawn into to his intense emerald eyes. As if she was pulled deep into his soul. "I'm asking you to come here."

Live a little, you're masked, they're masked. No one would ever know. The devil voice won out. Miranda slipped her hand into his strong, warm hand and took a deep breath before she acted the part of voyeur.

Chapter Three

ॐ

The sight before her was like something out of a sensuous novel. A fantasy she had secretly longed for, for a long time.

A woman with alabaster skin and long blonde hair lay spread-eagle on a large inviting bed. Her skin flushed with pleasure as she moaned and writhed in ecstasy as an ebony man drove into her, hard and fast. He had one hand on the bed to steady himself as he fucked the woman on the edge of the bed. The man's other hand rubbed the woman's swollen clit.

As if sensing her presence the man turned and his hazel eyes, sparkling from behind his red velvet mask, bore into her. He looked at her as if he was a hunter and she was his prey. He gave her a long sexy smile before turning back to the woman he was pleasuring on the bed. He quickened his pace. The man's smile and predator-like gaze heated her blood. She could feel her pulse beating a fast tattoo at the base of her neck.

Miranda felt herself grow wet watching them. She had never been one for porn. She barely tolerated watching it with her former boyfriends. Somehow this was different, this felt like a show, a seduction just for her. She also acutely felt the need to have a man.

She needed to feel a man pressed against her. She needed to be filled up, to feel the beating of a man's heart keeping in time with her own. Her cunt began to ache, a delicious feeling. Her skin began to heat and her cheeks grew hot with a flush as she thought of herself on that bed with her companion driving into her, giving her all that she wanted.

Without thinking, her hand trailed down over her breasts where her hard nipples were trapped by the strict confines of her bodice. Her hand kept trailing down over her corseted belly to the thick folds of her skirt.

"I know what you want," he whispered into her hair as he slid his hand over hers, cupping her pussy through her skirt.

"What?" she asked.

He lifted her hand and tugged her toward the end of the hallway where tall mahogany double doors were opened invitingly. She could see the bed as large as two kings, waiting patiently for her there.

He pulled her inside and closed the doors. He leaned back against the doorway and his green eyes seemed to drink her in as they roamed freely up and down her body. Her ache increased and her clothes felt even more constricting. She felt trapped and she couldn't breathe. She wanted to be naked. She wanted him naked.

He didn't say anything. So quickly he was at her side. As if reading her mind he said, "Allow me to help you."

He began to undo the laces of her bodice. She felt immediate release as her breasts were freed. It may have been an old-world design but thankfully Dee had added zippers to the skirt of her mantua.

"Interesting, such a wonderful little invention," he said, examining the zipper on the skirt briefly. He smiled up at her. "But it's not that interesting."

He made short work of the voluminous layers of her skirts. She stepped out of them and he tossed them over his shoulder.

Miranda was surprised at herself. She never, under any circumstances, had the lights on with a new man. She had no shame tonight as he pulled off her shift and she stood naked in nothing but her heels, stockings and a velvet choker.

"God, you're beautiful. I've waited a long time for someone like you."

So Monsieur Valquet wanted to act out the myth of the immortal owner of Violet Hall. Well, she could play along. It might prove to be fun.

"Yes, I'm sure it has. How long has it been since you fucked a girl senseless?"

He looked surprised by her words but not deterred. She could see the evidence of his arousal in his breeches.

"Too long," he said, his voice cracking. "Now I want to taste you."

She felt her knees buckle. "Pardon?" she asked.

"Taste you. On the bed, *ma chere*," he ordered.

She clambered up on the bed quickly, eager to comply.

"To the edge and remember you said you would do as I asked."

Miranda obeyed him, scooted to the edge of the bed and spread her legs wide. He dropped down to his knees and before she could prepare herself she felt his hot, wet tongue slide down between the lips of her cunt.

"Oh my god," she cried out as she propped herself on her elbows to watch him.

He smiled up at her. "Good, stay like that. I want to watch your face as you come."

With his finger he spread her folds and went straight for her clit. With slow, leisurely strokes of his tongue he licked her clit, causing jolts of pleasure to course through her.

Miranda moaned, she couldn't help it. The sensations of him licking her pussy and the sight of his tongue licking her clit was such a turn-on in itself. He opened his mouth wide and began to suck. She tensed and as if sensing her orgasm was near, he lessened the pace of his tongue.

She whimpered in frustration but as she settled down he started with a quick assault again and her pleasure built up inside her until she felt ready to explode. The feel of his tongue in one of her most intimate places, his teeth gently grazing her labia was so sensual, so divine, and it pushed her over the edge. She gave in to her climax. It came fast, it had been too long since she had a man and somehow after tonight a vibrator wouldn't cut it anymore.

As the sensations washed over her a vision came to her of them swimming naked in the river by the moonlight. She couldn't quite make out the features of his face but she knew it was Monsieur Valquet by the feel of him touching her, holding her.

She lay back on the bed with her eyes closed and breathing heavy as the last shock waves of the most earth-shattering climax coursed through her. She felt the bed dip and knew that he was lying beside her.

She opened one eye and he was on his side, propped on one elbow. His finger stroked her arm.

"Is that all you've got?" she asked, playfully rolling on her side.

His eyes flew open in surprise and he chuckled. "The night is young. Why, are you tired, *ma chere*?"

Miranda shook her head. "I promised to do whatever you want," she whispered. "What is it that you want, monsieur?"

He leaned over her and kissed her passionately. "What I want is you. That is all. Will you give yourself to me?"

"I thought I just did?" she answered.

He frowned and Miranda wondered what she said that was so wrong. He sat up on the bed, his back to her. She sat up, tucking her legs under her. *Great, the first sexy man in over a year and you screw it up.*

"Did I say something wrong?" she asked.

He looked at her, his eyes smoldering. "No, it's me."

Miranda sighed and stood up. *Well, so much for that. She had messed up a good thing and she didn't even know how.* She walked to where her costume lay in a heap on the floor. She could feel his eyes boring into her back.

"What are you doing?" he asked curiously.

"Getting dressed."

"Why?"

Miranda spun around, holding her skirt in one hand. "I thought you were finished with me."

He laughed seductively and lay across the bed. "I was promised your utter obedience tonight, that you would do anything that I desired."

Yes, thank god! "What is it that you desire?"

"Ride me."

Miranda's heart beat faster. *Ride him.* She got an instant mental image of riding him. Instinctively she knew it would be so damn good. She had never been on top before. Of course she was doing a lot of things that she had never done in her life before. It was this Masque of Desire tonight that brought out this nymphomaniac in her and she liked it.

He stood up and slowly undressed. She watched him peel off his clothes and she felt like she was standing in her most erotic dream. Only it wasn't a dream, it was real and it felt so good.

He stood up and tossed his waistcoat over his shoulder. From under his black mask his green eyes fixed on her intently, glittering in the flickering candlelight. Shadows from the flames on the tallow candles licked at his body like a lover's tongue, like she wanted to.

She licked her lips, moistening them as they had gone incredibly dry. She wanted to taste him, to run her tongue over his body. She felt the blood in her veins begin to heat, her pulse began to quicken.

With his eyes locked on hers, he slowly began to undo the buttons on his linen shirt.

"Well," he asked. "Will you do me the honor?"

"What?" Miranda choked, coming out her trance.

"Would you like to ride me, or shall I ride you?"

Try it, you never have before, her inner voice told her. "I'll ride you, monsieur, since you offered so politely. You shall have your turn though."

"I intend to, *ma chere,* I fully intend to." He chuckled huskily.

Miranda admired the vast expanse of his smooth chest. His skin was bronzed, probably sun-kissed from St. Tropez or some other exotic French Riviera location. *You're ruining the masquerade. He's not Monsieur Valquet, billionaire, he's your lover. You're his, play the part.*

Still, she could admire his fine physique and it was damn fine. Miranda's eyes wandered down his rock-hard abs to his tight breeches, where evidence of an erection was stifled under the stretched, taut fabric.

"Shall I help you with your pants, monsieur?"

"By all means, help yourself."

She seductively strolled over to her lover and ran her hands over his hard chest, her light touch leaving gooseflesh on his bronzed skin.

"Touch me, *ma chere,*" he whispered in her ear.

"Where?" she asked. "Guide me, monsieur."

"It does not matter where, *ma chere.* My pleasure does not matter tonight, only yours."

"Why only my pleasure? I'm a good Catholic girl. Do unto others—"

"You talk too much." He cupped her face in his rough hands and kissed her. His tongue stabbed past her lips, ravaging her tongue in a toe-curling kiss.

She pressed her body against the hard plane of his body. His hands left her face and grabbed her hips, pressing them against his hard cock.

She broke off the kiss, pushing him down against the pillows. Miranda suddenly had the wild idea of tying him down.

"There are silk scarves in the drawer of the bureau, right there," he said as if reading her thoughts.

She looked over her shoulder and smiled. "Are you sure, monsieur?"

"If it is what you desire, then yes, I am sure."

Miranda slid the drawer open and pulled out four long, black silken strands. She bit her lip as she slid the strands between her fingers. The coolness of the fabric sent a zing of desire through her. The silk cold, like ice, against her hot skin. She pictured him tied to the bed, naked, unable to touch her while she rode him.

She leaned over him and wrapped the silk strand around his wrist and tied it tightly to the bedpost. He was smiling up at her, his eyes twinkling behind his black mask.

Miranda quickly fastened his other arm and then leaned over him.

"Oh, *ma chere*, you don't know how I long to cup your breasts," he said. Miranda leaned in closer and his mouth found one her breasts. She gasped and felt herself grow wet again as he tongue flicked her sensitive nipple. She groaned and he stopped suckling. He lay back and chuckled.

"I am at your mercy."

"That's right, monsieur, you are."

Miranda slowly unbuttoned his trousers. They were tight and she could see the outline of his erection, pushing against the velvet of the fabric. She paused and ran her finger lightly over the length, stretched taut under the fabric as he moaned. He was so hard—she could hardly wait to feel it inside her. She undid the rest of the buttons and tugged the tight breeches over his hips, revealing his hard, pulsing cock.

She tossed the breeches over her shoulder and lashed his legs to the posts at the foot of the bed before she leisurely made her way back up to what she most desired.

She couldn't believe the size of his cock. She had never seen one so large before, other than in the movies. For one fleeting second she thought that she may not be able to fit it inside her.

"What are you waiting for, *ma chere*?" he asked, his voice cracking.

She smiled wickedly and ran her tongue up the length of his scrotum. He jerked, the headboard creaking slightly from the silken bonds that held him tight.

"*Mon dieu*," he cried out.

She licked around the head, where a bead of moisture lay glistening on the tip, before she took his entire length into her mouth. She moved her mouth up and down the length of him, sucking him and tasting him. His hips rose involuntarily to keep in rhythm with her mouth and tongue. She could feel that he was close.

"I want to come inside you," he cried out. "Please, let me come inside you."

She listened to him and removed her mouth. He was breathing heavily, rasping for air.

"Are you all right, monsieur? Shall I continue?"

"No, not that way," he panted. "I want to be inside you. I want to come inside you."

She laughed and sat astride him. He bucked up toward her and she pinned him down, her breasts brushing against his chest.

"I shall control the rhythm of this dance, monsieur."

She grabbed his cock and guided it to the warm opening of her pussy. She teased him by rubbing his head against her soft lips.

He was groaning through gritted teeth, straining against the bonds that held him.

He felt so hard in her hand, so hard against her soft core. She raised her hips and slowly allowed his long cock to sink deep inside her. She shuddered at the feel of him stretching her, filling her.

She cried out at the feeling of him inside her. The feeling of his rock-hard shaft against her clit.

"Ride me," he said roughly. "Fuck me."

She raised her hips, pulling herself along the length of him before she impaled herself with it again. She continued slowly, riding him up and down at a slow tempo, luxuriating in the feeling of him buried deep inside her, penetrating her to her soul.

He was moaning and the headboard was creaking. His muscles were corded and his teeth gritted. She quickened the tempo as she felt her orgasm begin, coming to her in waves.

She threw her head back, enjoying her ride when she heard a snap. Her eyes flew open in surprise as she felt his hands encircle her waist.

"I am sorry, *ma chere*," he said as he grasped her hips and increased her tempo, holding her down on him.

She cried out as she felt him throb deep inside her. He made up for his impatience by rubbing his thumb against her clit, urging her to come with him.

She felt her orgasm build and then explode around her as he came deep inside her. She shuddered, her body shaking as she fell against his chest. Her strawberry-blonde hair fanned against his bronze chest in sweaty tendrils. She listened to him breathe heavily as she lay draped over his chest. She closed her eyes and savored the feel of him under her, the last jolts of an electric orgasm coursed through her. The spicy scent of his arousal caused her blood to heat again. She wanted more, so much more.

His arms came around her, wrapping her in his warmth and strength. She felt so safe listening to his heavy breathing as he stroked her back tenderly. *What are you doing?* she thought to herself. *Come on, Miranda, what are you doing? You don't even know this guy, don't fancy yourself in love with him. This is all an act—he's your client, for crying out loud. It's just a masquerade, just for fun.*

She pulled away. She rolled to her side, her back to him. What was she doing? How could she go to work on Monday and face him at the board meeting? *He won't know it's you, the hair extensions for this ridiculous getup will be gone and you'll be safe behind your pinstriped business suit.*

"*Ma chere*, what is wrong?"

"Nothing," she lied.

"Hmmm, I think something is wrong. You pulled away so quickly." He cuddled up behind her, his warm body spooning her. "Tell me you're not finished with me yet. The night is still young."

"Well, I have busy day on Monday."

"Monday, that is two days away. It is not even midnight yet. The masquerade still continues, listen, they still dance below."

Miranda could hear the weak strains of a minuet wafting up through the floor. She could almost see the dancers in their mantuas and powdered wigs dancing in the stifling heat. This whole thing was a fantasy. A fantasy she had enjoyed but now it was time to get back to the real world.

"I should go," she said, sitting up and scooting to the edge of the bed. He frowned under his black mask.

"Why?" he asked.

"I told you why. Besides, I'm tired."

"You promised me that for tonight you would obey me," he said fiercely and it freaked Miranda out.

"So I did."

"A contract is binding, is it not?"

Her heart beat faster. *Damn, he knows who I am. Why would he suggest I would know about legal contracts if he didn't know I was a freaking lawyer?*

"I guess it is," she said quietly. "What do you want me to do?"

He smiled. "Well, for starters you could release my legs from the bindings."

After she released him from his bonds she rubbed his ankles. He stood up and pulled his pants and a billowy linen shirt on.

All those romance novels had it right—a man looked good in a billowy pirate shirt. She chuckled to herself.

"What is so funny?" he asked, buttoning up his shirt.

"Nothing, nothing at all." She wandered over to where her mantua lay in pieces and cringed at the thought of having to trap herself in its bindings again.

"No, *ma chere*," he said, taking the heavy skirts from her hands. He opened up the armoire and pulled out a silk gown. A simple shift that was definitely not historically accurate by the presence of the zipper and designer label.

"Uh, they didn't wear these in the eighteenth century."

"I know, I thought it would be more comfortable for you."

"Thanks," Miranda said relieved, slipping the cool fabric over her head. She presented her back to him. "Zip me up."

He did and his hands lingered on her shoulder. "Would you do me the honor of walking the grounds with me? There are things we should talk about, things that I need to tell you."

"Of course," Miranda agreed. She hoped that it would not take too long. She wanted to leave, to forget about this night of passion. She had to concentrate on her job. She didn't want him to think less of her because she had spread her legs for him. She was a businesswoman, she was a killer in the courtroom and that's the way their business relationship should stay.

He led her out of the room and down a back staircase. More chambers lined the hall and from each chamber she could hear the sounds of people acting out their fantasies.

Down the narrow staircase he led her into a dark summer kitchen and they wandered out onto the back part of the property. The dew from the night air was wet but after the sweltering crush of bodies inside Violet Hall she welcomed the refreshing feel beneath her feet.

He took her arm and said nothing as they wandered the grounds of what must have been a vast and profitable plantation in its heyday. She could almost hear the past calling to her in the stillness of the night.

If she closed her eyes, she could almost see the fields of cotton and tobacco. She could hear the sounds of carriages clattering up the gravel drive and she could hear the faint lull of a gypsy violin.

"Do you know the history of Violet Hall?" he asked suddenly, banishing the ghosts that had been slowly sneaking up on them.

"Only what your doorman told me. About the curse of the owner, the myth that he comes back every Halloween looking for his true love."

"Do you believe that?"

"No," she said. "Why would I? Your doorman said a body was found inside the crypt."

"*Oui*, there was a body but who is to say that it was the cursed plantation owner?"

"I guess one just assumes," Miranda said as a chill ran down her spine.

"Shall I tell you the whole story?"

"Would you like to tell me?" she asked.

He stopped and looked deep into her eyes. "I would, I would like to tell you everything and I hope at the end you believe."

"Doubtful, but do tell."

He seemed bothered by her response. "What do you mean by 'doubtful'?"

"I just don't believe in curses or myths or anything like that," she said and she regretted her words as soon as she said them. He looked bothered, angered by her response. *Call it a night. You had some mind-blowing sex with him, that's what you wanted. Leave.* "Look, maybe I should go." She turned to leave again but he latched onto her arm.

"You will stay and listen," he said sternly. "And at the end you shall let your heart, not your head, decide what is true."

"I don't think—" Miranda sputtered.

"That's it, *ma chere*, don't think."

"All right," she acquiesced. "I'll listen and I'll try to keep an open mind."

He smiled warmly at her. She leaned in and kissed his sensuous mouth. He chuckled and pushed her away gently.

"May I continue?"

"Of course." She could feel herself blushing. Her cheeks grew hot. *What had brought on that impulsive kiss?* she wondered. She was doing so many things that contradicted her nature. Having great sex with a stranger, putting a man in control of her actions, it was so unlike her. *Tonight is Halloween, Mira. A time for deceit, a time to wear different masks and to be someone different.*

"The family that built this plantation was Valquet."

Aha, so I was right. "Go on."

"You know this name?" he asked.

"I've heard of it, continue," she said smugly, pleased that her guess of her lover's identity was correct.

"*Bonne,*" he said pleased. "The Valquets came here in the late 1600s, looking for new opportunities. Europe was becoming too crowded for their tastes. Monsieur Valquet at first came to the West Indies, to Haiti, where he met his bride. She was a Russian princess. Their first son was born here, on this land. They called him Aleksandr."

"Very Russian name for New Orleans."

"*Ma chere*, even then New Orleans was a melting pot of cultures. It did not matter."

"So, is Aleksandr the man of the curse?" Miranda whispered seductively, leaning into the crook of his arm.

"Yes, he was the man of the curse. Alek grew up on the land of Violet Hall. His bride was a French lady whose father owned land abutting Violet Hall plantation. So Alek married to increase the plantation's land. Such was the way of things."

"Smart man," Miranda said.

"You think so, *ma chere*?"

"No one married for love back then," she replied. "He probably knew this."

"Well, then I concur, business-wise he was smart to marry his French lady and increase his property, but as with all loveless marriages he began to wander. He grew tired of waiting for his French wife to have his heir. They were married for over ten years and no heir was forthcoming. So instead Alek wandered and he fell in love with a Russian gypsy by the name of Mira."

Miranda almost choked. It was almost too coincidental. Almost set up. Valquet, Alek or Alex and Mira. It was as if Monsieur Valquet was fabricating this whole web of lies to add to the seduction. She wanted to slug him and tell him to be straight up with her. He didn't need these lies and stories about some ancient curse to lure her into his bed, he had already done that. What was the point?

"I'm listening," Miranda said cautiously.

"Mira and Alek fell deeply in love. They met every night in a small cottage deep in the bayou. He kept her there, safe and in comfort. His wife found out and she was not pleased. She was not as it seemed, she knew a bit of black magic, or voodoo, from her slaves.

"Mira became pregnant, with a long-desired heir and this enraged Alek's legitimate wife. She would not let a Russian gypsy's bastard take over Violet Hall."

"So she killed them."

"In a way, yes."

Miranda chuckled. "What do you mean, in a way yes? Either she did or she didn't. You can't sort of kill a person."

He kissed her hand and sent electric tingles up her arm. "You are thinking with your head again, *ma chere.*"

"Sorry, go on."

"She sent their souls into limbo. The unborn child and Mira's soul disappeared. Alek's French wife cursed them into oblivion and they were to return in two hundred and fifty years. Alek was crushed, for no man was immortal. He knew that he would never see his true love again."

"What happened to his wife?"

"She met her end, at the end of the gallows. She was charged as a witch and she was charged by Alek. Her slaves were quick to offer up proof of her black ways for their freedom."

"Wow, the poor guy. Did he every remarry?"

"*Non, ma chere.* Mira's grandmother gave him a gift. She was a powerful sage and she gave him the gift of immortality. He would live for two hundred and fifty years or until his true love returned. When Mira and the soul of their unborn child returned to Earth then he would be free again. Free to love, his soul would no longer be bound to the earth. He would live out his life with his love and his child as he should have done."

"And after two hundred and fifty years?" Miranda asked, feeling a sense of dread.

"If she is not found then Alek's soul and Mira's soul will remain forever in limbo. Never finding peace again."

"So where did he go?" she asked. "I mean, this place has been in disrepair as long as I can remember. I've lived here my whole life."

"I know, *ma chere*, I know."

A tingle ran down her spine as she found herself standing in front of Aleksandr Valquet's crypt. The bust of Alek staring down into her, as if looking into her soul, it terrified her and thrilled her. The wind picked up and she wrapped her arms around herself. Suddenly she had the strangest feeling that she had been here before, standing in this spot before.

A vision washed over her and suddenly she found herself standing back in time when Violet Hall was first built and she was standing in front of Aleksandr. Alek who was on the ground holding a lifeless body in his arms, weeping. She approached him and saw the face on the body was hers. Her lifeless eyes stared up into the sky. She cried out and saw Alek's wife with red eyes standing behind her, laughing, her black hair swirling in the wind. She wanted to scream, to run and do some serious harm to that French bitch but she felt her lover's arms go around her and she was brought back to present time. The ghosts of the past evaporated into the mist that had begun to roll across Violet Hall's grounds.

"I've been here before, haven't I?" she whispered.

"*Oui, ma cherie*. Welcome home."

Miranda backed away, terrified at the thought that just came to her. She knew it to be true, deep down she knew what he had been telling her had been real.

"Mira, don't be afraid of me."

"Who are you?"

"You do not know me?" he asked, confused.

"You can't be Alek, he's dead."

"No," he said, coming closer toward her. "I am not dead. I am here."

"No, you're not. Why would Alek allow Violet Hall to rot away into nothing? He wouldn't, he loved this land too much."

"I had to leave it, Mira. When that witch sent your soul away, I couldn't stay here. I loved you. I returned every Halloween, just hoping you'd find your way home early."

"You're crazy!" she screamed, backing up against the crypt. "You can't be Aleksandr and I'm losing my mind."

He came closer and took her hand. He stroked it with his fingers. "I am Alek and you are Mira, my Mira." He kissed her hand.

She began to cry. *What the hell is wrong with me? I'm going crazy.* She found herself again, back in the past. In a beautiful cottage deep in the bayou, making love to Alek under the light of the moon, in a large hammock strung between two juniper trees, wrapped in each other's arms, watching the sun rise over the water.

A clock chimed midnight from inside the plantation house. Miranda could hear the clapping and the cheering as everyone celebrated the end of Halloween.

"Unmask, unmask, the midnight hour is here. Unmask!" someone from inside shouted.

"Shall we then, Mira? Shall we unmask?"

Miranda didn't say anything. She just stared as he untied the black fabric of his mask. She watched as he pulled it from his face and watched as it fluttered to the ground.

She slowly looked into his eyes and saw his face. Saw the same face that was on the marble bust. Aleksandr Valquet stared back at her, his eyes, warm and full of longing.

"Will you unmask?" he asked.

"I'm not sure," she said.

"Please, it will all become clear to you. I promise. Unmask, Mira, please."

Miranda nodded and slowly pulled the mask from her face. The elastic snagged in the tendrils of her strawberry-blonde hair. She let it drop to the ground and slowly raised her eyes to meet his.

Her heart lurched in her chest, as she recognized him and she suddenly remembered who she was. She had never believed in anything like reincarnation, or magic. Yet, standing here, with him, she knew him. She remembered him and she remembered that she had loved him.

"Mira?" he asked cautiously.

"I really don't know. I don't know what to believe, my name is Miranda."

"Yes, I know. I hired the services of your law firm when I saw you. You were the spitting image of Mira. I knew I would have to be patient before your memories returned."

"I never met you at the firm."

"I know, I had to hide until tonight when I knew the spell would be broken."

"You knew all along."

"I set everything up this night to remind you of who you were," he said earnestly.

"Alek, I'm scared," she whispered. For the first time in her life, she felt terrified of what might lie in the future. "Hold me."

He came to her instantly and wrapped her in his strong arms. Whispering to her in Russian and she understood every word that he said.

He promised her that she would never be harmed again, that they would never be apart again.

Suddenly he was kissing her feverishly. All over her face and down her neck. She melted, pressing her body against him.

"Don't ever leave me again," Alek whispered in her ear.

"I won't, I promise." She felt the cool air against her thighs as he lifted her skirt above her waist. She eagerly unbuttoned his trousers and welcomed his cock into her warm, waiting depths.

She cried out and wrapped her legs around his waist and he plunged into her, fucking her hard and fast against the cold marble of the crypt. She felt her orgasm build and her eyes became blurry as if Alek was disappearing as her pleasure increased.

"Alek, don't leave me," she cried out.

"I'm here, Mira. I won't leave you," he replied as he came deep within in her.

She wrapped her arms around his neck and let herself go around him. She cried out as the pleasure washed over her.

"I love you, Alek," she whispered before her eyes closed and darkness washed over her.

* * * * *

Miranda stretched and felt the warm sun beaming on her face. She rolled over and let her hand wander but the bed beside her was empty. She opened her eyes and gasped. She was in her bed, in her Snoopy pajamas. The sun was filtering through her white gauze drapes and her window was open, letting in a cool autumn zephyr.

She bolted straight up in bed. She rubbed her head as her eyes adjusted to the daylight. She saw her Halloween costume, the mantua that Deanna made, hanging on the hanger on her closet door.

Was it all a dream? She ran her fingers through her hair. *What the heck happened?*

"Well, if it was, it was the best frigging erotic dream I've ever had," she mumbled to herself.

She heard the sounds of Deanna clattering around in the kitchen. She clambered out of bed. She stormed into the kitchen and Deanna chuckled when she looked over her shoulder at her.

"Wild night?" she asked as she continued to scramble eggs.

"I don't know."

Deanna chuckled. "If you don't know then it must have been a wild masquerade ball."

"So I did go to the ball?"

Deanna gave her a strange look as she poured a coffee. "Of course you went to the ball, Miranda," she said knowingly, wiggling her eyebrows.

"Oh." Miranda sat down at the kitchen table. Deanna placed a black coffee in front of her and she gladly took it and sipped the caffeine slowly, savoring it. "What time did I get in last night?"

"Oh, I don't know, after midnight, I think." Deanna gave her a querulous look. "Did you come home with a man by any chance?"

"No, I don't know, why?" Miranda asked quickly.

"I thought I heard you come home with someone," she teased again.

A shiver ran down her spine. *It was real, it was all real.* She took a sip of her coffee letting it all sink in. Then she remembered it all, she was Mira Romanov, a Russian gypsy, reborn. She remembered who her parents were, she remembered her life wandering in a caravan. Nights of music and dancing around a bonfire. She remembered the first night that she met Alek, the night he wandered into their gypsy camp.

43

She was dancing—it was her first night dancing. The provocative sway of the music, the violin and tambourine causing her pulse to quicken as she danced and twirled. While she danced she could feel Alek's eyes on her, watching her from the other side of the bonfire. She knew she could make easy money if she slept with him, she didn't know that she would fall in love with the man who took her virginity.

Miranda put her face in her hands and began to cry as all the memories came flooding back to her. She felt Deanna's arm go around her shoulders.

"Miranda, oh my god, what's wrong?"

"Nothing, Dee. I'm fine." She wiped the tears from her eyes. "I met a man and I'm in love."

Deanna looked surprised. "Miranda, I was only kidding about letting loose. What happened, did someone hurt you?" she asked, concerned.

"No, nothing is wrong." She finished off her coffee. "I have to go...back to Violet Hall. I have some work I have to finish off before the big meeting on Monday."

Chapter Four

ℬ

After showering and making herself more presentable she hopped into her PT Cruiser and pushed the speed limit across the city, making her way out to Violet Hall.

What was she going to say to him? Had it really happened, or was this some sort of wild dream that she believed to be true?

"It's real, it has to be," she told herself as she turned her car up the gravel drive of Violet Hall. The memories she had, she didn't just imagine them. They had to be real.

It looked so different in the daylight. It didn't look as magical as it had the night before. In the daylight it looked like an old home that was being restored. Teams of restoration crews were out and about today and the remnants of last night's party were being carried away by the party planner.

She parked her car and then realized that she had parked where the crypt should have been.

Where had it gone, where did it go? How could a large stone mausoleum disappear?

She turned around and scanned the grounds and bumped smack into the man that had posed as the doorman last night.

"Ah, Ms. Carter, how are you?"

"I'm fine, thank you. I have some papers for Mr. Valquet to sign, legal stuff." She brandished a small black portfolio in his face.

"Of course, he's in the study," the man said. "Have a nice day, Ms. Carter."

He turned to leave and she grabbed his arm. "Wait, remember last night, the myth about the crypt."

He looked at her, confused. "Crypt?"

"Yes, last night, when I arrived. You told me about the crypt and the curse of Violet Hall."

The man looked at her as if she was crazy. "There's no curse of Violet Hall, nor has there been any crypt on this property."

"But...I don't understand."

"Violet Hall has been in the Valquet family since it was built."

"No, Mr. Valquet purchased it. I helped arrange the transaction. I helped him arrange the restoration."

"Purchase, no, Ms. Carter. You're his fiancée."

"Pardon?" Miranda choked. She looked down at her portfolio. "Then what are these papers for?"

The man shrugged. "I don't know, Ms. Carter. You are Monsieur Valquet's lawyer, that's how you met."

Miranda let him go with an uncertain nod. The man waved and continued on his way. She looked back over her shoulder at the house. *What is going on? Am I losing my mind?*

"Mira," came a small voice from behind her. She turned and saw a small old lady behind her. She was dressed all in black, her dark brown eyes were very familiar to her. Then she knew it was the woman she had spied the night before. The gypsy woman in the trees.

"Do I...do I know you?" she asked.

"Walk with me." The old lady headed off toward the back of the plantation to a gazebo in the midst of a beautiful garden. Miranda followed her until they reached the gazebo. The old woman sat down on a bench and patted the seat next to her. Miranda sat down.

"Who are you?" she asked the old woman.

"I am your grandmother. I am the one that put the curse on Alek, so that he could live to wait for you."

"My grandmother?" Mira asked, confused. She ran her fingers through her hair.

"Well, only an echo of the past," the old woman said, patting her hand. "The curse of Violet Hall has been broken. No one will remember what transpired in the past, only you and Alek will remember."

Miranda felt her eyes well up. She felt the tears rolling down her cheeks. *It was real, all of it was real.*

"Now Alek is mortal. He will age and grow old and eventually die but all the past wrongs that his wife did to your innocent soul and your son's innocent soul have been righted."

"My son?" Miranda asked.

"That will come with time. All that was broken has been made whole again." The old woman smiled and patted her hand again. "I am so glad that you have returned from limbo, that you're home and safe. Now go to Alek. He is waiting for you."

Miranda embraced the small old woman. "Thank you, Grandmother. Thank you."

She got up and ran down the path toward the open French doors. She turned around to thank her grandmother once more but she was gone.

Miranda thanked her silently again and made her way inside. Through the French doors she found herself in Violet Hall's study. At the desk, in a pair of khaki pants and white linen shirt, with his back to her, was Alek.

She whispered his name and he slowly turned. Her pulse quickened as their eyes locked from across the room. Those green eyes she remembered all too clearly, those eyes that had been glazed over in passion behind his mask. She knew those eyes.

He held out his arms, wide open and she flung herself into them. Their mouths met and she remembered the kiss that she had tasted many times last night.

He said nothing to her. He scooped her up in his strong arms and carried her out into the hall, up the stairs toward the room that they had shared last night.

She giggled to herself when she saw the remains of the silken bonds from the night before still strewn across the sheets.

"All these servants, monsieur, and you can't even make your bed."

He laughed out loud before kissing her quickly. "I wanted to make sure that you remembered last night. I was concerned that your rational, logical mind would convince your heart that this could not be true."

"I tried to convince myself that it wasn't true. Believe me, for a while I thought that if I believed that you were over two hundred years old and that I have been in limbo for that length that I would be losing my mind." She kissed him quickly as he pulled her T-shirt over her head and then removed her bra. He began to suckle her nipples. "Maybe I am a bit crazy," she whispered, running her fingers through his hair.

"I am crazy, I am crazy for you. I've been waiting for so long. I had not been with another woman for over two hundred years. Last night was so hard for me to keep control, *ma chere*. Being buried deep inside you again was like heaven."

"That is a long time to remain celibate, monsieur. It looks like we have some making up to do."

He chuckled as he pulled her jeans over her hips and then quickly discarded her underwear.

"I plan to make up those two hundred and fifty years that we were apart every day and every night," he said huskily as he unbuttoned his shirt and then pulled down his pants. He covered her body with his. She ran her hands down his back.

"And what if I am giving birth, surely I will get some respite on that night."

"Of course, but that means we will have to make up doubly for it the next night."

Miranda giggled as he began to nibble on her neck. "I don't think I will ever get tired of this." Miranda sighed as she felt Alek sink deep inside her.

"You better not," he whispered in her ear. "I won't let you."

Their talking ceased as they greeted each other properly, not once but twice. Afterward, Miranda lay in his arms.

"How did you know?" she asked dreamily.

"I knew that I would find you again. My heart knew you as soon as I saw you. I knew that you would remember, I just had to make your heart remember who you were."

"And you knew that I would remember."

"Of course I knew you would remember. I saw your soul and I saw your face and eyes. Your memories were buried deep inside you, I knew you would remember. If I believed that you would not then what would I have to live for? Living without you for so long has been a curse. Like a living hell."

"So, you found me and devised an elaborate masquerade to make me remember my past."

"*Oui* and it worked, did it not?" he asked, nibbling her ear. "You're here in my bed and in a month we'll be married."

"Such an elaborate scheme to trap me into marriage, monsieur," Miranda teased. "Are you sure it was worth it?"

"It was worth it," he said.

"You were so sure I would fall for it and fall into your arms."

"It was clear that you wanted me. I could see it through your mask, you wore a mask of desire."

Miranda silenced him by kissing him and never letting him go.

BETWEEN A ROCK AND A HARD-ON
Cindy Spencer Pape

ᴇᴏ

Dedication

∞

*Dedicated to the wonderful friends I've made among my
fellow authors in the Pond — and to the big frog herself,
our editor Helen. Happy Halloween.*

Chapter One

** හ**

He couldn't fucking believe it.

One of the most sacred nights of the pagan calendar and his boss was making him hang out at a party. Not that he was particularly religious, but his sister Dana was going to tear a strip off his hide if he missed her coven's ritual tonight after he'd promised to be there. Besides, this was a *children*'s party and Bram wasn't all that comfortable around children. Not to mention the fact that if any of his brethren saw him standing here in a hotel ballroom, passing out candy in a black acetate cape and cheesy plastic fangs, he'd never hear the end of it.

"You're not Dracula!" One tow-headed boy of about six, who smelled strongly of sugar and candy-maker's wax, tugged hard on Bram's cloak.

"No, I'm not." Bram's voice was slurred by the fake fangs. "He gets invited to much better parties on Halloween. I'm the low-budget version. A second cousin on his mother's side." He pushed just enough genuine power into his words to make the boy's eyes go wide. Nodding as if that answer made perfect sense, the kid took the candy bar Bram held out to him, then scuttled off to the next station.

"That wasn't very nice." The voice in Bram's ear didn't have a body to go with it, so Bram knew who it had to be. There was only one ghost on the team of paranormal enforcers the mayor had put together.

"Hey, Frank." Bram gave a grim smile to another group of approaching youngsters. "How come His Honor doesn't have you doling out goodies?"

"There's the small matter of my hands—not to mention the rest of me—being incorporeal," Frank reminded him. "Actually, he had me stationed in his pathetic excuse for a haunted house. Fortuitously, all of the urchins have now completed that portion of the entertainment."

Bram laughed. Trust Mayor Pendleton to have a real ghost working the haunted house at his Halloween party for underprivileged kids. He passed out treats to the three kids in the next batch, then spoke to Frank again. "Yeah, well this party better finish up pretty quickly. I've got places to be tonight."

"Ooh, a hot date? Do tell." He could hear the envy in the ghost's disembodied voice. "I remember those."

Poor Frank. Bram decided to take pity on him and tell him the truth. "Nah, not a date. I've got a Samhain ritual I promised to attend." His tongue tripped over the plastic fangs and he damn near drooled. Uggh! Enough! He surreptitiously spat the stupid things out into his hand and shoved them in the back pocket of his black chinos, then allowed his own canine teeth to lengthen. To hell with the mayor's "better ideas"!

Another group approached, made up of a bunch of smaller kids this time, shepherded around by a grown-up. Bram had to look twice to figure that out—she wasn't much taller than the kids, but judging by the generous rack that filled the front of her cheap, black witch's outfit, she was an adult. One more look had Bram adjusting his damn cape to hide the sudden hard-on that had sprung up in his pants. But the mayor had screwed up when he'd dressed her as a witch instead of a fairy princess. Long, platinum-blonde curls tumbled out from the pointed cardboard hat. She had big, slightly tilted, green eyes and plump, glossy lips that would look just right wrapped around his cock. He only hoped none of the kids she was wrangling were hers.

"Trick or treat!" Five of the kids chorused the refrain, but one small one began to whimper and point at Bram. He felt a frisson of power and cursed mentally. That kid was a damn wizard, or would be one day. Unfortunately His Honor seemed to have forgotten that kids with magic could usually see through the façade of humanity that Bram wore on a daily basis.

"Don't cry, sweetie, he's just a pretend vampire." The ersatz witch picked up the sniffling toddler and cuddled him close while Bram passed out goodies to the others.

"Here's one for the little guy." He held out a lollipop to the woman as the teary-eyed urchin hid his face in her generous cleavage. *Lucky kid*! Privately, Bram thought the tyke had already gotten the best treat in the place. Bram would happily trade every last piece of candy in Philadelphia for the chance to bury his face between those breasts.

"Thanks." Her voice was soft and breathy and her bright green eyes twinkled as she grinned at Bram. A human wouldn't have been able to discern color in this half-light, but Bram had excellent night vision. "Sorry about Kevin."

She reached up to pluck the candy from his hand and just for a second, their fingers touched. And where they did, they burned. Just a momentary flare of heat, but it was like nothing Bram had ever felt before. If he'd thought he had a hard-on before, now he was going to have trouble walking, his body was so stiff. He actually felt dizzy for an instant as all the blood left his brain. She pulled her hand away like it was burning, so she must have felt it too. It wasn't just a shock of static electricity, it was magic, and Bram knew he was going to have to ask the mayor about her when he got the chance. Maybe the little fake witch was a real one. Wouldn't that make his sister laugh?

* * * * *

Twyla hurried through the woods of Philadelphia's Fairmont Park, cursing the mayor and his stupid party. She'd promised her roommate Katie that she'd be at the Samhain ritual and she was pretty sure she was too late. She shivered and speeded up to a jog. She'd pulled off the tacky witch's costume on the way and magicked it back to her apartment so she wouldn't offend any of the real Wiccan practitioners, but the tank top and running shorts she had on underneath were nowhere near enough for warmth on a chilly October night.

What had possessed Mayor Pendleton to insist that his entire staff work the children's Halloween party? Other than next year's election, of course. Did he have to include his team of paranormal advisors? Most of the mayor's staff thought Twyla was just an educational consultant—couldn't he have let her off the hook? Not that she minded helping out at a party for orphans, but did it have to run so late on the actual holiday? She'd told him herself that Samhain was a holy day to a lot of people. Twyla wasn't normally very big on ceremonies, but Katie's coven was inducting three new elders tonight including Katie, and Twyla had genuinely wanted to be there for her friend's investiture.

She reached the clearing that Katie's coven used for rituals and could tell immediately that it was too late. The glade was empty, but there was still a strong aura of residual magic in the air, along with the scents of sage, cinnamon and other incense.

She paused at the flat granite boulder the coven used as an altar and laid her hands on the rock, murmuring a short prayer of regret for missing the ceremony. The warm tingle of leftover magic crackled through her fingertips and pulsed through her body, straight to her core. It was almost as sexual as the jolt she'd gotten from the guy dressed as a vampire at the mayor's party. He hadn't felt black or empty, so she knew he wasn't a real vamp. But he had been—something. She had no idea what, but she'd never felt quite such a strong sexual pull in all of her six hundred years. One touch and her nipples had sprung to attention and her panties had gotten soaked. Fang-boy had sent all of Twyla's senses humming with nothing more than a casual brush of their hands. If she hadn't been in such a hurry to get to the ritual, she'd have stuck around to find out who — or what — he really was.

Leaning over the altar stone and just thinking about the pseudo-vamp had her tingling all over again and her pussy actually ached for attention. Then she realized that a good bit of the sexual energy she was feeling was emanating from the boulder. There had been sex magic in tonight's ritual, damn it, which wasn't something Katie's coven of white witches usually dabbled in. Whatever the reason, Twyla knew she'd better head back to her apartment and her trusty vibrator. The zing of residual magic was like a feather brushing rhythmically against her clit. It was enough to keep her in a perpetual state of arousal, but not enough to get her off. At times like this she almost missed being at her mother's court, where you could always count on finding a randy faun or pixie when you needed one for a quick roll in the clover. Sex was a lot more complicated here in the human realm where she had to be constantly careful to keep her — er, *family connections* a secret.

Twyla started to straighten, ready to return home, when she felt a sharp blow across her shoulders. She cried out and tried to turn, only to find herself pressed facedown into the rock.

"What?" She kicked backward, connecting with something hard and evoking a grunted whoosh of fetid breath from her attacker. "Let me go!"

"Looks like we got us a pretty one, Tirg. Feisty, too!"

The voice came from off to the left, so Twyla struggled against the weight on her back, finally managing to twist her head and get a look.

"Oh shit! Satyrs!"

Twyla might be feeling horny, but no way was she interested in being the filling in a satyr sandwich. Aside from being supernatural rapists, the goat-boys were known for inflicting pain on their victims. Real pain, not just harmless

S&M games. And on top of that, judging by the one pinning her to the rock, they smelled like week-old shit. She managed to wriggle 'til she was facing that one, then slammed the heel of her hand up into his nose, not even caring when the blood sprayed down the front of her tank top. Not as long as he let her go.

"Get her, boys," he grunted, clutching his face. Oh fuck, there were more than two! Before she could run, strong arms grabbed each of hers, stretching her out as if for crucifixion. She barely had time to register that indignity when she felt the sharp bite of cold iron clapped around her left wrist. The burning pain dropped her to her knees while the satyrs yanked both arms behind her back and shot the handcuff around her other wrist as well, doubling the sting.

Now she couldn't run and she wouldn't be able to cast a spell. The effect of the steel cuffs scrambled her sense and made it hard not to vomit. "What the hell are you boys doing in Philly?"

One of the satyrs looped a length of chain around the circular base of the altar stone and ran it between the linked cuffs and Twyla's back before padlocking the ends together into a tight ring around the bottom. Now her hands were dragged down to the ground and she was effectively chained to a ton and a half of granite.

"Looking for fun." The one she'd hit licked the blood off his lips and rubbed his engorged red phallus, making Twyla swallow some more bile. "Only night of the year we don't have to put clothes on." Of course. On Halloween no one would look twice at the horns on their shaggy heads or the furry legs ending in cloven hooves. People would just assume they were really good costumes. Unless they got a look at those disgusting and oversized cocks.

"Help me pick her up, Jagron." She kicked at them as they lifted her body and turned her 'til she was lying on her back on the altar stone, her arms hanging down behind her head. Her wrists had gone numb, relieving most of the pain from the iron, but the rock was hard and rough against the tender skin of her wings beneath the thin tank top. Even worse, the sex magic from the rock was hitting her whole body now, making her go wet and pliant even though she wanted nothing to do with these monsters.

The ringleader approached the rock, still pumping his rampant cock with his hand. Blood continued to drip from his broken nose, but it didn't seem to be slowing him down any. Twyla screamed as he reached down and ripped her tank top right down the middle, exposing her unbound breasts to the cold night air.

* * * * *

Bram hurried through the woods. His human guise was still in place but he made use of his extra strength and speed to move faster and with less effort. Damn the mayor for catching him and wanting to chat just as Bram had been trying to leave. He was sure he'd missed the ritual by now and Dana was going to be pissed.

A scream ripped through the night. Since it was coming from the ritual glade, Bram broke into a dead run, shedding all pretense at humanity. His claws lengthened and his teeth slid down and into place. He pulled off his shirt to let his wings unfurl and his skin hardened into a pattern of bronze-colored scales. His sister might be in that glade and nobody was going to hurt her and live. Not while Bram was alive to do something about it.

He burst into the clearing and felt a moment of relief. The ritual was apparently over—there was no crowd in the glade. Just three men and one woman.

Fuck. Make that one woman and three satyrs. One of the bastards had just ripped her shirt open and two others were holding her feet, spreading her legs wide for their friend.

"Leave. The. Woman. Alone." Bram threw all of his power into his voice, knew the human's ears would be ringing, but if he saved her from being raped, that was a small price to pay.

"Go get your own." The satyrs didn't even turn and look at Bram. One of the ones holding a foot was jacking off with his other hand. The one in the middle pulled the woman's running shorts down to her knees before ripping them apart with both hands. "This bitch is ours."

"I don't think so, goat-boy!" The woman was still putting up a fight, even though she was pinned and outnumbered. "Sooner or later you'll have to let me up and then I'm going to rip your intestines out and dance on the remains."

"I said, let her go!" Giving his full dragon's roar, Bram bounded into the clearing. One of the satyrs finally looked at him and screamed, dropping the girl's ankle.

"Dragon!" The others looked up at that and all of them paled.

Bram exhaled smoke through his nostrils. "You've got two seconds to run. After that I'm having goat for dinner." He let a small stream of flame escape his mouth.

Two of them fled even before he finished his sentence. The third one, probably the one in charge since he was the one on the woman, just straightened and glared. Blood dripped down his face. Good girl, she'd apparently busted the bastard's nose.

Bram huffed out a little more flame. "One."

The satyr growled something unintelligible, then dashed off into the underbrush after his pals.

Carefully, Bram approached the altar stone. "Miss, are you all right?"

She twisted a bit and moaned. As he walked, he resumed most of his human appearance, leaving claws and teeth in case the bastards came back.

"Miss?"

He got close enough to see her, saw that her hands were chained to the base of the rock, leaving her laid out on the altar defenseless. God knew he wasn't a sicko like the satyrs, but the position was inviting as hell, especially with her big, full breasts bared to the sky, the nipples drawn into knots, whether from fear or cold. Then he noticed the long white-blonde hair and groaned. "No fucking way."

It was. As he leaned over her, wide green eyes gazed up at him. It was the witch from the mayor's party. "Thank you," she whispered.

"Are you all right?" There was blood on her torso and he carefully wiped it away with the shreds of her shorts. His arousal was inappropriate, but overwhelming. He wished circumstances were different so he could pause and play with the sexy little diamond barbell piercing her navel.

"Not mine." She was twisting under his touch, almost as if she wanted—more. "I think I broke the leader's nose."

"Looked like it," he agreed, trying to will away the massive boner in his pants.

"Are you really a dragon?"

Looking into those eyes, he couldn't lie to her. He might have to do something about it later, but right now she deserved the truth. He turned so she could see his wings. "Half. My mother was human."

"Cool. I knew you weren't a real vamp the moment I touched you." Okay, she was at least a witch and he breathed a little easier. She was no stranger to things that went bump in the night. She closed her eyes for a minute and hummed, still squirming. "There was sex magic here tonight. Can you feel it?"

"Like a drug shot straight into my veins." Thank the gods she felt it too. At least now he wouldn't have to apologize for the hard-on. The sight of her offered up like a virgin sacrifice sent all the blood in his body straight to his cock.

"Me too." She gave a little laugh. "Katie's coven had to pick tonight to try that. There's so much oozing off the rock I can't even feel the steel in the cuffs anymore. I don't suppose you're into bondage, are you?"

His answering moan echoed through the clearing. "Goddess help me, I am."

"Maybe you wouldn't mind helping me out then? Right now I don't think I could walk, even if you could get me loose."

"You want me to fuck you?" This couldn't be happening. He didn't want to think he was like the satyrs, taking advantage of a helpless female.

"Only if you want to. But goddess, I wanted you right there at the damn kiddy party. Now it's all but unbearable."

"We should get out of here." He was already unbuttoning his pants.

"After." She lifted her feet to the rock and bent her knees to widen her legs. Bram caught a glimpse of neatly trimmed pale blonde curls. Damn, she was a natural blonde! Then he caught a whiff of her musk and no force in the world could have kept him from burying his face between her thighs.

"Yes!" She bucked against him and cried out as he licked her dripping pussy in one long slurp. She tasted of salt and earth and sex. He ran his tongue lightly from anus to clit, teasing without offering relief. "More!"

"What's your name?" He lifted his face from her cunt just enough to speak, blowing gently on her engorged clit as he did. "No more 'til you tell me."

"T-Twyla," she whimpered, rotating her hips against his face. "I'm Twyla."

"You're beautiful, Twyla." He lowered his mouth back down and circled her clit with the tip of his tongue. "My name is Bram. And I wanted you at the party, too. But only if you're really willing."

"I was planning to go home after the coven meeting and think of you." She huffed out the words between gasps. "While I got myself off. Then I was going to ask the mayor about you tomorrow."

Yeah, that had been pretty much his plan too. With the energy from the rock, the weird magnetism between the two of them and the taste of Twyla on his tongue, his conscience was outnumbered. He reached up with both hands and palmed her breasts while he feasted. The pale nipples were as hard as diamonds under his calloused hands and she moaned when he rubbed them. Oh yeah, she was more than willing. He'd lay money on the fact that she liked being tied up, as long as it wasn't satyrs doing it.

He nibbled on her plump labia and sucked lightly at her clit, earning himself another whimpered "Yes". He barely paused to breathe—he couldn't stop himself from wanting to devour her, to wring every last drop of pleasure he could from a situation that had started so badly. His tongue slid along her folds, circled her puckered rosebud anus, then drew back up to stab inside her. He was pretty sure they heard her scream in Center City as he tweaked both her nipples at the same time as he licked her. She came in a rush, even more of her sweet juices running down between her thighs and coating Bram's chin as he continued to lick and suck until her tremors ceased.

"Do you want me to stop now?" Maybe now that the worst of her tension was relieved, she'd change her mind and decide she didn't want to fuck a total stranger while she was chained to a rock.

"Try it and I'll kill you."

The intense, downright painful arousal had ebbed a bit when she came, but Twyla still wanted him inside her almost more than she wanted her next breath.

He straightened and she could see his hands shaking as he unzipped his fly, toed off his loafers, then shimmied out of his trousers. Goddess, he was perfect—long and thick and delicious. Her cunt throbbed in anticipation of having all that up inside her. She writhed against her bonds. Her wrists had gone totally numb after their prolonged exposure to the toxic metal. She was turned on by the restraint but at the same time longing to get her hands on that magnificent body. "Hurry."

"I'm right here, babe." He braced his arms on either side of her chest and leaned over her on the boulder. "How about a kiss first?"

"Please!" She knew she sounded pathetic, but she didn't care. As he leaned close she could see the glint of moisture on his face, smell herself on his skin. She hadn't thought she could be more turned on, but impossibly, she was. His longish dark hair dusted over her cheekbones as he bent down. Then his lips brushed hers and she flat-out forgot how to think.

Nothing in her experience had prepared her for this. Every other man she'd ever been with faded into oblivion beside the sheer beauty of his lips shaping hers. His hands weren't even touching her and his hairless chest barely brushed the tortured peaks of her nipples, but the flood of sensation from the kiss set every square inch of her skin tingling. When he ran his tongue along the seam of her lips she opened readily, greedily sucking him into her mouth. He tasted of coffee and Twyla's own arousal as he explored the cavern of her mouth. Her tongue danced and slid alongside his, while she lifted upward, trying to rub her nipples against his chest.

"Oh goddess!" He broke the kiss, leaving both of them gasping for breath. Then he knelt on the stone between her legs, nuzzling the side of her neck and then down between her aching breasts. "You are amazing, Twyla." The words were a whispered caress as he circled one nipple with his tongue, shifting his weight off one hand so it could cup and squeeze the other peak. She pulled against the bonds holding her arms over her head, turned on further by the restraint. When he sucked the beaded point into his mouth, she cried out, arching her back up off the stone to force her nipple deeper into the hot cavern. He got the hint and suckled harder, pinching the other nipple with thumb and forefinger. She was so turned on she could almost come again just from this. Then he pulled back and switched sides, nipping softly on the swollen nub.

Colored sparks of light flashed in front of her eyes as she came, a wordless cry forcing its way past her lips.

"That's two," he murmured, laving the abused nipple with soft licks. His voice was deep and rumbly, husky with desire. "Want to stop now?"

"Not done yet." She could already feel her body coiling up for another round. She wanted him so much her womb actually hurt—more than she'd ever wanted anyone before. "Inside me this time. Please."

"Your wish is my command, princess." He'd retracted his claws and now he used one big, long-fingered hand to test her pussy, probing and sliding two long fingers inside before he scissored them open, stretching her tight channel.

"More!" His fingers soothed the empty ache in her womb, but only slightly. She wanted him all, every long, thick, hard inch. And she wanted it now, with an urgency she knew was only partly due to the sex magic spilled here tonight. A good deal of her need had been there the moment she'd laid eyes on him in that hokey fake vampire costume, with his shining dark chestnut hair, glowing golden-brown eyes and gleaming white fangs.

And then he pulled his fingers out and took his cock in hand, positioning it between her swollen labia. He rubbed it against her, coating the fat, dark head with her juices. She craned her neck upward to watch.

"I'm not going to last long, princess." His voice was thick and deep.

"Thank the goddess! I want it *hard*."

"That I can manage." He pushed into her in one powerful shove. He was so big it would have hurt if she hadn't been so fucking turned on.

"All right?"

She looked up into his eyes, which were glowing in the moonlight with a gold metallic sheen. The pupils were just slightly elongated, though she didn't think they'd been at the party. It was as if he was too aroused to control his appearance. Every muscle and sinew was taut beneath the smooth skin that showed just the faintest trace of scale lines. Even the fangs were in evidence when he smiled and Twyla hummed her approval. "Perrrrrfect."

Then he started to move and she forgot how to speak.

Even though she was wetter than she'd ever been in her life, his size made sure she felt every bit of his slow slide out and forceful thrust back in. Her back scooted a few inches up the rock and she cried out at the abrasion to her wings.

"Sorry." He leaned over and slid his hands under her shoulders, wrapping the fingers around to hold her in place. He raised one eyebrow and grinned, but didn't say anything when his fingers brushed against the tip of her wings. The move put his face above hers and it was the most natural thing in the world to crane her neck upward, silently begging for his kiss. He gave her his lips, sliding his tongue into her mouth at the same time as he pistoned his cock back into her pussy, and he swallowed the little whimpers of pleasure she couldn't help making as he fucked her fast and hard.

It was only a few strokes later that their breathing became too labored to maintain the kiss and Bram's head fell to the side while Twyla gasped for air. Before she could even catch her breath, he caught the tendon on the side of her neck with his teeth, biting just hard enough to trigger some sort of pain-pleasure nerve she didn't know she had. At the same time, he slammed into her one last time, setting off the most powerful orgasm she'd ever experienced.

Colored stars filled the grove around them as Twyla screamed, and her pussy clamped down on his cock. That must have done it for him—she felt his whole body tense even further, then with one final thrust, he held himself deep and came, the warm, wet spurt of his seed jetting into her still-pulsating womb. The eroticism of the moment sent her over another peak and she strained against her bonds and cried his name as the stars exploded in front of her eyes brighter than ever before. The sensation was so overwhelming that the world faded to dark.

Chapter Two
ℬ

Holy shit, she'd passed out. Bram had enough strength, barely, to push himself up with his arms and not collapse on top of Twyla. She was so damn tiny he'd probably suffocate her, and that would not be a good way to end what had turned out to be a pretty fucking good evening. Though he still wished he'd had a chance to take the asshole satyrs apart with his bare claws. And maybe teeth.

He pushed up to his knees, then used one hand to brush her tangled blonde curls away from her face. He trailed a finger down to the two small puncture marks on her throat. They were tiny wounds, meant to mark rather than draw blood, and the hormones in his saliva made sure they were already healed shut. What the hell had he been thinking? He'd never bitten a lover before in his life. That was strictly a mating ritual for dragonkind.

Now that he could breathe, could think again, he realized he had to get Twyla out of here. Those cuffs were iron and a lot of the Fae were susceptible to the stuff. It was probably draining her strength even while she was unconscious. He slid off the boulder and examined the cuffs that bound her hands. Swearing at the satyrs, he let his claws out and used one talon to pick the lock on the left cuff. He swore some more when he peeled it away and saw the red, angry burn that circled her pale, tender skin. He released the cuff chain from the longer one that circled the boulder, then climbed back onto the rock and pulled Twyla into his lap to remove the other bracelet. By the time he was done, she'd come to and was smiling up at him.

"Thank you."

He grunted, not sure if she was thanking him for freeing her or for the sex. "You okay?"

She giggled and licked her lips. "Marvelous." She stretched, causing the lower edge of her wing to rub along his cock, which had only gone down to half-mast in the first place. Then she winced. "Okay, a little sore, but I can live with that."

"You've some pretty nasty burns from the iron on your wrists. And I'd like to take a look at those wings in better light, make sure they aren't torn from the rock."

Her eyes darted away and she bit her lower lip. "Busted, huh?"

"'Fraid so, princess. On the up side, I won't need to mess with your memory about seeing mine. What are you anyway? Faery? Pixie? Sprite? You're definitely not a dragon."

"Pixie," she answered in a tiny voice. Then she shivered.

There weren't a lot of pixies running around the mortal realm. They tended to be a bit too flighty for things like jobs and mortgages, but Bram supposed there were exceptions to every rule. He shook off the thought. He could worry about that later. Right now, this little pixie was cold and that was something Bram had the power to do something about. He gathered her close in his arms and sent a warm breath down her spine. Sometimes there were advantages to being a half-dragon.

"Mmm. That was nice." She snuggled into his embrace like she belonged there. "I suppose my clothes are completely trashed, aren't they?"

"Pretty much. Can you conjure yourself some more?" He couldn't remember exactly which magicks went with which branch of the Fae.

She wiggled in his lap 'til her hands were free and her face was no longer burrowing into his chest. Her eyes closed and her lips moved, but nothing else happened.

"Apparently not. The iron cuffs probably sapped things for a while."

She cuddled back against his chest, which Bram had to admit, didn't bother him a bit. Well, it bothered part of him, but only because his cock was starting to think about round two. But then she yawned and he knew he was going to have to wait. It didn't for a second occur to him that this might have been a one-shot deal. There was no doubt in his mind that he'd be seeing Twyla again. Right now though, he needed to get her somewhere warm, somewhere he could take care of the burns and abrasions.

"Okay, princess, time to get moving." Without dislodging her from his arms, he stood and stepped down from the boulder. "Can you stand?"

"Sure." She unfolded her legs and obediently stood on the ground. After one shaky moment when she grabbed his arm for support, she seemed to be fine, so he let her go and took a few seconds to pull on his pants and step into his shoes. She picked up a small purse that had been dropped beside the rock and he handed her a pair of flip-flops, which were apparently the only things she'd had on that the bastard satyrs had left intact. Then he lifted her back into his arms.

"I could walk, you know." But she wrapped her arms around his shoulders and nestled her face into his neck, so he figured the protest was just for show.

"I can move faster, unless you think you can fly. My shirt's a few hundred yards back up the path. Then neither of us will be in trouble if a cop spots us."

She didn't bother to answer and he was already moving. In just a few seconds he was at the bend in the path where he'd dropped his shirt. He set her on her feet and pulled the blousy white linen over her head, though it almost seemed like a sin to cover those curves. "Nice dress."

She laughed at his remark. "It does come to my knees. Thanks."

"Don't mention it. You have a car around here someplace?"

"No. Cars have too much iron in them. I can ride in them, but they never seem to work right when I try to drive. I took the bus."

"Okay, mine's not far. Come on."

* * * * *

She didn't know why she was suddenly apprehensive about getting in a car with him. She'd just let him fuck her literally senseless and all he'd done when she passed out was free her from her bonds. Shaking off her doubts, she didn't demur when he clasped her hand and started walking toward one of the many parking areas scattered throughout the park.

The shirt smelled like him, strong and masculine with a touch of something unfamiliar. It was the sexiest scent she could imagine and she knew it also clung to her skin where they'd touched, almost as if he'd marked her with it. She inhaled deeply and the potency of his musk had her creaming again, as did the stickiness of his semen drying on her thighs. What was it about him that turned her into a nymph? Pixies were pretty sexual beings, but it had never been like this before. Even now, her fingers tingled where they interlaced with his.

"Where do you live?" Was his voice always deep and gravelly like this, or was he still as turned on as she was? A glance down at the front of his pants had her licking her lips. Oh yeah. They were just getting started!

She gave him directions to her apartment in Manayunk while they walked. With every step she let some part of her body brush against his and had to hold herself back from jumping him there on the trail. When they got to the secluded parking area it was still and deserted, with just one car in the corner. She watched as Bram sniffed the air, as if making sure there was no one around.

"No satyrs. No humans. Good." His voice was a rumble, the pitch so deep she could barely hear it—and she had keener hearing than a human. He planted his feet slightly in front of him and leaned back so he was not quite sitting against the front fender of a big vintage muscle car. Then he yanked her into his arms.

She whimpered and practically climbed up his body trying to get her lips on his. Why'd he have to be so damned tall? He must have got the hint, because his strong hands slid up under the oversized shirt and palmed her ass cheeks, then lifted her up, crushing her breasts to his sculpted chest and settling her dripping pussy right over the enormous bulge in his pants. She ground shamelessly against it while they kissed, his lips and tongue devouring hers.

"Goddess, are all pixies as hot as you?" He leaned back, taking her weight on his body, and slid one hand into the crack of her ass, then forward, slipping and sliding through her wet folds.

"Don't think so." She dropped kisses all over his cheek and neck while she squirmed, trying to get those long, talented fingers into her cunt. "I'm not even normally like this. I mean, sex is fun, but I've never needed it like this. If you don't fuck me again soon, I'll go insane."

"Pretty sure I'm already there, princess." He bit down on her throat again, but this time without the fangs. At the same time he stuffed his middle finger into her pussy and wiggled it, finding the knot of nerves that set her screaming. When she started to come he took his thumb, which was slick with her cream, and ran it in a small circle around her anus.

"Yes!" She choked out the word, barely able to breathe. When his thumb breached her sphincter and went into her ass, she convulsed, coming so hard she was afraid something was going to break.

He waited 'til she stopped coming before he shifted her enough to reach the straining zipper of his pants. As soon as she figured out what he was doing, she slid down him, dropped her feet to the ground and replaced his hands with her own. Then very carefully she slid one hand inside his waistband to protect him from the zipper's teeth as she worked it down. He bucked against her hand and gripped the edge of the car with both hands. His spine bowed out as he leaned back over the hood. When his pants dropped down around his ankles, she pulled back a second just to take in the view. The single light in the parking area gleamed off his hairless chest and the glistening tip of his magnificent penis. His cock was pointed up at the stars with the head already weeping.

He'd gone down on her on the rock, now it was her turn. She leaned forward and rested her hands on his chest. "Stay still."

His odd, intense, otherworldly eyes bored into hers. "Whatever you want, princess. As long as it's *soon*!"

She hummed low in her throat. "Oh yeah!" Then she leaned forward and nipped at one bronze nipple.

"Fuck!" She felt his cock grow impossibly larger against her belly.

"We'll get to that," she assured him. Then she sucked his other nipple into her mouth and swirled her tongue around it.

"Damned straight, we will!" His breathing was harsh, fractured, and she could tell it was taking a whole lot of willpower for him to keep his hands on the car and not move.

She trailed a line of kisses down his belly, rimmed his navel with her tongue. When she reached the sparse nest of hair above his cock, the only body hair he seemed to have, she inhaled deeply, soaking in the scent of his musk mingled with the traces of her cream and his cum from before. "Stars, yes!" She had to taste that cock, never mind that she knew he wasn't all going to fit in her mouth.

He bucked against the car, his hips coming away from the fender as she licked her way up his shaft, tasting every inch of his skin along the way. She'd never been with anyone so big before and she wasn't about to waste any of it. She wrapped one hand around the shaft, unsurprised when her fingers didn't touch in the back. Her other hand slid downward to cup each of his heavy balls in turn. She was delighted to find them drawn up tight and taut.

The tip of her tongue circled the flared head of his penis, tracing the underside of the glans before running up along the slit and licking up the thick drops of pre-cum that beaded on the tip. His taste was salty and slightly bitter but hit her like a drug, making her pussy clench and her knees wobble. Unable to wait another instant, she sucked the entire head into her mouth, wrapped both hands around his shaft and squeezed.

Bram literally saw stars in front of his eyes when she slurped his cock into her hot little mouth. She set up a rhythm with her hands, rubbing up and down in time with the swirls of her tongue and the suction of her throat. Her cheeks hollowed as she sucked and he had to lock his knees in place so he didn't slide down the side of the car. He was pretty sure his claws were going to leave marks in the hood of his prized possession, but right now he couldn't bring himself to care, not when Twyla was doing her best to swallow his cock. He felt it bang against the back of her throat and she gave a pleasant hum, sending waves of vibrations through his penis and all the way up his spine.

He wasn't going to last this time either. Fucking her mouth was another way to mark her as his and every cell in his body was determined to do that, with or without his brain's consent. She kept making little noises as she sucked him hungrily, like she couldn't wait to taste a mouthful of semen. Her plump, sexy lips caressed the outer rim of his glans and her busy fingers were hitting every nerve ending up and down the length of his cock. He groaned out loud as his balls drew up even tighter, preparing to spurt down her lovely throat.

"Fuck, yes!" He heard the screech of metal as he pulled his hands away from the hood. He retracted his claws and relaxed his hands so he could bury them in her hair. He gently

74

gripped her scalp and held her head in his lap. He tugged a little on the hair, wanting her to know he was paying attention and she moaned again, deep in her throat, all the way around his cock. He pushed in a little farther, stretching her jaw, and pumped his hips.

"Now!" Even he wasn't sure if it was a command or a warning, in case she wanted to pull back before he erupted. Instead, she took her hands off his cock and dug them into the muscle of his ass, holding him close and deep. She swallowed, forcing his cock farther down her throat and swallowed again, the muscles of her throat milking his penis. That was all it took and he let out a full dragon roar as he shot down her throat, spurting jet after jet of cum into her mouth. Each time she swallowed it triggered another spurt until, completely spent, he fell back onto the hood.

Or so he thought. He learned otherwise when she crawled up his chest and impaled herself onto his still semi-hard cock. Her wordless little cry and the sudden spasming of her vaginal walls around him had him fully erect again in a second. Damn, they were liable to kill each other before they ever even made it out of the fucking parking lot!

Bram stopped driving his cock into her and lay on his back on the hood of his car with a limp pixie sprawled on his chest.

"You okay for now?" He wasn't, not even close, but he figured he could just about make it to Manayunk before he fucked her again. He wasn't even going to pretend it wouldn't happen again the second he got her behind a closed door.

"Yeah." Her answer was little more than a sigh against his chest.

"Then let's get you home, princess."

"'Kay." She stretched and peeled herself off him, grinning when their skin stuck together for a second. "Or we could go to your place. I've got a roommate."

"My place it is, then. If you don't mind."

"I know I should just go home and try to sort out what the hell is happening here. But I don't want to, Bram. I want to be with you tonight, wake up with you in the morning."

"Hell yeah!" He had an idea about what was going on, but didn't think she was ready to hear it just yet. For that matter, he wasn't sure he was ready to acknowledge it yet either. He hopped down from the car and pulled his pants up, while she smoothed his shirt back around her curves.

He handed her into the passenger side and was pleased when she scooted across the wide bench seat to sit in the middle even though he knew it was a bad idea with his control the way it was. He slid in beside her and dropped a kiss onto her forehead. "Over there. The way this is going, we don't dare risk touching while I'm trying to drive. I want us in one piece when we get to my place."

Which reminded him of her wrists and wings, damn it! She moved to the far side of the seat with a rueful chuckle. "Yeah, I guess that's a good idea."

"First, give me your hands."

She paused in the middle of strapping on her seat belt. "Why?"

"Dragons can get kind of rough during sex. So our saliva has a hormone in it that reduces pain and promotes healing." She held out both hands and he took them one at a time and swiped his longer-than-human tongue gently around the abrasions on her wrists. "Better?"

"Just drive. Fast." She slumped back in her seat, breathing heavily.

"How do you know the mayor?" He figured it would take about fifteen minutes to get to Old Town. Ten if there wasn't a lot of traffic. That was plenty of time to get to know each other, wasn't it?

"He's put together this task force of paranormal advisors. It's a cool idea and it's soothed out a lot of the racial tensions in the city, even if most of the humans don't know we exist."

She paused and tipped her head. "I wonder why he doesn't have you on it."

"Because I'm on his other task force. Paranormal Enforcement. He uses us if somebody's getting too out of line. I'm actually a paid member of the police department, but we report directly to the mayor."

"That's cool." She nodded. "So he made you come to the party too. What were you doing in the park after?"

"Looking for my sister Dana and her coven."

"Me too. The coven, I mean. My friend Katie is a witch. I think I've met a woman named Dana at one of her parties. Is she a half-dragon, too?"

Bram nodded, merging into traffic at the highest speed he considered safe. "Different mothers, but both human." Time to change the subject. He didn't really want to discuss any more about dragon family relationships. "So what are you doing in the human realm? Pixies don't come over here all that often."

He saw her shrug from the corner of his eye. "I like it here. Sometimes the Pixie Court can be kind of — confining."

"Court, huh? So you really are a princess."

"Yeah. Queen Mab is my mother. Since you've been calling me princess, I assumed you knew."

"Nope. I didn't. But when I saw you in that crappy witch costume, my first thought was that Pendleton had goofed. He should have cast you as a fairy princess."

"Not fairy, but close." She gave another little laugh. "Just like I knew you weren't a real vamp, but you were just as dangerous."

"Never to you, baby. You know that, don't you?"

Maybe not physically. He might like it rough, but she knew he'd never really inflict damage on a partner. But what about to her heart? Twyla chewed on her lower lip and stared out the windshield of the muscle car in silence. She'd never fallen for a guy like this—not ever. And even though she couldn't have pulled back from him if she'd wanted to—which she really didn't—the whole idea of a relationship was still almost as scary as the damned satyrs.

He parked in a small brick-paved lot in the oldest part of the city—a place where some of the streets were too narrow to accommodate a car. She loved this part of town, the mellow red brick of the buildings had always seemed so warm and cozy. Bram led her down one of the narrow lanes to a three-storey townhouse. The soft glow of the streetlamps showed a red-painted door and a bronze doorknocker in the shape of a dragon. She touched the metal sculpture, admiring the sleek lines that managed to convey both strength and courage.

"Truth in advertising?"

He laughed. "A bit. The humans just think it's a piece of artwork. And if any of the non-human bad guys come snooping around, I consider it fair warning. Nobody's tried to get past the wards on the place and break in yet, anyway."

He unlocked the door and drew her inside. A lamp glowed from the parlor off the tiny foyer, showing a comfortably furnished room in keeping with the three-hundred-year-old character of the house, but not fussily so. Before she could look any closer, Bram closed the front door behind him and scooped her up into his arms.

He took a few long strides into the parlor. "Not going to make it upstairs this time, princess."

"Good." She was already wet, just from sitting next to him in the car. She didn't want to wait.

After one deep, wet kiss, he set her down on a plush sofa then strode over to the fireplace, which already had logs and kindling waiting in the grate. He pulled back the screen and blew gently, his fiery breath igniting the newspapers and twigs. Then he replaced the screen and stood before the hearth on a thick, fluffy fake bearskin rug. "Come here."

She didn't even have to think about it. As she moved toward him, she pulled his shirt off over her head and tossed it aside. "Your wings are gorgeous." She'd seen them in the moonlight and the parking lot, but now the flickering flames reflected off their metallic bronze scales. They were bigger than hers, muscular, with pointed tips and tough, scaled membranes. She reached out a hand to touch the sleek folds, pleased when he shivered at her touch.

"So are yours. How badly do they hurt?" He took her by the shoulders and turned her around so he could examine them. His voice was low and resonant, thick with desire.

"Not much." They were pretty scraped up and more than a little bruised, but not seriously torn.

"Poor princess." He dropped little kisses and licks along her small dragonfly-shaped wings, the drug in his saliva soothing the sore spots. She looked down at her wrists and realized her burns were more than half healed already. Damn, he should bottle the stuff. She moaned when he took the sensitive tip of one wing into his mouth and laved it with his tongue. The pleasure it gave her was both relaxing and sexual. Meanwhile one of his hands snaked around her hip to palm her mound.

"I'd love to tie you up again, but I don't want to hurt your wrists." He licked up her spine between her wings. "So we'll save that for another night."

There was going to be another night? Thank the gods and goddesses! He could tie her up anywhere, any time he wanted. She even had some velvet-covered handcuffs he could use. But right now she wanted him inside her without anymore fun and games. Her legs gave out beneath her and she sank to her knees on the rug. "Now, Bram."

He followed her down, kneeling behind her. He bent his head to her ear to nuzzle and whisper. "Lean forward on your elbows."

Oh yeah! She bent forward at the waist and braced her elbows on the rug, which canted her ass upward. The fluffy rug teased her nipples as her breasts swung beneath her. Bram's hands gripped her hips and his rock-hard penis grazed her butt before he flexed his hips and drove inside her weeping pussy in one fierce thrust. He was so deep he seemed to fill up every bit of space inside her.

He leaned over and nipped the point where her neck met her shoulder. The sensation was so erotic and compelling she pushed back with her butt, driving his cock even deeper into her already-pulsing cunt and cried out his name.

"Twyla!" He straightened his spine and pounded his cock into her pussy, hard and fast and deep. She gripped the rug hard with her hands, rocking back against him as each stroke rubbed her hyper-sensitized nipples against the artificial fur. Another mini orgasm shook her body each time he filled her. "Take me inside you, Twyla. Take all of me."

"Everything," she vowed. "Anything you want. Just keep fucking me like this forever."

"Always!" She knew it was just sex talk, but she'd never wanted to believe anything more. "You." Thrust. "Are." Thrust. "Mine!" With one more deep thrust he sent them both over the edge into a screaming kaleidoscope of an orgasm and colored lights burst around the room like fireworks. Her pussy contracted hard to grip his penis tightly, trying to milk every drop of his hot, spurting seed. She whimpered when he pulled out after the first rush to pump himself with a fist, but it turned to a moan of pleasure when he cried out her name and sprayed the rest of his cum all over her back and wings and ass.

Chapter Three

🔖

She fell forward onto her arms, her pert little heart-shaped ass sticking way up into the air. He let go of his still-hard cock and used his tongue to spread her juices and his semen around her vulva, then all the way up to her puckered rosebud sphincter.

"Temptress." He used one hand to rub the head of his cock up and down the crack of her ass. "You're even wet back there."

"So do it." She wiggled her ass, tormenting him even further. "Just be careful, okay? You're not exactly small."

"Be very sure, princess." He leaned over and let his hot breath caress her throat. This was it, the final step in the mating ritual. He'd marked her neck with his teeth and her skin with his seed. He'd come down her throat and spilled into her womb. If he fucked her in the ass, he'd be bound to her forever. And every fragment of his being wanted that, wanted those bonds with a desperation he'd never dreamed it was possible to feel.

But he discovered that he couldn't make her his without her permission. The choice had to be hers.

"If we do this, it's the same as a marriage vow to a dragon." He was so hard he hurt, so aroused his words were barely intelligible. "So be very sure you want to be a dragon's bride, princess."

"Are—are you proposing to me?"

"I guess I am." And if she didn't say yes, he wasn't sure he'd survive.

"You've never done anal before? Is that what this is about?" Her tone was curious, but her breathing was as ragged with desire as his own. "You can fuck my ass without marrying me. I want you in every way I can get you, Bram. Even there."

"Goddess!" He hadn't thought he could get any harder, but he was. "It isn't that. I've played more sexual games than you can imagine. But dragons have this whole sequence of things we do when we find our perfect mate. And princess, we've already gotten to all but this one. This is the last step. Afterward it will be too late to change your mind."

"Perfect mate?"

Shit, had he really said that out loud? Too late to take it back now. "Yeah. Fucking perfect. For me. If you let me complete the ritual, I'll never be able to let you go. And both half-dragons and pixies live for a really long time."

"So I can look forward to several hundred years of your alpha-male bossiness?" She rolled so swiftly he didn't have time to react. Then her wide, tear-bright green eyes were looking up into his.

"Yeah. I'll try to control it, but I doubt I'll always succeed." He'd try to be an understanding mate, but it was his nature to be dominant, protective. And she was a pixie, a being who needed to be free. What the hell was he thinking to fall for her?

She pursed her lips and narrowed her eyes. "Is this something you want, Bram? Or just some physiological thing you think you need?"

"It does involve a physical reaction for me, but it's not involuntary, and it's not arbitrary. It's happening to me now because I want *you*." How could she doubt it? "From the moment I laid eyes on you in that damn witch outfit, I knew you were something special. Yeah, there's some weird biochemical or maybe metaphysical link between us. But it's not just physical. I like you, Twyla. I already know you're brave, you're a fighter and you have a hell of a sense of humor. You won't let me run roughshod over you and you'll give every bit as good as you get. But if you don't want me, aren't willing to have me as a part of the rest of your life, I'll walk away right now, even if it kills me."

Tears leaked down her cheeks but she made no move to wipe them away. Every bit of her attention was focused on Bram's strong, handsome face. His fangs were out a little with his pupils slightly elongated. She wondered abstractly if he knew that happened during intensely emotional moments — how sexy it looked.

She'd never planned to marry. Most pixies weren't into long-term commitments. She'd come all the way from her mother's kingdom just to gain her freedom. But to deny Bram — to give him up — would hurt more than if someone ripped the very wings from off her back.

Goddess help her, she'd gone and fallen in love with a half-dragon. Well, at least neither of them would freak when their kids came out with wings. She looped her arms up around his neck.

"I accept."

"Twyla!" His mouth crushed down onto hers, his lips hard and fierce. "Thank you, my love, thank you!" Then his tongue slid into her mouth like it belonged there, which she supposed it did. He stroked it along her own and caressed the inside of her cheeks and lips before thrusting in and out in an imitation of sex.

He called her his love! Had he meant it? She suckled his tongue, loving the taste of him, sweet and salty all at the same time. They ate at each other, drank in each other's passion, 'til Twyla couldn't wait any longer to have him penetrate her in that one final way. She wrenched her lips from his and drew in a long, shuddering breath.

"Take me, Bram." He loosened his grip enough to let her roll back to her knees. "My dragon!"

"Goddess, you have the most beautiful ass!" He used his hand to spread her lubrication, making sure her anus was slippery and wet. He dipped his thumb into the rim of her sphincter, ensuring she was wet inside as well. Then he leaned over and licked at it with his tongue. The pointed tip darted inside her hole and Twyla nearly leapt up off the rug at the intensity of the sensation.

"Take me!" She wanted him inside her in every way possible. In her mind, in her heart, even in her ass. She quivered, trying not to move as he scooped some of her own cream to lubricate his penis. The sound of him stroking himself was one of the most erotic things she'd ever heard.

"With pleasure, princess!" First one finger, then two penetrated her anus, stretching her wide. The hormone from his tongue must have prevented her from feeling pain. It didn't hurt at all when he added a third thick digit, then a fourth. She was breathing in little gasps and moans, but she didn't think it was turning him off. Not judging by the size of the erection that replaced his fingers when he positioned the tip of his cock at the entrance to her ass.

"You're sure?" She'd have sworn his voice almost broke over the question.

"Completely. Claim me, dragon. I want to be yours."

"Forever?" She knew he was just trying to give her one last chance to come to her senses, but she had no desire to do so. If this was crazy, she wanted to stay insane for the rest of her life.

"Forever!" She pushed back against him, forcing the bulbous head of his cock partway into her ass. "Fuck me, damn it. Now!"

"Mine!" His roar shook the walls of the townhouse as he rammed himself home. She'd never been so stuffed, so filled, so — whole.

She'd never be a docile mate and he couldn't be prouder of her.

He held himself still, deep inside her ass. "Are you okay?" He could hardly believe she'd taken him all in one thrust, though his slippery saliva had probably helped ease the way.

"Goddess, yes!" Her hips bucked against his groin. "But I need you to move!"

And that was all it took. Her sweet little rosebud hole gripped him tighter than he could with his own fist and the heat of her roared through his veins. Her wetness and his hormones provided enough lube to allow him to slide, but not enough to dull the magnificent friction. He started slowly, gliding out until just the tip remained inside, then pushing himself back home. His claws gripped her hips, holding her in place for his strokes. She'd probably have small puncture wounds when they were done, but right now she didn't seem to mind. Something deep inside him roared with triumph at the thought of her wearing ten more of his marks.

It was impossible to hold back, to keep it slow. Not when her internal muscles sheathed him so tightly, when her broken little cries accelerated with every thrust. He pistoned harder, faster and deeper and when he felt his balls draw up tight to his body, he bent over her and pounded into her even more passionately.

When the explosion came, it was the strongest one he'd ever had. He was pretty damn sure he'd blown the top of his head off. Twyla screamed and shattered around him as he flooded her ass with semen, her muscles clenching him, prolonging his orgasm, wringing every last drop of moisture from his spent and exhausted body.

When it was finally over and even her twitching aftershocks had subsided, he pulled out and collapsed beside Twyla, wrapping her in his arms. This was where she belonged and he was never letting go of her again. As a half-dragon, he'd never been totally sure that the mating frenzy would happen for him, but now that it had, he couldn't be happier.

"We could go upstairs to bed," he whispered several minutes later, when he'd remembered how to breathe again. He smoothed her tangled curls away from her pink and sweat-dampened face.

She stirred and stretched, smiling up at him. "Sounds like a plan. I think I could sleep for a week."

"You've had a busy night." First there was the party and then the park. He thought about the satyrs and had to fight down a murderous rage. If he ever saw those assholes again, they were dead. And yet without them, he might not have found Twyla, at least not tonight. So he hugged her close and set the rage aside.

"You too." She ran one tiny hand through his hair, then tapped him irreverently on the nose.

"Best night of my life," he told her. And it was no less than the truth.

She turned to face him, her smile warm and wonderful, her glorious green eyes brimming with emotion. "I love you, Bram. I know pixies are supposed to be fickle and flighty, but I'm not like that. I can't believe it happened this fast, but I've fallen in love with you."

"Good." Goddess, were those tears clogging his throat? That was not supposed to happen. Grown half-dragons did not cry, especially not from happiness. He distracted himself by licking the small claw marks on her hips. "Sorry about those."

"Don't be." Her grin turned sultry. "I like knowing I bring out the wild side of you."

Could any woman be more perfect for a dragon's mate? Bram didn't think so. He started to tell her that when he heard music blaring from her purse.

"It's Katie." Twyla knew her friend would be worried, so she sat up and reached for the bag. She pulled out her phone, flipped it open and spoke. "Hey, Kate. Sorry I missed the ritual."

"Are you all right?" Katie was a worrywart.

"Never been better." She laughed, a sound Katie couldn't mistake as anything but sexual satisfaction. "And tell your friend Dana her brother is just fine too." Incredibly fine as a matter of fact. She reached out with one finger and traced a line down Bram's left wing.

"Thank the goddess! We were worried about both of you. Umm… You do know that Dana and her brother aren't totally — human, don't you?"

"Oh yeah. But since I'm not either, it isn't a problem."

"Did you run into him at the park?"

"Yeah. But it turned out we'd already met at the mayor's party tonight, by the way. Who knew he had a team of paranormal cops as well as our advisory task force?"

"Really? I only met Bram a couple of times, didn't know what he did. I'm glad you didn't make it to the grove, though. There was a group there ahead of us, so we had to move our ritual to Lexa's garden. I tried to call you." One of the witches in Katie's coven had a big estate out in Bala Cynwyd.

""I had my phone off for the party and must have forgotten to turn it back on."

"Well, I'm glad you're ok. I'm pretty sure that they were doing a fertility ritual, so we cleared out pretty quickly."

"Fertility ritual?" She managed not to shriek, but her hand flew up to her mouth. Bram grinned and raised one eyebrow in question. Lying stretched out on his side on the furry rug, he was still the sexiest damn thing she'd ever seen, even if she was totally worn out.

"Yeah. Anybody who hung around that grove tonight had better be using double or triple protection for a while. It was pretty powerful stuff. I could sense it from like a hundred yards away. So we split."

"I see." Stars and moon, she and Bram hadn't used anything! Not on the rock, not in the parking lot, not here on the rug! "Anyway, Katie, I'll stop by tomorrow to grab some clothes, okay? I think I'm going to spend a few days here with Bram."

Yeah, like the rest of her life. But she wanted to tell Katie in person, with Bram by her side. And they'd have to go tell her mother, as well. Wouldn't that be fun? Mab was not likely to be overjoyed at having a dragon for a son-in-law.

She hung up the phone and turned to Bram, her mouth completely dry. It took a second to get her voice to work. "You heard?"

"Somebody did a fertility rite in the grove?"

Twyla nodded, her hand going down to cover her womb. "Do you think…"

Bram shifted and sat up to pull her into his lap and take her in his arms. His hand slid down to cover hers. "It could happen," he said agreeably. "Would you mind?"

"I—I don't think so." Her mind whirled and she clung to him for stability in the storm. "I just wasn't thinking about it so soon."

"Then we won't worry about it one way or the other. I love you, Twyla. That isn't going to change, not now, not ever. I'd like to have kids with you, someday. Now or later doesn't matter. I watched you tonight with those orphans. You'd make a marvelous mother."

And he would be a fantastic dad. Whenever it happened. She smiled and laid her cheek against his chest. "I suppose it's too late to worry about it anyway. I'm either pregnant or I'm not and we'll find out soon enough. But the mayor is going to have kittens, after he's tried so hard to keep his two groups of non-humans apart."

"Pendleton will cope." Without shifting her from his arms, Bram stood and carried her to the stairs. "Time to go to bed, princess. We've got plans to make tomorrow."

"Yep." After a quick shower together, she snuggled into his chest, not wanting to be anywhere else in the world. He took her to what was obviously the master bedroom, set her down carefully beside the big, rumpled bed.

"You know the black comforter and curtains are going to have to go," she teased. "The parlor was fine, but this room just screams 'bachelor pad'."

"Even the silk sheets?" He drew back the duvet to reveal glossy black sheets. She allowed him to pull her down beside him, felt the smooth glide of the fabric against her skin and smiled.

"They come in other colors, fang-boy."

His chuckle was warm and seductive. He pulled her full-length against him and kissed the top of her head. "I can live with that. There's a room across the hall that will work as a nursery if we need it."

Twyla yawned. They probably would, if not right away, then eventually. "We'll worry about that tomorrow." She glanced at the clock. "Or more accurately, later today."

"Now my beautiful mate needs her rest," he agreed, then yawned himself. "And so do I. Glad I'm not on duty tomorrow morning."

"Me too." She relaxed into him, reveling in the feel of his hot, hard body lying so peacefully next to hers. "Love you."

He bent and pressed an exquisitely sweet kiss on her lips. "I love you, Princess Twyla, with every bit of my body, heart and soul. This has been the best Samhain ever."

Happy tears leaked from the corners of her eyes but he kissed them away. "I want you again already, woman. So if you want to sleep, you'd better tell me to go away."

"Don't go away, Bram." She shifted over him, then lowered herself to capture his cock with her cunt, loving the feel of him filling her, completing her. He groaned as she slid down to fully take him in and she looked into his incredible eyes. "Don't ever go away."

MISCHIEF NIGHT

Cris Anson

ഔ

Trademarks Acknowledgement

ℭℴ

The author acknowledges the trademarked status and trademark owners of the following wordmarks mentioned in this work of fiction:

Outlook: Microsoft Corporation

Playgirl: Playgirl Key Club, Inc

YouTube: Google, Inc.

Chapter One

ဢ

"Naked men, Miss Fortier?"

Annabelle Fortier's breath hitched. Her fingers gripped around the day's first cup of coffee. Her long legs refused to move her out of the doorway and into her office as she took in the man who stood behind her desk. Her boss Lowell Smith, the man she'd had X-rated fantasies about since she'd come to work here six months ago, held her clandestine Playgirl calendar aloft. Mr. June stared back at her, clad only in his muscular splendor and a sensuous half-smile.

Heat raced up Annabelle's face. She knew that such a provocative item had no place in an office, but the model reminded her of Mr. Smith—the piercing blue eyes, black swept-back hair, angular jaw—and she used it as a pacifier. Well, okay, as her meditation cue when her workload overwhelmed her. But she kept it inside her top center drawer. Way in the back. Closed.

For a long moment she felt like a schoolgirl caught ogling the star quarterback in the boys' locker room. Then outrage kicked in. "Why are you rifling through my desk?"

"Please come in, Miss Fortier."

Electricity arced in the air between them as his intense gaze bored into her. She had the strangest sensation he knew why that particular month was so dog-eared.

"Believe it or not," he said, a half-smile of his own breaking out, "I was looking for your calendar."

Finally Annabelle's sense of self-preservation kicked in and she strode up to him. "My calendar is viewable on everyone's computer. We have Outlook, remember? I keep all my appointments there, so anyone can see what my schedule is."

"I already checked it. It didn't show anything for this evening, and I thought that this might be your...personal calendar. I wanted to be sure before I asked you."

Not that she'd sully all those hunks by writing on them. Then the dawn broke. "Ask me what?"

"If you're doing anything tonight."

Annabelle narrowed her eyes. "Why?" If she had to go to another meeting of the planning board, she'd scream.

He indicated the calendar. "I know now that you're the right person to ask. Would you like to go to a Halloween party?"

Would she like to go to a party with Studley Do-right? Was water wet? Her mind did a one-eighty.

"I'd love to, Mr. Smith." Dare she hope he saw her as more than just a competent assistant designer? The heavy-lidded look in his eyes at this moment said he did.

"Good. It's at the Savidges' home in Wayne. Eight o'clock."

Wayne was an upscale suburb of Philadelphia, a place of sprawling mansions and outrageously high property taxes. She'd passed through it, browsed the shops on the Main Line, but had never been invited to a home in the town. This would be a treat. "Is it a costume party?"

"Yes." He glanced at the gold watch at his wrist. "Take the rest of the day off and find yourself a costume."

She blinked. She'd never taken a sick or vacation day, often worked late with him, tried to make herself indispensable to this workaholic boss. It wasn't yet noon and he was giving her all this time to get ready. Her fantasies shifted into high gear.

"Is there a theme?"

"I don't know. They're making the downstairs into a haunted house kind of thing. Here's the invitation. Directions are on the back. You'll have to present it at the door."

She would? Fighting to keep any expression from her voice or her face, she parried, "We'll be going in separate cars?"

"Mr. Savidge is our most influential client. He sent me an invitation that I can't use because of an important meeting that just came up. I didn't want to insult him by not putting in an appearance after I had already accepted."

"But if you can't go, how will you put in an appearance?"

"The invitation." He swept an arm in the direction of the invitation lying on top of the sketches on Annabelle's desk. "Each ticket is numbered in the upper right-hand corner. He'll know."

She must have looked like Dumb Dora, because he added, "We both belong to an exclusive club. That's my membership number. He'll probably be at the door himself, checking identities. No one is admitted that he doesn't know." He smiled at her, the full, kissable lips parting to reveal strong white teeth. "If he asks, you just tell him you're coming in my place.

"And," he said almost as an afterthought as he turned to leave, "I'll try to wind up my meeting early, so I might see you there later."

At least he'd dangled a carrot in front of her, Annabelle thought later as she returned home with her packages. She had gone to three costume shops before she found something that would knock his socks off — provided, of course, he would actually manage to get there before the party wound down. And since it was a weeknight, she didn't want to stay too late waiting for him. She had an important meeting tomorrow.

But seeing as how she'd lusted after him from the first day she'd interviewed, and seeing as how Lowell Smith, bachelor extraordinaire, was too involved in work to notice her as a woman—although she admitted having caught him looking speculatively at her when he thought she didn't know it—she considered this evening a golden opportunity to make him see more than just the MBA in architecture that he'd hired over twenty-some other candidates.

Did the rich keep to schedules? she wondered as she drove down Lancaster Avenue in Wayne at exactly eight p.m. Should she arrive on time? Fashionably late? Or maybe, she thought sourly, she should concentrate on the directions to be sure she arrived at all. This was the last week in October, so darkness had long since fallen, and even though the streets were well marked, they certainly weren't spotlighted.

She found the address in short order and steered her little two-seater into a driveway which carved a semi-circle out of a lawn still green and raked free of fallen leaves. Luxury cars were parked off to the side by valets, one of whom hurried to her door. Maybe she wasn't rich, but her hair was. Instead of her usual braid or French twist that was her work style, it fell in soft auburn curls halfway down her back, accenting the vivid green of her eyes.

As she slid out of the seat, her costume rode up her long, slender legs. The valet gave her an appreciative once-over and made Annabelle feel a little better. She would have fun tonight, with or without Mr. Smith.

The front door was opened by a strikingly handsome man dressed all in black, including a cape slung across his shoulders—either a vampire or a man on his way to opening night at the opera. He held out his hand and assisted her across the threshold.

"And who do I have the pleasure of welcoming?" he said in a deliciously sexy baritone.

Oops! She needed to present the invitation. "Annabelle Fortier," she replied, fumbling in her beaded purse for the ticket.

He glanced at it. "Lowell will be joining us later?"

"I hope so," she blurted out, then added, "he was upset that he had to meet a client at the last minute."

"Understood. May I take your wrap? By the way, I'm your host, Robert Savidge."

"A pleasure." She turned and allowed the pashmina to slide off her shoulders.

"I knew Lowell had exquisite taste."

Annabelle turned around, a question in her eyes at the comment.

"You will undoubtedly be the second-most beautiful woman here tonight," he said smoothly. "After my fiancée. You look like a wood sprite, or a fairy. Or…I know, the delicate creature on that water bottle who's kneeling at the edge of a pond to see her reflection."

Annabelle could feel her face heat up at his compliment. If only Mr. Smith would see her in such a light. But maybe he did. The way he'd looked at her while holding that calendar…

She felt her costume suited her. It consisted of a short white slip with white silk squares applied here and there like dangling handkerchiefs, and tiny wings of gossamer thinness tacked on near her shoulder blades. And white stiletto sandals that wrapped up around her ankles.

"Would you like a mask?"

"I think not." She considered her eyes her best asset and didn't want to hide them, but more importantly, she wanted to be sure Mr. Smith didn't mistake anyone else for her. If he showed up.

The hint of a smile played around her host's lips then he ushered her from the foyer into a large living room. "Help yourself to something to eat and drink, then when you're ready, please walk through that door…" he indicated one on the far wall, "and enjoy our Haunted House Tour."

As a budding architect, Annabelle considered how one would make a haunted house out of this 1900s mansion. With fourteen-foot-high ceilings and a foyer bigger than her living room, she could just imagine room after room sprawling out in an H, perhaps. Or a U.

Draining the last sip of champagne, she sauntered to the door and walked through.

The door slammed shut behind her and she found herself in pitch-black darkness. Instinctively she reached her arms out and was reassured to feel a velvety wall on her left. She wasn't claustrophobic, but it was slightly unnerving.

"Okay," she muttered. "It's only a figment of someone's imagination. Skeletons will pop out and clack their bones, no doubt I'll brush against synthetic cobwebs, there'll be maniacal laughter and rubber-hose snakes. You can do it. Move it, feet!"

They did. She trailed fingertips over the velvet, feeling it curve to the right. Directly ahead, a vignette appeared, lit by a dim blue light. Annabelle stopped abruptly. A naked, voluptuous blonde woman stood under the spotlight. Behind her, a vampire—her host?—curved his black-clad arms around the woman's waist. Her chin was raised, exposing a graceful neck. The man dipped his head and opened his mouth, displaying, yes, she was sure, fangs. He sank them into the white throat and Annabelle flinched. Tears of blood dripped at the point of contact. The woman undulated her hips and the man slid his hands down her belly to the soft blonde hair below, and the lights faded.

Annabelle took a deep breath. *Wow!* This was like no haunted house she'd ever tripped through.

"Please keep moving," said a disembodied voice.

Right. She was pretty sophisticated, she wouldn't let a little thing like a naked woman being stroked and bitten and bloodied throw her off stride.

She took a few more steps, then when nothing happened, a few more. Suddenly the front of her bare thighs hit what felt like a barrier of open hands, cool and dry, one from each side of the corridor. She stopped in shock, pressed her hand against the wall to keep a grip on reality. Two other hands closed in on the backs of her legs, big, masculine hands whose fingers briefly tightened against her muscles. Their palms ran lightly down her legs, front and back, to her knees then back up, brushing under the hem of her costume and against the crotch of her panties with light, teasing strokes. Her pussy tingled, shocking her more.

Resolutely she pressed forward. The hands gave way and she almost bumped into a wall. The hallway apparently made a ninety-degree angle. Following it, she saw a red glow and another vignette. As she approached, she felt her jaw drop. Another naked woman came into view. She was kneeling on a cushioned platform, cheek resting on a pillow, ass haystacked in the air. Her arms stretched forward. Red scarves tied to unseen posts held her immobile. A well-built man in tight leather pants and nothing else stood behind her, holding a wooden paddle.

Annabelle must have gasped, because the tableau came to life. The man swung his arm, and a resounding *smack* echoed through the dark hallway. And another, and another. The woman wiggled as if to demand more, and the man complied. Annabelle could see the red marks blossoming on the woman's pale ass cheeks and thighs as the paddle struck again and again. Then the red light darkened to maroon then black then disappeared altogether.

Wow! What kind of club did Mr. Smith belong to? Was he a regular participant in such activities? Did he think this was the best way to see if she wanted to join in the…fun? And how would he—and she—have responded if he'd accompanied her through this journey?

Oh God, that's what he meant when he'd said, "the right person to ask" while he waved Mr. June in front of her nose. He was warming her up—she hoped—for some extracurricular activity. In the back of her mind Annabelle thought it a good thing her costume was so skimpy. Just thinking of what they could do together had her blood heated until she probably had a rosy glow all over her skin. If she had worn, say, a body suit or a form-fitting cat costume, she'd be too hot to move.

Shaking her head, she continued walking. And bumped into a body.

The full Monty. A full-frontal, naked male body.

Instinctively she moved to regain her balance in the darkness, clasping massive muscled arms in her grip. Holy Hannah. Definitely a male, because she felt the probing jut of his manhood aimed right between her legs.

His hands went around her, connected with her butt, and he lifted her with the greatest ease, rubbing her against his hard-on, up and down in slow, sensuous movements. The faint scent of sandalwood and aroused male wrapped around her.

She couldn't help it. She dipped her head, lowering her lips to the side of his head and licked whatever she could reach. His neck, smooth-shaven. The lobe of his ear, which she gently tugged with her teeth.

Common sense warred with her awakening lust. Did they time how long it took to traverse this Haunted House? Who was this anonymous man? Maybe she could have some fun in the dark...

Sheesh! She must be out of her mind. What if Mr. Smith was waiting for her at the end of the tour and she took forever to come out? She'd never be able to look him in the eye again.

So with no small regret, she pushed herself away from his rock-hard pecs, his washboard abs, and felt his reluctance as he gently set her back on her feet. And just like that, he disappeared behind a hidden escape hatch.

Now she just hoped the end was in sight. What if the other guests would be watching to see her reactions? Should she act lust-filled? Shocked? Jaded? Heck, maybe they'd snicker. Or ignore her. Or maybe they'd be doing in public what had been hinted at within these black confines.

Keeping her fingers in contact with the left-hand wall, Annabelle came to an opening. Faced with the prospect of making a U-ey or following the other side of the wall, she peered closer to see how wide the opening was. Maybe the wall continued after an interval. Or it could be a doorway she should walk through.

She gripped the jamb and swung her body to the left to explore the opening, her right-hand palm out in front of her. And connected with what was unmistakably a woman's heavy, full breast. By now Annabelle was so attuned to her sensual side and the darkness was so complete that she didn't recoil. Instead, curiosity asserted itself. She stroked it, hefted its weight in her palm, grasped the nipple between thumb and forefinger to test its resilience.

The woman in turn fondled Annabelle's breasts with both hands. Lightning streaked from her nipples to her pussy and her hips jerked. She felt moisture gathering in her panties. Any more stimulation, she thought, and it would be rolling down her thigh.

As if her hip movement were an invitation, the woman grasped Annabelle's waist, bent down and found Annabelle's breast with her mouth. It was too much. Although she was far from a prude, she'd never entertained the idea of dallying with another woman. She took a step back to give herself time to absorb the possibility of a woman-on-woman encounter.

Again, the performer took her cue from the guest and faded into the darkness, leaving her alone and tingling.

"Please enter through the opening," the same disembodied voice instructed.

It took Annabelle a moment to move her feet. She had the presence of mind to reach out both arms to discover the parameters of the darkness and found that the path indeed turned back on itself. Like a cornfield maze, she thought. Except tactile, not visual. Okay, she could deal.

Or not.

Because the sight that greeted her at the end of the short hallway infused her with a longing to hold and be held, to be kissed, caressed, to be loved.

Or at least fucked.

She shook her head to clear it. It wasn't like her to use such words. She didn't consider herself crude or earthy or promiscuous. But at this moment in time, with these stimuli, with the hope that Mr. Smith and his intense look would be at the end of her journey...

Gingerly she approached this new tableau, warmed by golden lamplight. Two men and a woman were arrayed on a bed, the woman lying face to face and on top of one of the men, the other kneeling to one side, caressing both of them. All three had the glossy bodies of models and all looked intent on their mission—kissing, touching, moving body parts one against another in apparent bliss.

Annabelle stared, entranced. Her nipples were so sensitive, so engorged, that they felt abraded by the silken slip with every breath. The aching center between her legs begged for attention and she let her hands wander down her belly to stroke it. Her breathing roughened. Her hips moved in sync with the woman on the bed.

Suddenly the man on his knees stared directly at Annabelle, and she realized she had moved so close to the tableau that the golden light fell on her as well, making her equally visible to them. He raised one hand and beckoned. Mortified, Annabelle lowered her eyes, leaned forward to rest her head on the glass—and discovered there was no barrier between her and the trio on the bed.

In shock she jerked her head up. The man's dark eyes burned into her green ones. His hand—and his rampant cock—reached for her.

She wet her dry lips with her tongue. Lord, but he was perfection, curly blond hair reaching almost to his wide shoulders, a thick splash of hair matting his muscled chest between the flat brown nipples, a thicker nest encircling his cock.

For a long moment Annabelle stood rooted to the spot, her gaze clinging to that magnificent specimen of manhood, her temperature spiking and her pussy juices overflowing her panties and trickling down her thigh.

Oh she was tempted. But no, she wasn't a wanton. It was like watching an adult movie, that was all. It was the day before Halloween, Mischief Night, and this was a Halloween party. She was there as the guest of her *boss*, for heaven's sake, and she'd better find the gumption to walk away and find the end of this tour because how would she explain to Mr. Smith that she'd participated in a sexual foursome?

Pivoting on one stiletto, she managed to grope her way down the hallway, through a couple of twists and turns in the pitch-blackness until she stumbled onto a small sign, lit by a night-light, that proclaimed, "This way out."

Relieved, but with a touch of regret, Annabelle grasped the doorknob and walked into a dimly lit room that looked like a solarium. Glass walls, glass ceiling, large plants and ferns and tropical trees in huge pots, wicker furniture with plump, brightly colored cushions. Men and women in all kinds of costumes standing in small groups and holding glasses. A bar, a bartender.

Just what the doctor ordered.

She sauntered — she hoped that's what it looked like — to the bar and ordered a gin and tonic, tall glass. Some of the men looked at her with avid interest, some of the women nodded or smiled, but no one acted as though she had a scarlet letter pasted on her chest.

Annabelle felt as though she'd passed some kind of test. She took several gulps of the refreshing drink.

And saw Mr. Smith approaching her.

But holy Hannah, not in her wildest imaginings did she visualize the pagan god striding toward her. His black hair, untamed and curling down to his neck—he must use a gel to keep it in place during work hours, she thought—was somewhat held down by a beaded Indian headband. His face and muscular, hairless torso were decorated with streaks of white, ochre and several other shades of a powdery substance. As to a costume, the only thing covering him was a tan leather loincloth held up by another beaded band riding low on his slim hips. She could see the unbroken line of his golden olive skin from chest to hip to thigh to moccasins on his long feet. She gulped. No tan line.

He was magnificent.

And he was standing in front of her, devouring her with his eyes.

"Mr. Smith," she whispered, the awe in her voice evident.

"You are a goddess," he responded, and bent his head down to brush a kiss on her unresisting mouth.

She opened her mouth, her mind, and her body language to him. Accepting her unspoken invitation, he deepened the kiss, delving delicately with his tongue. She felt the glass being removed from her hand then he pulled her to him, breast to chest, hip to hip, thigh to thigh, and wrapped strong arms tightly around her. He smelled like fine cognac mixed with leather and earth and man. It intoxicated her more than any liquor she could imbibe.

A tiny part of her mind wondered briefly if her costume was dry-cleanable, as the war paint on his chest was probably transferring itself to her dress—after all, she was rubbing against him like a cat. Then feeling the impressive bulge of his cock under the leather loincloth, she forgot all about the complexities of clothing. *She* did that to him! To the untouchable, unemotional Mr. Lowell Smith.

She felt herself being waltzed backward. Blinking her eyes open for an instant, she realized he was steering her behind a thick patch of bamboo, in effect screening them from other guests. She closed her eyes and just let herself *feel*.

Feel the strength of his embrace, the rigidity of his cock, the thrust of his tongue now more urgent, her back against the wall and her legs being hoisted up and around his hips, skin to skin...

His hand fumbling between their bodies, fingers burrowing under the elastic of her skimpy silk panties, reaching for her clit, stroking it, dry-humping her while she writhed and angled herself closer and yet closer to him so she could —

And she did. A fierce climax overwhelmed her, shooting shards of lightning into every cell, every gene in her body, his talented mouth capturing her moans, two fingers inside her pussy, thumb rasping against her clit. And a voice trying to distinguish itself from all the thunder and fireworks exploding inside her head, a voice coming from one side of her, another pair of hands grasping her shoulders and shaking her —

"Miss Fortier! Annabelle! What are you doing?"

Chapter Two

∞

"Mr. Smith! God, there are two of you!"

Mortified, Annabelle dropped her legs to the floor, pushed away from the Indian and found she was too wobbly to stand unaided. Her gaze bounced between the Indian and the pirate, seeing the subtle differences between them that the war paint had obscured. Or maybe it had just been her fervent desire that it be Mr. *Lowell* Smith and not some poseur who may or may not be brother or cousin or merely look-alike but could still answer rightfully to "Mr. Smith".

Which, if she'd admit it to herself, was how she'd addressed him when he'd approached. Formally, as though they were still in the office.

Well, it was his own fault, she decided. If Mr. Smith wasn't so damn prickly and rigid about office protocol, she'd have been calling him Lowell and this damn imposter, even if he was another Mr. Smith, wouldn't have tricked her into having a mind-bending orgasm under false pretenses.

Oops. Oh yeah, orgasm. Remembering how richly her juices had flowed, she surreptitiously pulled her thighs together and squeezed her Kegel muscles tight, hoping to forestall any more moisture seeping down her legs.

The two men stood on either side of her, glaring at each other while gripping one of her arms.

Ye gods and little fishes, what was she going to do now? She'd bet her next month's rent that the oh-so-proper Miss Manners didn't have an answer for this particular social contretemps.

"Beat it, Lowell. We're busy."

"You were out of line, Chaz."

"The lady made her choice. I didn't have to tie her up to–"

"Dammit, will somebody please clue me in here?" Annabelle shoved against the Indian's rock-hard chest. And noticed how smeared his war paint was. Glancing down to her own chest, she winced. Felt heat rise in her cheeks and up into her hairline. Could her actions have been any more obvious?

As if she'd ordered them to do so, both men looked down at her chest. The handkerchief squares that had been applied at strategic points of her costume seemed to have been dislodged in her rubbing frenzy, and small tears appeared where the corners had been sewed into the fabric. Wild streaks of paint decorated her costume. The silky garment exuded static cling, molding to the contours of her breasts. Her nipples jutted out like sore thumbs.

To say nothing of the wet patch covering the spot where the tops of her legs joined.

Mr. Smith—Lowell Smith, that is—lifted his gaze to her, the stern look on his face totally in keeping with the rakish pirate look. "You made a mistake, Miss Fortier."

Annabelle blinked. "It was a perfectly logical assumption—"

"I'm going to teach you how to tell us apart." Placing both hands firmly on her shoulders, he pushed her downward until her knees buckled and she found herself kneeling at eye level to his crotch.

His bulging crotch.

She'd never seen him in anything but Italian-cut suits, but those tight leather trousers and poet's blouse with billowing sleeves and a deep vee front made him look as gorgeous and as rippled as Mr. June. Better, because he was *here*. In the flesh.

Holding her in place with one hand still on her shoulder, he loosened a jaunty red scarf he'd tied around his neck then swiftly covered her eyes with it, tying it in a tight knot at the back of her head.

"Wait a minute, what do you think you're—?"

The rest of her words were captured by his mouth, softly nibbling at her lips with light scrapes of his teeth interspersed with mild suction.

Oh God, *was* it Lowell? Or was it Chaz? Wasn't that the name he'd called the other man? She reached out her hands for tactile clues, her mind equating pirate—leather and linen. Indian—almost naked.

Her hands were grabbed and swung behind her and tied at the wrists, all while Lowell—Chaz?—kept up a sensual assault on her mouth. Lowell hadn't introduced him, hadn't explained why they looked so much alike. Why didn't he clue her in to the rules of this game he was playing?

She concentrated on the feel of the very masculine tongue making such delicious forays into her mouth, licking its way around the edges, touching her tongue, stroking the roof of her mouth. Concentrate! Was the feeling similar to when the Indian had ravaged her mouth?

No. This was more tender, more coaxing. Lowell. It had to be Lowell. She gave herself up to the reality of finally, finally kissing her boss, and leaned forward to make her silent statement.

"Don't move." The command was roughly whispered, as if he didn't have total command of his voice. Lowell's voice. She was sure of it.

Wasn't she?

She heard the rustling of fabric and lifted her head to concentrate. Without vision, her hearing had sharpened. The slight squeak of leather rubbing against itself, the whoosh of a softer fabric. Was he disrobing in public? What kind of party was this, anyway?

Remembering the vignettes in the Haunted House, she answered her own question. This was a place where anything goes. Did she really want to be here? In this particular situation? She flexed her arm muscles but her wrists didn't budge. Tied like a Boy Scout's knot. A voice disrupted her thoughts—a deep, sexy rumble that made her body shiver in anticipation.

"Now pay attention, Miss Fortier."

Definitely Lowell's voice.

"Open your mouth."

Okay, what would he do, pour champagne down her throat? Surprise her with an ice cube? Run his fingers across the edges of her teeth? Feed her a strawberry?

She felt a large hand cup the back of her head. At the same time something warm and smooth and round slid between her teeth and into her mouth. Instinctively she closed her lips around it.

Ohmigod, she was sucking on Lowell Smith's cock!

She hoped.

The feel of it, rock-hard and velvet-smooth at the same time, thick in circumference, the vein rubbing against her tongue, made her giddy and horny. Hornier. He pushed in as far as he could go without forcing then withdrew slowly. He held the tip at the entrance, prompting her to lick the drops of pre-cum from the opening, to feel the bulbous head, the thick ridge, the veins standing out.

Oh man, she wanted to touch him, to cup his balls, to run her fist up and down that hard shaft. If he thought he was punishing her, he certainly was!

Again he pushed inside in a controlled stroke and withdrew totally. She felt bereft.

A silent moment passed when nothing happened. Then he cupped her skull again and glided his cock inside her mouth. It wasn't the same. Oh, it was still huge and hot and rigid, but the flavor was different. The scent was different. It wasn't Lowell.

Her heart lurched. Two gorgeous hunks—totally nude, she presumed—had her on her knees and sucking their cocks with each other's complicity. Annabelle forced herself to take a mental time-out and consider her predicament. Tomorrow in the office, what would Mr. Smith think about her wanton behavior tonight?

Well hell, he really wanted her to do this, or else why would he have invited her here tonight? He was the one who'd forced her to her knees, blindfolded her, allowed his look-alike to join them in a *ménage*.

In subtle indication that she knew who was who, she slackened her cheek muscles and turned her head to one side. The cock slipped out. A low curse followed.

"Something wrong, Miss Fortier?"

Lowell's voice. To her side. She was right. The one who'd cursed, whose cock no longer enjoyed the ministrations of her mouth, who'd stood in front of her, had to be Chaz.

She lifted her chin. "It wasn't you."

No response came from Lowell. Annabelle tensed.

Finally, he said in measured tones, "I think we should adjourn to a sitting room."

He slid his arms to her waist and raised her to her feet. She felt the soft linen of his shirt, heard the rasp of leather against leather, and realized he hadn't gone naked, he'd just moved the garments out of the way enough so they wouldn't inadvertently brush against her and give away his identity.

Well, the Mr. Smith she'd known at work wouldn't walk naked through a roomful of strangers anyway.

But wait. Didn't he say he was a member here? So he'd known what to expect, had probably been naked and seen others naked in this very room. Her pussy began to tingle all over again.

A few twists and turns as he guided her through what sounded like small groups of people variously talking, breathing hard, grunting, murmuring or kibitzing, then the soft clink of a door closing and the sounds faded.

"Now, Miss Fortier, we will continue."

Large hands cupped her jaws. Thumbs traced her lower lip. Light kisses dropped across her cheeks, her nose, her temple. A tongue stroked her mouth, teasing her. Annabelle had no doubt it was Lowell. By now she knew his scent, his touch, the rasp of his tongue. She tried to lean toward him, to capture that tongue, to feel his lips pressing hers as though he couldn't get enough of her. But he held her face just so, keeping her at arm's length so to speak, teasing her with just a taste, just a touch.

She moaned softly. "More."

"Patience, Miss Fortier."

Shivers raced through her at the husky timbre of his voice.

"Behind you is a bed," he said. "Take one step back and sit down on it. But first…"

Annabelle felt two sets of knuckles grasping both sides of her costume at its shoulder seam. Fabric ripped then slid down her torso, her legs, in a caress. She felt her nipples pucker even more as two indrawn breaths were taken. Hopefully they liked what they saw, her shimmery white bra cupping her 34-C breasts, the slender waist dipping in then swelling out to curvy hips covered in a matching, very wet-crotched thong.

She took the step back and sat. The luxurious feel of satin sheets tickled the backs of her bare thighs as she sank into the pillowy mattress.

Her arms still tied behind her, she kicked her feet free of the costume and wiggled a bit to get comfortable and balanced, feeling the plump globes jiggling into each other as she did. Murmurs of approval greeted her action.

"Exquisite," said Lowell.

"Agreed," replied Chaz.

Suddenly sensations bombarded Annabelle. A feathery touch down one arm, a soft wet suckling at one breast, fingertips skimming the inside of her thigh, teeth nipping the

111

delicate skin where shoulder met throat. With each second, Annabelle's awareness of her body heightened. Tiny electric shocks zinged through her, centering on the spot they studiously avoided, the spot where she most wanted their mouths, their fingers. Their cocks.

She felt her bound wrists loosen, and the tie fell away. With a sigh of relief she moved her arms around to shake some circulation into the pins-and-needles feeling.

Annabelle shivered again to remember that two men were plying her with sensual stimulation. She'd occasionally wondered how she'd feel as the filling in a man sandwich, but had never lusted after it, never daydreamed about it.

They were fast changing her mind.

Her right hand was grasped then moved, her fingers positioned to encircle a hard, hot cock that jutted upright. The Indian? She could feel no evidence of leather or linen as a hairy thigh brushed against her arm. Then her other hand was similarly positioned, and a similarly bare leg moved against hers.

God. Two cocks, thick and long and burning, in her hands. She wanted to dip her head and capture one with her mouth. Slowly she began an up-and-down movement, both her palms sliding over the bulbous mushroom heads then back down the shafts to their roots. Felt the wiry pubic hair tickle her wrists.

Behind the blindfold she tried to discern which cock was Lowell's then quickly gave up. What did it matter? Both felt so deliciously decadent, especially as their owners continued to bombard her skin with feather-light caresses.

One of them found the front clasp of her bra, opened it, slid the straps down her shoulders. He knelt, his cock popping out of her grasp. She wiggled her arm out of the bra strap that had restricted her movement and reached for any part of him that she could touch. His head nestled between her breasts as her hand settled on his hair. His curly hair. The Indian.

His teeth closed around her nipple, biting and scraping softly. Instinctively her back arched, pushing her breast further into his mouth, and her left hand squeezed around the cock she still held — Lowell's cock — forcing a groan from him.

Annabelle reveled in the power implicit in that sound. All her senses were on red alert. Her breathing had accelerated to short, panting breaths. Her nipples zinged with every pull of the Indian's mouth, every stroke of Lowell's fingers skimming her slit through the wet fabric of her thong. She widened the space between her knees, inviting him, or both of them, inside.

Suddenly Lowell's mouth found hers and she opened herself willingly to his searching tongue, sucking it fiercely into her mouth. Simultaneously his fingers slid under her thong and impaled her. Annabelle's head spun in sensual abandon. One man kissing her fervently while finger-fucking her dripping wet pussy, the other suckling one nipple and pinching the other. One man's scorching-hot cock fucking her fist, the other rubbing his cock against her bare thigh. It was all too much. She felt the orgasm building, building, she was seconds away from exploding into a cataclysmic reaction —

"No!"

Lowell's firm voice cut into her haze of passion. She felt herself being lifted to her feet and shaken like a wayward child being castigated. Disoriented, she vaguely noted strong hands holding her at the armpits to steady her as she regained her sightless balance on her stilettos. Her breaths came in harsh rasps. Her pussy throbbed, wept, her juices flowed down her thighs. Her stone-hard nipples ached from the loss of stimulation.

"What —?"

Fingers at the back of her head untied the scarf around her eyes. As it fell to the floor she blinked several times and found herself staring up into the intense visage of Mr. Lowell Smith.

"I want to see what it's like to have you totally dependent on me for your pleasure."

Annabelle blinked again. Was he kidding? It would be a dream come true.

Lowell's sapphire-blue eyes glowed as richly as the jewels they resembled. "Will you cede control to me?"

She had already ceded control, she realized. To both men standing naked before her, their cocks rampant and eyes full of lust, their faces and bodies similar enough to be brothers. Still, she needed some answers.

"First," she asked with a falsely sugary voice, "do you think you could introduce me to the man whose cock I just spent ten minutes giving a hand-job to while he was sucking my nipples?"

Lowell's eyebrows raised. His mouth twitched, but if he'd had the urge to smile, he suppressed it easily.

"Annabelle Fortier, meet Charles Smith, also known as Chaz."

Hiding her exasperation at the cursory intro, she turned to Chaz. Perhaps he'd be more forthcoming. "How are you two related?"

"Our fathers are twin brothers. He's my first cousin."

"And do you switch places often?"

Unlike Lowell, Chaz had no compunction to hide a brilliant smile, which he used to devastating effect on her. "Only when the subject is such a beautiful woman. When I saw you, I didn't know you knew Lowell. You whispered my name. Mr. Smith. I thought the guy who threw this party had told you who I was."

He reached to her face and stroked her cheek with his knuckles. "Frankly, I was flattered that you sought me out."

"Enough of this chatter," Lowell butted in. "If you will be kind enough to answer my question, Miss Fortier?"

Annabelle bit back a response. She knew that Lowell's speech at work tended toward the stuffy. Then a thought slammed into her. Being a member of a sex club, for it couldn't be anything else, he probably just pretended to be stuffy at work so no one would guess his true nature.

If that was the case, she thought—and said, "Yes."

A glance around her surroundings showed that they occupied a small room fitted with a large bed, two boudoir chairs and a dresser. Sort of a guest room. An ajar door led her to hope it was a private bathroom. Her eye snagged on a mirror at the far wall. The sight of herself, wearing only a thong and her heels, flanked by two gorgeous, naked hunks with hard-ons made in heaven, weakened her knees and made her juices flow again. Her baser self immediately wanted a photo, or better yet, a video, of what would transpire here. Her saner self overruled it. She didn't want to find herself on YouTube. But yes, she wanted to watch in that mirror.

"On second thought, Miss Fortier, you may assist in bringing about your own pleasure by suggesting a way to incorporate both Smiths into your fulfillment."

Annabelle's mouth opened, but nothing came out. He wanted *her* to…

A flush suffused her skin, starting at her cheeks and flowing down to her shoulders, her breasts and, it felt, all the way to her toes. She could easily visualize herself on her knees with Lowell pumping into her from behind, and Chaz on his knees in front of her while she sucked him off.

But to put it into words? To actually say it out loud?

"I think," she began, swallowing around the dryness in her throat, "that maybe you could…"

She cleared her throat. "That is, you and I…"

Dammit, how could she just come out and say it? *Okay, Lowell, I'll lie down on the bed and you climb on top of me and…* No. She just couldn't do it.

Chaz seemed to understand her sudden shyness. He came up behind her, wound his arms around her sides and cupped her breasts. "Repeat after me. 'I can kneel on the bed and Chaz can fuck me from behind and Lowell can watch as you ram into my tight, sweet pussy'."

"That's out of the question," Lowell snapped, his narrowed eyes glued to the way Chaz was manipulating Annabelle's nipples, at the way her nipples responded.

"Then you come up with a scenario, cuz. Can't you tell she was raised to be a lady and can't articulate her deepest desires?"

The two men glared at each other with Annabelle between them. At last Lowell stepped closer, forcibly removed Chaz's hands from her breasts, and grabbed her hips, grinding them into his erection. He captured her gaze with his own intense one.

"I'll be the one whose cock rams into that tight, sweet pussy. Chaz can watch, or he can lie alongside while you jerk him off—if I let your mind stray enough to pay any attention to such a minor, secondary diversion."

From behind her, Chaz nuzzled the spot where her neck met her shoulder, nipping small bits of skin with his teeth, sending shards of electricity up and down her spine. "Maybe the lady can find some middle ground here. How about if Lowell lies down on his back and you sit on him? Your legs will be wide open on either side of his hips, and that opens up your rosebud to me. Would you like that? Have you ever had a cock in your ass before?"

Dear God, Annabelle had never been so turned on, sandwiched between two naked, thoroughly male bodies and listening to what each of them wanted to do to her. Her pussy throbbed, and her breasts felt heavy and aching.

"And remember," Lowell murmured as his lips brushed hers in a teasing, taunting kiss, "no one else in this house will give you a climax if I so decree it, since you did cede control to me. We could set you down in one of the Haunted House scenarios, to be brought time and again to the brink with no relief in sight. But regardless, you would be unfulfilled unless I allow you to come.

"The choice is yours." Still gripping her hips tightly against his engorged cock, he leaned back a little to stare into her glazed eyes. "Your wish is our command."

Annabelle gulped. "I want...I want you to...to...can I show you instead?" She simply could not utter the words.

Lowell gave a terse nod. Both men stepped away from her, and Annabelle involuntarily shivered at the loss of their scorching heat. Shaking herself from the spell they'd cast, she climbed onto the bed, positioned herself in its center on her hands and knees then beckoned to Lowell.

"Please. Behind me," she said as she swept one hand around to her rump.

Lust flamed in Lowell's eyes as he crawled over the mattress, stopping inches away from her flanks. He grabbed the elastic of her thong with both hands then ripped it on one side then the other. "We won't need this anymore."

He balled up the tattered garment and brought it to his nose, inhaling deeply. "Mmm. Smells like heaven."

Nudging her knees farther apart, he dipped his head and began dropping kisses on her inner thighs, her hips, her spine. Annabelle closed her eyes and reveled in the feel of his mouth, his hands touching her, arousing her all over.

She barely heard Chaz say plaintively, "What about me?"

Suddenly Lowell gave her ass a hard smack with the palm of hand. "You didn't forget your duty so quickly, did you?"

Her skin sizzled where his imprint no doubt showed. It was so erotic, like a direct connection between his hand and her pussy, she wanted him to do it again. Deliberately she ignored Chaz.

"Miss Fortier!" Another smack.

In reaction, Annabelle's ass lifted in a silent plea for more.

Lowell chuckled. "I'm in charge, not you. For that transgression, you will…"

He stopped speaking, stopped moving, lifted his hands from her. Annabelle waited on a withheld breath for another smack. And waited. She held back a groan on realizing he was punishing her in a different way. She bit the inside of her cheek to keep from earning another punishment, for she had just come to realize a truth. Punishment wasn't merely the inflicting of corporal pain, it could also be mental, a withholding of pleasure.

"Ah, you are beginning to understand that I control your pleasure." She heard the crinkle of foil. "For that I will give you…" In one smooth stroke he slammed his cock deep inside her pussy and held himself tight against her.

Annabelle cried out in delirious pleasure as her inner muscles spasmed against him. So big, so burning hot, he filled her to bursting. Against every instinct to move, to feel him sliding in and out of her sheath, she held herself still.

"What about Chaz?" Lowell's voice.

Her muzzy brain processed the question too slowly. Chaz. There was something she had to direct him to do…

She felt Lowell's cock sliding out of her pussy. She clamped her muscles down to hold him inside, but he was stronger. On a moan she realized this was yet another punishment, for she hadn't completed Lowell's directive.

"Here," she gasped, lifting one hand to beckon Chaz in front of her.

"No." Lowell's fingers dug into the soft flesh of her hips, holding her immobile. "You must specify what you want to do to him."

"Please, I can't…"

Lowell's cock teased the entrance to her pussy. "Say it."

Oh God, she wanted him inside her, needed him to pound into her. "Chaz, I-I need you to kneel in front of me so I can — so I can suck your cock."

Her reward was another swift, hard thrust of Lowell's cock into her welcoming pussy, then another and another as he entered then withdrew. Lord, he felt good. Her inner muscles clenched around him, increasing the pleasure of his thrusts.

The mattress dipped as Chaz positioned himself at her direction. Then he guided his cock into her waiting mouth and she drew him greedily in. With one Mr. Smith in front and one behind pleasuring her in this daring new way, she wondered why she'd ever hesitated to say what she wanted.

She gave herself up to the myriad sensations, Chaz slowly easing his cock in and out of her mouth as he held her head just so with both hands, Lowell hunched over her, one hand stroking her clit and the other tugging her nipple while pounding his hips into her, his taut balls slapping into her. Her pleasure gathered, strengthened, drawing itself together from her mouth to her breasts to her belly and, finally, intensifying into that pinpoint of feminine cells, her clit, which suddenly exploded into a thousand fiery pieces and redistributed themselves into every atom of her being.

Boneless, she wondered why she didn't collapse onto the mattress then realized that Lowell was still fucking her, his hands now holding her hips in a death grip, his breaths harsh against her shoulder, his hips pounding into her in a frenzied cadence, the slap of skin on skin resounding around them.

And Chaz was doing the same, his hips pistoning into her mouth as she increased the tautness of her lips and tongue on his cock. She reached up with one hand to cup and massage his balls, felt them tighten in her palm as his climax neared.

She felt Lowell tense and swung her free hand behind her to clutch his ass cheek, trying to hold him one more millimeter closer as he too neared the end of his control. And then Chaz was shooting his cum into her mouth and she swallowed and swallowed to capture all of it, while behind her Lowell shouted hoarsely, pounded her viciously once, twice more, then roared his own climax as she experienced another orgasm so powerful, she didn't realize she'd blacked out until she again became a sentient being aware of the two spent males keeping her tethered to earth.

Chapter Three

ഇ

"Good morning, Miss Fortier, did you sleep well last night?"

Annabelle's head jerked up as Lowell—make that *Mr. Smith*—poked his head into the outer office where she was reviewing the day's calendar with her assistant. A quick scan told her he hadn't changed his persona one bit. Still the slicked-back hair, curling just the slightest at his neck. Still the superbly cut Italian suit, silk tie, hand-tailored shirt with monogrammed cuffs.

The eyes, though. His eyes seemed to glow as he looked at her. She wanted to pounce on him, but remembered her assistant Delia's presence. In her late forties, Delia Thompson had been with the firm since its inception eighteen years ago and mothered all the staff. It wouldn't do to fuel any office gossip. Annabelle was the latest hire and would be the one to go if things turned sour.

Should she tell him she'd never had a better night's sleep since childhood? That she'd even fallen asleep in Mr. Savidge's car while being driven home? That a valet had followed with her own car? That her pussy ached and her nipples hardened just from looking at him this morning?

She dipped her head in greeting. "Fine, Mr. Smith. I hope you did, too."

"I'd like to discuss the Wesley drawings with you this afternoon." He glanced at Delia. "How's her schedule, Miss Thompson?"

Delia checked Annabelle's calendar in her computer. "Miss Fortier has the morning blocked off to finish the plans for the library addition for their two o'clock meeting."

"Oh, is that meeting today? Well then, I won't disturb you. Why don't you stop by my office after they leave." He nodded to them both and continued to his corner office.

Delia sighed as she followed his exit with greedy eyes. "I'm happily married, but it's no sin to look. He's such a hunk. Honestly, I don't know why he doesn't do anything about it."

"About what?"

"The way he looks at you sometimes. Like he wants to eat you up. Then he goes into that 'Miss Fortier' routine and walks away." She shook her head. "I just don't get it."

Annabelle bit her tongue against the urge to confess that Mr. Lowell Smith had indeed "done something about it." The news would spread like a rash in a poison-ivy patch.

"Mixing business with pleasure," she said neutrally. "I'm way down on the totem pole in this firm. He's a senior partner."

"Pffft." Delia flung her hand up negligently, dismissing the argument.

Annabelle had scheduled the time today for a final review even though she'd completed the design last week. Good thing. She spent the morning at her CAD-CAM program, staring at the screen and thinking about last night and all the mischief Mr. Smith — the two Mr. Smiths — had gotten her into. How would Lowell greet her privately as opposed to the office where anyone could and did see how they interacted? Could she hold her head up if he decided there were separate standards for him and for her? What on earth was she thinking of to have allowed herself to be talked into a threesome with her *boss*? Was the Wesley account just a cover to get her into his inner sanctum so he could hem and haw and finally blurt out that he could no longer have such a wanton working for him?

Her stomach twisted in knots. He couldn't fire her. He *couldn't*. After all, he was a member of what was apparently a sex club and he'd invited her to go, gave her time off to find a costume, had bullied her into accepting his dictates once there. And he didn't even ask her about a safe word! Of course she'd never before been in a situation before where a safe word might be needed, but she'd read more than a few erotic romances and knew her way, theoretically, around the BDSM scene.

Delia knocked once then stuck her head inside the doorway. "The Library Board is here. I put them in Conference Room B."

"Thanks." Annabelle glanced at the half-eaten turkey wrap Delia had brought her two hours ago, but it wasn't the upcoming meeting that had her stomach too jumpy to eat much. She squared her shoulders and strode into the conference room with a façade of confidence. Three hours later, she was shaking hands with the Board as they departed. They would convey their verdict to the senior partners in a few days.

Now all she had to worry about was Lowell. *Mr. Smith*, she corrected herself.

Retrieving the Wesley plans from Delia's desk, she said good night as her assistant left for the day then walked to the corner office and knocked on Mr. Smith's open door.

"Come in."

She took a deep breath and entered.

"Please close the door, Miss Fortier."

Not good. His demeanor was stern, like he'd had a hard decision to make and he'd stoically accepted the one he reached. He stood rigidly behind his high-backed executive's chair, one hand resting on the leather as if it would help keep him upright.

The door clicked shut behind her. She approached him gingerly, laid the plans on his polished walnut desk.

His mouth moved, but no sound came out. He might have said her name, but Annabelle wasn't a lip-reader and couldn't be sure. His sapphire-blue eyes glowed the way they had last night when he'd mentioned punishment.

Finally he spoke. "Are you wearing panties?"

Annabelle gasped, jerked her head around to be sure the door was still closed and no one had crept in to hear his unbelievable, totally un-PC question. "Mr. Smith, this is no place—"

"All day long," he overrode her objection, "I've burned to know the answer to that question, Annabelle. Lift up your skirt and show me."

Which came first, she wondered bitterly, the rock or the hard place? She should have known—did know—better than to fish off the company dock.

"Mr. Smith, I think it's better to keep personal matters separate from the office."

He stood unmoving behind his chair, his eyes boring into hers with an intensity she'd never seen before. No, that wasn't true. He'd looked at her like that last night. But this was the office. With staff still coming and going. And no foreplay.

Crap. *Cancel that image.* To break the spell he'd cast, she bent down and began to unroll the plans, setting his brass pencil holder at one edge to hold the blueprint down.

"Annabelle, look at me." Usually he phrased orders as a request, but the texture of his voice held an edge of domination, of command. Her head jerked up.

"This office is rather formal in deference to its founding partner. So when we are in business mode, I will continue to call you Miss Fortier and you will refer to me as Mr. Smith. But when I call you Annabelle, it means something else entirely."

Lowell stepped away from the barrier of his executive's chair, unbuttoned his suit jacket and stood at the edge of his desk. Annabelle's eyes snapped to his crotch. To the massive bulge making a tent of the silken fabric of his Italian slacks.

"Yes, you do that to me, Annabelle. Please. Sit down so I can do the same."

"Mr. Smith, you wanted to discuss the Wesley drawings. Are you ready to do so?"

The twitch of a smile came and went on his face. "Fine." He gestured to her.

She sat.

So did he. "By the way, Miss Fortier, since you've now been here six months, you've passed the probationary period. If you stop by the payroll office tomorrow to fill out the new forms, I've arranged for a fifteen-thousand-dollar raise effective immediately."

Outraged, Annabelle jumped to her feet, plunked her palms on his desk, looming over him. "Are you trying to bribe me into — into — "

He stilled, like a predator waiting to pounce. Annabelle wrestled herself back into control. He didn't mean it like it sounded, she rationalized. He wasn't suggesting he would pay her to be his doxy. She'd earned this raise, dammit, and it wasn't fair of him to muddy the waters by discussing two such disparate ideas in the same breath.

But…but…

"Is that what you think?" He'd shifted into a no-nonsense voice, prickling the skin on the back of Annabelle's neck.

She lifted her chin, straightened her spine. "What should I be thinking? 'Oh, what an odd coincidence'? Obviously I made a massive error in judgment. You'll have my resigna — "

"Annabelle." Standing as well, he held up his hand in a traffic cop's "stop" gesture. "Annabelle," he said more softly, almost lovingly. His gaze softened, warmed on her. She swallowed hard. He wasn't making it easy for her to leave.

"Aha, I thought I might find you in here."

Annabelle spun around to find the founding partner standing in the open doorway. She hadn't heard the door open.

125

Joseph Butler sauntered toward her, liver-spotted hand outstretched, a wide smile on his weathered, creased face. "Just got off a conference call with the Library Board. They are absolutely delighted with the plans."

Scrambling to shift gears, Annabelle accepted his handshake in a daze. "Uh, that didn't take long."

"I knew they'd love it. You've been doing a first-rate job, Miss Fortier." Shifting his gaze to Lowell, he asked, "Have you told her yet?"

"We had just started discussing it," Lowell said, his suit jacket already discreetly buttoned.

Discussing what? Had he told *Mr. Butler* about last night?

"Splendid." Still gripping Annabelle's hand, the senior partner continued smiling at her. "I had suggested ten, you know, but Mr. Smith held out for the entire fifteen thousand budgeted. And after the call I just had, I'm glad he prevailed. You'll start seeing the results in this week's paycheck. Congratulations on passing your probationary period in such exemplary fashion."

"Thank you," she said weakly as he finally let go of her hand.

Mr. Butler glanced at his gold watch. It was past six, as Annabelle noted on the pendulum clock on Lowell's credenza. "Take the rest of the afternoon off," he said jovially as he walked out into the hallway, leaving silence behind him.

"I'm sorry," she said quietly. "I jumped to conclusions."

"Perhaps I'm at fault as well," he replied. "I'm not the most tactful person nor the world's best—what's today's jargon?—people handler. I should have made your well-deserved raise the first and only subject. But," he said as he ran the fingers of both hands through his slicked-back hair, "I take one look at you and all I can think of is having you under my thrall."

Annabelle felt her pussy spasm, her juices begin to flow. She wanted that too. Wanted to rip off her panties and let him see how quickly he made her cream with just his words, with the anticipation of what he might do to her.

"By the way," he added. "Since we're putting all our cards on the table, you should know that the partners made this decision Monday afternoon. Well before I realized I had a conflict in last night's schedule."

His eyes bored into hers. "I asked you to the Mischief Night party because I'd been fighting my own inclination. I've never been a fan of office romances, but I couldn't keep my mind on my work for thinking about you." He distractedly messed his hair up a little more, leaving finger tracks in the rumple, and curls in their wake.

"It occurred to me this could be a sink-or-swim proposition. You'd get a taste of the Platinum Club and you'd either accept it or you wouldn't, and no harm, no foul back in the office. But it wasn't until I saw your men's calendar that I dared invite you in the first place."

She shifted in her chair, looked down at her twined fingers. "I kept it because Mr. June reminded me of you."

"I wondered why it was so dog-eared." He chuckled. Then his eyes darkened. "When I saw you with Chaz, when I saw your legs wrapped around him, it took all my willpower not to deck him. Although that certainly gave me an answer as to your level of sensuality."

"The mistake I made was perfectly logical," she argued. "He looked just like you under all the war paint, and he didn't correct me when I called him Mr. Smith, and —"

"Annabelle."

She shut up.

"Now I'll ask you again. Are you wearing panties?"

A line had to be drawn. She knew it. She had to keep her — their — private affairs out of the possibility of discovery. "Mr. Smith, I'm going to close up my computer and have a celebratory drink at The Mojito." The Mojito was a bar a block from their office, popular with the white-collar crowd. She'd gone there a couple of times after work, but had never warmed to the idea of being a barfly.

"Perhaps *Lowell* would like to join me in a toast to the milestone of passing my probationary period. I would appreciate it if you would tell him that I won't be wearing any panties there."

And she walked out of his office, closing the door quietly behind her.

Chapter Four

ೞ

"That was quite an exit line."

Lowell had just walked up to where she was seated at one of the bar stools. Annabelle took a sip of her mojito before speaking. "I'm sorry. I simply couldn't bring Mischief Night into the office. There's too much at stake, for both of us."

"No apology needed. I admire your courage in standing your ground."

The bartender came by. Setting a twenty on the bar, Lowell ordered a beer then leaned forward to whisper into Annabelle's ear. "Now you will tell me, Annabelle, if you are wearing panties."

She swiveled on the stool, letting her knees brush him at crotch level. "You'll have to find out for yourself."

His eyes narrowed. "Annabelle. You disappoint me."

She set down her drink and slid off the stool. "Listen to that music. Just made for dancing." Wrapping her arms around his neck, she began to sway to its tempo, brushing her body lightly against him. In her high heels, she was almost at eye level with him. She nuzzled her cheek against his then whispered into his ear, "And you can find out the answer to your question...Lowell."

Instantly she felt herself plastered to his torso, his hands spanning her waist then running down her hips to her butt and back up again. "I don't feel a panty line," he murmured.

"That's because there isn't one."

Lowell's soft groan made Annabelle smile. Her eyes drifted shut at the heavenly feel of him in her arms, holding each other tight and swaying gently to a Sheryl Crow ballad.

She'd dreamed of this too. Not just making love with him, but the closeness, the tenderness.

"One Rolling Rock, no glass."

At the bartender's intrusion, Lowell pulled away just enough to see Annabelle's face but kept his hands on her waist and spoke in a low, hoarse voice. "I wish you were wearing a roomy skirt that you could lift up when you sit down on the bar stool, so your bare pussy touches the leather. It would be almost like you sitting on my chest, your legs spread wide apart and your juices drizzling onto my skin. But in the latter instance, my thumb would be stroking your clit. I don't think they'd allow me to do that here if you were sitting on a barstool."

Annabelle swallowed hard.

Lowell's gaze roamed the perimeter of the bar. "Aha. There's a group leaving the corner booth. Quickly," he spun her around and gave her a nudge, "lay claim to it. I'll bring our drinks."

She was settling on the padded seat, her back to the wall, when he walked up. "No. Sit on this side," he hissed as he sat their drinks on the not-yet-cleaned table.

"But this way I can see—"

"So can everyone else. This isn't the Platinum Society. I'm not going to share you with anyone. Not even let them look."

"Why? What are you going to—"

"Annabelle, you have already earned a demerit by questioning me. Sit here." He pointed imperiously. "Now!"

Moisture flooded her pussy as she absorbed his dominant stance, his scowl. She slid out of her seat and into the opposite side of the booth. He crowded into it right behind her.

"Spread your legs," he ordered, wrapping his right arm around her shoulders. "I'm going to see if you obeyed me."

Oh God, she would have to have this suit dry-cleaned. She could feel how much moisture was seeping to the lining of her woolen skirt. She moved her knees apart, tucking her thigh firmly against his. And heard his sharp intake of breath. *Good.*

Breathing softly into her ear, Lowell stroked his tongue around its outer shell, making her shudder. Slowly he ran the fingers of his free hand down her arm, onto her leg, bunching up the material of her skirt until he reached the crease between her torso and leg. With every hard-won breath she fought to stay unaffected.

Until his finger touched her unclothed pussy.

Her hips jerked forward. He laughed softly into her ear. "You obeyed. That deserves a reward." With the arm he'd already flung around her shoulder he managed to tip her head toward him. He captured her mouth with his, kissing lightly, darting his tongue inside and withdrawing, all the while stroking, stroking her pussy lips, tangling his fingers in her auburn curls.

"Here, let me take these empty glasses," the waitress said from behind Lowell's shoulder.

Annabelle stiffened.

"Don't move," he whispered against her mouth. "It's too dark to see. Just stay…absolutely still…" and he pressed his thumb against her clit.

Annabelle made a rough sound in the back of her throat. Lowell adroitly captured it in the continuing kiss and rubbed with the thumb still hidden under her skirt. She squirmed, but whether to move away in embarrassment or to move closer for more of Lowell she couldn't have said.

"Excuse me, Miss, I've got to wipe up this wet spot right by your arm. That last group was a bunch of slobs. Beer can stain your suit in a big way."

Lowell took that moment to plunge two fingers into her dripping wet pussy. Annabelle's arms automatically lifted as she turned into him, her right hand reaching for his neck to hold him closer to her, closer to his sucking mouth, his thrusting tongue, his two fingers fucking her pussy right in front of the waitress and all she could think of was more, more, she needed him inside her, needed to come right this minute…

Lowell removed everything, his mouth, his fingers, his warmth away from her. Dazed, she fluttered her eyelids until she could focus on him. "Why didn't you…?"

Then her focus widened to take in the murmur of voices, the smell of stale beer and whiskey and body odors and perfumes. Oh God, they were in The Mojito and she almost came from a finger-fucking right in the middle of all of it.

Hell, she still wanted to come. "Lowell," she gritted out. "I need you! Let's get out of here."

His chuckle grated on her nerves. "You still need to be disciplined for your error of judgment back in the office."

Her eyes widened. "We agreed not to mix—"

"Correct. But you did not trust me. *That* has to be punished. I want you to know, to believe, that I will always put your welfare first and foremost. I was a fool to wait six months to inform you of my interest. No. More than interest, it was an obsession. One that I hope will never diminish. Put your hand on my cock."

She hesitated, darted a look around.

"Now! Or you'll get another punishment."

Gingerly she let her left hand settle on his thigh then creep upward to the bulge under his trousers.

"The zipper. Pull down the zipper and tell me what you find."

She let out a gasp.

"It's okay, she won't be back until I signal her." He angled his body toward the corner, toward her, and away from prying eyes. "Go on," he urged.

Annabelle discovered that she needed both trembling hands to finesse the zipper down around the warm, hard obstruction. Then gasped again.

His cock sprang free, huge and hot and…naked in her hand. Her eyes popped up to capture his gaze. Her mouth formed a big round O. "You're not wearing underwear."

"That's right, darlin'. If you could do that for me I will do the same, and more, for you."

Annabelle's eyes sparkled. "Then you'd better hold absolutely still, because there's a favor I want to return."

And began slowly stroking his throbbing cock with her loose fist, up and down its thick length, her other hand grazing the thick ridge encircling the head, smearing the drop of pre-cum around the silky skin, driving him slowly crazy until he agreed.

They had to get out of there. Fast.

Chapter Five

❧

"I don't care what you say, Annabelle. This is a special occasion."

Annabelle looked at the face of her beloved. Six months had passed since Mischief Night, and they'd had a devil of a time keeping their relationship out of the office and in a "Mr. Smith" and "Miss Fortier" mode. No one knew, although many might suspect. The lingering looks, the flushed faces, the opportunities to be alone—they tried to avoid those. As well, he'd asked her to move in with him any number of times, but she'd always refused. She still felt she had to prove herself as a junior staff member and didn't want anyone to accuse her boss of favoritism.

They were dressed for a party. Tonight was Joseph Butler's retirement after thirty-one years as an award-winning architect. He would continue as Partner Emeritus, but was turning over the day-to-day running of the offices to his younger brother, the new Managing Partner.

She stood at the mirror in a corner of Lowell's office inserting her emerald stud earrings. She had brought a strapless cocktail dress to work, a rich emerald green silk with fitted bodice and softly flowing skirt, and changed in the ladies room. Lowell looked devastatingly handsome in a tux that fit him so well it had to be hand-tailored and not a rental. He came up behind her and murmured, "You look ravishing."

She met his eyes in the mirror. "So do you."

"Good enough to eat. No one would blame me for trying to kiss you in the office tonight." He bent down to kiss her bare shoulder, skimming a finger where the edge of her gown exposed the plump tops of her breasts. "Almost too much cleavage for everyone to see."

She smiled at him, tingled at his touch. But she wore panties. With this dress and in this milieu she didn't want to risk a wet spot. "Jealous?"

"Maybe. Do you ever think about another go-round with a third party?"

"No. Absolutely not. I don't want to share you and I don't want you to share me."

"Good. Anybody who puts their hands on you in a sexual way, I'll punch his lights out. I just want to make sure you don't miss having *ménage a trois*, the way we did at Halloween."

Annabelle sighed. "I'll say it for the hundredth time, I thought that Indian was you. And since I was already, shall we say, wrapped up in Chaz and didn't know what your intentions were, I went along with a threebie. Yes, I'll admit I was curious to see what it was like. And yes, it turned me on, but that was because you were the dominant force in that group. I would never have done it with any two other men in the world. Regardless of how many vignettes I saw in the Haunted House."

"Good," he said again.

"Of course," she added mischievously, "if someone wants to watch…"

"We'll play that by ear. I'm getting pretty possessive."

"Good," she echoed.

"And I'll say it again. This is a special occasion." He spun her around and pushed her back against the mirror then knelt at her feet. "This is just the kind of skirt I had in mind for you to wear," he said, his voice muffled under the handkerchief hem of her gown.

"Dammit, you're wearing underpants." Undaunted, he licked her clit through the silk. Instantly her pussy flooded, a Pavlovian response because she knew how well he could ravage her with his tongue. She felt his teeth scrape against her pubic bone, felt him pull her crotch aside and thrust his fingers into her.

"Lowell—Mr. Smith, stop it!" She had to brace herself against the wall, her palms flattening, in order to stay upright.

With a low chuckle, Lowell continued eating her, fingering her, licking the slit until she unconsciously spread her legs wider. When she let out a soft moan, he rose up and with a movement so quick all she saw was a blur, she was leaning over his desk, her elbows holding her weight and Lowell about to enter her from behind.

"Lowell, no! Condom!"

He took a harsh breath. His fully engorged cock halted against her pussy then detoured to rub between her ass cheeks. "Annabelle, I want to feel what it's like to be truly inside you."

She tensed. "Lowell, please. You know I'm on the pill, but I don't want to take the chance…"

"Shit," he swore softly, then stood upright, lifting her as well. He gently turned her around, cupped her face in his big hands. "Annabelle, I love you. I want to have a family with you."

Annabelle's eyelids fluttered closed. "Oh, Lowell, I love you too."

Dipping his head to plant a few soft kisses on her face, he murmured, "I wasn't going to ask you until after the party, but…" He dug into his trousers pocket and retrieved a small velvet box. "Will you marry me and bear my children? Will you let me call you Annabelle every day? Will you let me dominate you?"

"Yes! And yes and yes. And…sometimes."

Lifting her in a bear hug, he spun her around a few times then set her down next to the desk. "Please. Try it on."

Annabelle opened the box and lost her power of speech. A dazzling diamond flanked by two square emeralds sparkled at her. With shaking fingers she lifted the ring from its velvet nest and slipped it on her third finger, left hand.

Perfect fit.

Her eyes were full of love as she looked up at him. "Maybe after the party we can, you know, try —"

As if he knew what she wanted to say, Lowell spun her around. Positioning her to face the desk, he lifted her skirts, jerked down her panties and plunged into her pussy in one powerful thrust.

"Annabelle," he croaked as he stayed motionless inside her. "You feel so good. I don't want anything to come between us. Ever."

"Oh God, Lowell, don't stop, Lowell please, please..." She wiggled her ass.

He began moving his hips, pumping harder and harder with each stroke until she thought she would go crazy.

"Annabelle, Annabelle, Annabelle," he chanted. "You'll not refuse me ever again. Not in the office, not at home. No more calling you Miss Fortier. You're my Annabelle and always will be."

A half dozen powerful strokes more and Annabelle exploded, holding the pad of her palm to her mouth and biting down to keep from shouting. Two, three, four strokes more and Lowell came as well, his fingers holding her hips so tight she'd have bruises for days.

"Lowell?" A voice sounded outside the door. "Don't forget, you're giving the intro. We'll be starting in five minutes."

It took Lowell a long moment to catch his breath. "Be right with you."

And to Annabelle, "See what you can do in an office?"

"Thank goodness you have an executive washroom," she retorted, making an effort to lock her knees so she could stand upright.

He thrust a wad of tissues in her hand. "I have to get to the dais and get ready for my welcoming speech. See you there."

"I'll be there as soon as I...ah...clean up."

Laughing like a carefree boy, Lowell unlocked his office door and strode out.

A few minutes later, cleaned up and makeup repaired, Annabelle followed the crowd to the largest conference room. Lowell, his eyes sparkling as much as her brand-new diamond, looked at ease on the dais, speaking without notes.

The crowd applauded when he finished, and Joseph Butler took center stage. He spoke of his firm's accomplishments, acknowledged the contributions of his partners, then said, "Of course, my leaving the firm opens up a spot for a new partner. I'm happy to say that the board has unanimously agreed on a candidate to fill it."

His eyes roved the assembled group, lit up when they rested on Annabelle.

"I'm delighted to announce the new Senior Partner, Annabelle Fortier."

Amid the cheering and applause, Annabelle took a stunned moment to process what she'd just heard. As she stumbled up to the dais, she noted Lowell whispering in Mr. Butler's ear.

Just as she got to the stage, with Lowell reaching out a hand to help her up the three steps, Mr. Butler added, "And I understand we'll have to order another set of business cards in a couple of months, as she will soon become Mrs. Lowell Smith."

Nudged to the podium to make an acceptance speech, Annabelle looked at the smiling faces of her co-workers. Apparently she was a popular choice, because the applause continued for an embarrassingly long time. Finally she cleared her throat.

"Thank you, Mr. Butler, and all the Partners. I'm honored to be chosen. I'll do my best to live up to your expectations." She gripped the podium with damp palms.

"We all know Mr. Butler is a gentleman of the old school, and we all appreciate that. He has given us respect and support, and it's an honor to be the first woman to be made Partner in this firm." Her eyes glinting with mischief, she added, "However, you won't need to worry about my business cards. I've made my mark as an architect under the name of Annabelle Fortier, and I'm sure Mr. Smith will agree that I should continue to use my maiden name for business purposes."

She turned to Lowell with love in her eyes. "In all other ways, though, I wish to be known as Annabelle Smith." Giving him a chaste peck on the cheek, she whispered for his ears only, "And any time you call me Mrs. Smith, I'll be ready and bare-assed for you."

SPELLS AT MIDNIGHT

Jenna Castille

ഔ

Chapter One
෨

"You're crazy, girlfriend. You have to be completely crazy to try something like this," the small, dark-haired vampire shook her head in dismay as she slid sideways on the couch to face her "insane" friend.

Renee refused to listen, turning her back to stare at the two empty plates and chairs she'd placed at the door in honor of her parents. It wasn't like her friend was telling her anything she hadn't already considered. There were simply no other options left open to her. "Laurel, you can think I'm crazy all you want but I'm not giving up. I've got to keep on living."

"This isn't about living. This is about looking to one of *them* for love," Laurel sneered, her lips curling back with each word, flashing wickedly sharp fangs. "You can't tell me you're not. The timing of this spell proves you're looking at the nonhumans. I know it's been a while but you can't have forgotten what they did."

Renee tucked her silvery hair back behind her left ear, showing off the scar that bisected her cheek to full advantage. "Do you really think I've forgotten? But let's face it, very few of us human paras fall into the immortal category. If we want to survive as a species we're all going to have to start thinking outside the box. I'm sick of being alone, sick of searching. I'm leaving things up to the God and Goddess but I have to keep my options open."

Laurel pursed her overly red lips but nodded. "This sucks and not in a good way. You sure you know what you're doing, at least spell-wise? You're not going to pull some demon over are you? 'Cause I gotta say, I'm so not looking forward to cleaning up the spot one of those would make outta you."

"I can do this, Laurel. It's an untried spell but I did the research. Nothing can harm me here." Renee chewed on her bottom lip and rubbed at the scar on her cheek as she glanced around at the wards meticulously built into the very architecture of her home, checking for any sign of weakness. Nothing human or paranormal could hurt her in her house. Her parents' death in the last great battle between the paranormal drove home the need for perfect security.

"So much has changed in the last decade, Laurel," she whispered, eyes closed against the memories. "So many deaths and for no good reason."

Her friend frowned and twirled a silky length of black hair. "I know. The whole damn war made no sense. I wouldn't have fought in it myself if it hadn't been for my sire. What the hell does it matter if you were distantly related to humans or something else entirely? Either way you bleed and you die. And you're right. There isn't a paranormal race in existence that isn't staring down the brink of extinction. Hell, things aren't all that great in the immortal arena. Turned vampires outnumber natural vampires two to one and you know that not all turned vamps come out sane on the other end." Laurel had a wistful look that tugged at Renee's heartstrings. She hadn't realized her friend was unhappy. "But we don't really know what's happened in the Otherworld in the last few decades. Hell, for all we know they could be gearing up for the next big attack. Your spell could be inviting over some purist who wants us all dead."

Renee tried to push the last image she had of her parents firmly from her mind. Barely in their nineties. She should've had sixty years or more with them. But she couldn't afford to let fear or hatred keep her from her goal. She wasn't going there. Contrary to all the bad horror flicks released this time of year, Samhain was about hope, not despair. Respect the dead but welcome new life. "I'm careful. You know I'm damned careful."

"Yeah," Laurel replied, not sounding entirely reassured. "I just wish I could be here to watch your back. It's almost as hard finding a para friend as it is a lover. Are you sure I can't stay and help?"

She'd known Laurel since before the wars and trusted her implicitly. If she could have anyone stand by her during this spell Renee would choose Laurel. But it *wasn't* possible. "This is a solitary casting. If you stayed the added dimension could cause it to backfire."

"Well, Renee, I don't entirely agree with what you're doing but I understand." Laurel grimaced. "I know you didn't ask me here to give you permission, just some moral support. So here's my say before I leave. Without magic you'll be lucky to find your soul mate. There's what, nine of us paranormals within a two hundred mile radius? Most of those are shifters. You could move to a bigger city with a more diverse population but there are no guarantees that would work. So you're not going to get me yelling at you for doing something about it. I just want to make sure we don't lose any more of our kind. So no getting yourself killed. Deal?"

"Deal," Renee replied, a soft smile spreading across her face. "Now get out of here so I can get started."

Laurel hopped off the couch, holding both hands above her head. "Okay, okay, but remember, dusk tomorrow and I'm here pounding at your door. So if things work out and you're all horizontal, leave a note or something. I don't want to storm in and get an eyeful of your naked ass."

A snicker threatened to spill from Renee but she managed to control it. Laurel might have a strange turn of phrase but she meant every word. As soon as she could she'd be checking in to make certain Renee was safe. "I'll be sure to keep that in mind."

"Do that. Now I'll take my leave. Got a date with a hot little attorney. Thought I'd check out his briefs." Laurel gave Renee a wink and a leer as she smoothed her short, black silk dress and gave her ample hips a shimmy. When Renee smiled

145

at her bad joke and antics, Laurel gave her a sly look. "By the way, if you have any say in this whole thing, see if you can't find a sex machine while you're at it. You need to get laid, my friend. Love's good and all but what's life without a little chemistry?"

Laurel floated out of the room, a disturbing habit Renee had noticed in most vamps over the age of two hundred. Finally the door clicked and she was left alone with her last desperate attempt.

Renee stared down at the myriad herbs, crystals, candles and tools spread out before her on the altar she'd made from an antique coffee table. She bit her lip again and raked her fingers through her waist-length mane as she considered one last time if this was what she truly wanted to do. It was risky and there was no guarantee that it would even work.

Gotta decide soon, she thought, glancing at her grandfather clock. *Midnight on Samhain, the hour that the veil between worlds stretches to its thinnest, is the only time this spell will work no matter what side of the veil my soul mate lives.*

But did she dare try to force destiny to fit her timetable? Sometimes fate had a sick sense of humor and just plain liked to fuck with you. What if her mate came from the other side like she suspected? What if he *was* a nonhuman para? What if he hated her on sight? What if she disgusted him?

What she was about to attempt was unethical at best and dangerous at worst. To compel another being to come to you went against everything that a good witch stood for. It was the kind of action directly proscribed against in the Cross-Para Peace Accord—no magic-using being should compel another to do his or her bidding. To bring her love to her, even if she didn't force him to stay, tread a fine legal line and a finer karmic line.

She'd tried more benign spells that kept her open to the love around her. No one approached her with more than a lustful grin. Not to mention her friends kept giving her strange looks, probably because of the smells some of the potions left behind. She'd tried other versions of this very spell, even on other sabbats, but they hadn't worked either. The most she got was a new familiar, an annoying tomcat that disappeared for days on end no matter how much tuna Renee fed him.

What if my soul mate was lost during one of the battles? He might have fallen beneath a Fae blade or under demon claws. Maybe he had been on the other side of the battles, ripped to shreds by shifter teeth or hexed by another witch or warlock.

She had to know. She had to know if she stood a chance at love. A skillful witch could live to one hundred and fifty years old or more — over a century of loneliness to look forward to.

Desperation led to desperate actions.

She straightened her shoulders and braced herself for the work to come. There were many elements she'd woven together in her spell. She needed to keep her wits about her so as not to forget a single piece.

First, to prepare herself for the casting she placed a handmade wreath of myrtle flowers and leaves on her head. She then poured herself a glass of plum wine to which she'd added ground cardamom — lust and love combined.

Sipping her concoction with a wrinkled nose and a grimace, she walked to the windowsill where she'd placed chunks of dried dragon's blood resin. She sat on the built-in bench and lit the resin. She fanned it gently and let it smolder, both to attract her lover and to help keep evil away from her casting.

Satisfied with the incense, she walked to the middle of the room and sat down cross-legged. She took a deep cleansing breath in through her nose and let it out through her mouth. She completely cleared her thoughts, concentrating on the present moment. No past. No future. Just the now. Once her mind and body felt completely centered and completely at peace, she focused her intention in her casting — love, in whatever form it chose to take. She held the idea, the ideal, fast in her mind as she let the world flow through and around her.

Mentally prepared, she opened her eyes and rolled her shoulders. Resisting a groan, she stood and walked back to the fireplace. She took the brass cauldron from its hanger, filled it with rosewater and then added wine-soaked lemon balm before placing it back over the flames. As it started to bubble slightly she added cinnamon oil and the red juice of a crushed bleeding heart flower.

Three minutes later she took the entire brew off the flames and poured it into a large rose quartz bowl to cool. She stared into the mixture as she waited, channeling her thoughts and desires into the potion with pure, silent, dogged determination. After it cooled to the point she could touch it without burning herself she added the last ingredient—a piece of alexandrite from the ring her father had given her mother when they first met. It had hurt when she'd ground the stone down into a fine powder but she told herself it was for a greater cause, something her parents would understand. She sprinkled the precious dust into her now vile-smelling mixture, stirring it evenly.

Finally she drained it three times through cheesecloth, leaving only a muddy-colored liquid behind. She stripped out of the long white robe she wore but left the myrtle that crowned her head and waited.

When the clock struck midnight she took the liquid and coated herself from head to foot. Every last inch of her body was covered in her noxious-smelling, unorthodox potion, a mixture of what she considered the most powerful love- and lust-attracting herbs.

This finished, she knelt in the center of the room, her heart opened and tears filling her eyes.

Please God and Goddess grant to me my most heartfelt request. Please bring to me the one person in all the worlds meant to live by my side. Human para or nonhuman I do not care, as long as I am loved truly and well.

She remained there beseeching the God and Goddess for so many hours her knees ached. Finally too exhausted to do even that, she rose from her silent plea. Mind nearly blank, she took a damp towel to wipe off the worst of her concoction before falling into her bed and into a deep, numbing sleep.

Chapter Two

ℬ

Warm wet heat slid across her clit, threatening to drag her into full consciousness. A skillful tongue lapped over her labia before teasing her again with a quick, flicking tip. Renee moaned and wiggled as her placid dream shot straight into pure eroticism. She tossed in her bed and reached out for her dream lover, needing an anchor. Her fingers sank deep into thick, riotous curls that snaked around her fingertips and slid under her nails. In response that skillful tongue lapped at her aching pussy and stabbed playfully into the swollen, leaking slit that begged for attention. A brutal shot of arousal bowed her body.

"Goddess," Renee cried, eyes scrunched closed against the threat of reality intruding on this wonderful dream. How long had it been since she had a lover play her body? She bucked forward, deeper into the warmth, as the scent of a thousand autumn nights embraced her.

A rich, rumbling voice chuckled in the darkness as that wonderful mouth moved away from her and left her whimpering. "Not quite, lover," a deep voice purred, "but thank you for the compliment."

Then the moist embrace closed over her clit again, mercilessly taking her further into carnal delirium. The flicking motion along with the hard suckling pressure against her aching flesh sent her soaring toward orgasm at record speed. It had been so long since another person met her desires. But this mystery lover of her dream's creation read her needs like no real man ever had or ever could. Bringing her so close. So close.

"Ahh!" Renee cried out, words impossible in the face of her eruption. Her heels dug into the mattress as wave after wave crashed through her hungry pussy. The man lying between her thighs moaned and slurped, licking up every drop of her nectar.

Renee whimpered and sagged back into her plush bed as that wonderful mouth slowly released her.

"Turnabout's fair play," that dark voice teased as strong arms slid around Renee's waist, rolling her passion-slaked body to her stomach. "Time to turnabout." Yanking her hips up, the man reached over and slipped an overstuffed pillow beneath her. He parted her thighs with his shoulders and arranged her to suit his fancy. Nimble fingers and tongue opened her pussy, piercing her and loosening muscles. She felt like a virgin again beneath the impassioned assault. When that facile tongue slid into her, opening her, she moaned. An unnaturally passionate heat unlike anything she'd ever felt before spread through her womb, pulsing through her entire body with each beat of her heart, leaving her spellbound. Every place he touched tingled and glowed. Her fingers clawed at the thick flannel quilt beneath her. She didn't realize she was thrusting back into the caress until a stinging slap across the ass shocked a gasp from her.

"None of that now. Don't wanna rush things," the man said, using those wonderful fingers of his to circle her engorged clit while massaging her warm ass with his other hand. "Need to go slow with a tight little pussy like yours. You'll get it in time, don't worry. A nice hard cock filling you up. After I'm done eating your pussy I'll pound you good. I'll make you sore but aching to be taken again in the morning. Do naughty, nasty, wonderful things to you. Make you crave it. But for now, be still."

Renee whimpered, fingers digging deeper into thick blankets, scrabbling at the sheets as she struggled to comply with his command. *Be still. Have to be still. But it's so hard. I need, need now. What's happening to me? Goddess, how did he make me this hot, this hungry, this quickly?*

Mouth and fingers. Tongue slick and sliding. Grunt of approval, then more caresses. Fingertips sinking deep, rubbing across something inside that made her groan again and again. Making her ache.

The man murmured and the bed dipped. Hands pulled Renee's thighs farther apart. A hard cock probed at her entrance as thick hair rubbed against the backs of her legs. Tight, she was so tight in this position. And he was so thick. Slow pressure, almost painful, as a wide cock head pushed its way into her. Too full. Stuffed. The man groaned as he slid home, his balls slapping against Renee's ass.

"Damn, you're a perfect fit," the man growled, rubbing her back as he pulled out and plunged in deeper. "God and Goddess but you feel perfect under me. Gonna make you feel so good you'll beg me not to leave. You'll pine for me until I take you again. You will."

The man eased out ever-so slowly, making her feel every second of friction, and slammed back in with tooth-clenching intensity. Renee braced herself on her elbows as best she could as he set up a heavy rhythm, fast and pounding. She felt herself approach the edge of pain, only to have it turn into such intense pleasure she couldn't stop the hoarse cries flowing from her trembling lips.

A warm mouth rained nips, licks and kisses across her shoulder blades. Strong hands wrapped around her waist to reach her clit, flicking it to the same punishing rhythm he shoved into her. Again a strange, muscle-tightening wave of heat bore into her. Sweet and bitter need rippled through her heart and soul as her body shook at the edge of the abyss.

"Take me. Take all of me. Be part of me as I am of you." With those words her dream lover spilled himself deep inside. And the man did something with his hands, something warm and magical. Placing them flat on her womb, a wave of tingling warmth shot into her and sent her spiraling out of control. With a heartfelt cry she collapsed face first on the bed, the comforting weight of her lover blanketing her back.

Thank you, God and Goddess. Whatever the cost, thank you for this night.

Chapter Three

ഔ

Warm sunlight sparkled through her stained-glass picture window. The intricate design of color and magic created a spell of protection from any who meant her physical harm. Those colors danced across her face, teasing her back into wakefulness. Renee yawned, a smirk twisting her mouth as she remembered her dream. She might not have gotten her perfect mate like she prayed to the God and Goddess for but the consolation prize seemed damned nice of them.

She tried to stretch her arms and start moving only to find something soft wrapped tightly around her wrists. Her eyes snapped open and her heart skipped a beat.

She lay naked and spread-eagle on her bed with wrists and feet bound.

"Awake finally. I'd begun to wonder if I broke you last night."

Renee's head jerked in the direction of the deep rumbling voice. Her mouth dried and throat clogged. A strange man sat in the deep blue wingback chair she kept in the corner of the room. Or at least she guessed the guy qualified as a man. He was definitely strange. Thick curly fur the same texture and russet color as the hair on his head covered both of his legs. He wore no clothing. His heavy flaccid cock lay lax across his thigh. His hooves were crossed at his ankles. Muscular arms crossed a wide, well-cut chest, a chest that dared a person to lick it. Golden brown eyes twinkled in an appealing, youthful face. His lush lips curve up in a teasing half-smile. And peeking out of his thick hair were two small blunt-tipped horns.

"Satyr," Renee breathed, eyes going wide and hands jerking frantically at her bonds. *Shit, shit, shit. Here was fate's fucking sick sense of humor. Instead of true love, or even a steamy erotic dream, I'm gonna be screwed to death.*

The man rose, crossed the room and gave a mocking bow with a flourish of his arm. "Zachary, at your service. Sorry about the binding but you can't be too careful these days. You witches are a tricky, bloodthirsty lot. Seen quite a few of my kind fall under your spells. I'd be a fool not to remember that. And you did bring me to the mortal realm without asking my permission. Not exactly a peaceable move." Here the satyr's smile widened. Mischief flashed like golden fire through his eyes. "Not that I'm complaining about the trip considering my hot little reception last night. Best damned sex I've had in centuries. Makes my ears twitch and my horns itch just thinking about it. But it does leave me to wonder exactly what you wanted from me in the first place. Why did you call me here?"

"I couldn't have called *you* here. Not you," Renee muttered, tugging harder at what appeared to be her entire collection of scarves woven together into a surprisingly strong rope. Not only could the satyr tie a mean knot, he seemed to have a gift for enchantment, at least when it applied to bondage. While some dark little part of her found that fact to be both fascinating and tempting, she was trapped. She wasn't getting out of here without help. And no help was coming until nightfall.

"Oh but you did call me," Zachary replied as he stepped to Renee's side. "I heard you clear across the veil begging for me and offering me anything I wanted just to come to you. Pulled me out of a nice little dance with a group of nubile young wood nymphs. I couldn't stop myself from coming to you but at least I got to come *in* you once I got here. So *that* I don't hold against you. I still want to know what you thought you were doing, calling me here in the first place."

"The spell wasn't meant for you."

"Then who was it for?" Zachary asked with a toss of his head and the stomp of one hoof. The sound of that hoof on hardwood echoed through the room like a mini-explosion. "Now you're making me jealous. I'd hate to think that wonderful fuck last night was meant for someone else. All those sexy little screams and that hot cream really belonging to another man. Who were you calling if not me?"

Renee sagged in defeat at the thought. Last night she'd put together something special—the most powerful spell she could cast. She swore she'd felt the God and Goddess acting through her but it hadn't worked. She was still alone, no better off than she had been before. *Hell*, she thought, looking at the satyr, *maybe worse off*. "I don't know who I was calling. That's the point. I wish I did."

The satyr sat on the bed next to her and stared intently at her empty face as the void of hopeless emotions rolled over her. "Pull the other one," Zachary growled, leaning closer, so close Renee could smell his earthy musk.

"I wasn't asking for anyone in particular," Renee explained as she tried to edge as far away from the man as her bindings allowed. She didn't want to say more and give this para any details to use against her, use to hurt her. Why should she open herself up to ridicule from a creature who took what pleasure he could wherever he could and couldn't hold any stronger emotions? He'd been formed from pure lust so what more could he feel?

"Then who were you asking for in general?" Zachary prodded, refusing to take the hint. He cupped Renee's chin and forced her to meet his gaze. "Someone who wouldn't be missed? Someone to take out some old anger on? Someone to capture and enslave for your own purposes?"

Renee blinked in amazement. *How can the man think such a thing? What kind of a monster does he think I am?* "No! I wouldn't do something like that."

"Then what would you do?" he whispered, his face darkening. He loomed over Renee and glared. The full weight of his presence bore down on her.

"I just..." Renee stumbled over her words, unsure of herself in the face of the larger, enraged man.

"You just what?" Zachary demanded, arms bracketing her.

Renee jerked at the scarves again, hating herself for her own stupidity. She'd been so damned sure of herself and look where it'd gotten her. Things weren't supposed to end up this way. Love wasn't supposed to be angry or scary. It wasn't supposed to make you into less than you were. It was supposed to build you up and make you *more* than yourself. "Can you at least let me loose while I tell you? I feel dumb enough as it is."

"Nope," Zachary replied and sat back. He flipped over to lie beside Renee with his back against the headboard and arms crossed. He shook his head. "Can't trust you. At least not yet. Spill, lover, or I'll have to make you."

"Make me?" Renee squeaked, stilling as bloody images from her youth flashed through her mind and twisted her gut. Lust might be a satyr's prerogative but it didn't make him any less dangerous an enemy than any other nonhuman para. What exactly was this man capable of?

"All right. Don't mind if I do."

Renee didn't even have time to brace herself as the satyr pounced across her body. She closed her eyes since she didn't want to watch her blood spill, didn't want to see that final moment of her life spurt out of her as she had her father's. But instead of the quick sharp slice of pain she expected Renee felt warm breath and a hot tongue slide up her neck. Sharp teeth didn't tear and rend her flesh. On the contrary, they nibbled at her earlobe and scraped that tender spot beneath that sent shivers down her spine. Her pussy flooded with warm wet cream as her body arched forward to seek out remembered pleasure.

Instead of death, arousal swamped Renee's senses and ripped a gasp from her. She twisted her hands in her ties, using the support to pull herself closer to the source of sensation, closer to that wicked mouth as it danced over her neck and shoulders seeking out every tiny hotspot. Her feet jerked at their bindings, wanting to be free to wrap around Zachary's waist. So fast and so hot. What was he doing to her?

Incoherent babble fell from her lips as a strong, calloused hand slid down to cup her aching pussy. Electric, magic-filled heat encompassed her entire body. Zinging pulses of pleasure built higher and higher, hotter and hotter.

"Yeah, babe, that's it," Zachary murmured as he lapped at Renee's neck again. "You know you want what only I can give you — unimaginable magical pleasures. Dark and deep passion. You just have to give me what I want in return."

"Anything," Renee gasped, losing herself as she pushed into Zachary's hand and arched her neck into each warm caress. That unfamiliar level of lust clouded her mind again and swamped her senses. But it felt wonderful to lose herself in the thrill, to know someone else was there to catch her.

"You realize this body belongs to me for as long as I want it, don't you?" Zachary whispered as he worked his mouth down Renee's body to join his hand. Nibble, lick, suck, kiss.

"Yes, yours," Renee whimpered at the raging fire filling her. "All yours."

Zachary's hot breath played across Renee's straining breasts. Zings of pleasure shot from the aroused peaks as his teeth closed over the tips and his tongue flicked across the needy flesh. He released his grip to chuckle as Renee gasped and arched toward his mouth. With long laps across her nipples, he eased the aching flesh at the same time his caress drew both to hard points.

Palming and kneading both mounds, he moved down her body inch by quivering inch. Reaching her wet, clenching pussy, he blew a cooling breath against hot skin. "Mine to play with," he added with a quick flick of his tongue to collect a droplet of cream dripping down her thigh. He purred, "But that little mind of yours is mine too. Everything in it, every thought and desire belongs to me now."

"Please," Renee begged, her ties rubbing her flesh raw as she struggled to free herself, to wrap herself around her tormentor.

The satyr moved his hands from her breasts and reached above her head to stop Renee's movements. He loosened her bindings slightly and massaged the sore flesh of her wrists with gentle thumbs. "I will please you," he breathed as he slid his hands back down Renee's sides, leaving a trail of longing and magical heat in his wake. "After you please me. Just answer my question. A few simple words and I'll give you more pleasure than you can stand. I'll take you places no other creature ever could."

Renee scrambled to clear her mind of the erotic fog. She searched for some question she'd been asked. What was the fucking question? It was there skipping at the edge of her consciousness. Why couldn't she remember? What was happening to her?

Seeing Renee's frantic confusion and growing dismay Zachary prompted, "Why did you call me here?"

"I didn't call *you*," Renee whined, scarves squeaking against the wood of her headboard as she twisted against her bonds again. Why wouldn't he listen? She'd told him this already. *Why won't he listen?*

Zachary began petting her heaving chest, soothing and calming her. She bent beneath each caress, feeling those warm hands reaching inside and rubbing her soul. She wallowed in his crisp, wild scent. She wanted more, wanted a connection. But still the man asked questions.

"Who did you call?"

Tears blurred Renee's vision, dripping out to the corners of her eyes as she tossed her head. Her skin felt tight, about to burst with vibrating energy. Her throat clogged but she managed to answer. "I called on the God and Goddess. Begged them. Just wanted love. True love. Someone to care for and care for me in return. So lonely. Please. I didn't mean to hurt anyone."

Zachary reared back, hands falling to his side, his face a picture of abject amazement. "Love?" he murmured as something akin to hope filled his golden eyes.

"Yes, *love*, damn it!" Renee snarled, pitching and twisting, her every movement frenzied. "Now untie me and fuck me already. You want me. You must want me. Fuck me!"

With hands trembling so slightly Renee almost missed it, Zachary untied her bonds. She launched herself at the satyr, wrapping her arms and legs around him and dragging him down on top of her. A voice in the back of her mind said that this unbearable need had to be part of Zachary's magic but she didn't care. She needed to feel again. Last night rocked her but it still seemed like a dream, unreal. Zachary made her *feel*.

"Whoa, little one," Zachary said, pushing up on his arms to give Renee room to breathe. The position pushed his hard cock against her stomach, so close to where she wanted him. He stared down as if he wanted to memorize every inch of Renee's face. Instead of taking what he wanted as she expected, he dipped his head for a second to lick across the scar on her cheek before whispering, "You're going to hurt us both if you're not careful."

"Don't care," Renee whimpered and nipped at Zachary's neck. "I want you. *Now*."

The shocked expression faded from Zachary's face, an ancient, knowing smile replacing it. He cupped Renee's face in his hands and kissed her gently, his full lips lingering but his tongue not thrusting inside and claiming. "Yes, you do want me. You always will. And you shall have me. But not like this, not drowning in my power. I want this time to be with you and only you."

The satyr pried Renee's arms off him and gave her a quick shake. "Are you with me? I need you with me."

Renee blinked, jarred as the clawing mating urge subsided a bit. She still wanted Zachary, no doubt about that. But it didn't feel like she'd die if she didn't get him. "What now?" she snapped, her voice filled with need but no longer out of control. "Wanna know my lineage? Need a recommendation from my last lover? That'll be hard to come up with. It's been awhile. I'm not even sure where to find him now."

Zachary chuckled and cradled Renee against his shaking chest. "Nope. I just want to take a moment to change places. I want to see your face this time. I'm giving you the chance to take me." A lascivious grin spread across his craggy features. "Now come over here."

The satyr pulled her forward into their first real kiss, an exploration of the mouth not a quick teasing smooch. Renee hadn't known what she'd been missing until that moment. Pure, sweet, dark fantasy. His kiss alone undid any calm he'd managed to instill in her with his little talk. The taste of her satyr lingered on her tongue, bitter and sweet like dark chocolate. Lips and teeth nibbled at the tender flesh just inside her mouth. The sharp tip of his tongue tickled the roof. Then he plunged in, exploring every nook and cranny he could reach.

So very good and so very wicked at the same time.

When they parted their mouths clung together as though their lips didn't want to let go. Zachary licked at the corners, tasting her smile. "Gods, I could get used to this," he whispered before giving a wink and a wry smile. "But don't leave me hanging, lover. I offer to let you ride me and all you can do is tease"

161

Pulling back, Renee smirked. Eyeing Zachary, she pursed her lips and cocked her head.

Renee scooted back to sit across Zachary's fur-covered legs. She took a moment to lick at the tip of his massive cock, stabbing the tip of her tongue into the small, weeping slit. A wild cry spilled from his lips as he jerked beneath her and almost knocked her off him. Enjoying the thrill his reaction gave her, Renee tilted her head to mouth his balls for a moment, savoring each moan as she laved them with her tongue.

"Damn, woman," Zachary cursed, setting his sweat-damp curls dancing across his head. He panted as he fought for control. "Keep that up and I'm gonna shoot before you take me in you."

"I thought satyrs were known for their stamina and ability to go all night and into the next day. How else do you last through those week-long orgies you're famous for? Are you saying you're a one-hit wonder?" Renee teased, taking a moment to suck a single ball in her mouth and roll it from one cheek to the other.

"Fuck you, no," Zachary growled as he squirmed beneath Renee's tender assault. "But damn, there's something about you and you're too good at that."

Renee smirked. She took his cock in hand, flattened her tongue and licked from root to tip. Salty, intoxicating spice flooded her mouth and filled her with the desire to taste even more. His eyes rolled back as he bucked into the caress. He was hers to do with as she pleased this time and she'd see him beg her. Devilish mischief danced in her eyes as she closed one hand over his tight balls and sucked the fingers of her other hand. She continued massaging them as she sank a single slick digit into his ass and gave his prostate a quick rub.

Zachary gasped and bore down on the tempting finger, taking it as far as it would go. "Please, babe. Can't take much more. Get on with it."

"Oh I will. Don't worry." That was the only warning Renee gave before she pulled out her finger and took his cock as far in her mouth as she could. She bobbed her head, swallowing on each downstroke until he hit the very back of her throat and his flavor coated every inch of her tongue. This was something she missed, the taste of a man. The power in having a strong lover squirming beneath her mouth, hard length sliding and vein throbbing against her tongue. Zachary howled and arched into her hot mouth. When he seemed about to lose control she pulled back.

Renee moved off and licked her lips. "Think you're ready to take me?" she whispered darkly, getting into her role as the satyr responded to her every touch. "Big, bad, paranormal sex machine. Think you can handle one little witch?"

"Damn it," Zachary growled as he bucked beneath her. "Ride me now."

"My pleasure."

Renee slid forward, bending over to nip at his nipples. Slow and easy she lowered herself onto his cock, watching his face tighten as she clenched around him. The satyr tossed his head, snarling and crying out to the gods. But he also clawed at the sheets, demanding, "More, give me more. I want to watch as you take me in you. You've got more than that. Ride me. Ride me hard!"

Renee took him at his word and set a brutal rhythm as she took him as fast as she could stand. She watched Zachary's eyes glow that wicked, molten gold. His lips curled back in a silent sneer as he finally lost it, cheeks twitching as his cock spurted rope after rope of thick cum deep in her womb.

The sight of this man so overwhelmed by his own pleasure, a pleasure she gave him, sent Renee over the edge. Eyes locked with his and uttering a hoarse cry, she came rippling around him.

Exhausted by the power of her orgasm, Renee collapsed across his chest. With the last bit of strength she possessed, she tried to roll off to the side and reach for the edge of the blanket. But Zachary wrapped his arms and legs around her, murmuring in protest and keeping her close and warm.

Renee let herself be tucked under the man's chin and fell into a deep sated sleep. A contented smile graced her face.

Chapter Four
ഔ

Zachary held the still-sleeping Renee tight, staring at the minute cracks in an unfamiliar ceiling. *A freaking human para. Who would've thought the gods would pair me up with a human para, after all her kind did to mine?*

But strangely enough he didn't doubt Renee's word. As far as he could tell the woman didn't have a deceptive bone in her pretty little body. His power let him see into his lover's soul when watching her eyes during orgasm. Even after surviving the war, Renee retained a kind and generous spirit.

So he trusted her story. Thanks to an appeal for love here he was, lying in a strange bed, wrapped around a woman who could very well complete him. She had all the markings of a lifemate fated by the God and Goddess themselves. A woman with the ability to send Zachary into peaks of arousal he'd never found before. She even managed to wear him out. *Him.* After a few centuries of wild debauchery, that was saying something. The spicy smell and rich taste of her, sweetly addictive, clung to his memory and burrowed into his heart.

A single day and his life had changed forever. One moment he was dancing another meaningless dance with a few of the remaining satyrs and a handful of nymphs before another round of empty if scorching sex, the next he found himself inextricably bound to this precious woman.

But who is this Renee, really? he thought, staring down at the thin scar cutting across her cheek. *Why did the gods choose her to be my one?*

His powers told him that she was a survivor just like him. A woman who'd lost so much but still kept her heart open and hoped for the happiness of all her people. She was lonely and frightened for her future. He could see that she felt drawn to him but knew life with Zachary wouldn't be anywhere near easy. The para communities still weren't comfortable with all their members and certainly not with mixed species couplings.

There would be hatred and prejudice to face. Why had fate or the gods put them together like this? There had to be some greater purpose behind it.

Something drew him to Renee beyond the fact that the woman was just plain sexy. She with her slight, waiflike body, her flowing starlight hair and her one imperfect scar adding humanity to the almost magical perfection of her pale face.

And the only way he could find out what was behind it all was to leave this wonderful woman and go back to the Otherworld. There he had people he could ask for answers and help for him to stay with her.

He'd have to go back to Otherworld if he wanted to save his little witch from the ticking time bomb of her mortality. Looking down at her smooth face, he guessed his mate had maybe a century left to her, give or take a few decades. Meanwhile Zachary's kind weren't born at all and weren't tied to any archaic "circle of life". They rose fully formed from the firmament of Otherworld, molded from the lustful dreams and erotic desires of humankind. He was unaging and barring murder would never die.

His heart would rip in two when his mortal mate passed, leaving him to keep on living alone. He'd pine away and become a wraith. He had to speak with the elders and have them petition the God and Goddess on her behalf. He needed an answer to why they chose Renee and to find a way to save this woman who was his heart.

The God and Goddess seemed to enjoy causing difficulties and mayhem for their magical people. Maybe it was a punishment for the havoc all the paras caused each other during the wars. Maybe they had a plan beyond his understanding.

"What's wrong?" Renee whispered as she snuggled closer, burrowing her hands under Zachary's waist to hug him tight.

He let his hand slide up and down Renee's back and breathed in the sweet floral scent of his mate as he planned his next move. Already Renee was his touchstone. He couldn't leave her but saw no other way to proceed. He certainly couldn't take her with him. It was too dangerous. "Nothing's wrong, and everything."

Renee didn't say anything at first, her silence enough of an answer. She lay heavily across Zachary's body, an unmoving blanket of security and warmth. "When do you leave?" she finally whispered.

Zachary's hand stilled on Renee's back, clutching her to him for a moment. "What do you mean? Ready to get rid of me already?" he tried to tease, uncomfortable with how well she was reading him in such a short time.

She grimaced and wouldn't let him get away with making a joke of things. "I don't want you to go but I'm no fool." She paused for a moment and buried her face in his neck, refusing to meet his eyes. "I know you can't stay with me forever. Your kind lives in Otherworld for a reason. You're more comfortable there and the human population isn't accepting of you, not since the age of myths passed. I'm just wondering how long I get to have you here before you leave me."

It disturbed Zachary how quickly Renee let go of him. Hell, he hated that Renee could give up on him at all. This woman was his mate, the other half of his soul. She shouldn't be able to just toss him by the wayside. The thought alone should rip her and leave her emotions bare and bleeding, just as it did him.

"First let me make one thing clear," Zachary snapped, more harshly than he intended as he wrestled with the chaotic roll of unfamiliar emotions. "You said the God and Goddess brought me here as your love. I think they're right. I could easily love you. Hell, I'm halfway there already. From everything I see in you, you would make a fine mate."

"But?" Renee whispered.

Zachary heard the tears threatening to choke that single word, his heart aching when he thought that he was the cause. "But there are other things to consider, things I need to work out. Things that will take time."

"Things you can't do here," she whispered against his chest.

Zachary squeezed her tight as he heard the despair dripping from those words. He took a moment to gather up his own bitterness and plant a soft kiss on the crown of Renee's head. "I wish I could do everything here and not leave your side. I want time to spend with you. Time to get to know you. Court you. But I can't. I have to go back."

"When?"

"Soon, while the veil is still thin enough for me to cross."

"Will you come back?" Renee murmured both their greatest fears.

Heart aching at the thought, Zachary couldn't lie to Renee, not if she was his soul mate. "I don't know. I'll do everything in my power to return. But I don't know if it *will* be in my power."

Renee shifted on top of him, instinctively seeking comfort in the touch of skin on skin. "How long?" she asked against Zachary's neck, the brushing of her lips giving him chills.

"I'm not sure," Zachary muttered, pulling her closer. "Could be a long time. Will you wait for me?"

Renee pushed up to look into his face. She cupped Zachary's cheeks and stared down into his eyes. "I've waited this long to find you, what's a little more? At least now I know you exist and I know why it's taken so long to find you. I know that you'll miss me as much as I miss you. Just promise me that you'll come back."

"If I can, I will."

Zachary gave her one last, lingering kiss before rolling Renee over and prying himself out of her soft, warm bed. "If I don't leave now I never will. You beneath these blankets is just too tempting. I don't think either of us wants to face the consequences for that."

Renee hugged herself and stuck out her lower lip. "Your people would be mad if you stayed?"

A humorless laugh fell from Zachary's lips. "What do you think?"

No attempt at humor could hide her fear and sorrow. "I think I'll miss you. And I think I'll hurt like hell 'til you get back."

Zachary resisted the urge to take Renee in his arms again. That would only delay the inevitable. "Don't worry. I won't forget you."

"Better not," Renee threatened, eyes narrowing in mock anger. "I'd hate to have to go to the Otherworld just to kick your ass."

"Don't even dare joke about it," Zachary replied, a slice of terror winding its way through his heart at the thought of what could happen to Renee in the Otherworld. "You risk yourself like that and I'll beat you myself. And not in a happy fun way."

Renee tried to give him a parting smile but failed miserably. "Well, do I a least get to spend the day with you? You may not be coming back. You said so yourself. Surely the God and Goddess wouldn't begrudge us one short day."

Zachary's smile started sad but he couldn't keep a grim expression on his face. "And what would you want to do during your one day?" he teased, walking back to lean over her. "Or can I guess?"

Renee slapped at him as she crawled forward on the bed. "Not that." She paused for a moment, casting a coy look from under heavy lids. "Well, maybe a *little* of that. But I was thinking we could go out. I'd show you my shop. We could have a picnic. Maybe go dancing at a club I know. You satyrs love to dance, right?"

Zachary eyed her bare body, lean and fit. He could just picture her flowing to the music beneath open skies. He'd have to tear his brother satyrs' eyes out. "Yes, but the kind of dancing we do is best done in private. Do I get to meet the family?"

"No family to meet. But my friends would be interested." She grinned with mischief as she gazed at his bare chest and half-aroused cock. "Hell, some might be a little *too* interested. I'll keep you away from them. Don't want to waste any of my day refereeing the fight to get at you. Guess you can't tone down the sexy?"

"Nope, part of the whole package. I can amp up the wattage, take you to places you've never imagined. But I can't rein it back that much." At her cross expression, he gave her a sheepish look and a shrug. "Nature of the beast."

Renee rolled her eyes but didn't look *that* upset with him. "Do you need help blending?"

Looking down his naked body, Zachary quipped, "What, cloven hooves and goat legs not the fashion these days?"

"Yesterday you could've gotten away with it, being Halloween and all. But today not so much. I've got just the thing." Renee hopped up and raced across the room to a wooden box sitting on her dresser. She pawed through the contents, dragging out tangled gold chains and bangle bracelets in her search.

Zachary couldn't help but laugh.

Glancing back over her shoulder, Renee asked, "What?"

"It's just that you're so cute when you're all excited about showing off some of your magic. That *is* what you're digging around to fetch, right?"

Renee had the grace to blush. "Not like there's anyone else around here to appreciate it," she mumbled.

The melancholy tone in his lover's normally cheerful voice struck Zachary deep—heart deep. "Well, you've got an audience now. Show me your stuff."

"I think you've seen my stuff already," she quipped, flipping her hair over her shoulder and leering back at him. "But if you want to watch me cast something, too late. I'm thinking charm. I have a glamour charm I put together for a costume party that I never actually went to. Too lazy to shop for a costume like everyone else and not into it enough to actually show up. Anyway, I never triggered it so I think I can change it to work on you."

Zachary held out his arms. "I'm all yours."

"You trust me?" Renee asked, holding a heavy medallion over his head.

"More than I should," he answered in a tone too serious for one of his fun-loving breed. "More than I ever thought I would a human para. But we have to start somewhere, eh?"

"Yeah. I'm just hoping we don't have to stop here too," Renee mumbled under her breath as she dropped the charm over Zachary's head.

Zachary felt a cool blanket shimmer into place over him, leaving behind a prickling sensation tripping across his skin. It felt a bit like mint oil flowing over his body. Looking down, he couldn't see any change.

"Here," Renee said, handing him a mirror. "It wouldn't be any fun if you couldn't see through it yourself. But it shows up in reflections."

Zachary looked at the reflection of his face. Not much of a change really, until he tilted the mirror up to see his hair. No horns. He reached up and could feel them but he couldn't see them. Using the mirror, he glanced down. A plain white t-shirt covered his chest and brown slacks the same color as his fur met shoes the color of his hooves.

"Like I said, you can feel and see it but no one else can." Renee grinned, obviously pleased with herself but unsure of his reception. "You like?"

Zachary smiled at the crack of insecurity he heard in that question. "Very nice. Subtle. You're a skilled worker to know when *not* to go overboard."

Renee gave a mock bow but her face filled with pride. "Thank you, kind sir. From a being that lives surrounded by magic and creatures most skilled at casting glamours, I'll take that as a rare compliment."

He couldn't resist Renee's pleased little smirk. Zachary swooped forward to capture her mouth. A nibble and flick later and his tongue plunged deep between soft, full lips. Her sweet flavor filled his mouth and hardened his cock.

Renee whimpered and wrapped her arms around Zachary's waist, pulling him near.

Zachary pulled back, placing a soft kiss on the tip of her nose. "None of that if we plan on leaving."

"Whose idea was it to go out again?" Renee pouted.

"Yours and it was a good one. If I have to leave I'm leaving you with some damn good memories to keep you warm."

Renee held him close, her head tucked beneath his chin. "Don't know if they'll keep me warm but they'll keep me yours. We could start with a picnic. I know the perfect place, just outside of town. It would be a short hike but this time of year it should be deserted. Just you, me, a little food and the open air."

"That sounds just my speed."

Chapter Five

ະຈ

Zachary looked down at the delicate hand held loosely in his own—soft and smooth but vibrating with great power. Bright green eyes shone with intelligence as Renee talked about her life in the small town she'd moved to after the death of her parents. So different from the vapid gaze of the nymphs he usually kept company with, Renee sparkled with life and honest merriment.

He squeezed her hand tighter and filled his lungs with the crisp autumn air. What more could a satyr want? A warm fall day, no humans or paras for miles and his woman at his side. A perfect moment.

Renee tugged at his hand, pulling him off the path and down a small incline. "This way," she said as she ducked under a branch and scrambled through some bushes.

Lifting the picnic basket he carried in his other hand up over the brush, he followed her to a small glade completely surrounded by trees and brush. A private sanctuary. Zachary sat the basket in the shade of a large oak and stepped back as Renee flipped open the lid and started rummaging through the contents. He took a blanket from the growing pile and spread it across a flat area.

She turned from her search and smiled up at him. "Perfect," she murmured.

Zachary's heart clenched as his thoughts echoed her words. Perfect—she was utterly perfect with patches of sunlight dancing between branches to flash across her pale, oval face. Sweet, sexy and beautiful. The only word that could describe her was perfect.

"I couldn't ask for a better day," she murmured as she laid out the plates of finger foods she'd whipped up for them. "Maybe the God and Goddess want to be certain you understand exactly what you'd be giving up if you don't return."

Zachary stared up at the clear blue sky and pushed back the darkness that threatened his mood. "I don't want to talk about that now. This moment is for the two of us. Let's see what you have to tempt me with."

Renee smiled softly and nodded. Zachary made certain he ohhed and ahhed over each bit of food she offered him, wanting nothing more than to please her and distract her from his imminent departure. He didn't know if it worked or not but she smiled at him and continued feeding him tasty tidbits as if she hadn't a care in the world. When nothing remained she scooted down beside him and put her head on his lap.

"So is it very different here than where you come from?" she asked, looking up at him with innocently curious eyes.

Zachary leaned back against the tree, closed his eyes and slid his fingers through her soft hair. "Yes and no. We have trees and clear skies, fresh air and beautiful days. But there are differences, colors and smells. Magic permeates every inch of Otherworld, almost a presence all its own. And there are no humans to worry about." He paused for a moment and weighed his dissatisfaction. "But it gets monotonous too. Stifling. Everyone understands what you are and accepts you but nothing ever changes."

"So you weren't happy there?"

"Content but not happy."

"Could you be happy here?"

Zachary looked around. Beautiful day. Sweet, wonderful little witch. He might understand lust better but he recognized happiness and the beginnings of love when he felt them. The God and Goddess knew their people well. He leaned down and placed a gentle kiss on her forehead. "Happy? I think I can be much more than *happy* here with you."

Renee snorted. "Thanks for the vote of confidence but you've known me for a day. The God and Goddess might think you're my perfect match but I realize you don't have to agree."

"Why wouldn't I?" Zachary asked, cupping her cheek and rubbing her bottom lip with his thumb. "Other than the fact that you're human-para, which doesn't matter to me as much as it would some of my brothers. You're beautiful, sexy, skilled and loyal. Is there something else I'd want?"

She grinned beneath his caress and inched her fingers up his thigh. "Maybe not. I mean, you might not be of human descent but I know I could love you."

Zachary eased down to lie beside her, cushioning her head against his arm. "Really? Why? Because the God and Goddess picked me for you? It seems you're putting more faith in them than I am."

"Well, I do trust their judgment and my own skill at spellcasting. But there's something about you." She chuckled at Zachary's automatic leer and eyebrow wiggle. "Something beyond the sex. I feel comfortable and safe when I'm with you. Does that make sense?"

His heart clutched in his chest only to race a moment later. "Oh yes. That makes perfect sense."

He leaned forward and kissed her. Not a kiss filled with ravenous hunger. Not a passion-filled foray. A gentle meeting of the mouths. A soft touch that sent an arrow of gut-wrenching emotion darting into both their souls.

It was Renee who pushed it further. Renee who whimpered and crawled on top of him.

Zachary pulled his lips away. "I thought you wanted your day with me to be filled with more than just sex?" he teased.

175

"And I thought you were all about the sex. Plans change. I say go with it."

Wrapping his arms around her, the joy inside Zachary built and built until it burst out as the purest laughter of his life. He rolled her, chuckling the entire time and stopping only when her voice joined his.

He lay on top of her, nestled between her thighs. He cupped her dear face in his hands. "So damn beautiful. I want to see you here with the sunlight dancing across your skin. Want to take you under the open sky."

"Please," she sighed, her fingers curving over the skin of his back. It must have taken quite a bit of energy to cast her spell but there was something to be said about clothing built from illusion.

Renee must've had the same thought. She arched and rolled him to the bottom. She jerked her t-shirt over her head, catching her ponytail clasp and freeing a cascade of hair in the process.

He cupped her breasts, thumb gliding over her nipples as she struggled with the catch on her pants. A puzzled look crossed her face.

"What?"

"It doesn't feel the same."

A moment of worry struck Zachary as he rose up, sucking her nipple and nipping at the tip. *Damn, she tastes sweet.* "It's just you and me this time. The only magic here is what we make ourselves. That okay with you?"

"Just you and me. I think I can handle that. Not that I don't appreciate your wild ride but a girl likes a little slow and easy sometimes."

"As long as she gets the hard, fast fuck she wants other times?"

"You got it, babe," she answered. A quick jerk and a muttered curse at her shoes and her bare skin met his. Her mouth nibbled at his, teasing his tongue out to play. Zachary

176

shivered, a slow burn growing at the base of his spine with each playful lap and curl. He petted her back, grabbing her ass in both hands. She groaned as he arched his back and rubbed himself against her soft stomach.

"I want in you," he whispered. "Wanna feel you surround me in your moist heat. I want to lose myself in you, forget everything. Everything I've ever seen or done. Be reborn inside of you."

"Please."

Zachary slid his hand down, parting her cleft with a single finger. So wet. She was already so wet for him, without using a bit of his sex magic. She wanted him. *Him*. Not easy sex. Not the claim of fucking a satyr. She was wet for him.

A gift from the God and Goddess. She could be nothing less.

And she was impatient. With a growl, she clenched her thighs and grabbed his ass with both hands. His eyes rolled back as she impaled herself on his hard cock.

"Yeah, that's what I'm talking about."

Zachary would've laughed at her self-satisfied tone of voice if she'd left him any breath. As it was, for once in his limitless life he found himself hanging on as someone else took *him* for a ride.

Hot, tight flesh rose over him, milking him. He bit his lower lip as he struggled to gather back his control. But she'd have none of that. Her eyes glowed with wicked pleasure at the struggle in his face. She knelt up and slammed down on him harder.

"Fuck, love. I can't. You have to slow down."

"No. You have to keep up."

"I can't hold back."

She gave a wild laugh, slinging her head back to whip the hair from her face. "I don't want you to. I want to take everything you have to give. I want to know that I can make you lose control the same way you turn me inside out. So come already."

Zachary slammed his head back into the ground. His eyes rolled back in his head as he felt that lightning shock of pleasure building at the base of his spine. His balls ached, tightening that last little bit before he shot his seed deep inside her.

As she cried out her own pleasure, he watched her eyes again. So much there, open for him to see. A clear shining soul and a possible future that held many centuries for them both together.

* * * * *

Hours later, near dusk, Zachary laughed as Renee skipped backward down the tree-lined walk leading to her house, chattering the entire time.

"I wish we'd had time to go see my shop. I'd like to know what you thought."

"Really?" asked Zachary. He let a lascivious smirk play across his mouth.

Renee clapped a hand over her lips but couldn't hold back the giggles. "Well, I would've liked to know what you thought of my place but I liked how we spent our time more."

"Just *liked*. Guess I didn't do my job right."

"You'll just have to make sure you come back and work harder next time."

Zachary's heart lurched at the reminder. He stayed silent the rest of the way to Renee's house. The moon rose high in the night sky as they stepped on the porch of her neat little cabin on the outskirts of town. An unlit jack-o'-lantern grinned up at them and the words "Magic Happens" greeted them from a sign on the door. Renee struggled with the key.

Zachary gasped as he felt a tug deep in his chest. A familiar pulling dragged at his soul.

Renee stood in the half-open doorway, staring at him. "What is it?"

Hand at his chest, he glared at the moon just rising over the horizon. "My brothers. They've noticed my absence and call to me."

"You have to leave," Renee said in monotone as she followed his gaze.

Zachary stepped closer, taking Renee's face in his hands. He kissed her, hard and deep, imprinting her taste and feel on his senses. "I don't want to but I have to. I *will* be back."

"You'll try," Renee murmured, tears choking her words.

"I will." He reached up and took the medallion from around his neck and slipped it in her hand. "Keep this safe for me. I'll need it when I get back."

Staring at the cool metal lying in her palm, Renee said, "It's a one-time spell."

"Then recast it and have it ready for me," Zachary growled, shaking her until she met his gaze. "When I come back it'll be to stay."

She nodded and fought back tears as Zachary stepped away from her. A dark void opened behind him. The last thing she saw as he disappeared was the golden sparkle of his eyes.

An hour later Laurel found Renee curled on her steps, her sobs racking her body.

Chapter Six

Zachary's scream shattered the darkness, endlessly. Yet his voice hadn't broken, much less his determination. Most of his endurance had disappeared after the continuous months of trials. No sleep for more days than he could count. Only eating what food he could scavenge. No sex at all, devastating for one of his race. But he'd never lost sight of his goal—Renee.

Until now.

The elders brought him here to this dank, stone-lined room for months more of "tests". They finally accepted that he meant to have her, that *maybe* the God and Goddess had a hand in their meeting. Now he just had to survive the creation of the ambrosia to make her immortal and get the answer to his question of why they were mated. That was it. But that was so much more than he could stand. Tied to a stone slab with deep gouges cut into it, pain became his constant companion—pain and the voices.

"Are you certain this witch is worth it, brother?" a tempting voice whispered in his ear as flames seemed to lick through his every nerve. His constant companion during his trials, this voice didn't want him to succeed. Hatred laced its every word. "Are you certain you want to go through with this, all the agony? Ambrosia never comes without great cost. It would make your mortal witch more powerful than any other of her kind. That is dangerous. Are you certain you can trust her with such a gift?"

"I've seen her soul." Zachary tried not to flinch as his bindings tightened and cut into his flesh. "It belongs with mine."

"Does it? Does *she*?" another voice asked, ever taunting. "Or has her spell blinded you? Is it only lust you feel, the need for variety? Are the wood nymphs no longer enough for you?"

"Do you think I would come this far, let you tie me up and rip out a piece of my soul, if I weren't absolutely certain?" Zachary growled in return. "When I made love to her I saw my future in her eyes. She is my mate, the one I will live with forever. I'm a satyr. That shouldn't even be possible. But I *saw* it."

Silence was his only response. It seemed he'd given his tormentor something to consider. Maybe they *did* think he was that shallow, that led by his own lust. Even knowing the reputation of most satyrs the accusation almost hurt. Or at least it would've if every part of his body wasn't already in agony. No room remained for emotional pain.

Yet with the silence cold filled the stark room. The fiery pain that bowed his body slowly eased under the cool breeze. His shallow, labored breathing smoothed. He glanced to his side and watched as his blood and sweat traveled through the gouges in the stone to pool in a small crystal vial.

One of the ancients stepped out of the shadows, shape and form hidden in a purple, hooded robe. He took the vial in hand and muttered an incantation over it. The words were unfamiliar to Zachary but set the hair on the back of his neck on edge. The vial glowed as the liquid inside bubbled. Steam poured out the top as the contents turned a sparkling amber color.

Others released his bindings and help him sit up. As he rubbed at his abused wrists, the ancient one stepped forward again.

"You may take this and go back to her. But you must do so under a geas."

Zachary's heartbeat kicked up a notch but a slow grin spread across his sweat-soaked face. "Whatever you wish, I'll do it to be with her."

"It isn't my wish," the ancient intoned, his slitted eyes glittering beneath his hood. "It is the greater plan of the God and Goddess. They are not happy with their people. They wanted us to learn our lesson from the war but not die out because of our prejudice. That is where you and your mate come in. It will be through your connection with lust magic and her skill with love and calling spells that the God and Goddess shall bring us all to peace once more. They have a job for you to do."

Chapter Seven
℘

A half hour to midnight and Samhain again, Renee thought as she placed three chairs and three empty plates on a table near the door, two for her parents and one for Zachary. *Another fucking lonely day. And this time I don't even have the hope of finding true love. No, I found love only to have it ripped away before I even got used to the feeling. Not even the cute costumed kids could to cheer me up this year. Great way to spend one of my favorite sabbats.*

One night and one day, all the fates let her have was one stinking night and day. Then they tore him away from her. If Zachary didn't return tonight, what little hope she had left would die.

She'd been waiting a whole year and damned if it didn't look like a hundred more stretched out in front of her.

She pulled a tissue out of her sleeve as her eyes teared up again. It wasn't right and she knew that no amount of magic would make it right. Still, while she'd promised Zachary not to try to bring him back or go searching for him, she couldn't help but cast a few minor spells to encourage his return. She burned dragon's blood on her window again and wore another wreath of myrtle around her head.

And she'd prayed to the God and Goddess every night. Every invocation she made through the year she dedicated to him. The possibility that they didn't listen because they blamed her for giving back their gift terrified her.

After turning off the lights and putting the leftover candy in the cupboard, she sat on her window seat looking out over the few sparkling lights still shining downtown and waited. Again. Arms wrapped around her knees, staring off into the darkness, just like every other night for the past year. Waiting for someone who might never come.

She didn't even realize she'd fallen asleep until strong arms swept her up and carried her to her bedroom.

Renee's eyes flew open and she reached back to claw at her attacker.

"Really, lover, you'd think you weren't happy to see me," a warm voice laughed close to her ear.

Renee gasped as she stared into sparkling golden eyes.

"Miss me?" he asked.

She threw her arms around Zachary's neck and held on with the strength of all her pent-up emotions. "Where the hell have you been?"

"Been there among other places," he grumbled, a new bleakness shadowing his much thinner features only to be chased away by his innate merriment. "Back now though and I get to stay. Talk about it later. Now I want you. It's been too damn long since I've had you."

Renee smiled, eyes misting as she wrapped her arms around Zachary's neck. *Swept off my feet. Damned if the fool man hasn't swept me off my feet.*

"Omph," she gasped as the satyr dropped her in the middle of her bed. She still bounced on the mattress as Zachary followed her down, sealing her lips with his own. Oh Goddess, she'd missed his rich intoxicating taste.

"Missed you," he echoed her thoughts into her mouth and lapped at her lips. "Hasn't been anyone else since you. You got any idea what that does to someone of my breed? I'm fucking going out of my mind. I have to have you now. Can't wait. Sorry."

Renee sank her fingers into Zachary's thick hair, reveling in the silky texture wrapping around the tips as she pulled him down for another kiss. "Don't wait. I don't want you to wait. I want you now."

Zachary sat up. A flick of his hand had Renee naked.

Renee blinked, staring down her nude body before giggling. "Gotta love that satyr magic. Damned handy. You have to teach me that."

He grinned back and gave a negligent shrug. "If it has to do with having sex or getting down to sex, I can do it. Don't know if that's something I can teach."

"Then show me. I'm a quick study," Renee said, a half-smile curling her lips and a wicked glint in her eyes.

Zachary grinned, moving back to give himself more room. He didn't allow Renee any time for second thoughts. Focusing all his pent-up angst and repressed sexual energy in his hands, he put his palms on her stomach and shoved it into Renee.

She gasped and gave a high-pitched little cry, her entire torso bowing under the pressure of intense arousal. Her clit swelled to a hard little kernel and her pussy wept for attention.

Zachary pushed her back down on the bed, letting his hands run a glowing trail from her shoulders to her waist. He paid particular attention to her pert breasts. Renee tossed her head as the power rolled over and through her. She muttered incomprehensible words, the tone alone signaling her intense pleasure.

"You gonna come for me now?" Zachary asked in malicious delight. He pushed another wave deep into her. "Without me ever touching you where you want me most, you gonna come? You're feeling every second of need I felt over the last year. I denied myself even the comfort of my own hand. I had to prove to the God and Goddess how much you meant to me. No one for a full year. It's enough to make a satyr go mad. But I did it for you. Now it's your turn. Take everything I have to give. Are you gonna come?"

"So close, please," she whimpered, rubbing her thighs together. After a year, why the hell wasn't he fucking her already?

"Do you want it?" he taunted, grinning.

"Yes, yes," she begged. "Please, yes."

"Did you miss me as much as I did you?" he whispered as another rush of magical arousal slammed into her body.

Renee moaned as her senses became swamped beneath his erotic assault. She didn't understand his question at first. Why did he always expect her to be able to think after he got her so damned hot? "No one. No one but you. I haven't even been tempted since you left. No one was *you*."

Zachary knelt between her legs and breathed softly against her aching pussy, pushing a sliver more power into her aroused flesh. "Then come for me."

Renee screamed, heels digging into the mattress as spasm after spasm racked her body. Zachary smiled, pushing his face into her, licking her cream and bathing in her scent and pleasure.

Zachary pulled back and licked his lips. "Mmm, missed this. Missed the taste and smell of you — my mate."

"Fuck," was all Renee could manage to say between shivers.

Zachary chuckled. "Not yet, but soon."

Renee couldn't have moved if she'd wanted to. She lay spread across the bed. Zachary made a place for himself next to her and Renee snuggled into his side. "Seems like you're always taking care of me without my returning the favor."

"I wouldn't put it that way," he said with a self-satisfied smirk. "It's not like I don't enjoy the hell out of myself when I'm with you. And you'd be surprised at what I get out of sharing my power like that. Almost as good as the real thing. Better in other ways. So don't feel bad for me."

Renee came to her knees between his thighs to stare down at her lover. "But a whole year is a long time. Practically an eternity to a satyr without a touch of his lover." She slid a single finger down his chest, stopping to rub back and forth across his pelvis. "What say I return the favor?"

Zachary's abdomen twitched but he held himself still under her touch. "Gonna fill me with your magic and make *me* explode?"

"Something like that," was all the warning she gave before taking Zachary's cock straight down her throat.

"Shit!" Zachary cried, sitting up.

Without moving off her prize, Renee pushed him back down. Her cheeks hollowed as she sucked him with little art but much passion. She wanted to taste him, to know he was really there with her. She wanted to give him the same pleasure he gave her.

She reached up and pinched his nipples.

"Oh God and Goddess," he cried out, bucking under the onslaught of pain and pleasure. "Don't. Stop. Don't wanna come without you. Can't take it. Stop."

Renee released him and backed up, giving a striking imitation of his growl. "That what you want, me to stop?" She pulled long and hard on Zachary's cock with a firm hand, not giving him a moment of downtime. "But I missed your taste too. You want me to stop or do you want me to give it to you?"

"Give it. Now. Give it."

Head back down, she lapped at his cock as she fondled his tight balls. Caressing that little bit of flesh just behind them, she opened wide and swallowed him again. His groans and pleas became her music. They both needed to feel this, to feel each other, to feel at all after the half-life they'd lived the past year alone. This was what life really was about. Not battle. Not death. Not anger. Not hatred. Not prejudice.

Love and the purest expression of that love.

Renee felt tears stream down her cheeks as the man she loved came apart in her arms. She swallowed his salty, honey-flavored seed as he cried out her name.

* * * * *

187

Hours later Zachary came awake with a jolt as Renee rolled on top of him. Head resting on hands folded in a steeple, she asked, "So, you gonna tell me what took you so long?"

"I had to get something for you," Zachary replied with a yawn, wrapping his arms around Renee and snuggling her close. "Call it a wedding present. But I had to earn it first."

"Earn what?" Renee asked between nibbling kisses she rained on Zachary's forehead. "I don't need a damn thing but you. You should know that."

Spreading his legs to settle Renee more comfortably, Zachary replied, "My people are ageless. I have no intention of being a widower for the next millennia." He closed his eyes and grimaced at the thought. "Unlike some types of Fae or demons, my mate doesn't automatically get my extended lifespan. So I had to find a way to keep you with me."

"What did you find for me? And what did you have to go through to get it?" Renee asked, sliding her fingers through Zachary's hair and staring at his dear face with concern.

Zachary waved his hand in the air and plucked up the small crystal vial. So small it hardly seemed worth a year of her life, but Renee knew better than to judge magic by the size of the package. He handed it to her. "Ambrosia, specially formulated from me for you. If you drink it, it will link your lifespan with my own. Upside, you could live forever like me. Downside, if I'm ever killed you will die with me. There'll be no 'death do us part' here. This is forever. It's your choice."

Rolling the ornately carved vial between her palms, Renee replied, "Does make a normal marriage seem like child's play."

"Yes and it's much more binding. No possibility of divorce, no backing out later." Zachary closed Renee's fingers around the vial, keeping hold of her hand as he spoke. "You don't have to do anything right away. Take as much time as you need before you decide."

Renee stared at his dear face, a face she'd thought never to see again. "What, a year isn't enough?" Renee pulled her hand free, popped the bottle open and downed the contents before she had a chance for second thoughts. Fire, intense and painful, slammed through her, pumping in time with her heartbeat. She threw back her head and screamed. Sweat dripped from every pore as her body fought to cool itself.

Her back bowed and her muscles twisted. If Zachary hadn't held her down she would've flown off the bed.

As she contorted Zachary held her close, rocking, murmuring softly and petting her head. He didn't release her until the convulsions stopped.

"Sweet Goddess," Renee panted between chattering teeth, "I didn't expect it to be that bad."

"Eternal life never comes easy."

The darkness behind those words brought Renee's head up to look into Zachary's solemn eyes. "What did you have to give to receive it?"

"Some things I'll never tell you," he whispered. "Trials — tests of my determination and my feelings for you. Some were more difficult simply because my people still don't completely trust your kind. But in the end I gave my word to the God and Goddess."

An oath to the greater powers, something never entered into lightly. What exactly had Zachary given up to be with her? "Your word for what?"

Zachary sighed, a sad desolation filling his gaze. "You know that parakind as a whole is at a crossroads. It will be more difficult than ever for one to find his or her mate. But without true mates, we will all eventually disappear."

Renee pursed her lips and nodded. "It's why I resorted to a spell to bring you to me."

"Exactly." Zachary pulled Renee up to claim a kiss, savoring his lover's flavor. "Sometimes fate needs a little push. That's where we come in."

"We?" Renee asked.

"Yes, we," he replied, tapping a single finger on the tip of Renee's nose. "I promised we would do whatever we could to help others find their true loves, no matter how far separated or what race. We will help."

She could live with that deal. It was a fair trade. Hell, more than fair. Eternal life with the man she loved in exchange for playing the part of the paranormal world's version of a New Age Cupid.

Not a bad deal at all.

The End

GHOSTLY AWAKENING

Lacey Savage

 හ

Chapter One

ॐ

For the first time in over two decades, people strolled through the high double archways of the Bradley mansion. They poured into the main foyer on the hard soles of expensive shoes, their bright, elaborate costumes sending sharp flutters of color to bathe the neglected interior of the nineteenth-century manor.

Sebastian Bradley pressed his back against the far wall of the upper floor, watching over the wooden railing as guests surged into his home.

Only they weren't *his* guests. He hadn't invited any of them. He didn't know the woman wearing the Marie Antoinette wig that brushed the petals of the chandelier, nor the man with the wooden peg leg stroking his moustache in a blatantly suggestive manner as he leered at a Little Red Riding Hood half his age. Before tonight, Sebastian had never laid eyes on the chocolate-skinned socialite dressed as a zombie bride who stood in the center of the dining area and barked harsh orders at anyone unlucky enough to come within ten feet of her.

A flash of deep scarlet fabric caught Sebastian's eye and his heart gave a quick, tumbling lurch. He stifled a ragged sigh as a woman's curvy form came into view. She stumbled into the room on three-inch heels that mimicked the round-toed look of an athletic sneaker. A delicate ankle and impossibly long legs extended from the ridiculous platform shoe, drawing his gaze to a skirt that barely reached halfway up her thigh.

Sebastian swallowed hard. *Her* he knew. Celeste Winters was the reason strangers had stormed his home, invading his privacy, treating his family's property like their own personal playground.

"Listen up, everyone!" The zombie bride clapped her hands and the band playing a rough version of a classic rock song brought their music to a stuttering halt. "Thank you all for showing up to the most fabulous Halloween party in the entire country. Mine!"

She waited for the chuckles, which echoed somewhat belatedly. Frown lines appeared over the woman's upturned nose and her perfectly arched brows drew downward. "This night is very special to me. So drink, dance, enjoy yourselves. But don't you dare leave!" A hint of a threat lurked beneath the high-pitched warning.

Sebastian rolled his eyes as the band members picked up their tired song where they'd left off. He'd lost sight of Celeste. In an effort to find her again in the crowd, he risked moving away from the wall and crept closer to the balustrade. A few of the bolder guests had already thundered up the set of curved wooden stairs that led to the second floor, staking their claim to the perfect viewing area of the festivities in full swing below.

He carefully avoided the press of bodies, sliding sideways into an empty spot against the railing while attempting to take up as little room as possible. He curled his fingers around the old wood, his stomach clenching along with his hands.

Ah! There!

Celeste reached out and grabbed a flute of champagne from a waiter's tray as the man swept past her. She sipped at it once then seemed to decide that method was inefficient and gulped half the contents in one large quaff.

Sebastian smiled and shook his head. She was like no one he'd ever met in his life—before or after his transformation. For the past week he'd watched her as she'd tirelessly swept through his home, turning a dilapidated mansion ravaged by time and a neglectful owner into one of the most posh settings for a society shindig he'd ever seen.

Not that Sebastian had attended many of these gatherings in his youth. After his father's death, when he'd found himself with more money than he could spend in a lifetime and no idea what to do with it all, he'd wandered from bash to bender, always restless, endlessly seeking something he couldn't find.

And then, a week after he'd turned twenty-one, his life had come to a grinding halt because of one small, seemingly harmless error in judgment. What little hope he'd had of making something of himself had gone up in smoke, along with everything that had made him who he was.

Damn. He'd blinked and lost her again. The woman was more slippery than an ice cube against heated skin.

His mouth curved again as a delicious image of Celeste, spread out beneath him, breasts heaving and nipples perking to tight little nubs, flared in his mind's eye. He could picture that tight little body of hers all wound up, writhing and trembling with barely contained arousal as he trailed a slowly melting ice cube in the valley between her full, lush breasts. He'd dip the fragment of ice into the hollow of her navel then glide it lower to trail across her mound. If she were really good, he might even smear some of the cool moisture across her heated labia. The pink, quivering flesh would flutter as he'd slide a finger into the smooth, wet slit and —

"There you are." Celeste's husky, sensual voice had a groan ripping from his throat. His cock twitched, arching upward to strain along his bare stomach. "Didn't anyone ever tell you it's not a good idea to let a woman wait?"

Something strange and powerful washed through Sebastian — a feeling so deeply unexpected that it knocked the air from his lungs. He barely had time to identify it as hope, lust and the thrill of anticipation all rolled into one before he spun around rapidly, took a step forward and collided with Celeste's lush curves.

Celeste frowned and shifted from one foot to the other, her perfectly shaped brows drawing together over her upturned nose. For a moment, he couldn't breathe. Her breasts, full and plump beneath the tight, belly-baring cheerleader's shirt, pressed against his chest. He could feel her firm nipples scrape his pectorals even through the fabric of her clothes. The contact sent electricity sparking against his skin.

God, he'd never been so aware of another person in his entire life. The heat of her flesh seared him to the bone, awakening sensations in his body that had lain dormant for much too long.

Then, as if she hadn't already taken him to the edge of his self-control, she looked up at him — *right* at him — and smiled. A brilliant, jaw-dropping smile that had his already rampant erection raging out of control.

Her limpid blue eyes crinkled at the corners. Purple-tipped mascara tilted her long lashes at an angle, giving her all-American, girl-next-door appearance an exotic flare.

A mass of blonde curls framed her heart-shaped face. Sebastian couldn't help but reach out and stroke her soft hair, lifting a strand and twirling it around his thumb.

She frowned again, tilted her head and swept her fingers through her curls, causing the stray tress to slip out of his grasp. "Jonathan! Really, how many times do I have to tell you that if you're going to show up to one of these things, you really should let me know in advance you're going to be coming?"

"Well, darlin', I can't start getting predictable on you now, can I?"

Reality came crashing upon Sebastian in waves of agony. His heart knocked wildly against his chest.

She wasn't smiling at him. She didn't even know he was here.

Fuck!

How could she have known when no one had been able to see or hear him in eighteen years? Oh, he was free to linger among people and eavesdrop on their conversations. He could watch them go about their lives and desperately wish he could partake in even the worst of their human experiences. But he couldn't. He was cursed.

Cursed to always be on the outside looking in.

Humans—and animals for that matter—could feel and smell him. Taste him too, he supposed, not that anyone would ever be tempted to try. And if all that wasn't excruciating enough, he was given three hours every Halloween to spend in his fully visible, corporeal body. Of all the suffering that came with his curse, those brief hours of normalcy were by far the worst.

Gulping down a breath of perfume-laden air, he moved out of Celeste's way a moment before she threw herself into another man's arms.

"Damn you, Jon! How long have you been in town?"

Sebastian stepped behind Celeste, assessing the other man over the top of her head. Jonathan was the same height as Sebastian, but his easy smile and twinkling green eyes made him look far more comfortable in social settings than Sebastian would have ever been.

Jonathan leaned forward and brushed his lips over Celeste's right temple. "Only a couple of hours. I tried to check in to the motel downtown but all their rooms are booked. So I came here instead. Maybe I can room with you tonight?"

A spear of jealousy found its way into Sebastian's gut. It slammed home with a potency he hadn't expected, forcing him to dig his fingernails into his palms to keep from doing something he'd regret.

Sure, he wanted these people out of his house, but he didn't think sending a man flying over the railing was the right way to go about it. Especially not since Celeste seemed genuinely pleased to see the guy.

She shifted forward, her blue eyes sparkling with mischievous excitement. "You and me and Wes? Oh my!" She fluttered her hand in front of her face like a fan. "You did bring Wes, right?"

Jonathan winked. "We've only been dating for a month. Do you really think I'd unleash you on him so quickly?"

Relief suffused Sebastian's limbs at Jonathan's revelation. He'd never been so happy to hear of another man's sexual preference in his entire life.

Celeste pouted, drawing Sebastian's attention to her sultry lower lip. The playful pose caused another jolting rush of heat to pool low in Sebastian's groin. Any more of this and he'd have to find a quiet corner to take himself in hand and relieve the aching pressure in his balls.

There were some advantages to being invisible, he supposed, though they were few and far between. In the past week since Celeste had invaded his quiet, orderly life, he'd sustained a practically permanent hard-on. He wouldn't be surprised if the constant erection came with a permanent strain injury too.

But, God, it had been worth it. He'd had an opportunity to observe her as she worked tenaciously to get the place into top shape before the party, and he'd been able to stretch out on the floor beside her bed every night while she slept.

Although he could have easily followed her into the shower, he drew the line at that kind of blatantly depraved behavior. He'd allowed her as much privacy as he could, though he'd once glimpsed a shred of white lace as she'd pulled on a pair of tight jeans over delicate panties.

That image alone had been enough to keep him from getting a good night's sleep. Not that falling asleep with her scent in his nostrils and the sound of her shallow breathing in his ears was ever an option. He hadn't had a woman in his home in almost two decades. After tomorrow morning, he never would again.

For the next ten hours he intended to remember what it was like to pursue someone as though she were the only woman on earth who mattered. Celeste didn't know it, but for him, she truly was.

"Celeste!"

Her name reached Sebastian's ears on another high-pitched, instantly recognizable shrill.

Celeste rolled her eyes. "Her majesty beckons."

"She's still planning on announcing her engagement tonight?"

Celeste gasped and pressed her index finger to Jonathan's lips. "Shush! It's her big surprise. If this gets out, I'll never work in Georgia again."

She leaned in to whisper something in Jonathan's ear and Sebastian followed, pressing as close to the two of them as he dared.

"Besides, it's not just her engagement she's announcing. She actually made me hire an Orthodox priest to marry them tonight. The poor man wasn't thrilled about performing such a holy union on the most unholy day of the year, but money talks in any circle, I guess."

"Celeste!" The woman's second bellow carried up the stairs, over the sound of the band and the chatter of the guests.

"Gotta go. Stick around, okay? I have to be out of here by eight tomorrow morning. We'll have breakfast and catch up."

Jonathan agreed and a minute later Celeste was flying down the winding staircase, teetering wildly on her heels. Sebastian was right behind her as she moved around the large room, seeking out the woman who'd put her up to this— Lakisha Pernice, daughter of Michael Pernice, governor of the great state of Georgia.

Lakisha had been born with a silver spoon in her mouth and obviously believed herself entitled to push people around simply because of her daddy's social status. Worse yet, Sebastian had gathered that she'd recently become engaged to a pro-football linebacker with a multimillion-dollar contract, which gave her all the more reason to lord her wealth and status over anyone who came within shouting distance.

"I heard you were looking for me," Celeste said, stopping a couple of feet away from Lakisha. To protect her hearing no doubt.

"This party is dull," Lakisha proclaimed, propping one hand on an outward-jutting hip. The tattered pieces of her "decayed" dress fluttered around her feet. "We need a little excitement."

Celeste's lips pulled tightly over her teeth in a sickeningly sweet smile. "You told me not to do anything that might compete with your big announcement. Remember?"

Lakisha snorted, a decisively unladylike sound. "Nothing could possibly come close to what I have planned. So what have you got for everyone?"

"Aside from all this?" Celeste swept an arm around her to indicate the mansion and the two hundred guests milling about. Many were dancing while others had gathered around the lavishly decorated tables to enjoy the ample drinks and food provided by a topnotch catering crew. "Not much."

Lakisha's eyes narrowed. "I knew it was a mistake to hire you. You're nobody. An unknown in the event-planning world. And now my night...my *life* will be ruined because you couldn't pull off throwing a decent party!"

Sebastian's nails dug into his palms, carving another notch alongside the first. He knew better than anyone how hard Celeste had worked to make this party happen. Lakisha's expectations had been unreasonable from the very beginning, starting with the demand that the party should take place at the Bradley mansion.

Situated in the small town of Shady Dell, Georgia, the Bradley house had been voted the creepiest haunted house in the state. The mansion had earned its reputation through a series of eerie calamities, ranging from the sinister to the downright macabre. The property had belonged to Sebastian's family since the early 1800s, having been passed down through generations. Sebastian had even grown up in this home. As a child, he'd loved regaling his friends with creepy tales of his grandparents double murder or the story of his Uncle Phil, who some said still haunted the gardens where he'd been buried alive.

Somehow the Bradley family legacy seemed almost fitting in light of Sebastian's own misfortune while living in this house. Most people wouldn't have chosen to live in a place with such a disturbing history but Sebastian had always felt at home here.

Unconcerned with the outward appearance of the mansion, he'd made few changes to the place in the past decade. One important addition had been the state-of-the-art alarm. With the help of a brand-new computer he'd ordered through a mail catalogue, he'd been able to hire a local security firm to ensure trespassers and curious onlookers would be kept at bay. Sebastian guarded his privacy fiercely, needing no reminders of his inability to exist among the living.

Celeste however, had knocked down every one of his carefully crafted defenses simply by being stubborn and refusing to take no for an answer. When she'd first approached him, she'd sent him letters — two dozen registered letters to be exact — all of which he'd ignored. When that didn't work, she'd set up a tent on his front lawn and had dared him to either have her forcibly removed or give her five minutes of his time.

He would have activated the alarm and summoned the authorities if she hadn't pressed her face to the front window and looked through with those damned blue eyes open wide, a quirky smile tilting one side of her mouth.

It had been clear to him then she'd seen something in the old Bradley mansion that no one else had. Not only had she been determined to turn the place into prime party property, but she'd shown no fear when night fell and she found herself all alone in the middle of nowhere, miles away from the nearest neighbor.

She'd surprised him then, just as she continued to do so now.

Celeste crossed her arms over her chest. "You want something big...something that will make this party the talk of the socialite circle for years to come? Aside from your magnificence of course," she added with a tinge of sarcasm.

If Lakisha noted Celeste's tone, she ignored it. "You're not capable of anything that wildly exciting. Face it. You just can't cut it in this business."

Sebastian watched as Celeste tilted her chin upward. Her spine stiffened and her shoulders came up a fraction of an inch as though she prepared to do battle. If it came to that, his money was on Celeste. He'd never met anyone more passionately determined.

"Give me an hour. I'll have a special guest make an appearance."

"Oh yeah?" Lakisha tapped her foot. "Who?"

Celeste's gaze darted to the edge of the staircase landing, resting on a narrow door with brass and copper trimming.

Sebastian groaned. He'd agreed to her insane proposal because he'd felt something stir in his soul when he looked at her, something that told him she might be the *one*.

The woman who could end his torment by feeling something more than indifference toward him.

And then, just as quickly as the absurd idea had manifested itself, he'd pushed it away. He'd been a phantom long enough to know there was no escaping his curse. Yet he still hadn't been able to push her away. So instead of even trying, he'd spelled out two rules in the contract he'd dropped off in front of her tent.

One, she and all the guests were to be out of the house by eight in the morning. And two, she could go anywhere in the mansion except for the north tower. That was his territory. He warned her he'd be observing the gathering in case the guests devised crazy ideas about torching the place or doing something else equally ill-advised.

Watching her now, he could pinpoint the exact second she'd made up her mind to disobey him. His blood ran cold.

Celeste blew out a deep breath. "I'll bring you Sebastian Bradley himself."

Chapter Two

෨

Celeste stood in front of the door to the north tower with her hands balled into fists, staring at a deep groove etched into the wood just above the antique door handle. People bumped into her as they passed through the narrow hallway on the way to the guest bathroom at the end of the corridor. As that was the only functional bathroom in the entire mansion, the lineup was horrendous, looping halfway around the building. She'd set up portable facilities in the backyard, but respectable citizens apparently wouldn't hear of squatting in a plastic bin.

Yet one more thing she'd done wrong in a never-ending list and all the more reason to get Sebastian Bradley out here. She only hoped he was as monstrous in person as the town gossips speculated.

It stood to reason that there had to be something severely wrong with the owner of the Bradley mansion. She'd seen a picture of Sebastian taken in his teens and he looked like a handsome, normal kid. So why as an adult would he choose to hide inside this unkempt, crumbling mansion? Rumor had it no one had seen him in almost two decades, though local business owners asserted they dealt with him on a regular basis.

Having been born and raised in Atlanta, Celeste didn't know much about small-town living, but that seemed like an awfully long time for a man to spend indoors just to avoid his neighbors.

Blowing a deep breath out between pursed lips, Celeste wrapped her fingers around the copper handle and pressed down. The door didn't budge.

She swallowed past the wave of nausea that rose in her throat. Pestering a man until he agreed to turn his home into a posh party hideaway was one thing. Trespassing into intimately private property when she knew she wasn't welcome was entirely different.

Wood splinters scraped the skin of her index finger as she trailed her palm upward along the door's surface. Swearing low under her breath, she clenched her hand into a fist again and rapped on the door with her knuckles.

No response. She waited for almost a minute then tried again, knocking harder this time so she could be heard above the music and the incessant squealing babble of society's finest blaring behind her.

Nothing. She couldn't hear as much as a vague scuffle on the other side of the door to indicate anyone had heard her. Not that she thought the mysterious Mr. Bradley would bother to respond even if she banged and kicked on the door all night long. He'd made it perfectly clear that the north tower was his and therefore off-limits to the guests. And to her.

"Fuck," she murmured under her breath. What on God's earth had possessed her to promise Lakisha she could make Sebastian Bradley show his face at her party?

She'd been pushed into a corner, sure, but she should have stood her ground and made it clear to her presumptuous boss that she'd done her best.

Right. Like my best would ever be good enough for the likes of her.

A surge of anger welled up in Celeste's chest. She pushed it down, determined to squelch it before the all-too-familiar self-doubt reared its ugly head.

All Celeste had to do was pull off one party. One damned night could make or break her career. Everyone who was anyone in Georgia wanted what Lakisha had. If Celeste had to ride the woman's coattails to drum up business, well, so be it.

Abandoning the soft rap of the knuckles technique, she turned her hand and banged on the door with the side of her fist. The forceful slams shook the decayed frame but the door still refused to budge.

Gritting her teeth, she bent down and peered through the old-fashioned keyhole set just below the handle. Darkness infused the space with black shadows, but she couldn't make out a thing on the other side.

Then she heard it. A soft metallic click that was music to her ears. A shiver of excitement swept up her spine and her fingers trembled slightly when she gripped the handle. This time when she pressed down, the latch gave way easily. She pushed the door open and slipped through the narrow space without a second thought.

"Mr. Bradley?" she asked when she'd shut the door behind her. The darkness was absolute, without a sliver of light to help her make sense of her surroundings. Still, he'd let her in. That had to count for something.

She trailed her hands down the slightly slanted surface of the wood until she found the key and turned it in the lock, ensuring no one would follow her in here. Or worse, in a drunken stupor mistake this door for the one to the bathroom.

A tremor rippled across her skin as a light flared about ten feet away. She froze in place. Soft and golden, the light sent an ethereal mist to illuminate her passage. For the first time, Celeste realized she stood in another corridor, this one much narrower than the one outside the door.

She cleared her throat. "Mr. Bradley, I'm sorry to barge in like this but I need to speak to you for a minute. Do you mind if I come in?"

She waited for a response, hands clenched in front of her. When none came, she smoothed down her skirt and ventured forward.

The corridor stretching out before her ended in a stairwell that looped upward in a spiral. Judging by the look of the place, she'd expected a stale, musty smell. Instead, a spicy scent—like cinnamon and cloves—drifted down from the darkness above.

The bottom stair creaked loudly when Celeste stepped on it and peered upward. From her vantage point, she couldn't make out anything more than vague shapes and more black shadows. Beside her head, an old-fashioned lantern hung from a metal hook. It had obviously been lit by someone, but if Sebastian Bradley had been there a moment earlier, he wasn't there now.

Celeste took a deep breath and picked up the lantern. She debated with herself whether to continue acting like the heroine in one of those Gothic novels she used to read in high school or turn back and convince Jonathan to come with her. After a moment's hesitation, she decided one trespasser was bad enough. Two would likely ensure Sebastian kicked everyone out before Lakisha's big announcement and then Celeste could definitely kiss her career goodbye.

Besides, she hadn't as much as caught a glimpse of the man in the past week. If he'd wanted to harm her, he'd had plenty of opportunity to do so. As odd as it seemed, she'd never felt the least bit threatened in this house.

She crept upward slowly, testing each step before committing her entire weight to it. The wood felt fragile and decrepit, as though threatening to collapse at any moment. The lantern sent hollow circles of light to pool at her feet, guiding her careful steps.

The scent intensified at the top of the stairs. It tickled her nostrils as she inhaled deeply, smelling cinnamon, cloves and musk. The heady blend seemed to wrap around her as fluid as a dream. Lust hazed the edges of her mind.

Shaking her head to clear it, Celeste gripped the balustrade before raising her lantern.

She'd expected to finally come face-to-face with the owner of Georgia's top haunted mansion, but he wasn't there.

Instead, the light bounced off a low wooden table and more books than Celeste had ever seen gathered in one place. They were piled up everywhere—on the table, around it, on the matching chair and circling the neatly made bed pressed against the far corner of the room.

In fact, the bed was the only place that hadn't been taken over by books. Neatly made and lined with crisp white sheets, the piece of furniture looked inviting and cozy as it stood out like a beacon among the clutter. A small television set was perched atop a dresser across from the foot of the bed.

She shuffled forward, drawn by a dot of light on the table. It flared brightly, seeming to hover in midair. Too small to be another lantern and too bright to be a night light, it flickered from left to right a few inches and then bobbed up and down, leaving a phosphorescent arc in its wake.

Intrigued, Celeste moved to stand in front of the table and placed the lantern on top of a pile of books. It didn't take her long to realize what she was looking at. A firefly fluttered from one end of a closed jar to another, desperately banging into the glass walls of its prison.

Celeste's heart lurched. She never understood why people captured insects. It seemed unbearably cruel. Lifting the jar, she worked on unscrewing the lid to no avail. The top was firmly affixed to the glass and short of breaking the container altogether, there was no way she could free the firefly.

With a pang of regret, she cleared another space toward the front of the table beside the lit stick of incense that had to be responsible for the exotic scent permeating the air. She'd have a chat with Sebastian about the firefly too. If she ever found the guy.

As she set down the jar, she felt a hand graze her bare midriff.

The touch was so completely unexpected that she jerked her entire body backward, a scream catching in her throat.

She'd grazed the side of the jar as she pulled back and now it teetered on its side, wobbling dangerously close to the edge.

As Celeste watched, the swaying container stopped moving. It hung on an angle for a fraction of a second then righted itself and came to rest on its base. The firefly resumed its restless flight.

"Oh shit." Celeste wrapped her arm around her midsection, protecting her bare skin.

Could a person hallucinate a touch? It had felt so real...

Warm skin had brushed her flesh. If this had happened under any other circumstances, she'd have described the touch as a gentle, sensual cress.

No, she hadn't been imagining things. She'd felt that touch as though someone else were in the room with her, but she knew she was alone.

The light from her lantern illuminated the small chamber at the top of the north tower in its entirety. Books were stacked two feet high in places, but the piles were narrow, certainly not wide enough to give a grown man a place to hide.

She took a deep breath then another. "There are no such things as ghosts."

Sure, it sounded stupid when she said it out loud, but it alleviated some of the fear roiling in her gut. Turning around slowly, she took another look at her surroundings and tried to calm her hammering heartbeat.

Sebastian Bradley had to be here somewhere. This was his place. His sanctuary. Someone had let her inside. And that same someone had lit a lamp for her, practically guiding her up here. If there was a secret room beyond this one, she didn't know how to access it. Still, it was only a matter of time until Sebastian returned.

Unwilling to go back to the party empty-handed, Celeste picked up one of the books and flipped it open only to realize it wasn't a book at all. A soft leather covering lovingly protected the yellowed pages of a journal. The paper looked old, but certainly not as aged as other things in the mansion. The handwriting looped slightly to the left but it was bold and legible.

Guilt sank sharp claws into her. She moved to close the journal but her gaze skimmed over the discolored page. Despite her best intentions, she read a few lines of the crooked script.

Loneliness isn't as it's depicted in the movies. It's not melancholy and beautiful. It's harsh and cruel, leaving its mark on everything it touches.

The world is crumbling around me and I can't do a damn thing about it. Or maybe I'm the one who's crumbling. Trapped inside this place like a dragonfly in amber. Like that firefly over there. The two of us will grow old together. I'll die and it will continue to flutter in that jar forever because –

A warm gust of air brushed across Celeste's lips and she jerked her head up. Heat flared in her cheeks. The warmth returned, imbuing the air with the scent of cinnamon and mint. That's when she realized it hadn't been a gust of wind at all but someone's *breath*.

Soft, warm breath. It made her own respiration catch in her throat. She froze, listening to her heartbeat pound incessantly against her rib cage. And then the warmth intensified, followed by the tender pressure of lips against her own.

The journal fell out of her hands. It dropped to the ground with a thud, but the mouth demanding hers never faltered. It brushed across her lips, back and forth, slowly yet with a determination that sent a jolt of heat to swirl low in her belly.

She blinked rapidly, trying to discern a shape, a sound – *anything* – that would tell her she wasn't alone. Everything she felt screamed that there was someone else in the room with her, but everything she saw argued otherwise.

Still, she couldn't ignore the prickly stubble of a man's beard as it scraped across her chin nor the moist tip of a tongue as it slipped between her parted lips. A sigh escaped her throat only to drown and fade before ever making the slightest sound.

Fear mingled with excitement and throbbed low in her pussy. The scent of incense and male musk filled her nostrils. What was in that stuff? Was it messing with her mind? Making her hallucinate things that couldn't possibly be happening?

The kiss intensified, leaving her breathless. She thought about resisting but the entire situation seemed so absurd that she felt foolish running away from it. She was being ravished by her own imagination—nothing more. It had been too long since she'd been with a man—a real, flesh-and-blood man.

But this...this was different than anything she'd ever experienced. The kiss wasn't filled with arrogance or self-assurance. Her fantasy lover wasn't forcing himself upon her like so many other men who took what they needed without a second thought as to what she craved.

Which only served to reinforce her belief that whatever was happening was born of her own desperate need and the mysterious, eerie atmosphere in the Bradley mansion.

A finger stroked from the curve of her chin down the column of her throat. Her eyes drifted closed. The lips released hers and glided across her jawline, down into the valley between her breasts, trailing featherlight kisses all the way.

Broad palms slipped across her shoulders and down her arms. Fingers curled around hers, tugging her gently in the direction of the bed. She followed on an awkward stumble, her feet feeling weighed down with lead.

She collapsed upon the bed gratefully and rolled onto her back then held her breath as she waited for the fantasy to dissipate entirely. Reality had to come crashing back any moment now. There was no way she was making out with a ghost.

The bed dipped beside her, indicating another presence. Her eyes widened and she gazed into the empty space beside her. Despite everything her logical mind knew to be true, there was still no one there. She couldn't even hear the slightest sound aside from the fizzle of the lantern and the soft buzz of the firefly banging against the glass jar.

This is insane. I'm going insane.

As though to affirm that belief, something pinched her nipple. She groaned and glanced down where the tender bud had stiffened and tented the cotton cheerleader's shirt she wore. Teeth dug into her nipple, nipping at her, drawing the taut nub farther up.

As she watched, a stain began to darken the red material of her shirt. Her head spun with the implications. A broad palm cupped her cheek and a thumb traced the curve of her lower lip. She flicked her tongue out tentatively, sucking in a deep breath when she made contact with warm skin.

He tasted slightly salty yet not unpleasant. She tried to speak but the word came out as a hesitant croak instead.

She cleared her throat and tried again. "Sebastian?"

The lightest touch of a finger brushed against her clit through her silk panties. Her breathing quickened with anticipation and her voice broke when she uttered his name again...and again.

It had to be him. God, was he really dead? Had he haunted the mansion all this time? Had he watched her as she slept in one of the guest bedrooms? Followed her into the shower when she'd bathed?

A shiver arced through her. Fear and arousal gathered low in her belly and pulsed with a needy, growing throb.

None of this made any sense.

She clung to the only thing she knew — the jolt of pure ecstasy that had begun to build deep in her cunt. Cream seeped from between her folds. Warmth spread outward over her labia. Belatedly, she realized it wasn't her internal heat warming the fabric of her panties at all, but his moist breath as his mouth hovered just over her mound.

She swallowed hard and arched her hips. Her clit made contact with something firm. His jaw? She couldn't tell.

Rolling her head back on the pillow, Celeste squeezed her eyes shut and reached down between her thighs. Her fingers threaded in silky locks. She curled her fingertips and dug them into his scalp just as he pushed aside the fabric of her panties and wiggled the tip of his tongue into her slit.

A cry of delight built in the back of Celeste's throat. Waves of tingling warmth spread outward from her cunt. She trailed her palms downward, over his ears and along his stubbled jaw then down farther to a wall of solid muscle. She explored his shoulders, noting the broad width of them and the planes and valleys of his lean form. He wore no clothes she could discern as she wrapped her fingers around strong, firm biceps.

His tongue was as magical as the rest of him. It had to be supernatural because no one else had been able to have her writhing on the sheets within a few minutes of licking her pussy. She remembered the fumbling attempts of her previous lovers. Nothing had prepared her for this. Sebastian stroked, nibbled and sucked on her labia with the same gentle intensity he'd used to kiss her, eliciting myriad sensations in her body.

Her nipples pebbled, hard and stiff against the fabric of her shirt. Her clit mirrored them, engorging and throbbing with pent-up need.

This is wrong. So wrong.

And yet it felt so right.

She fisted her hands in the bed sheets, arching her back so she could grind her mound against his mouth. She needed more. Her cunt ached with the desire to be filled, to know him as intimately as he knew her.

She felt him part her slick folds and held her breath as he eased two fingers into her moist passage. His mouth moved slowly, drawing his lips sensuously over the top of her mound, encasing her clit in intoxicating heat.

Tension built in her pussy as he thrust in and out of her tight channel. His tongue swirled around her engorged bud, drawing another desperate cry from her throat.

Her fingernails dug into her palms through the fabric of the bed sheets. Her hips thrust upward, matching his strokes.

She drifted on a cloud of euphoria, no longer caring that what she was experiencing should have been impossible. Somewhere in the back of her mind, a sliver of doubt continued to nag at her but she pushed it aside and lost herself in the erotic sensations spreading through her cunt.

Sebastian added a third finger to the two already inside her, stretching her inner muscles. The walls of her pussy tightened in response, pulsing around the thick intrusion.

Tremors began low in her belly. She drew her lower lip between her teeth to keep from screaming, knowing she wouldn't able to hold back when her climax hit. As though sensing she hovered on the edge of a precipice, Sebastian positioned his lips around her clit and sucked gently, drawing the tender nub into his mouth.

The sudden release rocked her body in an explosive ripple. Light burst behind her closed eyelids. A cry ripped from her throat, echoing through the room. She clung to the sheets for dear life as her pussy spasmed and shuddered beneath Sebastian's expert ministrations.

He'd released her clit but his tongue now swept through her folds, concentrating on the entrance to her channel where his fingers continued to pump. He lapped her cream, adding another toe-curling sensation to those already pouring through her.

Her chest heaved from exertion. She waited for the world to stop spinning while a ghost trailed soft kisses along the inside of her thigh.

Impossible. No way this is happening.

Cautiously, she cracked one eye open and peered between her legs, preparing to once again face the fact she'd gone insane.

Golden lamplight pooled along the crisp white sheets, darkened the pale skin of her legs and sent golden highlights to shimmer in Sebastian Bradley's deep brown tresses. She recognized him instantly from his picture. Far from being the monstrous creature rumors had made him out to be, he was absolutely gorgeous.

His hair curled at the ears and a lock fell over his forehead when he looked up at her. He grinned, a pleased, boyish grin that made a dimple appear in his right cheek. His dark eyes sparkled with mischief as he curled the fingers that had remained embedded deep in her pussy and nudged a particularly sensitive area deep in her cunt.

Faced with the sudden appearance of a fully corporeal phantom lover — a stranger who had his fingers buried to the hilt inside her — and no longer under the sensual spell of impending orgasm, Celeste did the only thing she could.

She let out a bloodcurdling scream.

Chapter Three

છ્ર

For several heartbeats after Celeste's shriek had faded, Sebastian was unable to move. He simply sat there as her inner walls squeezed his fingers and gaped, openmouthed.

"You—you can see me?"

She scooted slightly back in an obvious effort to put some distance between them. He crept forward a fraction of an inch along with her, his fingers never budging from the moist heat of her body.

"Of course I can see you. I'm not blind," she snapped. The color returned to her cheeks, turning her skin a rosy hue. She lifted her chin a little, clearly trying to regain some measure of control over the situation. "And I'm not crazy."

Was she trying to assure him or herself?

God, he'd been a fool. He'd lost track of time. He'd planned to be here in his room, all alone when the clock struck midnight. He had three hours of full humanity and he intended to spend them as he'd had for the past decade— wrapped in the comfort of solitude.

Instead, he'd ended up lost in a sensual haze and had dropped his ethereal appearance at the most inopportune time. He cursed inwardly, knowing he must have scared her half to death.

He wouldn't know it to look at her though. Her almond-shaped blue eyes narrowed with suspicion and her full, sensual lips pursed in thought as she assessed him. Even though he clearly had the upper hand in this situation, her spunky, brazen personality quickly took over. One thing was clear—Celeste Winters definitely wasn't the kind of woman who allowed a man to think himself in control.

A smile quirked his lips. "So...if you knew I was here all along, why did you scream?"

Hesitation flickered across the limpid pools of her eyes. She drew her lower lip between her teeth, the only outward indication that she was as rattled by this as he was.

"You startled me that's all." Her rigid stance relaxed minutely and Celeste wiggled her hips. "It's a little hard to ignore you when you're doing *that*."

Okay, so she wouldn't call him on the fact he appeared out of nowhere for fear of looking like a nutcase. Good. He had no explanation for her anyway. At least, none he was willing to give.

"Oh yeah? How about when I do this?" He lowered his head again and splayed his mouth across the seam of her pussy, nudging her folds with the tip of his tongue.

She arched her back as a moan escaped her throat. "Sebastian."

He closed his eyes against the flood of emotion that poured through him at the sound of his name on her lips. In eighteen years, no one had addressed him by name. No one even really knew he still existed as anything more than a boogieman whose name scared children into behaving.

He pressed his lips to her warm cunt, tasting her musky flavor on his tongue. She was pure heaven. Even with his mouth exploring her most intimate part, he still couldn't quite believe she was real. She seemed more like a figment of his imagination, a dream he'd conjured to keep some of the oppressive loneliness he lived with at bay for a little while.

He feasted on her sweet, soft flesh until she was panting and writhing beneath him again. Heat scorched the air between them as he glanced up and took in the sensual curve of her throat, the way her nipples pebbled through her shirt, the slick sheen of sweat that beaded on her flat abdomen and trickled into her navel.

As long as she wasn't asking questions he wasn't willing to answer, he could get lost in the miracle that had brought her to him. When he'd first been cursed, he spent the few hours of true humanity he'd been given interacting with others. He'd even gone to the local pub and picked up a girl a time or two, thinking that an hour with someone's legs wrapped around his waist would remind him what it meant to be truly alive.

It always had the opposite effect. The women he'd been with left before his time was up, making it clear they wanted nothing more from him than a romp in the sack. Each time, he was reminded that his curse was all-encompassing. He was doomed to be inconsequential. Invisible—whether anyone could see him or not.

Celeste's inner walls trembled and pulsed around him as he stroked her deep inside. His tongue fluttered over her clit, matching the rhythm of his fingers' deep thrusts. He pleasured her inside and out until she was grinding and shuddering, her hips pulsing slightly as she tumbled over the edge.

He held her, his lips fused to her cunt while her release flooded her limbs. He felt her orgasm explode and rode it with her, grinding his cock into the mattress to relieve some of the pressure that made his balls ache.

When her trembling subsided, he placed a soft kiss to the blonde curls atop her mound. "Your pussy is so soft, so perfect," he murmured against her skin.

She chuckled, a wry, delicate sound at odds with the strength of her character. It sounded almost like a strangled sob. "Thanks…I think."

Loath to remove his fingers from her body but knowing she could use a break to recover, he pulled out of her channel. She gasped, arching her spine as her empty pussy gaped open for a moment before the delicate folds closed around the entrance, hiding the pink opening that beckoned to him.

Sebastian splayed his fingers across her stomach. His ghost-white skin contrasted with her soft, healthy tan, reminding him they lived in different worlds. Squelching down a flash of anger, he slipped his hand beneath the fabric of her shirt and cupped her full breast in his palm.

"Why are you here?" he asked, not unkindly.

She blinked at him, her tongue flicking out between her lips and sending another rush of naughty images and visceral heat to slam into his overheated mind — and into his groin.

"I came to ask you for something."

His heart hammered hard against his chest. The scent of her arousal mingled with the warm, natural aroma of her skin to form a heady, intoxicating perfume that seemed to mess with his brain and burrow deep into his cock.

"I think you know that whatever it is, the answer is yes."

She raised herself up onto her elbows and watched him through narrowed eyelids. The purple slant of her long lashes made her blue eyes take on a sapphire hue. She reached out to him slowly and then hesitated with her fingertips half an inch away from his cheek, as though afraid he'd dissipate if she touched him.

Funny, he felt the same way about her, but that hadn't kept him from tasting the sweetness of her pussy or bringing her to climax. Twice.

He leaned in to her caress. She jumped when her fingers made contact with his skin then seemed to think better of her apprehension and splayed her palm along his cheek and jaw.

Her caress was like water to a drowning man. He rubbed his cheek against her skin, suddenly unable to get enough.

"Those journals are all yours, aren't they?"

He nodded, emotion constricting his throat. No one had ever seen his journals. He'd started keeping them a year into his curse. Since then, he'd used them as therapy, knowing that he had to get his thoughts down on paper or he'd go mad. It was bad enough he didn't have anyone to talk to. At least writing things down made him feel as though he could share his most intimate thoughts with someone, even if it meant they wouldn't be found until long after his death.

"I'm sorry I looked through one," she whispered.

"That's all right. It's my fault for leaving them out in the open." He wanted to say more, to tell her that no one ever came up here, that he'd wanted her to see into the deepest part of his soul.

Only he was glad she hadn't read further. She wouldn't have liked what she found.

He swallowed hard and turned his head away, suddenly unable to face the curious probing in her gaze. A gentle pressure on his jaw made him tilt his face back toward her.

Their eyes met and for a moment it was as though a visible current of electricity slammed into him. It jolted his heart, his groin, reawakening feelings and sensations that had lain dormant for much too long.

Celeste rose to her knees. His gaze followed the lean lines of her legs, admiring the way her short skirt fell against her upper thighs, the slender curves of her calves, her delicate ankles. Even the ridiculous spiked heels that looked like faux sneakers only made her look sexier.

Leaving no doubt as to her intent, she slipped her fingertips down the length of his abdomen and cupped his rock-hard shaft in her hand.

"No one should be alone on Halloween," Celeste said as she stroked him from root to tip.

He nodded, too damn horny to do anything else. Knowing that whatever he uttered at that moment would be meaningless or imbecilic, he elected to keep his mouth shut. He didn't want to send her away. Not now. Not yet.

Not ever.

Except he didn't have a choice in the matter. She would go away. The clock was already ticking, quickly counting down to the time when he'd once again revert to being invisible.

He might have worried more about this night's inevitable conclusion if he could concentrate on anything but the way his cock stood stiff and erect only inches away from her pussy. If not for the flap of her skirt, he wasn't sure he could hold himself back from pushing her down and plunging deep into her heated cunt.

She bent forward slightly, trailing soft kisses over the soft curls on his chest then lower until her nose nuzzled the coarse curls at his groin. His fingers trembled as he wrapped his hands in her long, blonde tresses.

Her mouth seemed to move in slow motion. She slipped her tongue out first, circling the head of his cock before taking the tip between her lips.

The sensation that slammed into him was so intense he ground his teeth and cried out, willing himself not to come with every ounce of willpower he possessed. As though sensing his desperate need, she held back and squeezed the root of his shaft, forcing down the onslaught of orgasm.

For a while she simply held him in her mouth, giving him time to adjust to the feel of her slick heat wrapped around his cock. He refused to open his eyes, knowing that just one look at her ass thrust high in the air would make him lose control.

Instead, he fisted his hands in her hair and trembled as she swirled her tongue around the head of his cock again and again, alternating between slow, excruciating swirls and fast, eager swipes. He held himself back from thrusting between her lips and fucking her mouth until he spilled his hot seed into the back of her throat.

He wanted her to take all of him, to accept him for who and what he was when no one else had. Even through the haze of lust that enshrouded his mind, he knew that was a ludicrous wish. She'd be gone tomorrow and it was better that way.

Celeste sucked him deep into her mouth, milking the last remnants of his self-control. He slid his hands out of her hair and grabbed her shoulders, pulling out of her mouth.

She looked up at him, her full lips parted and glistening wetly. Without a word, she climbed off the bed.

Sebastian's heart gave a sudden lurch in his chest. She was leaving. He'd be alone again, forced to jerk off until he spilled his seed in his hand and the warm fluid covered his belly and dripped onto the sheets.

Celeste smiled. She bent down and unhooked the straps of her shoes before tossing them aside. It took Sebastian a moment to realize she was staying, but the relief that suffused his body was nothing compared to the scorching heat that lit his veins.

He watched her as she removed her panties, pulling them down from beneath her skirt and letting them fall to the floor. She stepped out of them and he could only stare, entranced by the beauty of her body. Her skirt followed her panties to pool on the ground. She shed her shirt just as quickly until she stood naked before him.

For a moment Sebastian couldn't breathe. The need in his groin bordered on pain. With almost ferocious intensity, he lunged for her, drawing her close against him. Her body molded to his perfectly, her lush curves complementing his lean lines. As his erection pulsed against her belly, her nipples grazed his chest, causing a swirl of sensation to slide through his nerve endings.

"I've waited for you. My whole life, I think."

He didn't know where the words had come from. That was certainly not something he'd wanted to admit, yet there it was, hovering in the open between them. He didn't give her a chance to reply but lowered his mouth to claim hers.

Clinging to her tightly, he kissed her with the fierceness of desperation. His tongue slid between her lips and stroked hers. She tasted of him and the knowledge filled him with raw, hungry desire that threatened to make him spill his seed right there with his cock trapped between them.

He lifted her off her feet and she wrapped her legs around him, letting him carry her back to the bed. Bending down, he lowered her onto her back. Her thighs squeezed his middle as he burrowed himself between her parted legs.

His cock sought her hot channel of its own accord, positioning itself at the entrance. The need throbbing in his balls threatened to send him over the edge. Still Sebastian hesitated.

Gazing deep into her eyes, he placed a tender kiss on her forehead. "Are you ready for this?"

Celeste opened her mouth as though to speak but raised her hips and impaled herself on his cock instead.

"What do you think?" she answered breathlessly.

A chuckle tore from his throat, so raw and unexpected that it sent a jolt of surprise low into his belly. She'd made him laugh. God, she really had turned his entire world upside down in the span of just one week.

He remained motionless for a long moment but Celeste wasn't having any of it. She squirmed beneath him, setting the pace until he took over and lifted himself so he could better watch her face as he thrust inside her.

"Celeste."

She smiled at him, her blue eyes shining with something akin to genuine fondness. Something he couldn't remember ever seeing before from anyone.

"Sebastian."

He groaned and plunged in deeper, grinding against her mound as he sheathed himself to the hilt. Her channel pulsed around him, squeezing him, welcoming him. He filled her perfectly and she took all of him with such intensity that it knocked the air from his lungs.

Her breasts bounced with every thrust. He drank in the sight of her large, dark areolas and distended nipples, the swell of her breasts, committing to memory each subtle nuance of her body. At last, he lowered his head and bit down on a perfect nipple, drawing a strangled cry from her throat.

He fucked her slowly at first then faster as the insistent undulation of her hips urged him on. His mouth moved across the top of her breasts and over her jaw to claim her lips in another scorching kiss.

Thrusting his tongue into her mouth, he mimicked the movement of his cock plunging deep inside her. She met him thrust for thrust, her tongue curling around his, licking and exploring with every stroke.

She whimpered softly as her inner walls tightened against him. He could feel her orgasm build from the inside. The thrill of impending release swelled his cock, traveling through his shaft to lodge into his lower belly. It hung there, suspended, like a ball of pure pleasure about to erupt.

And then Celeste shattered around him, screaming his name. His self-control unraveled and the orgasm that had been gathering for so long finally exploded in an arc of heat. Her body rippled beneath him, causing a mirror effect that had him spilling himself in hot, sudden spurts.

Sebastian's voice echoed off the walls, melding with Celeste's in a crescendo of passion. With one last thrust, he wrapped his arms around her, keeping her close against his chest. His cock softened inside her pussy and still he held her as if he might never let her go.

Much too soon, Celeste cleared her throat, bringing him out of the comfortable shelter of their afterglow. "You're not really human, are you?"

Chapter Four

ജ

Sebastian chuckled, although an undercurrent of anxiety traveled through the sound. He lifted some of his body weight off Celeste, aware he was crushing her beneath him, and propped himself on his elbows. Loath to slip his semierect cock from its comforting sheath, he held his hips pressed tightly against hers.

"You're asking because that was out of this world, right?"

Her brow furrowed. "This is going to sound stupid, but... Uh... Are you a ghost?"

He chuckled, hoping the sound came out more confident than he felt. "I'm willing to bet you haven't run into a lot of ghosts so let me educate you a little. They usually don't feel solid. And most of them can't talk."

She stroked her hand up and down the outside of his arm, sending shivers spiraling over his skin. "And you're the expert on paranormal phenomena around here?"

His smile faded. "Something like that."

"Professional interest or something else?"

Sebastian sighed. She was inching too close to topics that were off-limits, topics he had no intention of discussing, even with her. He averted his eyes, his gaze falling on the firefly bouncing in its jar. "Haven't you heard? My home is haunted. I've run into hundreds of the pesky critters. They get into everything."

She shook her head, clearly not buying his explanation. Smart girl. He wouldn't have bought it either.

"You wanted to ask me something," he reminded her, circling his hips so his cock settled deeper in her cunt. "That's why you're here, remember? So ask."

She frowned, wrinkling her nose in distaste. "There's a woman downstairs...Lakisha Pernice. She's the governor's daughter. Very influential. Anyway, she wants to meet you."

"Me?" He furrowed his brow, feigning surprise. "Why? I'm nobody to her."

"There are more rumors about you in the entire state of Georgia than there are about anyone else." She swallowed hard, suddenly not meeting his gaze. "Most aren't pleasant. I guess she wants to see for herself and show you off to the guests."

Sebastian shook his head. He'd encouraged those rumors and speculations since he'd taken over the mansion. It ensured he'd be left alone—for the most part. Oh, there were always thrill-seekers and rowdy teenagers who tried to trespass on his property, but the alarm system and a push of a button to summon the authorities usually got them off and kept them away.

Obviously it didn't always work. Persistent event planners who didn't take no for an answer weren't part of the security company's intrusion detection system.

"She'll be disappointed." Sebastian trailed his fingertips over the top of Celeste's breast, pausing to circle a nipple.

She trembled slightly, the quaking in her body traveling into his cock to stiffen it farther.

"I'm not," Celeste whispered.

Before he could react, she lifted her head and pressed her lips to his. The kiss was quick and abrupt, but it was filled with longing and acceptance. It sent a jolt of erotic energy into his groin.

He remembered the feel of her tongue in his mouth, the taste of her, and desperately needed to experience it again. Cupping her face in his hands, he tilted her jaw and ravaged her mouth, kissing her with passion, fierceness and near violence.

She responded to him with the same intense fury, raking her fingernails down his back, pulling her to him with more strength than he'd given her credit for. When the kiss ended, they were both panting and his cock raged out of control inside her pussy. He could do this for hours.

Hell, he could do this all night. Only he didn't have all night. With no clock in the bedroom to show him the time, he didn't know how many hours of true humanity he had left. One? Two? Not nearly enough.

"More later," he promised, withdrawing from her tight channel. Her disappointed groan sent a spear of pain to lodge in his heart. "Your friends are waiting."

"Serves them right," she said, sitting up.

She propped her back against the wall and grabbed a pillow. Cradling it in her arms, she watched him as he moved to the dresser and opened it in search of a suitable outfit to wear.

He hadn't been out in public for years. These days, even the unbearable solitude was preferable to the chatter of people who wouldn't remember him the next day anyway.

Rummaging through one drawer after another, he found nothing appropriate for a costume party. The only clothes he'd kept were now old and faded, but they weren't interesting enough to pass for a believable guise. "You don't mind if I get a little creative with my costume, do you?"

When she didn't reply, he glanced over his shoulder. And froze.

She'd reached for the top journal stacked on a dozen others beside the bed. Black with a golden trim that ran all the way around the binding, it was the most recent. And she'd had it for at least five minutes. Maybe more.

"Put it down." His voice grated against his throat, sounding harsh and foreign to his own ears. "Please."

Celeste looked up, her eyes wide and questioning. "What is this?"

Too late.

She knew. Everything.

"Maybe I didn't pay enough attention to my high-school English class when we learned about the folly of hubris. Arrogance. Pride. They were my downfall." She read the words slowly with inflection. Each one stabbed like a dagger into his heart.

"Stop," he whispered.

She didn't. "There was something about summer that called to me. Sultry, hot nights filled with sticky air and the promise of more heat to come. Unlike other college guys who used those nights to pick up girls and fuck them senseless in the back of pickup trucks, I had a different hobby."

Sebastian closed his eyes and leaned against the dresser. *Stop.*

He didn't speak the plea this time. He knew it wouldn't have mattered.

"I trapped fireflies. Hundreds of them. I kept them in jars and used them to light my way in the dark. I placed them everywhere. Every week or two, they'd expire and I'd catch more. I thought they were beautiful. And insignificant. Until one night, I caught *her*."

He couldn't see her, but he knew Celeste was eyeing him. "Her?"

Sebastian nodded. "Nurielle."

Celeste returned her attention to the journal and continued reading. "I didn't know what she was at first. She looked like a larger version of the fireflies I was so enthralled with. About two inches tall, she glowed like them, but it wasn't until I returned home that I realized she appeared human. I should have let her go the moment I figured it out. I should have—"

"Apologized," Sebastian said hoarsely, cutting her off. He blinked his eyes open. "Repented. Done anything and everything in my power to return her to her natural habitat. I did none of those things."

Celeste pressed her lips together but said nothing. Her silence unnerved him more than her ire would have done.

Swallowing hard, he continued. "She begged me to release her. It should have never come to that, but it did. I refused. I had a fairy in a jar! Hell, I'd hoped she could grant wishes! What twenty-one-year-old in his right mind would let her go?"

"I would have," Celeste said softly, glancing at the firefly bobbing in its jar. "Then and now."

"If I could change things, I would. But I can't. Nurielle punished me. She decided that since I was so unconcerned with the fact that no one would miss the fireflies or her for that matter then no one would miss me either. She wanted me to understand how it felt to be inconsequential. Invisible."

Celeste shook her head. "Wait a minute. You're telling me a fairy cursed you? That's what you're saying?"

He scrubbed a hand over his face, realizing how ridiculous this entire thing must sound to someone who hadn't lived the life he'd been living for the past eighteen years. He forced a laugh to bubble from his throat. "Had you going there for a second, didn't I?"

She pulled her lower lip between her teeth and eyed him skeptically. "You made that up?"

"I'm a writer," he said with all the conviction he could muster. "We're eccentric folks, y'know. I make up stories. It's what I do."

"A writer," she repeated, clearly unconvinced.

"A bona fide wordsmith. A recluse. As outlandish and peculiar as the rumors make me out to be. Only not a ghost."

At least that last part was true, he thought with an inward grimace. God, he hated lying to her. But what other choice did he have? If she thought he believed what he was saying, she'd run out of there faster than he could say *firefly*. And he wasn't ready to let her go yet.

Celeste closed the journal and placed it back on top of the teetering stack then tossed the pillow aside and lowered her feet to the floor. He watched in silence as she pulled her panties on, the scrap of flimsy cloth barely covering the delicate pink folds and soft curls beneath.

"That's quite the story," she said as she buckled the strap of her shoes around her ankles.

"Isn't it though?" Sebastian pasted another fake smile onto his features. "It's my favorite."

He turned back to the dresser and yanked on the bottom drawer, opening it to reveal a stack of neatly folded bed sheets and pillowcases. After a second's deliberation, he chose a white sheet, which he quickly wrapped around his body and tied over one shoulder.

Celeste straightened her clothes and ran her fingers through her curls, smoothing her hair back from her face. God, she was stunning, he thought as her eyes widened and she met his gaze. A jolt of electricity slammed into him. That...*connection*, whatever it was, threatened to knock him off his feet.

"What..." She paused to assess him from the top of his disheveled head to the tips of his wiggling bare toes. "Are you wearing?"

He swept his right hand up and down in front of his torso. "You like it? I made it myself."

"Uhh...I can see that." She raised an eyebrow. "What is it?"

"Ah! That's the beauty of this costume. It's whatever you want it to be. To one person, I might be a Roman senator in a toga. To another, I could be a ghost."

Celeste grimaced and suddenly he wondered if he'd gone too far. Something told him his lie hadn't been as convincing as he'd hoped.

He stalked toward her and captured her wrists in his right hand then forced her hands up over her head. She glanced at him, startled, her blue eyes filled with questions that had nothing to do with his outfit.

Questions he couldn't — wouldn't — answer.

"Forget about me," he murmured. "I want to know about you."

The tip of Celeste's tongue darted out to moisten her full lips. He was certain she'd intended the gesture to be innocent, but it looked delightfully wicked. "What do you want to know?"

"For starters... Don't you ever do what you're told?" He whispered the question in her ear before grabbing her earlobe and nipping it between his teeth. "I asked you to put down the journal but you refused."

A self-conscious giggle bubbled up from inside her. "Do I look like the kind of girl who obeys orders? That strategy didn't get me off your lawn. And it won't keep me from poking into places that aren't any of my business either."

"Mmm...do you know what happens to women who stick their noses where they don't belong?"

She shook her head, sending loose strands of blonde hair to brush against his face. He inhaled her scent, committing the citrus aroma of her shampoo to memory.

"They're punished."

"P-Punished?"

The word turned into a whimper in Celeste's throat as Sebastian spun her around and cleared the table of journals with his arm before pushing her over it. Her bare belly scraped against the edge of the table. The wood bit into her skin but

231

she barely felt it. The only sensation sliding through her veins was arousal.

Deep, overwhelming, mind-blowing arousal.

Truth be told, it scared the hell out of her.

She wasn't afraid of Sebastian, even when he folded her skirt over her waist and traced the fleshy cheeks of her ass with the flat of his palm. Or when he pushed the waistband of her panties over her hips and slid the fabric down to her thighs.

What she felt for him however, terrified her to the core. In a few hours he'd turned her world upside down. It had been years since she'd allowed herself to feel something more than superficial attraction for a man. Oh, she liked men well enough. But they were entertainment. A way to pass the time.

Sebastian was much more than that. He was unlike anyone she'd ever met. Funny, self-deprecating, shy, he came across as someone who barely possessed social skills. And yet there were moments when he showed fierce possessiveness and a rugged strength that caused cream to drip from her overheated cunt.

Like now.

His hand slid over her exposed bottom. "Good girls get to join their friends at the party and pretend nothing happened up here. Bad girls get spanked. Which are you?"

The stroke of his fingers against the crease of her ass sent a groan to lodge in her throat. "B-Bad. Bad girl."

"Good answer."

Before she could even consider feeling ashamed of what she'd said, the first smack landed against her ass. It stung but the prickle of awareness that fluttered over her skin was pure ecstasy.

She hadn't felt guilty for reading the journal. He'd told her it was his fault for leaving his inner thoughts out in the open and she'd believed him. Now however, she was thrilled she'd decided to take another peek. There was more to his explanation of being a writer than he was letting on. Sure, his reasons seemed plausible enough. Writers were an eccentric lot. But that didn't explain why she'd been alone in the room one minute and surrounded by pure masculine temptation the next.

And the punishment... *Oh God.*

She wiggled against his hand, arching her back when his palm came down to deliver another smack and another. Heat flooded her core, drenching her pussy. If she'd been wearing panties, the fabric would have been soaked through. As it was, liquid heat trickled between her legs, dripping over the inside of her thigh.

"You like this."

It wasn't a question, but she answered it anyway. "Yes."

"I'd give anything to be able to explore this side of your personality with you."

Sebastian's voice sounded wistful and sad. Before she could contemplate what that meant, another smack landed squarely on her right cheek, making her gasp aloud.

He thrust two fingers inside her, punctuating the strokes with deliberate, careful blows. She squirmed as fire traveled from her exposed cheeks into her cunt where his fingers slid in and out of her channel.

Her breathing came in quick pants as her body trembled with the spiraling heat that quickly blossomed out of control. It culminated in her clit, which throbbed and pulsed with every open-palmed slap against her skin.

Lost in the sweet flashes of pain and pleasure, she barely had time to react when the orgasm crashed into her body. It knocked the breath from her lungs as the pleasure soared and crashed, drenching her in raw, rapturous delight.

She didn't know how long she lay there, drifting in a fog of euphoria. She was vaguely aware of Sebastian bending between her legs and licking his way up her inner thigh, cleaning her cream.

He kissed each cheek, soothing the pain with soft, pliant lips and kind caresses. At last, he pulled up her panties and helped her to her feet.

Oh…fuck. He really was unlike anyone she'd ever met. He'd seemed to know exactly what she craved even when she hadn't been aware of it herself.

"Let's go," he said, taking her hand.

She folded her fingers around his, blissfully grounded by his presence. "All right. But after we're done with them, you're mine."

The fragile smile that curved Sebastian's lips made her heart flip-flop. He didn't reply, but she feared his silence was answer enough.

"We're not finished here," she insisted, squelching the nagging doubt that flittered through her mind, telling her he really didn't want her. "Not by a long shot."

Chapter Five
ఈ

The wedding was in full swing by the time Celeste and Sebastian slipped through the north tower door to join the other guests. Lakisha stood beside her fiancé at one end of the room, facing the crowd. Not one to miss a photo opportunity, she'd elected to make the priest turn his back to those assembled.

Holding tight to Sebastian's hand, Celeste slipped through the throng unnoticed. The crowd's eyes were on the happy couple as they said their vows, which they'd clearly elected to write themselves.

"As this night extends its dark tendrils into daylight, so my love reaches out for your touch," Lakisha bellowed as loud as her voice would carry.

Sebastian chuckled as they slid into an empty spot against a buffet table. "Is she always this melodramatic?"

"I wouldn't know," Celeste whispered. "I'd only met her once before she hired me. She said she needed a fresh take on Halloween parties. She was looking for someone who was far removed from the flourishes of high society. Come to think of it, I probably should have been insulted."

Sebastian reached up and smoothed a strand of hair behind her ear. She leaned in to his touch, relishing the heat of his flesh against her skin.

"If you ask me, that's a compliment. You're not like anyone here, Celeste. You're…"

Someone shushed him loudly from behind. Sebastian smiled at Celeste, lifting a shoulder in silent apology.

She brought her hand to her chest in an effort to calm the hammering pulse that beat wildly at the base of her throat. What had he been about to say? She wasn't the type of woman who fell all over herself at the sound of a few pretty words, but she knew Sebastian's statement would have been genuine. She was eager to learn what he thought of her. Was he as intrigued by her as she was by him?

Turning back to the ceremony, she forced herself to focus on the vows being exchanged but her mind kept spiraling back to the hours she'd spent in Sebastian's arms. She'd intended to bring him downstairs as quickly as possible and alleviate Lakisha's concerns. Instead, she'd lost herself in the heat of his body, in the sultry ecstasy of his touch, in the planes and valleys of his beautifully sculpted body.

No. That wasn't true. She hadn't lost herself in the north tower.

Somewhere between the passionate lovemaking and the rampant energy that flowed between them, she'd *found* herself. And now, squeezing his hand, she knew she never wanted to let go of the discovery she'd made—or of the man who'd awakened a part of herself she hadn't even been aware.

Before tonight, Celeste would have never considered making love to a stranger. Or reveling in the feel of his palm landing across the exposed curve of her ass. Yet somehow with Sebastian there'd been no embarrassment. No humiliation. No shame.

Only a sense of belonging, coupled with a wild, unmistakable need to get to know him better. She craved to know everything about him—what kinds of stories he wrote, why he chose to live like a hermit, whether he had anyone to confide in.

The exchange of vows seemed to take forever. Lakisha's overdone sentiments grew more elaborate and dramatic with each minute that passed until even her poor fiancé looked at a loss for words. Broad-shouldered with dusky skin and close-cropped hair, Jim Boden looked every bit the football player he was. He'd even elected to wear his jersey and tight pants to the party. Not the most creative of costumes but it certainly complemented his muscular physique.

Letting her gaze roam over the heads of those assembled, Celeste caught sight of Jonathan standing toward the front of the room. As if feeling the weight of her stare on the back of his head, he turned and met her eyes. His gaze immediately darted to Sebastian and his eyes widened. The questions she saw written across his face would have to wait, but the way he wiggled his eyebrows told her she had a lot of explaining to do.

Celeste's feet ached. She transferred her weight from one foot to the other, hoping to relieve some of the pressure that thrummed in her soles. If Lakisha hadn't been holding Celeste's career in the palm of her well-manicured hand, she'd march right back up to the north tower and let the happy bride handle her own damn party.

After what seemed to Celeste like an eternity, the wedding finally came to an end. She and Sebastian stood off to the side as the new Mr. and Mrs. Boden made their way through the throng of bodies that parted for them. As soon as Lakisha noticed her, she released her husband's hand and stalked over to Celeste, stopping only a few inches in front of her.

"Well?" she demanded, her high-heeled shoe tapping restlessly on the ground. "Where is he?"

Celeste forced a smile onto her features. "Lakisha Pern — err...Boden, meet Sebastian Bradley. He owns the mansion and was kind enough to allow us to use it for the purposes of the party. And your lovely wedding of course."

Lakisha rolled her eyes, looking bored. Off to the side, her small wedding party had already begun to organize themselves in a receiving line. "Fine. Bring him over here."

Celeste's thumb made a small circle against the back of Sebastian's hand, hoping to soothe the anger she could feel rolling through him. She'd known Lakisha had expected someone with a monstrous appearance, but there was no need to be rude.

Fighting to keep her temper under control, she turned to Sebastian. "He's—"

The words died in her throat. She still held on to his hand. She could feel every small nuance of his body's response to Lakisha's presence yet she couldn't see him.

No one could.

The only thing left of Sebastian Bradley was a rumpled white sheet, bunched in a heap on the hardwood floor.

Celeste swallowed hard. "He's...coming."

Lakisha's eyes narrowed. "Why you lying little bitch. You ruined my wedding! I told all these people they were going to meet the elusive Sebastian Bradley, and now what? I'll look like a fool!"

Her loud shrieking had already brought a crowd to gather around them. Creeping up behind Lakisha, Jim looked apologetic as he wrapped an arm around his wife's waist in an attempt to pull her away.

"I'm sorry," Celeste's voice wavered as anxiety welled up in her throat. "I'll tell them. It's my fault. I—"

Lakisha wouldn't have any of it. Her bellowing cries intensified and her name-calling grew even more creative than her wedding vows.

"I should have guessed you'd never be able to pull this off! What possessed me to hire an unknown, a silly little twit who couldn't plan her way out of a paper bag, I'll never know!"

Sebastian slid his hand out of hers. Celeste tried to cling to him, needing the reassurance of his presence even if no one else knew he was there but he broke the contact and moved away, leaving her standing alone to face Lakisha's wrath.

Celeste's cheeks heated. She didn't turn away from confrontation but the snickers and finger-pointing from those assembled made the situation a thousand times worse. So much for her one big break. She'd never get another event-planning job in Atlanta again.

The lights dimmed, flickered and then grew bright again, sending up a confused murmur from the crowd. Even Lakisha looked momentarily thrown off her stride. When she opened her mouth to continue her tirade, the lights flickered again, this time dying out completely.

"What the hell? Turn those back on!"

"Sebastian," Celeste whispered.

A hand clamped on her shoulder while another crept up the back of her thigh to caress the curve of her ass where the heated imprint of his palm still lingered like a permanent brand. She trembled, but not with fear. Her pussy heated with the memory of his touch and she allowed him to lead her up the stairs.

He opened a doorway and pushed her inside. By the familiar scent of incense, she guessed she was once again inside the corridor to the north tower.

A moment later he was gone.

The screams that erupted from below traveled upward, making her cringe. She heard glass crash and shatter along with platters of food being overturned.

Anxiety lodged in Celeste's throat. Feeling her way with her outstretched hands in the darkness, she left the safety of the corridor and moved forward to the balustrade overlooking the main room. She arrived just in time to see candles being lit in a wide, flaming arc. No one guided the blazing matchstick.

The lick of flame swept over Lakisha's head and she shrieked, her face going as pale as her unconventional wedding dress in the golden glow of the fire. She backed away into her husband's arms only to see a champagne bottle rising to float suspended in midair only inches away from her face.

She screamed again as the cork popped, narrowly missing her head. The contents of the bottle gushed out in a foamy flow, drenching her.

With another harrowing wail, Lakisha pulled her husband in front of her and used him as a human shield against any additional flying objects. Then, leaving a wild litany of curses about haunted houses and bad party planners in her wake, she stormed toward the door, pushing guests out of the way to reach the exit first. The priest bellowed out what sounded like an exorcism prayer but he too bolted.

The rest of the crowd followed, stepping over each other in an effort to escape the haunted mansion. Headlights poured through the front door to illuminate the now-empty hall and tires screeched on the gravel road that led up to the house.

Celeste collapsed to the floor, folding her legs beneath her and resting her back against the balustrade. She was finished. Done. The career she'd worked so hard for had just gone up in smoke.

She should have been devastated. Instead, a smile curved her lips as she recalled the look on Lakisha's face when that champagne bottle erupted.

A giggle bubbled up from her throat.

"Celeste? You in here, hon?"

Jonathan.

"I'm fine, Jon. Give me a few minutes…please?"

His footsteps rang out from below. She could picture him hesitating, his concern for her keeping him from leaving with the rest of the crowd.

"You're sure?"

She smiled, though she knew he couldn't see her. "I am."

Waiting until she heard him leave, she rose unsteadily to her feet. A breeze wafted over her legs, sending a shiver to travel across her skin.

"Sebastian," she murmured, knowing he was there. She could feel the heat of his skin. She had only to touch him and—

Ah. *There.* She ran the flat of her palms across his chest and up higher to frame his face. To all the world it would look as though she held nothing but air.

"Thank you," she said, knowing that didn't even come close to expressing the gratitude she felt toward him.

He cupped her breasts in his broad hands, running the tips of his thumbs across her nipples. The buds tightened painfully and a sharp jolt of moisture flooded her pussy.

"That story wasn't just something you made up, was it?"

He didn't answer, but she could feel him shaking his head. The stubble on his cheek scraped her palm.

A shiver traveled across her skin. "Let me help you. Let me..."

Love you.

It was too much too soon. She couldn't make her mouth form the words, but the feelings were there, rolling beneath the surface of her soul.

Hating to break contact with him but driven to do the only thing she could, she reached beneath her skirt and pulled down her panties. The skirt itself followed a moment later. After pulling off her shirt, she stood naked except for the three-inch heels.

Taking a deep breath, she turned toward the railing and curved her fingers around the old wood. She pushed her ass back and made contact with his groin.

Sebastian's erection throbbed against her skin. She rocked her hips, swaying her ass back and forth to rub along his cock. Seconds later, his massive shaft plunged inside her slick pussy, filling her with a blast of hot pleasure that bordered on pain.

A gasp caught in her throat. She pushed back against him, impaling herself on his cock until he was buried in her to the hilt. He cupped her breasts, pinching her nipples as he pumped wildly. With savage thrusts, he fucked her desperately.

Her phantom lover. The ghost who'd awakened her to the pleasure she'd been denying herself.

"Damn you, Sebastian. You're mine," she ground out between clenched teeth as her clit pulsed and her cunt stretched to accommodate him. "Mine. I'll take you in any way I can have you."

A roar echoed through the room, loud enough to shake the wooden planks of the balcony. It startled her, drawing a cry from her throat.

His cock spasmed, sending a flurry of concentrated pulses deep into her core as he pumped his seed. Tears filled her eyes and dripped over the lower line of her lashes. Her pussy responded to his release with a throbbing vibration that seemed to peak in her clit, sending a shiver of pure sensation to stream along her nerve endings.

She turned her head slowly as her orgasm subsided, fearing the cavernous emptiness of the space stretching out behind her.

Instead of the void she'd dreaded, she found a pair of dark eyes watching her with possessive fervor. Sebastian's brows were drawn downward, not in a frown, but in a look of abject astonishment.

Celeste grinned and slipped his cock out of her pussy. Turning around, she wrapped her arms around his neck and pulled him to her. "I told you we weren't finished."

"Thank God, for women who don't know how to mind their own business," he whispered against her mouth before bringing his lips down to hers.

Lost in the kiss, her eyelids drifting closed, Celeste almost didn't notice the bright pinpoint of light that fluttered above their heads. Her eyes snapped open as she followed the firefly's path.

It soared undeterred toward the front door.

CONJURED BLISS

Brigit Zahara

෨

Dedication

&

For Simarone and Rio

Trademarks Acknowledgement

&

The author acknowledges the trademarked status and trademark owners of the following wordmarks mentioned in this work of fiction:

Bellagio: Bellagio Corporation

Caesar's: Caesars World, Inc.

Guinness Book of Records: Guinness Publishing Limited Corporation

Jockey: Jockey International, Inc.

Chapter One
October 30, Las Vegas, NV

❧

"Hey, where's my tuna melt on rye?"

Callie leaned forward against the red-and-white-checkered countertop that fronted the steamy kitchen of the diner and, peering in, called out to the short-order cook. Busy flipping burgers and attending to other assorted grill items, his back remained to her even as he answered.

"Don't get your pantyhose in a bunch. It's coming."

Yeah. So was Halloween. Tomorrow.

The realization sent a stab of pain through Callie and with a stifled huff, she whirled on her heel, her long dark hair flying as she collided for the third time that day with the other waitress on shift.

"Jesus Christ, girl! One of these days you're going to knock us both out cold."

At fifty-something, equipped with a gravelly low voice thanks to her two-pack-a-day cigarette habit and wearing a ton of outdated makeup, Eleanor was the stereotypical greasy spoon server.

"Sorry," Callie mumbled. "I guess it's going to take me some time to remember the lay of the land."

At the tinkling sound of the bell hooked to the diner's door her eyes drifted over the older woman's shoulder to note the threesome who walked in. Bordered by two guys, the woman in the center had linked arms with one while she held the hand of the other. Laughing lightly and exchanging playful banter, the trio exuded all the indications of a very good and comfortable relationship. Callie's eyes quickly filled with tears.

"Hey, honey. Take it easy," Eleanor said, her voice softening as she laid a motherly hand on Callie's shoulder. "It's only a job. And you're doing fine, just fine. Give yourself a break. You've only been back a few weeks."

Yeah, back to her old job and her old residence that just so happened to be one in the same.

Quickly brushing an errant tear from her cheek, Callie sniffed loudly.

"It's not that."

"Then what?"

Callie's gaze moved over to the booth where the three newly entered customers now sat. The woman was still clasping the hand of the one guy across the table while mischievously nuzzling the neck of the other beside her. At the frisky, loving scene before her, a jab of reminiscence flooded through Callie, bringing with it the detailed and multifaceted memory of her first night at her former job.

She and the two magicians Vance and Hart who made up the then-brand-new act Abracadabra had just finished their opening night show at the Bellagio. Only weeks earlier she had been hired to be the guys' pretty, buxom assistant who would provide props, poses, participate in a number of the tricks and utter strategically placed *oohs* and *aahs* throughout the performance. In fact, Callie had jumped at the opportunity to quadruple her two-waitressing-job salary — the staggering sum the guys offered her all the more remarkable given the fact that she wouldn't have to take her clothes off. That was something Callie had vowed never to do, even though numerous others were cleaning up doing that very thing in Sin City — topless showgirls or out-and-out strippers able to generate some pretty good coin. But after her divorce, all Callie felt she had left was her pride and she was not about to sell that — or peeps at her bodacious bod — for any price. So while her costumes with Abracadabra were certainly sexy — the corseted bodices with plunging necklines beautifully exhibiting her naturally large full breasts and tiny waist, while the short-skirted chiffon dresses and high strappy sandals were seemingly specially designed to show off her long, shapely legs — by Callie's standards, they were acceptable.

Of course, it also didn't hurt that she would be working day and night with two of the most beautiful, sexy and overwhelmingly hot guys Callie had ever seen, let alone met. Where Vance was irrepressibly charming with his boyish good looks, startling turquoise eyes, dimpled smile and ever-present comical flair, the more serious Hart was dangerously attractive with his cinnamon-colored hair, silver eyes and low, hypnotic voice.

Not that any of that mattered.

From day one, Callie was determined that things would *never* go beyond a professional relationship with her hunky coworkers, that hard-and-fast decision stemming from what she saw as three very good reasons.

For starters, even though her divorce was almost a year old when she took the job with Abracadabra, Callie was still tremendously gun-shy about the opposite sex. A nearly permanent mark had been left thanks to the split from her rich businessman husband of six years, who very calmly announced one day over Salmon Wellington that he was gay, had a lover and was leaving her. Just like that. No warning.

Well, almost none.

In retrospect, Callie remembered wondering why her ex wasn't into some of the more intimate acts of sex, why she practically had to force him to make love to her and then when they did, why it was only every couple of months, only in the missionary position and always with the lights off. As he was the only lover she'd ever known, Callie was left to blame her husband's apparent disinterest on herself, assuming she must be doing something wrong. Maybe she wasn't attractive or sexy enough, or maybe, he just didn't *want* her — love her, yes — but more and more Callie began to suspect that the man she had married just wasn't sexually excited by her. In the end she was right.

After his stunning declaration, Callie threatened to sue him for alimony, but in yet another unforeseen occurrence, her dearly-beloved-no-longer literally sold their home—registered only in his name—out from under her and moved out of the state, leaving her penniless, homeless and heartbroken. Unable to deal with the additional stress of a messy divorce and forced onto the street as a result, Callie quickly secured work and a place to live all in one location—the shabby little in-law suite located in the back of the diner serving as her new home. It was a shock to the system but she became grateful for what she had, all the while keeping her eye out for the arrival of something better.

And *poof!* like magic, it appeared. When she saw the ad for Abracadabra and learned of the job's excellent pay and promise of keeping her personal dress code intact, dropping her day job at the diner and night shift as a cocktail waitress at Caesar's was a no-brainer. But getting involved with one of the two super-hot hunks that headlined the show? No way. Even if she could choose between the two, she wasn't eager to rush into any new romantic relationship.

So that was reason number one.

Secondly, Callie assumed that single guys as uncommonly beautiful and built as Vance and Hart just had to be gay—a preference that twisted the knife in her heart and strengthened her resolve to keep the two handsome heartthrobs at bay.

And just in case they weren't homosexual, Callie had always been a firm believer in the crude but good advice, "you don't shit where you eat and you don't fuck where you work". Regardless of the fact that both Vance and Hart had an amazing knack for making her heart pound and her sadly neglected "private place" react with only a look or smile. Never mind what the sound of their voices or a stray touch could do! Callie ignored the incredible chemistry between the three of them and pushed the desire to create a little magic backstage with one or the other of the guys to the back of her mind. It was the act's opening night on Halloween and it was going to be spectacular.

As it turned out, spectacular was the word. The audience was alternately stunned silent and worked into a nearly orgasmic applauding frenzy at the threesome's mesmerizing blend of spooky effects and supernatural displays. But that was nothing compared to the mind-blowing sleight of hand Vance and Hart had in store for Callie later on that evening.

Arriving back at the guys' sprawling bungalow where they all had spent the past six weeks very platonically rehearsing for their big debut in the home's large basement studio, the three prepared to enjoy an official celebratory toast to their newfound success. This on the heels of two bottles of champagne consumed in the limo on the ride back.

"So," Callie grinned, feeling only slightly tipsy but thoroughly delighted that the show had gone so well and she had finally settled into a good-paying, respectable job, "what are we drinking now?"

"How 'bout something warm and creamy?" Hart said with a sexy grin that in a flash set her thighs trembling and turned her knees to jelly.

Standing sideways at the bar, Callie found herself suddenly sandwiched in between Vance's and Hart's hard bodies, the soft scent of their different aftershaves combining to assault her nose in a way that quickly translated into a wild fluttering in her stomach. Her voice, when she sputtered out a response, was raspy.

"Ah… You mean like hot chocolate?"

"Nah, too sweet and too much. Maybe a shooter," Vance whispered from behind her.

"A shooter, yes," Hart agreed, gently pressing the front of his body against the front of hers. The pressure of his long, stiff cock turned his ivory pants into a mighty impressive pup tent and jabbed into her pelvis as he lightly pulled her against him. "I like the idea of shooting."

Similarly, Vance brought up the rear, his steel-like cock pressing in against the crease of her soft ass. "Ah-huh," he said in a low voice laden with lust. "How 'bout you, Callie? Do you like to shoot?"

Stunned, Callie tried to slow her quickly increasing breathing but the more she fought against her body's response, the more it revved up. Unaccustomed to such blatant displays of sexuality, she was surprised at how quickly and completely she was responding. Despite her resolve and damn good reasons for not going there with her two coworkers, she just couldn't seem to convince her body that was, at that very moment, revealing its true state at every turn. Her face, usually pale, was now flushed red, her torso vibrated with a long-repressed need and, completely foreign to her, the crotch of her satin panties was now positively soaked with the slippery fluid that had dripped from the throbbing region between her legs.

Reaching down and under her short skirt, Hart nudged her thighs apart with his fingers, only to palm her fabric-covered mons, his face registering surprise at just how wet the material of her underwear already was.

"I think it's safe to say that Callie likes to shoot. So how 'bout it, Satin? Do you want an orgasm?"

Satin was Hart's nickname for her, a term he'd chosen the first day they met when he shook her hand and claimed her skin was as soft as the silky textile.

Callie knew Hart was referring to the frothy white shooter but at the suggestive question, her liquid-laden feminine folds, cupped and pressed by his warm hand, twitched in response. Hart felt it but only smiled as he gave the sopping package he held a little squeeze.

"Oh I think she does," Vance replied for her, wrapping his arms around her to delicately fondle her now-aching breasts, the large, globes starved for male attention. His fingers lightly brushed over her painfully erect nipples through the sheer fabric of her bodice, causing her to gasp. "But I don't think one is going to be enough."

Hart quickly agreed.

"Nah-ah. I think Callie could use a bunch of orgasms."

Breathless and near swooning, Callie tried one last time to keep their relationship professional.

"Fellas, I-I really don't know if we should do this."

Hart's silver eyes locked with hers, the look of desire within further inflaming her growing need to be fucked.

"Sure you do, Callie," he said, his satiny voice caressing her as his hand continued to palpate the region between her thighs. "We *definitely* should do this. We want it, you want it and more than that, you need it."

"Need it?" she breathed heavily.

"Hart and I know that you haven't been fucked long and hard with a long, hard cock since your husband hit the highway over a year ago. And even then, well, let's just say, it wasn't nearly as much as a beautiful woman like you should be fucked."

Vance's raw and direct choice of words bowled Callie over, the trembling excitement that shot through her body at the dirty talk astonishing her even more. Sensing her strong response, the guys then launched into an erotic two-way conversation.

"Worst of all, his heart wasn't in it," Hart said. "Can you believe that, Vance?"

"Unimaginable."

"But don't you worry, Callie, our hearts are going to be in it."

"Not to mention our fingers and hard-ons. In it and deep."

"Poor Satin. Never had a decent fuck in your whole life and didn't even resort to taking matters into your own hands."

"So to speak. And no toys either! Girl, how have you lived?"

"You must be just aching for it."

"The craziest part is your ex wasn't into tongue sports and we all know what that means."

"Yeah, that sweet pussy of yours has never been licked and sucked and tongue-fucked like it deserves."

"Oh, but our gorgeous girl, it's going to be."

Callie could barely breathe. While Vance's and Hart's super-hot dialogue had left her more titillated than she had even knew was possible, she was also radically ill at ease with their obviously intimate knowledge of her love life.

"What are you guys talking about? Wha… How do you know all this? Have you been spying on me?"

"Easy, sweet," Hart said, his velvetlike voice soothing her. "It's nothing like that. We just are able to know many things. Call it a gift."

"We can smell it," Vance continued as he leaned into her further, the hard, rippled surface of his torso pressing against the smooth flesh of her back and threatening to distract her from the mounting force of his cock against her ass. "We can sense it. Feel it deep down. Everything we've said is the truth."

Shaken, Callie glanced down, bewildered, embarrassed and suddenly very overwhelmed. Additionally confused by the powerful sexual feelings she was experiencing for the very first time, she stared at the hardwood floor, not really seeing as tears welled up in her almond-shaped green eyes.

"I know but…"

Hart's voice once again was soft and reassuring.

"But it's not going to be your truth anymore, Satin. Vance and I are going to change all that. Now don't cry, pretty. You're one of a kind. A woman like no other."

He reached up and, placing a finger under her chin, lifted her eyes to meet his.

"You've made our show magic, just by being in it," Vance said.

"Made my *life* magic, just by coming into it."

"Mine too. And now we want to say thank you."

Leaning down, Hart locked his lips around one nipple and sucked softly through the partially translucent fabric of Callie's top and lacy bra. Startled, she drew in a ragged breath.

"I can't. I don't, I'm not ready. I didn't... I didn't see this coming."

"Yes you can and believe me, you're ready," Hart laughingly murmured as he moved to brush her ear with his lips. His tongue rimmed the curve of her earlobe for a quick moment before delving inside, the warm, moist sensation sending shivers down Callie's spine. She let out a heavy puff of air. "Good and ready. And as for not seeing this coming? Maybe you didn't. But I guarantee you're going to see a whole lot of coming from here on in."

"Better late than never," Vance murmured in her other ear as he began licking her neck.

With a feathery touch, Hart's hand shifted slightly to slip in under Callie's satin panties. Tilting his head so he could suck the sensitive skin on her neck, he gently inserted two fingers into her pussy and very slowly began to finger-fuck her. Moaning, Callie let her head fall back against Vance's shoulder, the frame of his strong arms about her waist the only thing holding her up.

While she had recalled that night many a time, Callie could never fully remember how the three of them got to a bedroom down the hall, only that they did. Once there, Vance and Hart both undressed her—deliberately and almost reverently—before laying her out on the king-size bed.

Then going at it from opposite directions, Vance at her head and Hart at her feet, they worked Callie over from head to toe, licking, nibbling and sucking every single inch of her writhing body. Extra-special attention was paid to her plump breasts with their large brown nipples that stuck out against the smooth velvet of her white skin. But the primary focus of their combined lapping loving was saved for her pussy. Engorged and pounding with the blood Vance and Hart had taken turns urging into it, Callie's dripping folds twitched, convulsed and endlessly poured out the creamiest of juices in response to the guys' relentless and talented oral attacks, the likes of which—as they had accurately stated—she had never before experienced. Pushing her effortlessly from one fantastic orgasm to another—another new and earth-shattering experience for her—Callie's previously ignored crease was given a series of tongue lashings that made her weep with pleasure and release.

But that was only the appetizer.

From there, Hart and Vance turned to one other, their hands and mouths playing up and down each other's bodies in a sizzling erotic display that left Callie breathless and wanting more.

Once the guys worked them all up to a crazed sexual state, their bodies all glistening with a combination of perspiration, saliva and cum, Vance and Hart alternately rammed their combined nineteen inches of pounding, granite-like rods into different openings on Callie's body, often simultaneously, even managing from time to time to bring the three of them to climax at exactly the same moment.

At one point when Callie interpreted Vance's hands on her wrists from behind as restraining and the weight of Hart's body on hers as too heavy, she panicked, whimpering and fighting at the sensation of being outnumbered and in danger. Abruptly the guys stopped and Vance, releasing her wrists, leaned down and kissed her softly on the mouth while Hart pulled out of her and gently pressed her knees together so she wouldn't feel so exposed.

"Ssssh, Satin," Hart said, stroking the outside of her thighs. "It's okay. We just want to make you feel good. Any time you don't feel comfortable, you just say so and we'll stop."

The matter never came up again.

The scenarios and positions that went down that night—and for the next eleven months—were too numerous to name, each one even more pleasure-producing than the previous one. But one that was forever burned in Callie's consciousness came back to her as she stood staring at the three customers who waited for her to take their lunch order. Swallowing hard, she shut her eyes as the long-remembered sensations coursed through her body.

Lying on her back with her legs extended in a wide V against Vance's torso, his hands clasping her ankles which rested on his ultra-broad shoulders, he seriously pummeled her cunt with long, hard, fast strokes. The speed and rhythm and force of his drives, coupled with the feel of his thick, long, hard cock stretching her slippery entry as far as it would go, easily made Callie come. All the while Hart's sexy dark voice spewed sexual encouragement and low appreciative chuckles from somewhere behind her, his warm breath and sharp canines brushing her ear, unexpectedly making her hotter than she'd ever been. Never was he more determined than when he sensed she was about to come. That's when he'd lay it on thick, lowering his voice to a husky whisper and choosing the dirtiest words possible, his vocabulary and voice working to push her to orgasm as surely as the hard, heavy thrusts of Vance's cock inside her while his hands lovingly caressed her hips.

"That's right, Satin. It feels soooo good, doesn't it?" he said breathlessly. "You fuck him, Callie. Fuck that hard cock. Fuck it real good. That's it. You're getting close, aren't you? Oh yeahhhhhhhh." It was as if his tongue and his mouth were on her swollen clit—a pleasure she now understood—and while she didn't understand the novel and surprising hold his voice had on her, she couldn't stop or even control her reaction to it. "Fuck it hard. That's it. Soooooo close. Push it good now. Oh yeah, Satin's gonna come, come on, sweet, juice that pole. Cream all over it."

And she would, moaning and groaning and countering every plunge of Vance's hard rod into her tight, clutching channel with a hard, frenzied thrust of her hips.

But one pleasurable peak wasn't enough for Vance and Hart. Call it making up for lost time but the more Callie came, the more Vance and Hart set out to make her come.

Kneeling at her head, Hart leaned forward from his waist, the move bringing Callie's mouth in perfect line with his massive, vein-ridged shaft. She desperately wanted to take his clearly aching pole into her mouth and suck the mushroomed head hard while her tongue flicked in and around the ridge but he wasn't quite in the right position for that. Still, she could give his balls a good going-over.

As they bumped against her face, she eagerly opened her mouth as wide as possible, taking in the bulk of both solid orbs and sucking very lightly on his sac. Reaching up, she grabbed hold of his cock and, with a solid, steady stroke, began tugging on his cock, the incredible pulse within thumping hard and fast in her hands.

Hart moaned, dangerously close to letting go of the reins and depositing hot, milky fluid all over her stomach, but determined to ride on the pleasure-Callie train a little more first, he ignored the growing sensations in his throbbing cock and focused on the cavern between Callie's legs.

Reaching down, he used the index and fifth fingers of his right hand to hold the outer lips of Callie's upper pussy apart to better expose her glistening, swollen nub. From his upside-down vantage point, he watched the bud that, poking out invitingly, twitched with every thrust of Vance's pole into her cunt. Just opening her outer lips increased the intensity of the rhythmical yank on the ultra-sensitive flesh, compliments of Vance's thrusts. Looking up, his eyes locked with his partner in crime and they exchanged a knowing smile.

Working as the team they were, Vance then pulled Callie's legs even farther apart and leaned forward a bit to change the angle, which in turn gave her clit an even stronger wrench. Slightly increasing his tempo, Vance then thrust even harder into her as both he and Hart looked down at Callie's pussy. Their plan had worked. Her already twitching clit was now being jerked noticeably farther down with every forceful shove by Vance. The change in slant, speed and strength was acknowledged by a mumbling whimper from Callie as her spread-eagled thighs, trembling at a furious pace, telegraphed the imminent approach of yet another momentous orgasm. The addition of Hart's voice into the mix made Callie's almost painfully swollen slit beat even harder.

"Yeah, that feels sooooo good, doesn't it? You're gonna come, aren't you, Satin? Explode some more of that tasty Callie cream. Yes…"

But Hart wanted something else too. He wanted to drive Callie crazy.

With his outside two fingers still holding her lips open, Hart took his two middle fingers and pressed them down on Callie's shuddering clit. Then, in perfect sync with Vance's forceful thrusts, he joined in on the strong, steady downstroke on her swollen flesh, further heightening the tugging on the ready-to-explode skin. The combination sent Callie over the edge in a violent and agonizing release. Just barely managing to cover her teeth so she wouldn't bite down on Hart's sac, she came hard, her cry of unbelievable enjoyment and release muffled thanks to Hart's bulging balls that packed her mouth.

Riding the waves of ecstasy, she unconsciously continued to lightly suck on his bag and apply a persistent double-fisted tug on his throbbing cock. Losing all sense of time and space, Callie's body was reduced to a bucking frenzy, her pelvis humping wildly forward in strong, rhythmic jerks as her slippery pussy clutched hard around the cock that battered her inside and pulled unrelentingly on her throbbing clit. Even as she came, Hart's fingers continued to ride the distended nub heightening her orgasm even more as he pressed down further and vibrated his fingers at an inhuman speed over the inflamed ridge. With a strangled scream of rapture, her legs, still held by Vance's hands, quaked spasmodically and her toes curled under as one rapturous wave after another rocked her body. Only distantly was she aware of Vance's vibrato-like ramming into her pussy and the loud, sharp exhalation that spoke of his own orgasm, the sound arriving just as the blistering explosive spray from Hart's jerking shaft shot out hard against her and Vance's pelvises, the shiny white droplets of cum glistening on their skin and in their pubic hair.

It was then Hart lowered his head and began sucking her belly button. Hard. At least it felt like sucking. Just sucking. Of course, now she knew better but back then she didn't. How could she? Not once did she ever feel teeth break her skin, so skillful were both the guys in the ancient art of bloodletting. In fact, it would be months before Callie realized that her new partners—onstage and in bed—were vampires.

"Hello? Callie?"'

"Huh?" Callie turned to look at the concerned face of Eleanor.

"Jesus, where were you just now?"

When Callie didn't answer, Eleanor picked up their conversation where it had left off.

"You were saying that it's not the diner."

"What is?"

Eleanor gave her a quizzical look.

"Whatever it was that has you so upset. You said it's not the diner. So what's the problem?"

Callie let out a long sigh.

"I guess I just miss my old job."

In a classic "I don't know" gesture with her palms up and shrugging her shoulders, Eleanor gave her a sweet smile.

"So go back."

"What?"

"Call them up and say you want to give it another go."

Eleanor didn't know all that had transpired and Callie wasn't about to start explaining it. At least, not all of it.

"It's not that easy."

"Nothing worthwhile is, hon."

"I left things badly. I left them at a bad time."

"There's rarely a good time to leave someone."

"You don't understand. Their biggest show of the year is tomorrow night and I just walked out a few weeks back, leaving them high and dry."

Eleanor enunciated every word.

"So go back."

Callie shot a glance at the clock over the cash register. It was almost six p.m. and the end of her shift. Eleanor's suggestion was terribly tempting and as of last night, she had more than one excuse to do it. The only question that remained was, should she?

Chapter Two

Vance awoke as he always did, ravenous and filled with a sort of youthful enthusiasm and excitement about the night that lay ahead. In the vast sea of humanity that existed just outside the door, pressing in and literally pulsating around him, there were so many experiences to be had, so many bodies to do in a dozen different ways. And, of course, there was so much blood to gulp down. Gallons upon gallons of the warm red elixir that in a perfect world filled his mouth and throat and soul while he simultaneously filled the squirming source beneath him with his hot cum. The thought of the endless opportunities made his head grow light and his cock hard but his sex-laden supper would have to wait. There was something to attend to first.

Leaping from his coffin he landed silently on the cold floor and sprinted barefoot downstairs to the main floor. The fireplace had already been lit, the stereo turned on and the brooding figure of his business partner lounging lazily on the loveseat facing the flames told Vance the former was in no better mood this evening.

"Hey. How's it going?"

The being on the sofa turned his head, his shaggy cinnamon-colored hair startlingly contrasted by the silver shade of his eyes. He raised one dark eyebrow.

"How do you think?"

"Oh, come on, Hart. Enough already. So she's gone. Big fucking deal. We'll get someone else."

"Will we really? Just like that? Funny, but it seems to me that the past three weeks of interviews have turned up exactly how many potentials again? Oh yeah. Zero."

"So what?" Vance flopped down beside him, playfully slinging a leg across Hart's. "We have another interview tonight, right? Maybe she's the one."

Determined to lighten the other's black state, Vance gave Hart one of his charming grins that never failed to make the slightly older vampire chuckle.

Only this time it didn't.

Instead Hart just regarded him, taking in the short fair hair, large turquoise eyes and smooth white skin, the latter sharply standing out against the black cotton shirt that was open to reveal his smooth chest. Vance's charm and sex appeal may not have made Hart laugh but it did manage to make a bulge shoot up in the front of his pants, the blood in his body racing to and stiffening his cock in record time.

Since things fell apart with Satin, Hart hadn't been in the mood for sex. At least not mentally. Choosing to use his incredible willpower to dam off the persistent and powerful tide of his supernatural sexual appetite, he had purposefully kept his distance from all potential lovers, including Vance. But the lack of physical stimulation and release would no longer be ignored, the sight of his hot prodigy so close to him rapidly giving him the mother of all hard-ons. Annoyed and frustrated, he looked back into the fire.

"We had the one and we let her slip away."

"*You* let her."

Hart's head snapped around but the look on his face was one of pain, not anger.

"Thanks a lot."

Vance raised his hands in mock self-defense.

"Hey, you had the argument with her, not me. I wasn't involved."

"You sure got that right. You *never* got involved. Just get in, get your rocks off and get out."

Surprised by the bitterness in Hart's voice, Vance nodded in urgent agreement.

"That's right. And I wouldn't have it any other way. Just look at the mess you're in now. You went and fucking fell in love with her. *In love* with an assistant and a mortal to boot. Hart, she was below us on so many levels."

Vance didn't see the lightning-speed punch coming, Hart's right fist cracking into his face with enough force to knock the fair-haired vampire onto the ground and split his lip. Licking the blood that sprang from the cut and dripped down his chin, Vance rose, his light eyes darkening in rage. And hurt.

"Don't ever talk about Callie like that again," Hart spat.

"I'd be happy never to talk about her at all. Now listen, I know you're torn up about this but you've got to get your shit together. We've got a show to do. Maybe the most important one of the year. In case you've forgotten, Halloween is tomorrow night."

"I haven't forgotten. I just…"

Hart rubbed his forehead, pressing his fingers in under each brow bone in an effort to get rid of the pounding headache that throbbed behind his eyes and in his temples.

Overcome with compassion, Vance crouched down on his haunches between Hart's knees and peered intently up into his face. His voice, when he spoke, was soft and kind.

"Look, man, if she means that much to you, go and get her."

Hart's hands dropped to his sides with a heavy sigh.

"I can't."

"Why not?"

"She left us, remember?"

"Yeah?"

Hart gave Vance a sad smile.

"If she really wanted to be here, she would be here."

Laying a gentle hand on Hart's leg, Vance asked quietly, "So what do you want to do?"

"I…" He stared at the floor, pushing past the pain to will himself into action. "I want to get ready for this interview and then get ready for the show."

Vance's gaze fell to Hart's bulky crotch where it lingered for a moment before lazily drifting back up to the other's face again.

"And maybe, get back to getting off?" He sounded hopeful. "After all, we have an eager applicant arriving in the not-too-distant future."

Hart couldn't help but laugh at Vance's insatiable lust.

"What if she doesn't want us?"

The stunned expression on Vance's face was comical. "Who has ever not wanted us?"

Hart opened his mouth to say "Callie" but closed it swiftly. There was no point in beating a dead horse. The three of them had a good thing going, a *great thing*, but now it was over. She was gone and he—*they*—had to move on without her. "Good point."

With a grin, Vance stretched up one pale slender hand and, pressing along the straining bulge in Hart's pants, began a leisurely torturous rub upon the immense lump.

"But ah, you'd better unload a bit first. One look at your too-big-to-believe package here and our potential new assistant will have a heart attack. Besides, if you don't, your precious jewels are going to blow to smithereens."

Vance was right.

Unlike their human counterparts, a vampire's semen production was always in constant overdrive, therein creating a very real and urgent physical need to eject the fluid, via orgasm, from the body. Failure to do so, at least every second day, resulted in an accumulation of liquid in the balls which, if not expressed, would bloat the guy's sac up to until it burst. Literally. It may take a month, maybe two until it happened but either way, it would not be a pleasant occurrence. The eruption, which like all other injuries to a vampire's body would heal, would not kill him, but it would sure make him wish he was dead. No, it would be best to go the infinitely more pleasurable route and get rid of the massive amount of fluid that had accrued over the past three weeks the old-fashioned way. His body designed to accomplish the formidable task, the backlogged male vampire could not only maintain an erection *ad infinitum*, he could and would experience multiple orgasms until the well was dry. But those first dozen or so, occurring with a hair-trigger response to the slightest thing, would be dillies, nearly knocking him unconscious with the force and volume of each ejaculation and shocking, albeit it pleasurably, those on the receiving end.

Hart grimaced, his head falling back against the couch as he clenched his teeth, his body immediately responding to the feel of Vance's expert hand movements along the rigid length of his stiffening rod to palpate his knob. He wasn't going to last long. The relentless and escalating pressure in his groin throbbed, the weeks of abstinence weighing heavy on his body that, along with his still-lengthening shaft, silently cried out for a painfully overdue release. Mortal men often made similar complaints with a shred of truth behind their more-times-than-not pleasure-seeking pleas, but nothing could be compared with the driving force and need of the suppressed male vampire. Now only seconds away from orgasm, Hart's canines had ripped through his gums and elongated like two porcelain hard-ons, the points drawing blood on his lower lip as he bit down hard, his body trembling continuously in a combination of anticipation and pre-ignition.

With a low moan, he shuddered roughly, his hips jerking forward toward the firm pressure of Vance's hand. Vance continued rubbing him with strong, steady strokes, letting out a low whistle at the feel of Hart's cock powerfully jerking beneath the constrictive fabric. Within seconds, his skilled touch easily made Hart come in his pants, a dark blotch appearing on the light-colored material, slowly expanding out in between and beyond Vance's fingers to entirely saturate the front of Hart's khakis.

"Yeah," Vance said slowly, as he undid Hart's zipper and pulled out his rock-hard rod which was now slathered with his own cum. Using the still-warm fluid as lube, Vance resumed a solid tip-to-base stroking rhythm of Hart's cock, only now with the added benefit of flesh-on-flesh contact. "You're ready to explode."

Explode he did, in four short strokes, the force and volume of the cadenced spurts that shot from his pulsing tool nearly ripping the slit from where they came. Powerful, almost angry gushes of molten lava shot from Hart's shaft while he helplessly convulsed, the vigorous contractions extracting four times the normal amount of semen with each heavy forceful squirt to land in a series of hard splatters against Vance's chest.

"I think you could be setting some kind of record here," Vance said as he ignored the glistening tracks of cum that streamed down his chest and adjusted his position to kneeling. "I mean it. I think we should be videoing this. Who knows? There might be a place in the *Guinness Book of Records* for you."

Taking note of the oversized bulk still hidden in the base of Hart's shorts, Vance pulled the band of his Jockeys back and looked inside. Shaking his head slowly, he clucked his tongue as he gently fingered the painfully overstretched mass of Hart's sac, his balls having ballooned up almost to the size of grapefruit. His touch, while tentative, still caused Hart to draw in his breath sharply. It was as he figured. Full-out massage of the distended, deeply discolored spheres would hurt too much right now but after he liberated several cups of cum from the swollen orbs, the pressure would let up a bit and light force against the bag would feel good.

"See what you've done to yourself? You do realize it's going to take you a lot of coming to get these babies back to normal."

With that, he returned his attention to Hart's gigantic cock, laying another good series of tight-fisted strokes on it only to end with one especially solid tug. Squeezing all the way up to finish with a pulsing fisted grip and twist on the purplish knob, Vance then used his thumb to make small circular presses on a small area just under the ridge of Hart's angry-looking head. Dizzy and panting, Hart let out a distinctly pleasurable groan, his eyes fluttering shut. His whole body was racked with the tempoed convulsions of his orgasm as he bombarded Vance's chest with another large and violent expulsion of steaming cum.

When his eyes next opened, Hart stared down the length of his torso, his cock jerking hard as he noted the glint of lust in Vance's eyes. With his mouth teasingly dancing around the tip of Hart's penis, Vance flicked his tongue only once against the distended taut skin, preparing to, with his legendary and masterful oral skills, continue on his mission to put an end to Hart's self-imposed sexual drought. As if knowing its own fate, Hart's thick, long shaft, a rigid blue vein coursing up its center, now twitched with the desperate painful need to be sucked good and hard until blazing jets of cum burst from it. Not that, in his present state, it would take a lot of sucking to achieve that goal. Quivering, he closed his eyes and waited.

Opening his mouth slightly to accommodate the tip of Hart's pulsing head, Vance guided the engorged cap very slowly into the wet, hot chasm of his mouth. Pursing his lips to surround Hart's tool with the soft inside of his lips, he sucked hard and lowered himself all the way, making a tight, moist cocoon around Hart's now-jerking rod as he swallowed hard, his throat muscles closing around it.

Sucking his cheeks in even more and tightening every muscle in his mouth, Vance pulled back to the tip of Hart's cock, which had now become granite. With each orgasm, Hart's cock grew only harder and longer, almost as if it knew the floodgates had been opened and it was damn determined to force every last drop of his pent-up semen from it as hard and as fast as possible.

Completing not even a dozen tight and wet top-to-bottom plunges on Hart's pole, Vance once again heard the sexiest sound in the world, the series of soft muffled thuds as Hart's semen was rhythmically pumped from his engorged sac and loaded into his cannon, ready to be fired.

"Ahhhhhh."

Hart groaned loudly, his body quaking violently as his hands suddenly clasped Vance's head, unconsciously trying to drive the hot, tight vacuum that surrounded him harder and faster upon his ready-to-pop cock. Making sure his own distended canines were covered with his lips, Vance squeezed his eyes shut and continued to suck Hart's now-jolting rod, bracing himself for the onslaught of cum that would blast into his mouth.

And it did blast. Harder and faster and hotter than he'd ever known. Vance swallowed repeatedly, trying to keep up with the massive amount of fluid that hit his tonsils and filled his mouth time and time again, but he just couldn't. Soon, a couple of milky streams oozed down other side of his face even as his mouth remained clamped tightly around Hart's twitching penis, his head dipping up and down in a fast steady pace.

As the spasms in Hart's body subsided to infrequent and minute tremors, Vance sucked all the way up Hart's still-erect cock and, pulling his mouth from the ever-ready-to-party cock that had lengthened to a vein-ridged ten inches, he smiled as he rubbed his own hard-on that, suffering from a week-long abstinence, was similarly raring to go. Or come, as it were. Prior to that, Vance had been taking matters into his own hands to facilitate his body's insistent need but anticipating the upcoming meeting, he had held off to give the woman a real treat.

"That's better. Now we're both ready for that interview."

Taking in the large wet stain on the front of Hart's pants and using his shirt to dry his glistening cum-splattered chest, he added with a grin, "Better shower and change first though."

Chapter Three

ॐ

Callie's hand trembled as she raised it and rapped lightly on the door. A long moment passed in which she stood quaking in her boots, her stomach feeling like it was filled with a mass of angry butterflies on speed. When her knock remained unanswered, with a degree of relief, she very quickly took the lack of response as fate and readied to go.

"Callie?"

Her back to the door, she winced at the sound of the voice she had so come to love over the past year. Sucking in a deep breath, she squared her shoulders and turned.

"Hi, Hart."

He smiled, that sexy grin, as always, making her feminine folds react hard and fast.

"Hi."

A long moment passed in which they just stared at each other. Then stepping back, Hart motioned to the space behind him.

"Did you want to come in?"

Reluctantly Callie did, her gaze quickly scanning the room for Vance. He wasn't there. What was, though, were the countless locations around the comfortable living room where the trio had repeatedly fucked and sucked their way to carnal bliss. The sofa, the love seat, the low wide coffee table, both of the high-backed armchairs, on practically every inch of the floor, the kitchen table barely visible around the corner just beyond and of course, smack-dab in front of the fireplace. Every spot held a vivid memory of the guys pounding her vagina, her sucking their cocks and swallowing their hot, salty ejaculate or getting her pussy flamboyantly French-kissed in a multitude of ways and positions. Blinking, Callie cleared her throat and, turning to face Hart, regarded him in silence. As always, his fabulous form looked hard and hot and ready to fuck, this time covered in a dark maroon shirt and tight gray pants — the crotch of which was conspicuously bulkier than she had remembered. Callie knew that his remarkably packed package, very clearly straining the zipper of his pants, meant Hart had not being having sex since she left — and the knowledge gave Callie a little encouraging thrill.

Another weird silence.

"So?" she began.

"So?"

"Where's Vance?"

"Upstairs."

Just then, the mantel clock on the fireplace's marble façade chimed loudly seven times.

"Was there something you wanted, Callie?"

"Wanted?"

"It's just that Vance and I have an interview at seven."

"An *interview*?"

"Yeah, for the new assistant."

Callie stared at Hart for a lengthy moment, then, with a soft chuckle, shook her head.

"What's so funny?"

"I think I'm it."

"What?"

"The interview."

Hart looked confused, a completely endearing expression on his usually serious face.

"Hart, Vance called me last night and asked if I would come over."

The expression of surprise on Hart's face revealed he was clearly out of the loop.

"He did?"

"Yes."

"What else did he say?"

"That you were miserable, unwilling to work on the show and being 'ridiculous'."

Callie's gaze dropped once more to the bulge in Hart's pants. When she next looked up at him, he was blushing.

"Is that *all*?"

"No. He also said that I was to blame."

"I never said that," Vance's voice from the overhead landing floated down as he sauntered down the stairs. "I said we all were partially to blame."

"Even you?" Hart posed a little sharply.

Vance nodded.

"Even me. I knew about your feelings for Callie and yet I didn't do anything to discourage them. In fact, I may have even pushed your buttons a little bit to play upon your jealousy."

"Jealousy?" Callie asked, clearly surprised. "You were jealous?"

Hart rolled his eyes and, with a deep breath, walked over to the fireplace and stared into it. Vance took the opportunity to answer for him.

"Hart had mentioned to me a few times about his concern that you and I were getting too chummy."

"Chummy?"

"That we were becoming more of a duo instead of a trio. In bed," he clarified. "You know, you and me instead of you, me and him. I knew it wasn't the case, I knew that it stemmed from the fact that he'd fallen madly in love with you."

Callie sucked in a quick breath. All along she had been fighting and hiding similar emotions for both Vance and Hart, never once suspecting that the feeling was mutual. She directed her next question to Hart.

"Is this true?"

He turned but didn't speak, his expression alone confirming Vance's assertion.

"Why didn't you say something?"

"Like what? You like him better than me, so I don't want to play anymore?"

"I don't know. But did you really think ignoring me and focusing more on Vance was the way?"

"That's just it. I wasn't thinking. I was reacting."

Vance jumped in.

"Just like you reacted, Callie, when you though Hart and I were edging you out."

"That's different."

"How, Satin?"

The endearment on Hart's lips shot through Callie like an arrow but she wasn't going to be sweet-talked out of her feelings.

"How? Have you both forgotten that my husband left me for another man? You think I want to be rejected by another man—in this case, two men—end up being a third wheel again?"

"Callie, Callie," Vance said, touching her tenderly on the shoulder. "Girl, you could never be a third wheel, not with us. This is just a crazy situation that got out of hand but never needed to."

"You can say that again," Hart said, his voice rising in volume. "None of this would have happened, Vance, if you hadn't pretended to feel for Callie in the first place."

"I never pretended."

"Bullshit! What was all that talk earlier of not getting involved?"

"It was just that. Bullshit."

Callie and Hart answered at the exact same time.

"What?"

Vance shrugged.

"Yeah, I know. It was an Oscar-winning performance but the truth is I love her too, man. As much as you do. As much as I love you."

Hart gave him a warm smile.

"Same."

Callie breathed heavily and glanced down, waiting for the next surprise to burst forth in this conversation of revelations. But it never came and when she next looked up, she saw both Vance and Hart regarding her expectantly. After their admissions of love for her and each other, the ball was in her court.

As much as she wanted to blurt out that yes, she loved both of them with all her heart and wanted nothing more than to pick up where they had left off, doubt and fear kept her from doing it. Instead, she backtracked and decided to tackle the supposed reason she had returned.

"Look, I think it's best if we put all that on the back burner for right now. Need I remind you that we have a Halloween show to prepare for?"

Vance and Hart swapped excited looks.

"So, you'll continue on with the show?"

"Yes. Just the show. And just until…"

"Until what?" Hart asked.

"Until you find my replacement."

Chapter Four
October 31

ಐ

A constant buzz rippled through the tiered auditorium of the Bellagio as the ten p.m. show crowd filed in and took their seats. Unlike other nights, Abracadabra held one show only on Halloween and unique to the night, the theme of the undead reigned supreme. Given the day, the crowd was ripe for spooky stuff of the supernatural nature so it was easy to play upon the masses' already psyched state right from the get-go. The ticket takers outside the auditorium were dressed in particularly ghoulish attire, one donning the unmistakable costume of a very realistic skeleton; the other wrapped in dirty tattered rags in an amazingly lifelike display of mummification.

Inside, a series of gasps and appreciative murmurs could be heard throughout the two-thousand-seat venue as people took in the magnificent layered set that sprawled out before and around them, the uncanny sight of wispy ghostlike apparitions flitting from time to time overhead or materializing in an empty seat, hovering strangely for a time before vanishing from sight. At the front of the massive multi-tiered circular stage, and looking every bit the medieval forest, a barrage of enormous leafless trees extended down either side of the space, making the crowd feel as though they were right in the woods. Looking positively gothic in their own right, the trees' gnarled branches were nearly black against the misty fog that drifted about the space. This despite the soft glow that, shining from the cloud-covered moon overhead, barely illuminated the entire area in an eerie blue light.

A not-so-babbling black-watered brook, flanked by a spotting of cragged, menacing-looking boulders, snaked down the center of the platform, fronting the gorgeous gothic castle that served as the focal point of the entire auditorium. Complete with a crumbling gray mortar façade, an authentic moat, a very unstable-looking drawbridge and a rugged octagonal tower, the castle's outer wall had been partially removed to reveal what would normally be the structure's inner courtyard on the other side. But in this theatrically altered depiction, the interior of the castle was exposed. Housing an ornately laid-out sitting room richly decorated in red, black and mahogany with a winding staircase near the rear that rose to a balconied second level some one hundred feet in the air, the entire enchanted area was lit by umpteen dozen candles strategically situated in candelabras about the room, their flickering flames working to heighten the hall's spooky atmosphere.

As the house lights slowly went down and the erotic pulse of the ambient music came up, a dreamlike mist bubbled and crept from the moat, extending forward into the forest and back into the castle, just as the hair-raising howl of wolves pierced the sudden stillness of the place.

Out of the fog from the right side of the stage came a lone figure, its full-length black cape and large circular hood hiding its identity. Clutching an oil lamp in its hand, the individual walked tentatively to the center of the stage, turning from time to time to look over each shoulder, even completing half a rotation at one point to face the rear of the stage, its movements insinuating that it was lost.

Or looking for something.

Another peculiar canine bay sliced the air and the figure whipped about to face the audience, the motion dropping the hood from its head.

It was Callie. With her long dark hair loosely caught up in a tousled bun, from which lazy tendrils fell to frame her narrow face, her striking emerald eyes outlined in black and her lips colored blood red, she was an absolute vision.

Just then a large black wolf entered the scene from the left, skulking toward his prey with a horrifyingly languorous but steady stride. Gasping, Callie took a couple of cautious steps back, but when she caught the edge of her full, long cape with one heel, the latch at her throat came loose and tore the garment from her shoulders. Underneath she wore her usual costume, a feminine flimsy shift, the bodice pushing her curvaceous breasts up, while the chiffon hem floated around her upper thighs. Stumbling, she fell to her knees and in a flash, the huge black wolf was on her, his large paws resting on either side of her shoulders as he pushed her flat.

As she let out a shrill scream, a blast of smoke shot up to surround them and seconds later Vance stood upright, holding Callie in his arms. The transformation left the audience baffled and thrilled as they erupted into a deafening applause.

Looking every bit the young hot hunk he was, Vance was clad in red and black, the latter constant in his pants and shirt, the color of blood blazing in the knee-length brocade overcoat that, in its brilliance, stood out against his fair complexion and platinum hair.

Glancing down at Callie, he gave her a quick wink before grabbing her cape and carrying her into the castle. As he did, a blue spotlight appeared high up on the terrace, the light shining on the mesmerizing figure of Hart. Looking more wonderful than ever, he was wearing tight ivory britches and matching leather boots, a billowing ivory shirt and a crushed velvet waistcoat that, brushing his knees and hiding the enormous bulk of his still-oversized cock and balls, was exactly the silver shade of his eyes. Raising his arms, he levitated forward, his body floating up and over the wrought iron balcony to very slowly glide the hundred or so feet down the ground. The crowd went wild, screaming, clapping and whistling, the supernatural display unlike anything they'd ever seen.

By now, Vance had set Callie on her feet and, sauntering over to them, Hart wrapped her in his arms, his eyes warmly locking with hers as he bent her backward and made as if he was sucking her blood. Normally he would mimic the motion but this time he gave Callie a tiny little love bite, again the suction of his mouth shielding her nerves from the prick of his teeth much the way squeezing flesh before inserting the tip of a needle practically eliminates the pain of the prick. While he took very little blood from her, the work of his lips and tongue on her flesh managed to raise the hair on the back of her neck and fill her pussy with cream.

As Hart nuzzled her, Vance lightly clasped Callie's ankles and stretched them out so she was completely horizontal while her upper body was still held in Hart's embrace. With one hand holding up her ankles in a freakish display of strength, Vance then used the other hand to place her cape over her body, extending it up and around where Hart held her. Adjusting the fabric to ensure she was well covered, Vance then released the hand that had been holding her ankles, slipping it under the material and up between her thighs, his fingers pressing firmly against her clit before trailing up and giving one breast a little squeeze—the undercover fondling completely undetected by the audience. As Hart released her and pulled away, Vance did too.

This brought on another gasp from the crowd who were astounded at the sight of Callie lying perfectly horizontal with nothing and no one holding her there.

Hart then covered her face with the cloth so now she was completely covered and continued to hover at eye level without any aid from either Hart or Vance. With one hard, fast movement, he pulled the cape from her body to reveal empty space. She had vanished.

Or had she?

A light fired up in the middle of the stairwell and there she stood, her arms raised high overhead.

More frenzied applause and cheers.

For the next two and a half hours, the night continued on with similarly astounding and inexplicable displays. In addition to a handful of "traditional" tricks like sawing Callie in half and Hart escaping from Houdini's water torture, there were more vanishings and reappearances, more transformations and more levitations and flying stunts, with Callie's favorite part of the show saved for the grand finale. With arms intertwined and ne'er a line or lead in sight, the three rose up and, flying over the heads of the flabbergasted crowd, soared to the ceiling and then to the back of the auditorium before touching down. In a flash of smoke, they disappeared.

* * * * *

With Abracadabra's Halloween extravaganza behind them, Callie retreated to her spacious luxury dressing room in the Bellagio. More a suite than a change room, in addition to an extensive closet and makeup area, it came equipped with a fireplace, bar, futon and conversational seating space centered by a quartet of overstuffed modern chairs and a massive polar bear rug. As she undid her hair and brushed it out, Callie wondered how long she would need to fill in until the guys found someone else. Maybe this was it, their very last show together.

Peeling off her costume, she headed for the shower, glancing en route at the connecting door to Vance and Hart's dressing room. How many times had they slipped in after a show and well, *slipped in*, the three enjoying a hard and fast fuck on the floor, Hart lightly closing his hand over her mouth when Callie's rapturous cries became a little too loud? Too many times to count. But not tonight. Not ever again. With a frown, she retraced her steps and silently flipped the deadbolt on the door, effectively preventing them from entering.

By now, it was well after midnight and the hot streams of water did wonders in relaxing her. Washing her hair and face after she had thoroughly soaped and rinsed her body, Callie emerged fresh-faced and damp, only to wrap one of the hotel's cozy terrycloth robes about her. Padding out into the room, she halted abruptly, shocked to see Vance and Hart lounging lazily in her suite. She didn't want to know how they got in there but would wager it was through their supernatural abilities. While both were freshly showered and barefoot, they had changed back into their street clothes. Where Vance was slumped seductively in one of the chairs, his legs spread invitingly apart, Hart was standing with his toned, muscular butt leaning against the futon, one hand resting casually on either side.

"All clean?"

"Ah...yeah."

Vance stood up.

"Wanna get dirty?"

Callie looked down and shook her head, a light smile begrudgingly spreading her lips. The moment was so bittersweet, she couldn't speak.

"We can make this work, Callie," Vance said soothingly as he sauntered toward her. "I know we can. There's lots of loving to be had for us all."

"I do love you. *Both*."

"We know that. That's why we want to give it to you. And we know you want to give it to us."

Callie misunderstood his words.

"So that's what this is all about? We're just going to be fuck buddies. Is that it?"

Vance looked shocked.

"Oh no! Is that what you think? Oh no, Callie. We want you back all the way—in the act, in our beds, in our hearts. The three of us, from here on in."

Callie looked at Hart, who wordlessly stood perfectly still, watching her closely.

"And what do you say about all this?"

"I agree."

"Mind elaborating a little?"

Hart knew she was trying to get him to confess his feelings for her, say those three little words that, while he had admitted to feeling them, he had yet to declare them directly to her. But given his serious, reserved nature, he wasn't about to do that. Not just yet.

"I want it the way it was before. The three of us. Just like Vance said."

"Why?"

"Because I…"

His beseeching gaze bore into her eyes, his own now dancing with looks of lust and love.

"You what?" she whispered.

Pushing himself away from the futon, Hart walked over to her and, taking her face in his hands, leaned down and kissed her, a slow, wet erotic kiss that said everything he couldn't. From behind she could feel Vance's hands on her back and hips, his palms moving and down in slow, soothing caresses.

Pulling back from Hart's mouth, Callie tilted her head back and, turning her face to Vance, kissed his lips, a long, lazy soothing set of kisses that both comforted her and fanned her passion as Hart's hands dropped down and undid the belt of her robe. Back and forth she kissed one after the other, each kiss deeper, longer and more intense than the last. The guys' fangs, having grown long and hard like little ceramic erections, nipped sexily at her lips and tongue.

As Hart pushed her robe off, Callie unbuttoned his shirt and then, turning around so she had her back to him, pulled at the waist of Vance's tee and yanked it over his head. Kissing him full frontal, their tongues swirling wildly about each other, Callie became aware of Hart's lips on her neck and ear. With a slight move of her head to the left, she reached up and back, guiding Hart's face forward. She then pulled back from

Vance's lips and with her hand, directed Hart's chin on toward Vance. When he realized her intent, Hart stopped and both he and Vance looked at her imploringly. Placing a soft warm kiss on both of their lips, she smiled and nodded. Turning to each other, Vance and Hart kissed, the sight of their increasingly hot and heavy exchange making her pussy pound like never before.

Reaching out, she unzipped Vance's pants, lowering them and his shorts to his ankles before guiding one foot and then the other up and out. His balls, looking like puffy flesh-colored oranges pushing against the constraints of his sac and stiff ten-inch cock, made her mouth immediately water. Kneeling before him, she stuffed his cock between her parted lips and, sucking in her cheeks, fell into a steady solid rhythm bobbing up and down on his cock. Wrapping her arms about his hips, she clutched the globes of his ass and wedging her fingers in along his crease, lightly dug in her nails on either side of his anus. He groaned, his hips jerked forward and a powerful surge of hot creamy semen hit the back of her throat again and again. Spluttering, Callie worked hard to gulp down the forceful sprays, immediately aware that the volume was more than it had been in the past and more than she could swallow. With Vance's hands now on either side of her head, holding her still as he pumped his shaft into the sweet vacuum of her mouth, Callie did her best to drink all of Vance's searing cum but the little stream that had started at the corner of her mouth very quickly turned into a river, the milky white liquid snaking down her chin and along her neck.

When Vance stopped coming, Callie quickly turned her attention to Hart's enormous cock. Easily two inches longer and one inch thicker than it had been only weeks earlier, the only thing more incredible than its twelve-inch length was what lay underneath. Still ballooned up, Hart's massive balls had stretched the skin of his sac so tight it was practically translucent and she could see the mass of veins on the freakishly large purplish globes contained within.

"Oh my God. Doesn't this hurt?"

When he didn't answer, she looked up. He was smiling that dead-sexy grin.

"Yeah. But it won't for long."

Leaning forward, Callie pressed a number of delicate kisses on his puffed-up sac before laying a bunch of end-to-end licks on his throbbing cock, breathing in the musky distinctive scent of his genitals as she did. With a heavy sigh, Hart slowly dropped to his knees and Callie shifted to all fours, allowing Vance the opportunity to walk around and fuck her from behind. But first he knelt down and tongue-fucked her, slurping hungrily from his anterior position at her dripping slit until her ass jiggled and jerked with the need to come. Gripping her hips, he then repositioned himself and rammed his hard cock into her pussy just as she took the bulb of Hart's delicious cock into her mouth.

Sucking slowly and strongly, Callie swhirled her tongue around the sensitive tip, flicking against the ridge in that special area as he had taught her. At that, the sound of Hart's inner pump, forcing an incredible amount of cum up out of his balls and very soon out of his twitching cock, thudded loudly, the strange sound perplexing Callie. Only when Hart steadied the back of her head with one hand and began thrusting his pole into the hot, wet cavern of her mouth did she recognize the noise for what it was, a warning. He was going to come and all things considered, it wasn't going to be like any orgasm before it.

Callie's jaw was starting to ache, so wide was her mouth stretched to accommodate Hart's still-growing shaft but she continued to suck heartily at his distended length as it plunged in and out. When the first violent blast hit her tonsils, she gagged, not even having time to attempt to swallow before a second and third and fourth spray battered the roof of her mouth, her tongue and the inside of her cheeks. This time, there was no containing the massive quantity of ejaculate that was flooding into her mouth every couple of seconds, the cum spilling readily from between her lips to drench her chin, neck and chest even as she tried to continue sucking his shuddering shaft. Hart groaned loudly, oblivious to the fact he was nearly drowning Callie and Vance crammed his explode-ready cock into her with increased force until he too came, the two simultaneously filling Callie's pussy and mouth with frenzied jets of their sizzling cum. Just as Hart finished and pulled himself from between her saturated lips, the intense pounding of Callie's pussy compliments of Vance's doggy-style fucking sent her over the edge. As she rode the wave, Callie heard Hart's voice softly in her ear.

"Mmmm. That's it, Satin. It's your turn to come. Now shoot it real good."

Having finished his orgasm, Vance worked to maximize Callie's by spreading the domes of her ass apart and using his supernatural strength to pump inhumanly hard and fast into her pussy. With a scream she exploded, unaware of Hart who had leaned down, biting into her shoulder and sucking the blood that bubbled up under his lips.

No sooner had she plummeted back to earth than Callie felt Hart wriggle his body underneath hers. Sliding down between her legs so that she was straddling his face, he stretched up and locked his lips around her inflamed clit even as Vance continued driving into her glistening cunt from the rear. Still close to her sexual summit, it wasn't long before the feel of Hart's mouth on the distended nub at the top of her pussy and the pressure of Vance's hard, thick rod inside her made her come again, her back end twitching and bucking with the force of her contractions. Feeling it grasping hard along his ready-to-burst shaft, Vance growled, his lips drawing back to reveal his long, hard fangs as he shot another steaming load of cum into Callie's increasingly tight, sopping pussy, lunging forward to bite and suck the side of her neck as he did.

Panting and lightheaded, Callie could only watch through eyes dazed with desire as the guys next rearranged themselves and lightly flipped her so she was on her back in a tried-and-true scenario with Vance at her head and Hart at her feet. Loving them was always an intense experience but on Halloween when the guys revealed their true natures to an unwitting show crowd, their stealthily veiled "coming out" heightened the fervor of their post-show celebration.

Reaching around to knead her now cum-slathered breasts, Vance pushed the voluptuous globes together to create a slippery tight valley. Straddling her torso, Hart then inserted his pole into the slick valley Vance had created of Callie's boobs and slid his cock back and forth, back and forth. From her perspective, Callie could see the bulky purplish knob of Hart's cock push through the tight crevice of her breasts every few seconds as he rhythmically stroked into the makeshift vagina, the telltale siphoning sound of his cum in transit once more announcing the onslaught that was about to take place. As Vance bent over and began suckling one of Callie's large tawny nipples, Hart quickly tilted her head back a little so she wouldn't be sprayed in the face. Then thrusting faster, his full-to-bursting balls swaying heavily with their weight, Hart threw his head back, his fangs glinting in the light, as the first spurt of cum struck Callie under the chin. Groaning over and over again, he spewed one painful blast after the other of his blistering semen against her neck, chest and breasts.

Moving down, Hart then took his place between Callie's legs. Vance released her now-dripping boobs and, hooking one hand behind each one of her knees, pulled Callie's legs up and apart, holding her in place while Hart fastened his lips around her clit once more. Callie moaned, her eyes rolling back in her head, as Vance softly encouraged them both.

"Eat that pretty pussy, eat it good. That's the way. Oh yeah, Suck that clit. She is loving that large."

Sucking hard and fast on the bump, Hart pulsed his fingers in and out of Callie's drenched cunt, mumbling against her nub as she came, the walls of her vagina clutching tightly around his fingers as they continued to drive into her. The feel of her tight flesh grasping all around him in a hot, wet circle of contraction just about made Hart come on its own and he knew right there and then, he had to bury his burning cock inside that sweet, snug sheath.

Rising swiftly to his knees, Hart sunk into her pussy in one fast movement, delving himself in all the way up to his balls, the girth of his throbbing hard-on taking Callie's breath away. Clasping her ankles and extending them skyward, Hart pumped mercilessly, the thump-thump-thump of his heavy sac landing with a cadenced thud against Callie's anus. While Vance turned around and, kneeling with one leg on either side of Callie's face, eased his still-jerking rod into her mouth, Hart crammed his foot-long cock into the snuggest, wettest pussy he'd ever felt, ruthlessly driving them both to four back-to-back orgasms in just under a couple of minutes. Vance wasn't far behind, a couple of quick expulsions of semen filling Callie's mouth and sliding easily down her throat, thankfully now in much smaller, more manageable quantities. His soft caveat of "Don't bite me, babe" reminded her of the tender tool in her mouth even as multiple orgasms ricocheted through her body. Gasping with each one, Callie could actually feel the force and heat of the voluminous violent spurts that blasted from Hart's cock inside her, a steady stream of blistering cum now dripping from her pussy to snake down and pool on the floor beneath them. She was so caught up in the magnificence and power of the moment, she almost missed the soft whispered declaration that fell from Hart's lips as he hammered her hard.

"I love you, Callie. I love you, I love you," his murmured, words giving way to a loud groan as another powerful gush of cum hit her cervix with incredible force, his orgasm instantaneously triggering hers, just as the hot, pungent liquid spilled from Vance's cock into her mouth while he quaked and came atop her too.

Rising, Vance then got up and moved around to take a new position behind Hart. Now with Vance out of the way, Hart could press his torso more fully flat against Callie and come face-to-face with her. With her legs still over his shoulders, this brought her feet up to dangle on either side of her head and for a long moment, they were still, staring into each other's eyes and softly kissing each other's lips, as Vance lubed up Hart's puckered hole. Then inserting his still-hard cock into Hart's anus, his hands clasped Hart's shoulders for traction and slowly he began the cycle of withdrawing and thrusting. Rocking in opposite directions—Hart pushing forward into Callie as Vance pulled out of Hart and vice versa—the three slowly increased their speed and force until they had bucked and clutched and fucked their way to a seemingly endless string of orgasms that left them all cum-soaked, gasping and pretty much void of all bodily fluids.

When it was finally over and the trio lay in a crumpled heap, drenched and sticky, exhausted but happy, hands lightly caressing skin and soft kisses being given and received in total silence, Vance's quiet voice broke the hushed serenity that enveloped them.

"Callie, there's something else we didn't mention."

Callie's heart skipped a beat.

"Oh? What?"

"It may change things between us."

Another skipped beat and real fear now had a death grip on the muscles in her chest. Rising up on both elbows, she looked at Vance who lay on her right.

"Go on."

"Well..."

Vance exchanged looks with Hart who, on her left, had now rolled onto his side and, smiling, propped his head up in one hand.

"What?" she nearly cried. "What is it?"

"We would like you to...move in with us."

Callie beamed.

"You would?"

"More than anything, Satin," Hart murmured into her ear.

"Never wanted anything more," Vance said, planting a light kiss on her shoulder.

"But what if…"

"What?"

Callie could barely bring herself to say the words.

"What if you get tired of me?"

A hush stretched out for what felt like forever before Vance and Hart started to laugh.

"Callie, sweet, that's never going to happen."

"Never."

"But when I get older…"

"Sssshhh," Hart said, silencing her with his index finger pressed lightly against her lips. "If you're really worried about it, we'll talk about that later. There are always options."

He grinned his sexy smile, the movement revealing his fangs that were still erect and as he ran his tongue over the tip of one, Callie knew he was hinting at the possibility of turning her into what they were.

"But as far as we're concerned, we'll never tire of you. In fact, I'm not tired now. Are you, Hart?"

Hart's eyes sparkled.

"Nope."

Looking from one to the other in amazement, Callie's gaze moved from Vance's massive hard-on over to Hart's. Their erect tools and full sacs, while basically back to normal size after the night spent expelling every bit of bottled-up semen from their immortal bodies, were nevertheless still ready to party. She laughed.

"Don't you guys ever get enough?"

"Of you?" Hart asked, to which he and Vance both answered at the same time.

"Never."

Then easing her back down on the rug, Vance and Hart and Callie christened the beginning of the rest of their lives together in another pulse-pounding time of love on the magical day that started it all — Halloween.

NOCTURNAL OBSESSION

Lolita Lopez

ഌ

Trademarks Acknowledgement

The author acknowledges the trademarked status and trademark owners of the following wordmarks mentioned in this work of fiction:

Chippendale: Chippendales USA

Civic Hybrid: Honda Motor Co., Ltd.

Rubik's Cube: Ideal Toy Corporation

Tod's: Tod's S.P.A.

Chapter One
ဆ

With her pale blue nightgown fluttering above her knees, her bare feet padded across the soft Persian carpet as she entered a room that was a veritable den of iniquity. The space was decorated in the style of a harem, yards of overlapping saffron silk draping the walls while contrasting panels of gauzy crimson curtained off an area directly across the room. Heady scents of jasmine, sandalwood and frankincense permeated the heavy night air. Lowering her eyelids, she breathed deeply, infusing her lungs with the aromatic aphrodisiacs. Smiling lazily, she opened her eyes and welcomed the rich colors and dim lighting. They encouraged relaxation, and instantly her stressful burdens began to diminish, fading away from her thoughts as she focused on enjoying the present.

Perusing the room, she approached a pair of short, square benches with tufted chartreuse cushions. Silver trays of chocolate delicacies and chilled champagne sat upon the cushions, and she obliged her sweet tooth by nibbling a square of chocolate and swallowing a tipple of the cold champagne. As she enjoyed the epicurean delights, she surveyed the room with a closer eye. To her left stood a plush sofa upholstered in stripes of orange and yellow chenille. A mosaic table in front of the sofa bore a crystal *hookah*, already assembled with a vase full of water, the *shisha* carefully packed into the bowl. On one side of the *hookah* were wooden boxes of charcoal, matches and assorted *shishas* for replenishing; on the other sat a bottle of absinthe, glasses, a bowl of sugar cubes and a carafe of ice water, everything required to mix up a perfect complement to the smoking experience.

Her champagne flute empty, she returned it to the silver tray. She crossed the room with a purpose, curious to see what lay behind the red gossamer curtains. Grasping the edges, she drew back the thin curtains and discovered a long, wide mattress resting directly on the floor. It was covered in glossy chartreuse sheets with dozens of satin pillows in various colors scattered across it. She tested the firmness of the mattress with her toes. It gave just enough that she was seized by an urge to fall back onto it, spread eagle, but she resisted.

It was odd really, but she couldn't quite remember how she came to be in this room or why she had come here in the first place. It almost seemed familiar but, well…wasn't. It was all very confusing, and as she tried to work it out, her forehead wrinkled and she pensively bit her lower lip.

Suddenly, she was aware of another presence in the room. Innately sensitive, she listened for the telltale sounds of footsteps and extended her protective aura in a defensive gesture. She felt no danger as she slowly searched the room with her gaze and slightly relaxed her tense muscles. And then she saw him stepping out from behind an intricately carved wooden screen.

He brazenly presented his nude form, confidently striding slowly toward her. Eyes widening, she raked a surprised albeit appreciative glance across his naked body. To say that he was a genuine Adonis seemed an understatement. He radiated raw sexuality with his bronzed and toned body, angular jaw and aquiline nose. Piercing azure eyes and tousled straw-colored hair added to his captivating nature, but it was something else that captured her attention — a sizeable erection jutting forth from a tuft of blond hair.

And what a cock it was! Thick, turgid and the head already scarlet with arousal. Instinctually, her tongue stole out to lick her lips as thoughts of taking that proud cock into her mouth rushed through her mind. She imagined the feel of his hot skin against her lips, her tongue caressing the tip, his hands in her hair, gripping her face…

Her cheeks flamed with embarrassment as she realized that she was staring, and she swallowed, suddenly self conscious. Seemingly amused, he boldly met her gaze and daringly crossed the remaining space between them. Her breath hitched in her throat as he stopped a foot short of her.

"Good evening, Desi," he said, his voice a smooth rumble, his accent distinctly affluent British.

"D-Dr. Cuvos," Desi stammered, overwhelmed by the woodsy, spicy scent of his skin.

"Ian," he gently corrected. His fingertips trailed the curve of her cheek and he tilted her chin up with his fingers. "I thought we had worked that out last night. When we're here, together like this, I'm just Ian."

"Yes," Desi murmured, her heart stuttering as his fingers followed the turn of her throat and traced the outline of her collarbone.

"How was your champagne?" Ian idly toyed with the strap of her nightgown as he slowly paced around her.

"Fine," she whispered, cautiously watching as he circled her. She shuddered nervously as he stopped behind her, snaking his arm around her waist, drawing her buttocks against him. She gasped at the feel of his cock stabbing the cleft of her ass and he chuckled with amusement.

"I think I've had enough of the pleasantries," Ian said, his lips against her ear. His tongue licked the sensitive area just below her earlobe and her knees buckled slightly. He turned her chin until their eyes met over her shoulder. "I say we skip the boring bits and get right to the fun parts. What do you think, darling?"

Desi thought that sounded divine but could only manage a mute nod. She was entirely focused on the sight of his descending mouth and moistened her lips in anticipation of a kiss. Ian's lips touched hers, lightly at first, but the pressure increased as the kiss deepened. His tongue swept the small space between her lips, gently prodding its way between them.

She groaned at the sensation of his tongue invading her mouth and twisted in his arms until her breasts were pressing against his naked chest. His hands drifted south from the curves of her waist, and he grabbed two handfuls of her luscious ass, squeezing and kneading through the thin fabric of her nightgown.

Moaning, Desi arched against him, her thighs clenching as hot fluid started to coat the inner lips of her pussy. Desire consumed her thoughts and she wanted nothing more than to lie naked on the bed with Ian, to have his hands roaming her body, his mouth tasting her skin. As their tongues danced, Ian worked the hem of her nightgown up over her ample hips and broke their sensual kiss just long enough to draw it past her mouth before carelessly flinging it aside and claiming her mouth once again.

In one seamless motion he grasped the backs of her thighs and lifted her from the ground. She wound her legs tightly around his waist as he carried her toward the bed. With the utmost gentility, he lowered her back to the mattress and lay down beside her, keeping one hand planted on her body as he continued to make love to her mouth. Sighing, she broke away from his lips, her eyes closed as she reveled in the feeling of his hands caressing her breasts. His tweaked a nipple with his right hand, teasing it before he placed it between his lips and swirled his tongue around the hardening tip.

Groaning, Desi bucked beneath him. The fingers of his left hand slipped between her teeth and she lightly bit them, rolling her head back in ecstasy. He shifted his position until he was leaning over her and she clutched at his ribs, running her fingernails up and down his sides. As she panted and moaned beneath him, he sucked and nipped her heaving breasts. Every time his tongue darted across a nipple, the sensation went straight to her stiffening clit as it clamored for his touch.

As if reading her mind, he flattened his palm, slowly sliding it down her front and tracing the outline of her navel before letting it settle on the fleshy mons. She inhaled sharply with anticipation as he petted her newly waxed lips. Desi lifted her hips in hopes of coaxing his fingers to touch her burning clit, but to no avail. He seemed to thrive on the teasing and moved his hand farther away from her pussy to stroke the insides of her thighs. He pressed soft kisses down her stomach, following the path his hand had taken until he was kneeling before her. He slowly parted her knees and whistled with appreciation as he trained his gaze on her glistening pussy lips.

"I can't wait to get my tongue on your clit," Ian said, his gaze locked with hers.

Desi's slick passage contracted as he spoke and her body ached for satisfaction, for his intimate touch. He situated himself between her thighs, and his hot breath fanned the delicate exposed skin. He placed feathery kisses along the sensitive insides of her thighs, delaying the inevitable and ratcheting up her anticipation for that first contact.

"Your pussy smells so good," he murmured as he inhaled the musky scent of her sex.

"Ian," she groaned, embarrassed but highly aroused by his frank statement. Desi watched in fascination as he tenderly parted the folds and revealed the shiny pink flesh. Her body tensed as she awaited that first touch of his tongue, but instead, he leisurely ran a finger up and down her slippery slit. Throwing her head back, she fought to breathe as he circled her clit and dragged his finger down to the small opening, playing at the entrance but never penetrating.

"Ian!" she desperately implored.

His icy blue eyes met hers over the gentle curve of her tummy, and he chuckled at the needy expression coloring her face.

"Say it," he instructed. "Tell me what you want."

"Please, Ian," Desi begged, her cheeks flaming at the thought of asking.

Smiling devilishly, he shook his head. "I know what you want, Desi, but I won't give it to you until you ask."

To prove his point, he started to back away from her. Slightly panicked by the thought of his ceasing, she gathered her courage. "Suck my pussy, Ian!"

"Yes, ma'am," Ian replied, leering triumphantly. By the slowest of degrees, he extended his tongue and swiped the broad plank against the firm nub hidden beneath its pink hood. She bucked and groaned with pent-up need, encouraging his attention. He swirled his tongue around her clit before sucking it between his lips and wagging his head from side to side. Writhing and fisting the sheets, Desi thought she might pass out. Her stomach knotted, her calves tightened and her toes dug into the mattress as Ian continued his expert ministrations. The wet sounds of Ian slurping her pussy echoed in the room and she closed her eyes, focusing on the feeling of his tongue against her clit.

As she lost herself in the perfection of the moment, her mind wandered. Perfect as this was, she couldn't help but imagine what it would feel like if this were truly a harem, if there were a handful of men just as dedicated to her pleasure as Ian seemed to be. What would it feel like to have multiple hands and mouths on her body?

While she shuddered violently at the thought of such an encounter, she became vaguely aware of a strengthening scent in the air. Cloves, she realized. Desi thought she heard a sound from somewhere off to her right, but as she lifted her head in curiosity, Ian renewed his suckling in earnest. She quickly lost interest in the sound and returned her attention to the pleasure at hand. He slipped a finger into her pussy and she instinctively squeezed it. He made a guttural sound of approval and began moving the finger in and out while he lapped at her throbbing clit. Eyes clamped shut, she panted as an orgasm built. She was close, so very, very close…

The tingling sensation of fingernails lightly scraping her arms caused her eyes to shoot open, and she stiffened at the sight of two strange men surrounding her. They were athletic Chippendale types in black leather collars who shamelessly displayed their nakedness. The one with wavy brown hair had a distinctive Mediterranean look about him while the redheaded man looked very Midwestern with his bulky shoulders and tight abs. As if to ease her anxiety, the men smiled at her, their ethereal copper eyes shining, but it did little to lessen her fright. Desi tried to bolt upright, but it was almost as if invisible ropes were restraining her to the mattress. Who were these men, and where the hell had they come from?

"Friends of mine," Ian said, halting his licking and suckling to answer a question that hadn't been asked. "Red and Nicco," he explained as he pointed them out. His expression suddenly matched Desi's frown. "Isn't this what you wanted?" he carefully asked, his eyebrows furrowed with uncertainty.

What she wanted? How was he doing that? Was he reading her mind? And how had he fabricated men from thin air?

"Later, my love," Ian said, smiling with amusement. "Soon it will all make sense, but for now, lie back and let us give you what you desire."

Desi wanted to argue, but Ian returned his mouth to her inflamed clit and suddenly, none of the details mattered. She was consumed by sexual need and it clouded her judgment. Later, when her passions had been sated, she would seek answers, but for now she was determined to enjoy this for what it was—a chance of a lifetime.

Nicco, the dark-haired slave, began massaging her foot while Red lay down beside her. Surrendering to desire, Desi reached for Red and drew his mouth closer, sensually brushing her lips against his. Lost in Red's erotic kisses, Desi gave little thought to the cool, smooth sensations wrapping around her thighs and arms. It wasn't until Ian stopped licking and she felt that first gentle tug on her limbs that she broke away from Red's kiss.

Sitting back on his heels, Ian watched his friends work with efficiency. Desi's pulse quickened at the sight of the white silk ropes that the collared men were looping around her extremities and waist. Five long, braided ropes suspended from ceiling hooks wound around her thighs and waist to hold her body horizontal, while loops attached to her upper arms kept them immobile and perpendicular to her trunk. At present, the slaves were bending her legs gently until her heels touched the backs of her thighs before using a series of loops and knots to secure her legs in place. Nicco pulled a length of rope from behind a pillow and began winding it around Desi's breasts, creating a halter-style bra of sorts.

Desi gulped, slightly terrified but mostly thrilled by the prospect of bondage. She had seen pictures of women bound in Japanese erotic bondage but never had she dared to dream that it might happen to her someday. While the ropes could be used in a variety of increasingly restrictive and painful ways, these loops and knots were a simple introduction to the erotic art form.

When the men had finished securing the ropes around Desi's body, Ian tossed aside a pillow and pressed a button hidden in the floor. Very slowly, the ropes dangling from the ceiling began to tighten, and as the slack left them, Desi was gently hoisted from the mattress. The pressure along her arms and thighs increased, but it was far from painful. The intricate coils around her waist bore most of the weight of suspension, and she found the horizontal position freeing and highly sensitizing.

Ian stopped the hoist when she was suspended a few feet above the mattress. Almost immediately, Nicco and Red descended upon her. There were tongues on her toes and fingers, and hands massaged her ass. With fiery possession burning his gaze, Ian approached Desi with an opal nipple chain hanging from his hand and halted next to her dangling head. Her breasts were already tender and heavy from being constricted by the crisscrossing ropes, and she hesitantly eyed the clamps. Wordlessly, Ian palmed her left breast, gently at first, but increasing the pressure of his squeezing as she acclimated to the feeling of his hand on her overly sensitive skin. He licked his fingers and used his saliva as a buffer as he tweaked her engorged nipple. Her pussy pulsed as he rolled the nipple between his fingers and when he finally attached the first nipple clamp, the mixture of pain and pleasure was so intense she almost came. He just smiled and repeated the same process on her right breast.

Stepping even closer to her head, he stroked the length of his raging hard-on. Desi hungrily stared at it and Ian decided to capitalize on the ravenous look. He nudged her mouth with the tip of his cock and she willingly accepted it, widening her lips as it passed over her tongue. He pressed it halfway into her mouth before withdrawing. She licked the head and tasted the salty hint of pre-come. Even though she was technically the helpless one, he was just as turned on as she was and at this moment, completely at her mercy. A wicked smile curled her lips.

It quickly vanished as Ian tugged on the nipple chain. The pain was fleeting but it served its purpose, reminding Desi who was in charge. Still, she boldly met his gaze, almost daring him to pull the chain again. He obliged and she bucked with pleasure.

Ian abandoned the chain and placed his hand on the back of her head. He guided Desi's mouth over his cock, this time plunging it almost to the hilt. Her jaw tightened in slight panic, but one tug on the nipple chain and she was forcing her jaw to relax, to accept his cock deep into the alcove at the back of her throat. Satisfied with her response, he withdrew his cock and thrust it into her mouth again. There was no malice in his action, no desire to demean her, so Desi allowed him to fuck her face with increasing speed.

By now, Desi was so aroused that she could feel her pussy juices dripping from her thighs. Even though there were two talented tongues on her body, her clit was feeling particularly neglected, and had she been able to move her arms, she would have rubbed herself to aid in reaching the release she wantonly craved. Ian seemed to sense her desperation and as he continued to thrust in and out of her mouth, he made a gesture in Red's direction. Red nodded dutifully and assumed a position between Desi's thighs. Nicco remained by Desi's feet and continued suckling her toes and kneading her arches with his thumbs.

Desi whimpered pitifully as Red probed the folds of her pussy with his pointed tongue, licking around the hood of her clitoris before circling the bud with more direct pressure. The competing sensations of Nicco's suckling and Red's insistent licks caused tiny quakes in her lower belly, and she bucked when Red buried a pair of fingers up to the knuckles in her swollen pussy. Moaning wildly around Ian's cock, she felt her pussy clenching in rhythm with Ian's thrusts.

Quivering and shaking, she was overwhelmed by pleasure. Each suckled toe was bested by a tongue lapping her clit or fingers pounding her pussy. Her mouth was stretched by Ian's cock and the ropes constricting her body heightened the pleasure of each touch. It was almost too much bear. Heat bubbled in her lower tummy and her clit became so sensitive she wanted to scream. A few more licks and she would tumble over the edge.

Red devoured Desi's pussy like a starving man. Desi's toes curled, her calves tightening, and her tummy shook. She panted and sucked air each time Ian's cock left her throat. Suddenly, she was gripped by that split-second wave of panic prior to orgasm. She unleashed a torrent of ecstasy, coming so violently that she couldn't breathe or scream. As Desi shook and clenched, Red continued licking her clit and Ian kept shoving his cock into her throat while he tightened and slackened the nipple chain.

Just as the first wave of orgasm swept through her body, Desi felt another building. She inhaled a ragged breath and cried out as Red's fingers and tongue brought her to another peak. It was absolute insanity, but Desi sacrificed herself to it, riding wave after wave of orgasmic bliss. Ian's breaths were quick and shallow now. She could tell he was close and locked eyes with him. She wanted to taste his come in her mouth, to swallow him as he pumped his seed down her throat. She wanted to milk his cock for every last drop and as she gazed into his eyes, she knew he was desperate for the same. His chest reddened with exertion and his jaw twitched. He was close. She could sense it.

"Come in my mouth," Desi begged, her pussy still quivering as Red's tongue swiped her juicy folds.

Ian growled and Desi shivered with anticipation. He was coming. He was almost—

"Desi! Wake up! It's happening again! Wake up!"

Unexpectedly, Desi was gripped by a pair of hands that began to shake her. In another confusing second, she was cruelly ripped away from Ian's cock, from the devoted attention of Nicco and Red and out of the ropes. Ian's distorted voice bellowed for her return, but it was useless. Desi was free falling, and in the next second she landed with a heavy thud. She blinked quickly, bewildered by the sudden turn of events.

"Are you okay?" Lauren asked, her forehead creased with concern. Swatches of foaming cleanser clung to Desi's roommate's forehead and cheeks, and her early morning bed-head had been tamed with a headband. "I was washing my face when I heard you howling and screaming again. I ran in here and I swear to god, you were clawing at the walls, Desi. Are you okay?"

"I think so," Desi eventually replied, still panting and covered in sweat. Her pussy ached and her nipples throbbed, but other than that she felt fine. Horny, but fine. "What time is it?"

303

"A little after seven," Lauren said, sitting on the edge of the bed. "I got up early to head into the library to work on my research paper." She regarded her friend with a worried eye. "You sure you're okay?"

"Yeah," Desi said, nodding weakly.

"It was another Dr. Ian dream, wasn't it?"

"Yes," Desi grudgingly admitted.

"Was it the same one as the other night? The one where he has you bent over his desk and he's paddling you while he gives it to you?" Lauren didn't even try to mask her interest in Desi's erotic dreams.

"Not exactly."

"Well, from the looks of what I saw when I came in here, whatever you dreamed about was pretty dirty. You gonna tell me?" Lauren's eyes widened and she smiled expectantly.

Desi flushed with embarrassment. She and Lauren had been friends and roommates since their freshman year of college, five years ago now, but this last encounter was a bit too intimate for her to share. "Suffice to say, it was a little out there."

Lauren pouted and huffed. "I can't believe you're holding out on me! It's already unfair that you're having all these sexy dreams. I haven't had a decent hookup in, like, six weeks, but you've fucked Dr. Ian almost every night for the past four."

"We're not actually having sex, Lauren," Desi refuted testily. "It just seems real because I'm so much more in touch with my dreams."

"If you're trying *not* to make me jealous by pointing out your witchiness, it's not working," Lauren grumpily retorted.

"Oh yes, because being a witch has made my life so incredibly fascinating and easy," Desi sarcastically replied. "You've seen what a constant burden it's been, Lauren. Balancing my college education with my witch duties hasn't been easy, and believe me, this dream thing may seem exciting to you but it's actually rather annoying. Dreams are a place for us to process the stress and uncertainties of daily life, but instead of me processing stress, I've got Dr. Ian running me through an Anaïs Nin play-by-play."

"Better Anaïs Nin than the Marquis de Sade," Lauren teased, dampening the conflict between them.

Desi rolled her eyes but agreed. "True, but still…" She sighed and shook her head. "I wish I'd never taken that stupid Concepts of Love seminar."

"How were you supposed to know that going to a few weeks of evening seminars would cause this much trouble? Besides," Lauren shrugged, "it was a good class. We learned a lot and Dr. Ian is an amazing philosophy professor."

Unable to argue Lauren's points, Desi shrugged her shoulders instead.

"Maybe this is just your mind's way of telling you that it's time to branch out, find you a man and try new things," Lauren suggested. "Like you said, our dreams are where we work through things, and with you being a super-stressed grad student *and* witch, you tend to overlook the romance department. It probably doesn't help that today is Halloween. You're probably tapping into some kind of cosmic short-circuit."

"Maybe," Desi reluctantly agreed. It was true that she was prone to wacky experiences and power surges near and on magical days like Halloween. These dreams could be some kind of subconscious message about tending to her love life. It sort of made sense that her mind would pluck a philosophy professor who specializes in love and lust from her cache of memories to influence her dreams and actions.

Lauren rose from the bed. "You know what I think?"

"What?"

"I think you need to get laid. I mean a seriously spontaneous, dirty fuck. We've got the Moonlight Masque tonight out at the Sigma Phi Epsilon compound. You don't need a crystal ball or tarot cards to tell you that you're guaranteed to find someone."

"I don't know," Desi wavered. "Aren't we a little old for frat parties?"

"You're not even twenty-four yet! And I'm still seven months away from turning twenty-five. We wouldn't have received an invitation if we weren't invited, and anyway, we've already bought our costumes. We're going. End of story."

"Fine," Desi sighed, recognizing the folly of arguing with Lauren. Once her mind was set, there was little chance of changing it.

"Good. Well, I'm going to get dressed and head out. I'll be back around six or so. When do you get off work?"

"I have class until three and work until seven."

"We don't have to be out there until nine," Lauren said. "That's plenty of time for us to grab something to eat and get into our costumes. So I'll see you later then?"

"Yeah. Later."

Lauren nodded and strode from the room, shutting the door behind her. Desi unwillingly hauled herself from bed and walked toward the bathroom attached to her room. With every step, her thighs slid together, rubbing in the sticky cream leaking from her core, and while her clit felt inflamed, the overwhelming urge of desire was slowly fading.

Desi reached into the shower, adjusted the water temperature and then stripped. Standing in front of the full-length mirror, she took a moment to consider her reflection. She saw skin the color of toasted almonds, green eyes with honey flecks, full lips, high cheekbones and loosely curled mahogany hair that hung to the middle of her back. While not thin like Lauren, Desi hardly considered herself fat. Sure, she filled out a size twenty nicely, but as far as she was concerned, she carried the weight well on her medium frame. Others might disagree and point out the dimpling of cellulite along her thighs and the pudge around her tummy, but Desi wasn't about to waste precious time obsessing over the roll of flesh padding her midsection. Besides, there were women out there who would pay good money for a rack like hers. Not every woman could have 44Ds or a rounded ass that just begged to be grabbed and swatted.

Turning sideways, she admired the way her tattoos accentuated every curve. A vivid tangerine tiger lily and a flamboyantly pink stargazer overlapped one another on her right calf, a Sanskrit protection poem spanned most of her back, and she wore the All-Seeing Eye on her nape. A solid purple triquetra on her left wrist symbolized the bond she shared with her grandmother and mother. The interwoven triple points also exemplified the natural progression of a witch through the maiden, mother and crone stages.

As she faced the mirror again, Desi saw tiny marks on her nipples that had escaped her earlier notice. Curious, she drew closer to the mirror and almost fainted. It was undeniable. They were clamp marks, impressions matching the ones the clamps in her dream would have left. And was it just her imagination or were there faded lines crisscrossing her thighs, arms and stomach?

Rope marks!

But that's not possible, her mind screamed. It was just a dream. Or was it? If her magical upbringing had taught her anything, it was that nothing was simple when it concerned a witch.

Chapter Two

ɛ๑

Still seething with frustration, Ian stepped out of a frigid shower and yanked a clean towel from the nearby rack. Damn that meddling roommate! She'd thwarted his nocturnal advances four times in the last two weeks, and it was becoming most taxing. He glanced in the slightly fogged mirror and noticed the dark circles beneath his eyes, the sallow pallor of his face. He shook his head in frustration. Being an incubus was already hard work without having to deal with interrupted liaisons where his astral self was robbed of the chance to spill his seed. That exchange of fluid with his prey formed the psychic link that allowed him to feed, and without feeding, he was expending large amounts of energy with no return.

And it was draining him more than he cared to admit. Normally he would have moved on to another woman, someone without an interfering roommate. Hell, he had never fed off one woman for more than two consecutive nights in his entire existence as an incubus, but when it came to Desi, he simply couldn't stop. She was addictive, and quite frankly, he wasn't ready to give her up.

Desideria de Soto. In his opinion no other woman had been more aptly named. Desideria. *Desire*. She definitely lived up to her name.

Towel secured around his waist, he ambled to the bar and poured himself a scotch, neat, and downed it in a single gulp. He exhaled roughly as the fiery liquid rushed into his empty stomach. He refilled the glass and slumped into the nearest chair. Leaning his head back, he closed his eyes and immediately his thoughts were invaded by visions of Desi. Heat rolled through his stomach as he remembered the feeling of her hot, moist mouth wrapped around his cock, and the enticingly musky scent of her pussy filling his nostrils.

Never in his wildest dreams could he have imagined that he would find his mate in Texas. Of all the places he had traveled and searched — Europe, Asia, South America, Oceana — he had never once met another quite like Desi.

Teaching philosophy at a college level was the perfect cover for an incubus. He got paid for doing something he enjoyed and, let's be quite honest, his packed classrooms were literally a smorgasbord of delicious, nubile young things ripe for the plucking — or fucking, as it happened.

In his thirteen months at the university he'd already sampled hundreds of Texas' best tarts, but he'd had a craving for something a little different. He knew that evening seminars on love would attract a different crowd than those who attended his lower-level courses. The payoff had been even better than he'd anticipated.

He'd been watching the small lecture hall fill up when she'd walked into the room that first evening of class. Sun-kissed skin, red tank top, wrinkled tan skirt with little bead embellishments and gold flip-flops. Her brown hair had been pulled up in a high ponytail with curls bouncing against her back, and the golden bangles encircling her wrist had jingled rhythmically as she walked. She had bubbled with vibrancy and had attracted the attention of just about everyone in the class that night. With every smile, Desi had enthralled him, too.

After class she'd introduced herself and as soon as their hands had touched, a jolt had coursed through him. He had been certain that she'd recognized him as an incubus just as easily as he had identified her as a witch, but she hadn't. For whatever reason, it had escaped her. That had surprised him, too.

He'd visited her dreams that night, not to seduce her, but just to watch and probe her mind for information. She had been an open book of information and he'd quickly learned that she wasn't by any means a magical novice. She'd been instructed in the Craft from birth by her doting grandmother and widowed mother and had acquired a great deal of skill in potions, divination and hexing. When her mother had later fallen in love with a New Age holistic healer, Desi had benefited from the vast store of practical knowledge imparted by her stepmother and had shown promise as a healer. He had seen that Desi planned to found a holistic healing and pagan supply center someday. He supposed that was why she had chosen to pursue a bachelor's degree in agribusiness and a Ph.D in horticulture.

He had started seducing her in her dreams shortly after that first dream visit. Her mind contained a plethora of erotic scenarios that she secretly wanted to act out—he was merely providing the conduit for experiencing those fantasies. And of course, with every sexual tryst, he had been able to recharge his batteries. Well, at least when he was able to finish their copulations without interruption.

That was another thing that had surprised him about Desi. Usually women visited by incubi felt physically and emotionally drained the mornings following their encounters. It was an unfortunate side effect of the dream mating and yet another reason Ian frequently switched partners. Less considerate incubi often fed on women until they were killed or driven to the point of madness before flinging them aside and seeking another.

But Desi seemed to be thriving on his visits. He'd been watching her for weeks now and she was far from wilting. He couldn't explain why she was able to withstand his erotic assaults but thought that her maternal bloodline might hold the key. She was such a powerful witch that she barely missed the little bits of energy he drained from her. Until now, he'd never tasted a woman who could match his carnal desires.

He was almost too frightened to even hope that he'd finally found The One, a mortal woman who could live as his mate. Having been born of hellfire after The Fall, Ian had known only how to torment and had made the mistake of a lifetime when he seduced and ruined the daughter of an ancient Sumerian conjurer. The conjurer's punishment had been swift and of a sort that could be considered a mixed blessing.

When that primordial conjurer had drawn him forth from the pits of Hell all those centuries ago, Ian's black soul had been implanted into a human body. With his new human form, Ian had retained his incubus powers but had gained free will that would always be tethered by the rapacious hunger for female psychic energy. From his southerly vantage point, Ian had always viewed humans as weak and simpering, but while living among them, he had become envious of all that was humanity.

Wanting Ian to suffer just as his daughter had, the ancient conjurer had included a single clause in his creation spell that would torment Ian for centuries with the promise of something he could never have.

During the full moon's void, free of malice or duress, claim Hecate's daughter in the flesh, obtain Cupid's pledge, and forever shall you be bound like Hades to Persephone, and only then shall you escape your unnatural hunger for innocents.

The clause was simple enough. As a witch, Desi fulfilled the role of Hecate's daughter, and if he could just convince Desi to sleep with him and declare that she loved him, Ian would finally be free. Desi was intelligent, witty and never ceased to amuse or amaze him. She was, in short, the perfect mate.

So he'd been testing the waters, visiting her dreams, giving her pleasure and teaching her to trust him. Tonight, the full moon, the Blood Moon, coincided with the moon's Void of Course—the time period between the moon's exit from one astrological sign, Aries in this case, and entrance into another, Taurus, tonight. Hardly an expert at astrology, Ian had consulted his online astrologer who assured him that the conjurer's prescribed lunar alignments occurring tonight would not happen again for another seven decades. Ian took it as an incredibly good omen that tonight was also Halloween. Surely he would find success.

He had one chance to get this right, to make love to Desi free of duress or malice and coax her to say those three little words sometime during a five-hour span that began just before one a.m. In the great scheme of things that was an incredibly short window of time. But a normal life—a loving wife, kids, a house, a dog, even a picket fence—were within his grasp, and he was about to claim them.

* * * * *

When he arrived at the sprawling Sigma Phi Epsilon compound later that evening, the party was in full swing. The lavish ten-acre estate was crawling with thousands of co-eds, including hundreds of barely legal delicacies in tantalizing costumes. It was hard to differentiate the faces behind their costumes. For his own part, Ian had chosen to rely on an old staple—black silk pajama bottoms, burgundy smoking jacket with black shawl collar and platinum toggle fasteners, and his favorite pair of claret leather Tod's. It was a comfortable ensemble, perfect for what he had in mind this evening.

Scouring the crowd for Desi, Ian had to admit that college students were incredibly creative. There were dozens of the requisite sexy nurses, trampy witches, abs-baring firemen and velvet-draped vampires, but Ian also spotted a milk carton, a calculator, a Rubik's Cube and even a voodoo doll. It was entertaining to say the least.

Navigating through the bustling crowd on the massive flagstone patio was tricky. If revelers weren't bumping and grinding against one another to the rhythm of booming hip-hop, they were chugging plastic cups of keg beer or nursing colorful cocktails. A small, brave group had taken the plunge into the heated pool where they were doing things he hadn't seen since the days of Caligula. Curious onlookers stood along the edges of the pool to indulge their voyeuristic penchants, some of them so aroused they pawed their partners with the same insistency as those gyrating in the pool.

He shook free from the lust-induced stupor that overwhelmed him. Environments like this tested his control over his demonic side. If he wasn't diligent he might accidentally out himself as an otherworldly predator, and that just would not do. Especially not tonight, not when he was on a mission to find Desi, make love to her in corporeal form and persuade her to accept him as a mate. He glanced at his watch. It was almost midnight and he had yet to locate her. The Void of Course would begin soon, along with his five-hour window. He had to get moving.

Pressed for time, he abandoned his current method and activated his keenly perceptive senses. His second sight, a sort of infrared, scanned the teeming crowd for her. He continued walking and craning his neck as he swept the party, quickly jumping from one aura to the next in search of hers. Less than ten minutes into his search, he found her. Through his second sight, she was a curvy black silhouette surrounded by vibrant, pulsing rainbow rings. The pure power that reverberated through Desi's aura was quite a thing to behold, but as soon as he switched back to his normal vision, he was completely floored by a most seductive sight.

Dressed like a naughty beer wench, Desi wore a miniature version of a German peasant's frock, red with black and green embroidery, over a white ruffled, short-sleeved top. A frilly white petticoat hung a fraction of a centimeter lower than the skirt of the dress, which barely skimmed mid-thigh. The corseted dress braced her midsection, lifting her breasts and displaying them over the daringly low white top. Braids, sexy white thigh-highs and a pair of black patent-leather Mary Janes completed the flirtatious ensemble.

He watched as she threw back her head and laughed gaily at some remark made by her friends. The gentle arch of her neck and back presented the heaving crests of her breasts, and he inhaled a sharp breath. His cock leapt and he consciously quelled the rush of need that coursed through him. He was overwhelmed by the need to bury his face between her breasts, to palm a cheek, to stab his cock into her tight channel.

More importantly, Ian suddenly realized that he wasn't the only one beguiled. He jealously eyed the group of men surrounding her and almost came unglued when one of them dared to reach out and sweep one of the braids off her chest, touching her bare arm in the process. As far as he was concerned, she belonged to him—and he wasn't one to share what was rightfully his.

He used his powers of persuasion to mentally push the mixed group of guys and girls to leave Desi's side. Most of them scuttled off within seconds of the time he implanted the thoughts in their weak minds, but Lauren, the roommate, was a tougher sell. Before he met Desi, Lauren was exactly the kind of girl he would have preyed upon, and in that Little Bo Peep outfit—complete with itsy-bitsy pink dress, pink fishnets and white hooker platforms—she was quite a visual delight. And yet, he gave her very little thought beyond wanting to shoo her away from Desi. Eventually, she too succumbed to his mental will, and soon, Desi was left standing by herself. Self-assured, she didn't seem the least bit bothered by her solo status and happily sipped her drink.

He carefully considered his plan of attack. In any other situation, he would have relied heavily upon his incubus powers and simply planted a suggestion in her mind, but not tonight. He needed her to choose him of her own volition, without coercion. Sure, he could coax her with gentle words and soft caresses, but ultimately, she had to choose to make love to him. He could only hope that the many nights of pleasure had influenced her trust in him. Right now that was his only advantage.

He sucked in a long, cleansing breath and strode toward her. It was now or never.

Chapter Three

 හ

Desi tipped her glass and finished the final few drops of her Texas Sunrise. Since she had lost the coin toss for designated driver, the nonalcoholic version was the closest she would come to tasting a Tequila Sunrise tonight. She was just about to head to the bar for another when she thought she heard her name over the din of laughter and music. Forehead wrinkled, she tilted her head and listened but didn't hear anything other than the normal sounds of a crazed co-ed party.

"Fraulein Desi?"

Startled by the sound of that oh-so familiar British voice behind her, she tensed and her heart jumped into the back of her throat. *No fucking way*, she thought. This was not happening! She was not standing there in some slutty beer wench costume while Dr. Ian, the ringmaster of her filthiest dreams, stood right behind her.

"Desi?" His warm fingers touched the naked skin of her shoulder and electricity jolted through her.

Gulping nervously, she twirled to face him. *Oh god*, she thought, knees weak. He looked positively sinful in that Hugh Hefner getup. The paper lanterns strung overhead cast their light upon the opening of his smoking jacket, highlighting the rippled ridges of his incredible abs. She wanted to trail her fingers down that washboard tummy, play with the blond happy trail that she imagined lay beneath the folds of the jacket and follow it straight down to his rock-hard —

Focus, Desi! she harshly reminded herself. *Words. Now.*

"Dr. Cuvos," Desi said, recovering quickly.

"Ian," he smoothly replied. "I'm not your professor any longer. You should call me Ian."

"Right. Sorry," she muttered.

He idly waved his hand, dismissing her apology. He gave her an appraising glance and smiled approvingly. "I love the costume, Desi. It definitely highlights your best assets," he said, eyes lingering on the swelling crests of her breasts.

She blushed beneath his scrutinizing glance. Was he seriously checking her out? She wanted to pinch herself to prove that she hadn't just nodded off and this wasn't simply another one of her erotic fantasies. Calm down. He was probably just being friendly. Best to play it cool.

"Thanks," she managed finally. "I like the smoking jacket. It suits you."

"I'm glad you approve," Ian purred, his sapphire irises locking with hers. "Do you come to costume parties often?"

"More often than you'd think," Desi laughed, loosening up around him. "You?"

"I seem to get quite a few invites to these kinds of things," he said wryly.

"Because the frat boys idolize you," Desi said without thinking. Her cheeks flushed as she realized her *faux pas*, but Ian laughed heartily, clearly amused by her candor.

"Is that so?" Ian asked, still laughing. "Care to explain?"

She considered playing coy, but that just wasn't her style. "Come on, Ian, you know that you're *the* epitome of a playboy. These guys see the way the girls drool over you. They want to be just like you. They want girls crawling all over them. And let's be honest here, you're the perfect bait for luring girls to these parties. They hear you're going to be here and bam!" She snapped her fingers for emphasis. "They're determined to make it here. The guys like that because it ups the odds that they'll score."

"Is that why you came here?" Ian squarely asked. "Because you knew I'd be here?"

"Hardly," Desi laughed, rolling her eyes.

"Then why?"

Mulling her options, Desi met his unwavering gaze. She could lie, but there was almost a daring quality to Ian's look. The hell with it, she decided. They were both adults. He could handle the truth if she could dish it out.

"I came here to get laid," Desi calmly, boldly explained.

"That's quite a coincidence," Ian replied without missing a beat, "because I came over here with the intention of seducing you."

It took every fiber of her being to keep her jaw from hitting the patio. Did he just say that? Did he just admit to wanting to sleep with her? She thought about the implications of his admission. She could have sex with him, *real* sex. She was almost reduced to jelly at the thought.

"So what you do say, Desi?" He was still talking. He tipped her chin with a crooked finger and ran his thumb across her pout. "Stand here for another hour making small talk or skip right to the best parts?"

Her stomach somersaulted, but before committing herself, she gauged the sincerity of his statement. There wasn't a hint of duplicity in his eyes. He was serious, she realized. He wanted her. They were surrounded by literally hundreds of horny, promiscuous girls, but he had approached her, chosen *her*. That realization thrilled her. Her mind was made up.

"Skip to the best parts," Desi stated, her voice surprisingly strong, considering the apprehension quaking in her stomach.

"Excellent choice," Ian said, grinning boyishly. He extended his hand and as soon as her palm rested upon his, he curled his fingers around it. Without a word, he turned toward the grand limestone frat house like a man on a mission. She trailed closely behind, unable to hear anything but the deafening thud of her blood pumping past her eardrums.

As they walked, she noticed curious stares in their direction. Unwilling to be fodder for the campus rumor mill, she raised her hand, whispered a quick incantation for a veiling glamour and made an inconspicuous gesture to trigger the magic. The faintest buzz of energy ensued and Ian unexpectedly cast a glance over his shoulder, his gaze confused. Desi held her breath, hoping he hadn't sensed her magic, and a second later he was facing forward again. Revealing her witch identity had always been a problem in the past, and she didn't want to end this relationship before it had begun because of something beyond her control.

Once they entered the frat house, Ian hooked a sharp right. They walked through a sitting room, a den and a massive dining hall before reaching the industrial kitchen. In every room there were at least three, but sometimes five or more couples engaging in heavy petting and, in one case, full-on sex. The kitchen was packed with stacked kegs and pallets of bulk snack foods. Ian led her around the obstacles in their way, his body language transmitting determination. They passed a closed door, but Ian suddenly halted and retreated. He tried the door, finding it unlocked. He peered inside the room and Desi tried to see over his shoulder but couldn't. He tugged on her hand, half dragging her into the presumably empty room.

It was a spacious laundry room with ten washers on one wall and ten dryers on the other. Multiple shelves holding laundry supplies sat along the far wall and long, stainless steel tables lined the center of the room. Miscellaneous towels, mismatched socks and a pair of green boxers were scattered across their surfaces, the remnants of careless frat boys.

She heard the door lock behind her and a moment later, Ian was embracing her, his smoking jacket already discarded. It was so bizarre, but he smelled exactly as he had in her dreams. The arms clenched around her body felt exactly as they had last night. His hands felt incredibly warm against her skin, almost unnaturally hot, but she chalked it up to his highly aroused state. His tongue insistently prodded her mouth and she welcomed it into her own, groaning as it swirled around hers. His cock strained against the flimsy silk fabric of his pajama bottoms and stabbed her soft belly.

"I want to fuck you so badly," Ian growled, sucking on the curve of her throat.

"Oh god," Desi moaned, overcome with lust. He sounded absolutely voracious, and she wanted him to ravish her. "I *want* you to fuck me, Ian." *For real…*

Ian spun her around and applied pressure to her back, bending her over the nearest table. Her breasts rested atop the surface and she breathed raggedly as he groped her ass, grabbing two handfuls of her girlie lace bloomers. One hand left her bloomers, snaking up to settle on her neck, and his lightly stubbled cheek rubbed against hers as he kissed the edge of her mouth. She panted loudly as his hand slipped inside her bloomers and followed the rounded globes of her ass. He tickled the cleft and she bucked. Her bloomers were damp and in a few seconds he would know just how hot she was for him. His fingers gripped the tops of her bloomers and he yanked them down around her thighs. Cold air met her blazing-hot ass cheeks. She lifted her feet as he pulled the bloomers down.

"Open your legs," he instructed, his voice thick.

She complied. Her pussy contracted as she awaited that first touch of his fingers, but it didn't come. She jumped when she felt his soft, wet tongue probing the folds of her pussy. She convulsed as slippery fluid gushed down the walls of her sex. No one had ever licked her from that angle, and it felt deliciously naughty. He dragged his tongue from the tip of her erect clit to the sopping wet hole and gently prodded it.

"Oh. My. God." Her staccato cries filled the room.

"Not quite," Ian said, a smile filling his voice as he paused his lapping to reply.

A split second later he was back at it again, licking and suckling the supple lips. Clutched by instinct, Desi wiggled her ass in an effort to guide his tongue right where she wanted it. Her legs shook as pleasure knotted low in her tummy and she gripped the edge of the table to keep from crumpling to the ground in a heap of quivering ecstasy. Ian's hands grasped her ample hips as he gave her pussy the licking of a lifetime. She was on the cusp of exploding when he abruptly stopped. His lack of action wrangled a tortured cry from her throat, but his only answer to her rasping plea was a flat-palmed slap across the fleshiest portion of her ass.

Squirming with need, she fought to breathe as his fingers nimbly flew through the lace back of the frock's corset closure. When the last lace had been pulled free, he spun her around and, grasping the front of the dress, pulled it down. Her breasts spilled forth, the areolas dark, the nipples tight and stiff. As he toyed with her nipples, his mouth met hers. Tasting her pussy on his lips was an odd but welcome sensation. It joined them in a deeply erotic manner, and she swiped her tongue across his lips for more.

Consumed by the need to give him pleasure, she pressed on his chest, turning him until his back was against the table. She squatted in front of him and freed his erection. It was fully engorged, dark red and quivering. A few glistening drops shined on the head and she swiped her tongue across them. Palming his balls, she took his cock into her mouth, taking him fully on the first plunge. His hand was immediately on her head, caressing her face as she used her other hand to stroke the shaft in the opposite direction of her mouth. She lavished his cock with a combination of her hands and mouth until he was tense and panting.

"Stop. Please," he begged, gently grasping her head.

She relented and he clutched the tops of her arms, lifting her to her feet, kissing her deeply and lifting her onto the table. She gasped as the chilly metal made contact with her blazing-hot skin, but the slight discomfort was quickly forgotten as soon as Ian's fingers began tracing the inner lips of her pussy. He slipped one finger into her, working her slick flesh until it was ready for another. With two fingers deep in her pussy, he used his thumb to rub slow circles around her clit until it was stiff and pulsing.

"Ian," she hungrily implored. "Please fuck me. I want your cock. I want it now."

Growling excitedly, he shoved his cock right into her, letting the slippery wet passage swallow him. She loved the way he stretched her, filled her so tightly that her entire pussy was awakened. She felt his cock stroking places that she'd never known existed and swore that with each stroke he was rubbing against that elusive G-spot. He fucked her slowly at first, but began picking up the pace as she clutched at his forearms frenziedly. He took her right hand, brought it to his mouth and sucked on the fingers before placing it against her clit.

"Rub your pussy," he ordered.

Her eyes widened at the unbelievably frank instruction but she did exactly as he asked. Her clit burned and it felt incredibly good to play with it. Her intimate muscles clenched his cock as it slid in and out of her. She was gasping with need, chasing her orgasm. While he thrust like a madman, Ian squeezed her swollen breasts and lightly swatted her nipples. She gasped as the stinging sensation spread through the sensitive flesh.

They were both so very close. Ian saw the way her skin was flushed pink and she noticed the rhythmic clenching of his jaw. Her toes curled around his ribs as she brought her knees closer to her chest, deepening each penetration. Fiery waves crashed through her stomach and suddenly, she was gripped by an intense orgasm. She arched off the table, screaming his name, begging him to continue fucking her. Holding his own release in check, Ian obliged.

The power of her orgasm was unbelievable and it felt like an hour had passed before she was able to relax her constricted muscles. Ian continued to pump her pussy, each thrust accompanied by clicking suction. She held onto his shoulders, locking eyes with him as he approached his orgasm. As he began to stiffen in anticipation of coming, panic clouded his gaze, but a second later it was gone.

And then something strange happened. Just as she felt hot semen spurting inside her, she watched in horror as his brilliantly blue eyes went completely black, both sclera and iris. Her heart seized in her chest as she realized what was happening.

Ian wasn't a human at all. He was an incubus.

Chapter Four
బ

"Get off of me!" Desi screamed as she placed the heels of her Mary Janes against Ian's bare chest and shoved. In a most unladylike fashion, she scrambled away from him, rolling across the table and hopping down to the floor. With the table between them, she lifted her hands in a defensive motion, gathering energy along her fingertips, ready to strike.

"Please, Desi, you have to listen to me!" Ian hastily tied the waistband of his pajama bottoms, concealing his shrinking erection. "It's not what you think."

"It's exactly what I think," Desi angrily retorted. "You're a fucking demon! You're a murderer!"

Ian balked at her assertion. "I most certainly am not a murderer! In all my centuries on this plane, I've never once drained a woman to the point of death. I'm not some cold-blooded, psychotic killer. But, yes," he said quietly. "I am an incubus. But you have to know that I wasn't trying to hurt you. I know that you're a witch, and I don't care."

"You're crazy!" Desi yanked her skirt into place with one hand and desperately tried to refasten the laces lining the back of her dress. It was impossible to do so she just left it.

"No, I'm not crazy, Desi. I fell in love with you the moment you walked into my lecture hall. We're meant for one another, Desi. I know you can feel it."

"You lied to me, and you used me, Ian! You've been invading my dreams, haven't you?"

"Yes, but it wasn't like that," Ian said, shaking his head. "I was just trying to establish trust with you, to show you the pleasure I can give you, to teach you —"

323

"I don't want to hear your twisted excuses," Desi shouted, cutting him off. "I'm leaving this room right now, and I swear on the souls of every de Soto witch who's passed before me, if you take one step closer I will curse you back into the seventh level of Hell!"

Ian gulped audibly and Desi received a perverse sense of satisfaction at seeing his obvious fear. She meant what she said. A few words, a flick of her wrist and he would be right back in the sulfurous hellfire where he had been spawned. Not wasting another moment, Desi scurried to the door but paused to look over her left shoulder at him. She was shocked by what she saw in his eyes. Not fear but sadness, extreme sadness, colored his face. For the tiniest of moments, she was gripped by the need to rush into his arms, to comfort him, but then she realized that this was just another one of his tricks.

"Don't follow me," Desi said firmly. She spit over her left shoulder, completing an ancient spell for holding a demon at bay. Instantly, an invisible wall of energy sprang up between them. She grabbed the door and rushed into the hallway. She fumbled in the hidden pocket along the right side of her skirt for her key ring. Selecting the key to her childhood home, one that she rarely used, she shoved it into the lock. With a little effort she was able to break it off inside the lock, ensuring that no other person would accidentally enter the room and become Ian's next victim.

She ran from the frat house. She could only imagine how disheveled she must have looked. Her dress was untied, the skirt and petticoat wrinkled, her braids were coming loose and she had left her bloomers on the floor of the laundry room. Desi looked everywhere for Lauren until a friend of a friend assured her that Lauren had left with Roger, an old flame. Certain that Lauren was relatively safe, she rushed to her silver Civic Hybrid, frantically clicking the button on her remote lock as she approached. As soon as she was inside the car, she locked the doors, hastily buckled her seatbelt and squealed out of the parking lot.

She reached the house she shared with Lauren in record time. The second she stepped through the door, she punched the alarm keypad, but she knew that wasn't enough to keep Ian out of the house. Dashing into her bedroom, she grabbed the box of polished agate stones that her grandmother had given her years earlier and began running around the house, placing them in every corner, whispering the proper protection spell. When the final stone was set into place, energy zipped through the air and Desi could feel a protective blanket humming around the house.

Her frantic heartbeat began to slow. The need to bathe overwhelmed her and she jumped into a scalding shower, scrubbing until her skin tingled. She wrapped herself in a bathrobe, emptied a can of salt in a circle around her bed and climbed under the covers. Her back resting against a mound of pillows, she silently cursed her stupidity.

How had she missed the blatant signs? The vivid dreams were the biggest clues, and she had simply brushed them off as simple fantasy. And come on! Dr. Ian Cuvos! Incubus. Sweet Persephone, he wasn't even trying that hard to hide his identity. She remembered their first meeting, the moment their hands had touched and that spark of power that had vibrated through her arm. Because she often accidentally discharged energy, she had just chalked it up to coincidence. What a fool she had been! She deserved everything that had happened to her.

And yet, even as she lay there, shivering and upset, there was a small part of her that was secretly excited by the prospect of being an incubus's lover. It was quite possible that he'd been lying when he told her that he loved her, but for some reason, she was inclined to believe him. That look on his face when she was leaving—that wasn't acting. Within her very core, she recognized that truth. However skewed his reasons and wrong his actions, Ian did love her. Out of millions of women, she was the one who had captivated him.

But it was pointless. Demons and witches only had a chance in stories and myths. This was the real world, and by rights, Desi should hunt Ian down and banish him. Just not tonight, she decided. She was so incredibly tired and so unbelievably heartbroken. Sleep. She just needed some sleep.

* * * * *

Well, I royally fucked that one up, Ian thought. Frustrated and growling, he tried to teleport out of the room but it was no use. And he couldn't even get close enough to the door to try to open it. Desi had hermetically sealed the room. He was a prisoner until she came back to let him out—or kill him. After seeing the blazing fury in her eyes, he wouldn't be at all surprised by the latter.

He had to admit that he had seriously underestimated Desi's abilities. He had known she was proficient, but not *that* powerful. He'd seriously miscalculated and now it was entirely likely that he'd soon find himself tossed back into the pits that he'd escaped thousands of years earlier. And for what?

For a chance at love, for something more organic, something longer lasting than unadulterated lust—that's why he'd gone through all this trouble.

He glanced at his watch. He'd wasted precious hours trying to break out of the room, but there was still time to fix this, to convince her to admit that she loved him, if he could just get out of this fucking room! It was fairly evident that she'd placed some kind of binding on the place when she'd spit over her shoulder. It was an old trick, but she'd played it well. He could only hope that the binding was purely physical and didn't involve the parallel astral planes. That was his only chance.

He hopped onto the nearest table and lay flat on his back. Closing his eyes, he inhaled measured breaths, calming his mind as he prepared to enter a trance. In mere seconds, his astral form was lifting away from his body and cautiously approaching the door. Steeled for the worst, he extended a hand, and to his immense relief, it passed right through Desi's spell and the door. He was a free man!

At least until sunrise, he thought glumly. Just like most spirits, he was incredibly vulnerable to sunlight when in his astral form. He had to be back in his body before dawn, but the most pressing deadline, the moon leaving her void, was even closer than that, less than an hour away. He had to hurry.

Confident in the land of Morpheus, Ian transcended time and space, using his astral form to move through the dream world on his quest to find Desi. She had easily withstood his dream advances in the past, but she had expended quite a bit of sexual and magical energy in that laundry room. She'd have a hard time staying awake tonight.

Soon he was standing outside Desi's house. While the protective blanket was invisible in the real world, here in dreamland, the house was wrapped in orange light. Ian stopped short of touching the orange barrier, terrified that it might vaporize him. He studied the protective wall for a moment before deciding that he had no choice but to breech the barrier. He was certain Desi wasn't foolish enough to activate a deadly barrier that would kill anything that dared cross the threshold. She would have included some kind of failsafe. He was willing to bet that only malicious persons would be kept out by the barrier, and as he bore her no ill will, he felt relatively confident that he could make it through without being snuffed.

Summoning all his courage and visions of love and security to the forefront of his mind, he poked the toes of his left foot against the orange light. If he was wrong, he could live without toes much more easily than any other appendage. Just as he had suspected, he was able to freely penetrate the barrier. Once on the other side, he discovered that he was no longer standing on a well-manicured lawn, but on the outskirts of a fully blooming English garden. By the looks of the plant life it was early summer and the skies were slightly overcast,

327

providing just enough shade to temper the summer heat. Neatly trimmed hedges formed a small square around the garden, and a pale stone path wound past antique roses, forget-me-nots, foxglove and beds of fragrant herbs.

This heavenly patch of Earth was her safe place, a dream where she sought refuge when life was particularly stressful or frightening. He moved slowly down the stone path, his bare feet making no sound. He rounded a curve in the path—and there she was, sitting on a wooden bench beneath a white arbor covered in climbing clematis. A hummingbird darted above Desi's head as she lazily turned the pages of a book, her head resting against a pink canvas pillow sandwiched between her temple and the inner edge of the arbor. Her feet dangled from the bench, wet grass clinging to her naked toes, while the short hem of her pale yellow sundress flapped in the light breeze.

Unable to move, he stared at the angelic vision before him. Unfortunately the moment wasn't meant to last because Desi visibly stiffened, as though sensing his presence.

"You arrogant bastard!" Desi bolted from her seat and hurled the book at his head, but he blocked it with his forearm. "How dare you invade my dream! Get out!"

"Desi, please calm down," Ian pleaded, raising his hands. "I'm not here to hurt you. You must know that. I wouldn't have been able to enter the protective field if I had bad intentions, would I?"

She frowned, thrown by the question. Unwilling to admit he was right, she crossed her arms over her chest and huffed loudly. "You're a demon. You're a skillful liar. You could have fudged your way through the barrier."

"No, I couldn't," Ian refuted, taking a step closer. "I was able to pass through because I love you, Desi."

"Don't say that! You don't love me! If you loved me, you wouldn't have betrayed me, Ian."

"Look, Desi, I made a mistake and I'm sorry. I couldn't help myself. You're just so beautiful and I had to have you. I wanted you so badly and visiting your dreams was the only way. I was afraid that you'd realize I was an incubus, and then you'd never give me a chance. I'm not a bad person. I needed to prove to you that you could trust me."

"You picked a really screwed up way of doing it, Ian," Desi replied angrily. "And being a good person has no bearing on this situation, either. You're a demon!"

"And you're a witch!" Ian gruffly retorted, moving closer, his anger propelling him forward.

"What the hell does that have to do with anything?"

"A few hundred years ago they were rounding up your kind, tossing you in lakes and burning you in bonfires. Sure, a handful of witches were really nasty, but they gave the entire population a bad name. It's the same thing with us," Ian explained. "People fear what they don't understand."

"Don't you dare compare my family to your...brood or whatever! We're nothing alike. You're a bunch of leeches —"

"I am not a leech!" Ian bellowed. He exhaled roughly and lowered his voice. "Yes, I feed off the psychic energy of my lovers, but I also give them immense pleasure in return. It's a fair trade, Desi."

Shaking her head, Desi covered her face with her hands. When she looked up tears shimmered in her green eyes and Ian's stomach clenched as he understood the emotional grief she was enduring.

"Why me, Ian?" she asked, sobbing softly. "Why are you doing this to me?"

"Because you're the only one for me," Ian confessed, his voice impaired by the lump blocking his throat. "In centuries of searching, you're the first who's ever matched me. You've been able to withstand my feedings. You're invigorated by them. I can be with you without the fear of killing you." He took a careful step toward her and met her tearful gaze. "You're my only chance, Desi."

"Only chance? For what?"

"A normal life."

"Normal life?" Her forehead wrinkled as her shoulders hunched questioningly. "What does that mean, Ian?"

"It means that I can be freed from this uncontrollable urge to feed. I can have a wife, a family, kids, the suburban American dream. I want to share all of that with you—if you'll have me, of course," he added gently.

"Ian, you're asking for forever and I'm...I'm not ready for that," Desi admitted, dashing his hopes. Guilt-ridden, she chewed her lower lip. "Maybe someday I might be able to give you forever, but not now. We barely know one another. There's no rush, Ian."

"Funny thing," Ian bitterly laughed. "There is a rush."

"How so?" Desi asked nervously.

"I was summoned into existence by a conjurer. The only way for me to be set free from his curse is for you to have sex with me, free of malice or duress, and then tell me you love me—all during a full moon's Void of Course. And I don't think just telling me you love me would work. I think we're going to have to make love again first. I'm pretty sure lying to you about my true identity was against the rules. You know, that whole 'without malice or duress' bit." He anxiously checked his watch. "But we have to hurry. This is the last intersection of a Void and full moon for the next seventy years, and the window is closing in about half an hour so you need to make a decision and—"

He abruptly stopped talking as peals of laughter met his ears. Nose toward the sky, Desi giggled madly.

"What?" Ian asked, clearly annoyed. "What's so goddamn funny?"

"You are," Desi laughed, hugging her sides as she drew near him.

"I'm glad you find my pain and suffering so hilarious," Ian sarcastically snapped.

"Calm down," Desi giggled, patting his bare arm. "Who told you that full moons and Voids of Course intersected only once every seventy years?"

"My astrologer," Ian replied defensively.

"I hope you didn't pay much for the services," Desi said, still smiling. "These intersections happen quite a bit. There have been two already this year. There's no rush, Ian."

Humiliation reddened Ian's cheeks and he cast his eyes downward. That was the last time he'd use an online astrologer! "You must think I'm a bloody fool."

"No." Desi reached out and touched his stubbled chin. "I don't think you're a fool, but it's pretty clear that you're not very thorough."

"I was pretty thorough in chasing you around all evening. I can't believe I put us both through this for nothing!"

"Not for nothing," Desi disagreed. Her lips parted and closed quickly. She searched for the right words. "Ian, I like you—a lot, actually. I'm flattered by the attention, and obviously the sex is fabulous, but I just…I don't love you, yet."

"Yet?" Ian's eyebrows arched. "Does that mean you might eventually?"

"There's no 'might' to it, Ian. I'm positive that I'm going to fall in love with you. It's just a matter of time."

"Then let's do this now! We'll make love. You can tell me you love me." He placed his fingers against Desi's lips as she began to protest. "It doesn't matter that you don't love me right now. You said it yourself. You will one day."

Desi laughed and shook her head. "You're really incorrigible, you know that? Patience is a virtue, Ian. It's time to practice that. Besides," she shrugged lightly, "you need to prove yourself to me. I need to know that I can really trust you. I need to know that you're truly committed to me, that you're not going to be tempted to run off and feed on some unsuspecting woman the first time we have a fight. You need to show me that you're serious about us."

"I can do that," Ian vehemently promised. "I can be a one-woman incubus, *your* incubus."

"Good." Desi smiled encouragingly and intertwined her fingers with his. Her lavender scent filled the air as they embraced, her cheek pressed against his bare chest. As they shared a steamy kiss, Ian's hands followed the natural curve of her back before settling on the fleshy mounds hidden beneath a fine layer of yellow linen. Giggling, Desi broke free from the kiss. "You know, Ian, relationships are about substance. It can't always be about the sex."

"You're right," Ian agreed, grinning slyly. "What about a ninety-ten split? I think I can control myself ten percent of the time."

"You're hopeless."

Ian didn't argue. He planted a long, loving kiss on her mouth, enjoying the softness of her form molded against his. He could stay like this forever, holding her, loving her…

Except that he couldn't. Not if he didn't want to be dust at sunrise.

"Desi," Ian said between kisses.

"Yes?"

"Do you think you could maybe undo the binding on the laundry room back at the frat house? I'd like to continue this, but I've got to hop back into my body before sunrise. Otherwise, it's going to be poof! No more Ian."

Desi closed her eyes for a moment and Ian felt the electric vibrations her body radiated. "It's done," she said, opening her eyes.

"Thank you," Ian said, kissing her again. "I'll be right back..."

* * * * *

Desi stumbled forward slightly as Ian disappeared in the middle of their kiss. She felt a strange tug behind her navel and then she was tumbling out of her dream. Her eyelids flittered open and she saw only the light blue walls of her bedroom. Pale orange early morning sunlight filtered through the curtains, and she was seized by panic at the thought of Ian not making it back to his body in time.

Before she could sit up, a toned, bronze arm landed across her waist. She glanced over her shoulder and there he was, affectionately spooning her. Smiling happily, Desi snuggled her buttocks against his pelvis, wiggling her hips as she settled under the covers. She felt the first stirrings of an erection and reached between them to play with his morning wood.

"If you don't stop that I'm going to have to start chiseling away at my ninety-percent quota," Ian sleepily said, his lips brushing her ear.

Desi smiled wickedly and continued stroking the length of his shaft, encouraging it to spring to life. Behind her, Ian growled.

"I warned you."

The next second, she was on her back and her squeals of delight filled the room. Desi ran her fingertips along Ian's ribs and abdomen as he lay over her. He was solid beneath her touch. As Ian kissed her, Desi's hand drifted lower. She glued her gaze to his and used her fingers to encircle the tip of his penis before moving her hand down the shaft, deliberately slowly. He was as hard as steel and seared her palm as she deftly stroked the length of his cock. Her tongue stole out to lick his lower lip.

"Let me ride you," Desi huskily requested.

"Absolutely," Ian agreed as he grinned sexily. Wrapping his arms around Desi's waist, he flipped them over so that Desi was straddling his knees and he was reclining against the pillows with his magnificent cock standing at attention.

Desi moaned, overcome with the need to ravish him. Smirking impishly, she lifted her right knee and almost instantly, Ian groaned at the feeling of her wet labia smashed against his thighs. She rose up on his lap and with her nimble fingers wrapped around the base of his cock, Desi lowered herself onto him at a torturously leisurely pace.

"Ah…" Desi moaned as her scorching flesh swallowed him inch by inch.

Gritting his teeth, Ian fought to maintain control over his body. He was in the most enviable position a man could possibly occupy. There was a gorgeous woman astride his lap and as her hips swayed back and forth, her bountiful breasts danced only inches from his face. Ian grasped Desi's hips, guiding her belly dancer movements and reveling in the sight of her body in motion.

Bracing herself with a hand on Ian's abdomen, Desi ground her enflamed clitoris against his pubic bone, sentient of her body's needs. Feeling the telltale tightening in her lower belly, Desi hastened her rocking, alternating her up and down strokes with circles. Ian's hands moved north, squeezing the full globes of her breasts as she rode him with greater fervor.

Realizing that she was being a bit selfish, Desi decided to include Ian in her journey to orgasm and grabbed his hand. Still bouncing on his rigid cock, Desi captured his gaze and brought the fingers to her mouth, running her tongue across them.

"Desi!" Ian growled at the sight of the erotic gesture. His thighs tensed as he battled the sudden surge of excitement.

With a naughty grin, Desi guided his hand down to her clit and, as she leaned back, placed her palms on his thighs to give him better access. Taking the hint, Ian placed his thumb against the hardened nub and rubbed side to side. He could feel her pussy clenching his cock as she approached the precipice of orgasm, and her fingers bit into his hamstrings as she climaxed, throwing her head back and screaming with ecstasy.

She was still shaking from the power of orgasm when Ian clutched her waist and spun her around, desire burning low and hard in him. All he could think about was ravaging her. Addicted to the submissive nature of being claimed from behind, Desi eagerly spread her legs and rested her elbows on the mattress as Ian moved behind her. His cock nudged the dusky pink slit, and without a thought for finesse, he sank into her, burying his penis to the hilt.

Jarring with the force of their primal mating, Desi fisted the sheets as she grunted with need. Her pussy was still throbbing from release and within moments, she was once again on the verge of climax. The squeak of the bed paired with the sounds of Ian's cock slamming into her reduced Desi to a quivering mass, and she pleaded for salvation from the torment.

"I want to feel you come again," Ian pleaded. He knew exactly what she needed and reached around to her front, sliding his hand between her legs. It took only a few flicks of his fingertips and she was jolting with ferocity, howling into the comforter. The sound of Desi's enraptured wailing catapulted Ian over the brink, and he roared as he came, jerking five times as his seed spilled into her.

Suddenly, torrents of blazing purple energy exploded from their bodies as they consummated their relationship. The walls shook, windows rattled in their frames and pictures flew off the walls as the radiating waves of energy pulsed through the room. Lamps jiggled across tabletops and the TV balanced precariously on its stand. As ceiling dust trickled down, they collapsed onto the comforter in a tangle of sweaty, trembling limbs, with Desi's hair sticking to Ian's damp forehead and cheeks.

"What just happened?" Desi asked incredulously.

"The conjurer's spell, I think," Ian panted, his cock still nestled in the warm cushion of her sex. He peered at the alarm clock now dangling off the edge of a bedside table. Technically, the Void of Course had ended almost nineteen minutes ago, but somehow, for whatever reason, their mating had triggered the conjurer's clause.

Desi glanced over her shoulder at him, her eyebrows furrowed in question. "Does that mean that we're, you know, bound?"

"I honestly don't know," Ian musingly admitted before he started to pull away from her. Desi moaned and her buttocks tensed as he withdrew. He snuggled up to her back, curling his knees beneath her buttocks and winding his arm about her waist. He planted a noisy kiss on her shoulder blade before pensively asking, "Does it matter, Desi?"

She hardly considered his question before the answer was on her tongue. "No. No it doesn't."

"Does that mean that you love me?" he tentatively asked.

"I think it does," she said. "Yes. Yes it does." She turned her head until their lips met in a short, sweet kiss. "I love you, Ian. I really do."

"I love you, Desi."

Blissfully happy, Desi grinned and burrowed against Ian's warmth. Last night definitely hadn't disappointed as far as usual Halloween wackiness was concerned — but she was going to have one hell of a story for Lauren!

Also by Amy Ruttan

༂

Love Thy Neighbor

About the Author

༂

Amy discovered her love of the written word when she realized that she could no longer act out the fantastical romances in her head with her dolls. Writing about delicious heroes was much more fun than playing with plastic men dolls with the inevitable flesh-colored "tighty whities".

She loves history, the paranormal, and will spew out historical facts like a volcano, much to her dearest hubby's chagrin.

When she's not thinking about the next sensual romp, she's chasing after two rug rats and reading anything spicy that she can get her hands on.

Amy welcomes comments from readers. You can find her website and email address on her author bio page at www.ellorascave.com.

Tell Us What You Think

We appreciate hearing reader opinions about our books. You can email us at Comments@EllorasCave.com.

Also by Cindy Spencer Pape

ℰℛ

Djinni and the Geek
One Good Man
Stone and Earth
Stone and Sea
Teach Me

About the Author

ℰℛ

Cindy Spencer Pape has been, among other things, a banker, a teacher, and an elected politician, though she swears she got better. Her degrees are in zoology, and she currently works in environmental education, when she can fit it in around writing. She lives in southern Michigan with her husband, two teenage sons, a dog, a lizard, and various other small creatures, all of which are easier to clean up after than the three male humans.

Cindy welcomes comments from readers. You can find her website and email address on her author bio page at www.ellorascave.com.

Tell Us What You Think

We appreciate hearing reader opinions about our books. You can email us at Comments@EllorasCave.com.

Also by Cris Anson

❧

About the Author

❧

Cris Anson firmly believes that love is the greatest gift...to give or to receive. In her writing, she lives for the moment when her characters realize they love each other, usually after much antagonism and conflict. And when they express that love physically, Cris keeps a fire extinguisher near the keyboard in case of spontaneous combustion. Multi-published and twice EPPIE-nominated in romantic suspense under another name, she was usually asked to tone down her love scenes. For Ellora's Cave, she's happy to turn the flame as high as it will go--and then some.

After suffering the loss of her real-life hero/husband of twenty-two years, Cris has picked up the pieces of her life and tries to remember only the good times...slow-dancing with him to the Big Band sound of Glenn Miller's music, vacations to scenic national parks in a snug recreational vehicle, his tender and fierce love, his unflagging belief in her ability to write stories that touch the heart as well as the libido. Bits and pieces of his tenacity, optimism, code of honor and lust for life will live on in her imaginary heroes.

Cris welcomes comments from readers. You can find her website and email address on her author bio page at www.ellorascave.com.

Tell Us What You Think

We appreciate hearing reader opinions about our books. You can email us at Comments@EllorasCave.com.

Also by Jenna Castille

๛

Magic of Three

About the Author

๛

It's always the quiet ones. Mild-mannered Jenna Castille lives a rather normal life with her husband and daughter in Las Vegas. Only her husband and closest friends know about the twists and turns her imagination takes. She's loved fantasy and horror stories since childhood. Then she discovered romance and romantica. As a writer, she never could figure out which genre she liked better, so she decided throw them all in a pot and see what came out.

Her husband still shakes his head every time she describes one of her plots, but he's always more than willing to help with any "hands on" research she might require. And her friends love to read her stories. They tell her that at least now they understand the glassy stares and all the mumbling to herself. Happily, they don't have to worry about her anymore.

Being a writer is much better than being committed.

Jenna welcomes comments from readers. You can find her website and email address on her author bio page at www.ellorascave.com.

Tell Us What You Think
We appreciate hearing reader opinions about our books. You can email us at Comments@EllorasCave.com.

Also by Lacey Savage

ℰℭ

All the King's Men
Diva in Denial
Fighting Chance
I, Nefertiti
Wed and Wanton

About the Author

ℰℭ

Award-winning author Lacey Savage loves to write about her dreams—or more specifically, she loves to breathe life into her steamy fantasies (and she's got plenty!). She pens erotic tales of true love and mythical destiny, peopled with strong alpha heroes and feisty heroines. A hopeless romantic, Lacey loves writing about the intimate, sensual side of relationships. She currently resides in Ottawa, Canada, with her loving husband and the mischievous cat.

Lacey welcomes comments from readers. You can find her website and email address on her author bio page at www.ellorascave.com.

Tell Us What You Think

We appreciate hearing reader opinions about our books. You can email us at Comments@EllorasCave.com.

Also by Brigit Zahara

❧

Aquamarine: Catch of the Day
Front Page Fate

About the Author

❧

A former operative for the CIA, Brigit Zahara unleashed her passion for excitement and adventure through her work, spending a good deal of her early adulthood traveling throughout the United States and Europe, with lengthy spells in New York, Los Angeles, Louisiana, Venice, London, Florence and Malta.

In her early thirties, Brigit retired, looking then to her closet habit of writing fiction as a means of indulging her need for pulse-pounding action. From there, her taste very quickly turned to the tantalizing arena of erotica.

These days, Brigit lives in a seaside villa in Majorca, spending the steamy days penning even steamier stories and the cool, ocean-breeze-kissed evenings researching love scenes with her heart's destiny and husband of nearly eight years. She welcomes hearing from fans.

Brigit welcomes comments from readers. You can find her website and email address on her author bio page at www.ellorascave.com.

Tell Us What You Think

We appreciate hearing reader opinions about our books. You can email us at Comments@EllorasCave.com.

Also by Lolita Lopez

୭

Pressing the Flesh

About the Author

୭

Lolita has been writing naughty tales to entertain friends for years because, seriously, how else was she supposed to fuel her co-ed procrastination? Study organic chemistry or pen a quick story for her girlfriends? No surprise that she's on a sabbatical from college, eh?

A newlywed, Lolita lives in Texas with her paramedic husband. If not snuggling on the couch with her husband while tapping away at her laptop, Lolita can be found roaming her local bookstores, sipping cocktails with her closest friends, or carrying on conversations with her favorite plants.

Lolita welcomes comments from readers. You can find her website and email address on her author bio page at www.ellorascave.com.

Tell Us What You Think

We appreciate hearing reader opinions about our books. You can email us at Comments@EllorasCave.com.

Why an electronic book?

We live in the Information Age—an exciting time in the history of human civilization, in which technology rules supreme and continues to progress in leaps and bounds every minute of every day. For a multitude of reasons, more and more avid literary fans are opting to purchase e-books instead of paper books. The question from those not yet initiated into the world of electronic reading is simply: *Why?*

1. *Price.* An electronic title at Ellora's Cave Publishing and Cerridwen Press runs anywhere from 40% to 75% less than the cover price of the exact same title in paperback format. Why? Basic mathematics and cost. It is less expensive to publish an e-book (no paper and printing, no warehousing and shipping) than it is to publish a paperback, so the savings are passed along to the consumer.

2. *Space.* Running out of room in your house for your books? That is one worry you will never have with electronic books. For a low one-time cost, you can purchase a handheld device specifically designed for e-reading. Many e-readers have large, convenient screens for viewing. Better yet, hundreds of titles can be stored within your new library—on a single microchip. There are a variety of e-readers from different manufacturers. You can also read e-books on your PC or laptop computer. (Please note that

Ellora's Cave does not endorse any specific brands. You can check our websites at www.ellorascave.com or www.cerridwenpress.com for information we make available to new consumers.)

3. *Mobility*.   Because your new e-library consists of only a microchip within a small, easily transportable e-reader, your entire cache of books can be taken with you wherever you go.

4. ***Personal Viewing Preferences.***   Are the words you are currently reading too small? Too large? Too… ANNOYING? Paperback books cannot be modified according to personal preferences, but e-books can.

5. ***Instant Gratification.***   Is it the middle of the night and all the bookstores near you are closed? Are you tired of waiting days, sometimes weeks, for bookstores to ship the novels you bought? Ellora's Cave Publishing sells instantaneous downloads twenty-four hours a day, seven days a week, every day of the year. Our webstore is never closed. Our e-book delivery system is 100% automated, meaning your order is filled as soon as you pay for it.

Those are a few of the top reasons why electronic books are replacing paperbacks for many avid readers.

As always, Ellora's Cave and Cerridwen Press welcome your questions and comments. We invite you to email us at Comments@ellorascave.com or write to us directly at Ellora's Cave Publishing Inc., 1056 Home Avenue, Akron, OH 44310-3502.

COMING TO A BOOKSTORE NEAR YOU!

ELLORA'S CAVE

Bestselling Authors Tour

UPDATES AVAILABLE AT

WWW.ELLORASCAVE.COM

erridwen, the Celtic Goddess of wisdom, was the muse who brought inspiration to storytellers and those in the creative arts. Cerridwen Press encompasses the best and most innovative stories in all genres of today's fiction. Visit our site and discover the newest titles by talented authors who still get inspired - much like the ancient storytellers did, once upon a time.

CERRIDWEN PRESS

www.cerridwenpress.com

Discover for yourself why readers can't get enough of the multiple award-winning publisher Ellora's Cave.

Whether you prefer e-books or paperbacks,

be sure to visit EC on the web at www.ellorascave.com

for an erotic reading experience that will leave you breathless.